THESE BROKEN STARS

THESE BROKEN STARS

Amie Kaufman & Meagan Spooner

LITTLE, BROWN AND COMPANY
New York   Boston

Little, Brown and Company
Hachette Book Group
1290 Avenue of the Americas, New York, NY 10104
Visit us at LBYR.com

Originally published in hardcover and ebook by Hyperion, an imprint of
Disney Book Group, in December 2013
First Trade Paperback Edition: November 2014

Little, Brown and Company is a division of Hachette Book Group, Inc.
The Little, Brown name and logo are trademarks of Hachette Book Group, Inc.

The publisher is not responsible for websites (or their content) that are not owned by the publisher.

Library of Congress Control Number: 2013010334

ISBNs: 978-1-4231-7121-8 (pbk.), 978-1-4231-8778-3 (ebook)

Printed in the United States of America

CW

10 9 8 7 6 5

For Clint Spooner, Philip Kaufman, and Brendan Cousins,
three men who have always been fixed constellations
in this ever-changing universe

"When did you first meet Miss LaRoux?"

"Three days before the accident."

"And how did that come about?"

"The accident?"

"Meeting Miss LaRoux."

"How could it possibly matter?"

"Major, everything matters."

ONE

TARVER

NOTHING ABOUT THIS ROOM IS REAL. IF THIS WERE A PARTY at home, the music would draw your eye to human musicians in the corner. Candles and soft lamps would light the room, and the wooden tables would be made of actual trees. People would be listening to each other, instead of checking to see who's watching them.

Even the air here smells filtered and fake. The candles in the sconces do flicker, but they're powered by a steady source. Hover trays weave among the guests, like invisible waiters are carrying drinks. The string quartet is only a hologram—perfect and infallible, and exactly the same at every performance.

I'd give anything for a laid-back evening joking around with my platoon, instead of being stuck here in this imitation scene from a historical novel.

For all their trendy Victorian tricks, there's no hiding where we are. Outside the viewports, the stars are like faded white lines, half-invisible, surreal. The *Icarus*, passing through dimensional hyperspace, would look just as faded, half-transparent, if someone stationary in the universe could somehow see her moving faster than light.

I'm leaning against the bookshelves when it occurs to me that one thing here *is* real—the books. I reach behind me and let my fingers trail over the rough leather of their antique spines, then pull one free. Nobody here reads them; the books are for decoration. Chosen for the richness of their leather bindings, not for the contents of their pages. Nobody will miss one, and I need a dose of reality.

I'm almost done for the night, smiling for the cameras as ordered. The brass keep thinking that mixing field officers with the upper crust will create some sort of common ground where none exists, let the paparazzi infesting the *Icarus* see me, the lowborn boy made good, hobnobbing with the elite. *I* keep thinking that the photographers will get their fill of shots of me with drink in hand, lounging in the first-class salon, but in the two weeks I've been on board, they haven't.

These folks love a good rags-to-riches tale, even if my riches are no more than the medals pinned to my chest. It still makes for a nice story in the papers. The military look good, the rich people look good, and it gives the poor people something to aspire to. *See?* say all the headlines. *You too can rocket your way up to riches and fame. If hick boy can make good, why can't you?*

If it wasn't for what happened on Patron, I wouldn't even be here. What they call heroics, I call a tragic debacle. But nobody's asking my opinion.

I scan the room, taking in the clusters of women in brightly colored gowns, officers in dress uniforms like mine, men in evening coats and top hats. The ebb and flow of the crowd is unsettling—patterns I'll never get used to no matter how many times I'm forced to rub elbows with these people.

My eyes fall on a man who's just entered, and it takes me a moment to realize why. There's nothing about him that fits here, although he's trying to blend in. His black tailcoat is too threadbare, and his top hat is missing the shiny satin ribbon that's in fashion. I'm trained to notice the thing that doesn't fit, and in this sea of surgically perfected faces, his is a beacon. There are lines at the corners of his eyes and around his mouth, his skin weather-beaten and marked by the sun. He's nervous, shoulders rounded, fingers gripping the lapels of his jacket and letting go again.

My heart kicks up a beat. I've spent too long in the colonies, where anything out of place might kill you. I ease away from the bookshelves and start to weave my way toward him, past a pair of women sporting monocles they can't possibly need. I want to know why he's here, but I'm forced to move slowly, navigating the push and pull of the crowd with agonizing patience. *If I shove, I'll draw attention.* And if he is dangerous, any sudden shift in the energy of the room could trigger him.

A brilliant flash lights up the world as a camera goes off in my face.

"Oh, Major Merendsen!" It's the leader of a gaggle of women in their mid-twenties, descending on me from the direction of the viewport. "Oh, you simply *must* take a picture with us."

Their insincerity is poisonous. I'm barely more than a dog walking on its hind legs, here—they know it, and I know it, but they can't pass up an opportunity to be seen with a real, live war hero.

"Sure, I'll just come back in a minute, if—" Before I can finish, all three women are posed around me, lips pursed and lashes lowered. *Smile for the cameras.* A series of flashes erupt all around me, blinding me.

I can feel that low, stabbing pain at the base of my skull that promises to explode into a fully fledged headache. The women are still chattering and pressing in close, and I can't see the man with the weathered face.

One of the photographers is buzzing around me, his voice a low drone. I step sideways to look past him, but my eyes are swimming with red and gold afterimages. Blinking hard, my gaze swings from the bar, to the door, the hover trays, the booths. I try to remember what he looked like, the line of his clothes. Was there room to hide anything under his dinner jacket? Could he be armed?

"Major, did you hear me?" The photographer's still talking.

"Yes?" *No, I wasn't listening.* I disentangle myself from the women still draped over me on the pretense of stepping closer to speak with him. I wish I could shove past this little man, or better yet, tell him there's a threat and watch how fast he vanishes from the room.

"I said I'm surprised your buddies on the lower decks aren't trying to sneak up here too."

Seriously? The other soldiers watch me head to first class every evening like a man walking down death row. "Oh, you know." I try not to sound as annoyed as I am. "I doubt they even know what champagne is." I try for a smile too, but they're the ones good at insincerity, not me.

He laughs too loudly as the flash explodes in my face again. Blinking away the stars, I stumble clear and crane my neck, trying to locate the only guy in the room more out of place than I am. But the stooped man in the shabby hat is nowhere to be found.

Maybe he left? But someone doesn't go to the trouble of crashing a party like this and then slip out without a fuss. Maybe he's seated now, hiding among the other guests. My eyes sweep across the booths again, this time examining the patrons more closely.

They're all packed full of people. All except one. My gaze falls on a girl sitting alone in a booth, watching the crowd with detached interest. Her fair, flawless skin says she's one of them, but her gaze says she's better, above, untouchable.

She's wearing the same hue as a navy dress uniform, bare shoulders holding my gaze for a moment—she sure as hell wears the color better than any sailor I know. Hair: red, falling down past her shoulders. Nose: a little snub, but that makes her more pretty, not less. It makes her real.

Pretty's not the right word. She's a knockout.

Something about the girl's face tickles at the back of my mind, like I should recognize it, but before I can dig up the connection, she catches me looking at her. I know better than to mix with girls like her, so I don't know why I keep watching her, or why I smile.

Then, abruptly, a movement jerks my gaze away. It's the nervous man, and he's no longer meandering in and out of the crowd. His stooped posture is gone, and with his eyes fixed on something across the room he's moving quickly through the press of bodies. He's got a goal—and it's the girl in the blue dress.

I waste no time weaving in and out of the crowd politely. I shove between a pair of startled elderly gentlemen and make for the booth, but the outsider's gotten there first. He's leaning close, speaking low and fast. He's moving too quickly, trying to spit out what he came to say before he's picked out as an intruder. The girl jerks back, leaning away. Then the crowd closes up between us, and they're out of sight.

I reach down to lay a hand on my gun, and hiss between my teeth as I realize it's not there. The empty spot at my hip feels like a missing limb. I weave left, upsetting a hover tray and sending its contents crashing to the floor. The crowd recoils, finally giving me an avenue toward the table.

The intruder has grabbed her elbow, urgent. She's trying to pull away, eyes flashing up, looking around for someone as though she expects help. Her gaze falls on me.

I get one step closer before a man in the right sort of top hat claps a hand on the stranger's shoulder. He has an equally self-important friend with him, and two officers, a man and a woman. They know the man with the fervent light in his eyes doesn't belong here, and I can see they mean to remedy his presence.

The redhead's self-appointed guardian jerks the man backward to stumble against the officers, who take him firmly by the arms. I can tell he's got no training, either formally or the rough-and-tumble sort they learn in the colonies. If he did, he'd be able to handle these desk jockeys and their sloppy form.

They start to turn him toward the door, one of them grabbing at the nape of his neck. More force than I would use, for someone whose only crime so far seems to be trying to talk to the girl in the blue dress, but they're handling it. I stop by the adjacent booth, still trying to catch my breath.

The man twists, breaking free of the soldiers, and turns back toward the girl. As the room starts to fall silent, the ragged edge to his voice is audible. "You have to speak to your father about this, please. We're dying for lack of tech, he needs to give the colonists more—"

His voice gives out as one of the officers delivers a blow to his stomach that doubles him over. I jerk forward, shoving away from the booth and past the widening ring of onlookers.

The redhead beats me to it. She's on her feet in a swift movement that draws the attention of everyone in the room in a way the scuffle didn't. Whoever she is, she's a showstopper.

"Enough!" She has a voice well suited to delivering ultimatums. "Captain, Lieutenant, what do you think you're doing?"

I knew I liked her for a reason.

When I step forward, she's holding them frozen in place with a glare that could fell a platoon. For a moment, none of them notice me. Then I see the soldiers register my presence, and scan my shoulders for my stars and bars. Rank aside, we're different in every way. My medals are for combat, theirs for long service, bureaucratic efficiencies. My promotions were made in the field. Theirs, behind a desk. They've never had blood on their hands. But for once, I'm glad of my newfound status. The two soldiers come reluctantly to attention—both of them are older, and I can tell it rankles to have to salute an eighteen-year-old. Funny how I was old enough by sixteen to drink, fight, and vote, but even two years later, I'm too young to respect.

They're still holding on to the gate-crasher. He's breathing quick and shallow, like he's pretty sure someone's going to fire him out an air lock any minute.

I clear my throat, making sure I sound calm. "If there's a problem, I can help this man find the door." *Without more violence.*

We can all hear how my voice sounds—exactly like the backwater boy I am, unpolished and uncultured. I register a few scattered laughs around the room, which is now entirely focused on our little drama. Not malicious laughter—just amused.

"Merendsen, I doubt this guy's after a book." Fancy Top Hat smirks at me.

I look down and realize I'm still holding the book I took from the shelves. Right, because this guy is poor, he can't even read.

"I'm sure he was just about to go," says the girl, fixing Top Hat with a steely glare. "And I'm pretty sure you were about to leave, too."

They're caught off guard by her dismissal, and I use the moment to relieve my fellow officers of their captive, keeping hold of his arm as I guide him away. She's effectively dismissed the quartet from the salon— again her face tickles my memory, who *is* she that she can do that?—and I let them make their enforced escape before I gently but firmly steer my new friend toward the door.

"Anything broken?" I ask, once we're outside. "What possessed you to go near them, and in a place like this? I half thought you were aiming to blow someone up."

The man gazes at me for a long moment, his face already older than the people inside will ever look.

He turns to walk away without another word, shoulders bowed. I wonder just how much he had riding on this manufactured encounter with the girl in the blue dress.

I stand in the doorway, watching as people give up on the drama now that it's done. The room slowly comes back to life, the hover trays zipping around, conversation surging, perfectly practiced laughter tinkling here and there. I'm supposed to be here at least another hour, but maybe just this once I can skip out early.

And then I see the girl again—and she's watching me. Very slowly she's taking off one of her gloves, pinching each finger deliberately in turn. Her gaze never leaves my face.

My heart surges up into my throat, and I know I'm staring like an idiot, but I'm damned if I can remember how my legs work. I stare a beat too long, and her lips curve to a hint of a smile. But somehow, *her* smile doesn't look as though it's mocking me, and I get it together enough to start walking.

When she lets her glove fall to the ground, I'm the one who leans down to pick it up.

I don't want to ask her if she's all right—she's too collected for that. So I put the glove down on the table, then find myself with no excuse to do anything other than look at her. Blue eyes. They go with the dress. Do lashes grow that long naturally? So many perfect faces, it's hard to tell who's been surgically altered and who hasn't. But surely if she'd had work done, she'd have opted for a straight, classically beautiful nose. No, she looks real.

"Are you waiting for a drink?" My voice sounds mostly even.

"For my companions," she says, lowering the deadly lashes before peering up at me through them. "Captain?" She tilts the word upward, as though she's taking a stab at my rank.

"Major," I say. She knows how to read my insignia; I just saw her name the ranks of the other officers. Her sort, the society girls, they all know how. It's a game. I might not be society, but I still know a player when I see one. "Not sure that was smart of your companions, leaving you unattended. Now you're stuck talking to me."

Then she smiles, and it turns out she has dimples, and it's all over. It's not just the way she looks—although that would do it all on its own. It's that, despite the way she looks, despite where I found her, this girl's willing to go against the tide. She's not another empty-headed puppet. It's like finding another human after days of isolation.

"Is it going to cause an intergalactic incident if I keep you company until your friends get here?"

"Not at all." She tilts her head a little to indicate the opposite side of the booth. The bench curves around in a semicircle from where she sits. "Though I feel I should warn you that you could be here for a while. My friends aren't really known for their punctuality."

I laugh, and I set down the book and my drink on the table beside her glove, sinking down to sit opposite her. She's wearing one of those enormous skirts that are in fashion these days, and the fabric brushes against my legs as I settle. She doesn't move away. "You should have seen me as a cadet," I say, as though that wasn't just a year ago. "Punctuality was pretty much the only thing we were known for. Never ask how or why, just get it done fast."

"Then we have something in common," she says. "We aren't encouraged to ask why, either." Neither of us asks why we're sitting together. We're smart.

"I can see at least half a dozen guys watching us. Am I making any deadly enemies? Or at least, any more than I already have?"

"Would it stop you from sitting here?" she asks, finally removing the second glove and setting it down on the table.

"Not necessarily," I reply. "Handy thing to know, though. Plenty of dark hallways on this ship, if I'm going to have rivals waiting around corners."

"Rivals?" she asks, lifting one brow. I know she's playing a game with me, but I don't know the rules, and she's got all the cards. Still, the hell with it—I just can't find it in me to care that I'm losing. I'll surrender right now, if she likes.

"I suppose they might imagine themselves to be," I say eventually. "Those gentlemen over there don't look particularly impressed." I nod to the group in frock coats and more top hats. At home we're a simpler people, and you take your hat off when you come inside.

"Let's make it worse," she says promptly. "Read to me from your book, and I'll look rapt. And you could order me a drink, if you like."

I glance down at the book I plucked off the shelf. *Mass Casualty: A History of Failed Campaigns.* I slide it a little farther away, wincing inwardly. "Perhaps the drink. I've been away from your bright lights for a while, so I'm a little rusty, but I'm pretty sure talking about bloody death's not the best way to charm a girl."

"I'll have to content myself with champagne, then." She continues, as I raise a hand to signal one of the hover trays. "You say 'bright lights' with a hint of disdain, Major. I'm from those bright lights. Do you fault me for that?"

"I could fault you for nothing." The words somehow bypass my brain entirely. *Mutiny.*

She drops her eyes for the compliment, still smiling. "You say you've been away from civilization, Major, but your flattery's giving you away. It can't have been all that long."

"We're very civilized out on the frontier," I say, pretending offense. "Every so often we take a break from slogging through waist-high muck or dodging bullets and issue dance invitations. My old drill sergeant used to say that nothing teaches you the quickstep like the ground giving way beneath your feet."

"I suppose so," she agrees as a full tray comes humming toward us in response to my summons. She selects a glass of champagne and raises it in half a toast to me before she sips. "Can you tell me your name, or is it classified?" she asks, as though she doesn't know.

I reach for the other glass and send the tray humming off into the crowd again. "Merendsen." Even if it's a pretense, it's nice to talk to someone who isn't raving about my astounding heroics or asking for a picture with me. "Tarver Merendsen." She's looking at me like she doesn't recognize me from all the newspapers and holovids.

"Major Merendsen." She tries it out, leaning on the *m*'s, then nods her approval. The name passes muster, at least for now.

"I'm heading back to the bright lights for my next posting. Which one of them is your home?"

"Corinth, of course," she replies. The brightest light of all. *Of course.* "Though I spend more time on ships like this than planetside. I'm most at home here on the *Icarus*."

"Even you must be impressed by the *Icarus*. She's bigger than any city I've been to."

"She's the biggest," my companion replies, dropping her eyes and toying with the stem of the champagne flute. Though she hides it well, there's a flicker through her features. Talking about the ship must bore her. Maybe it's the spaceliner equivalent of asking about the weather.

C'mon, man, get it together. I clear my throat. "The viewing decks are the best I've seen. I'm used to planets with very little ambient light, but the view out here is something else."

She meets my eyes for half a breath—then her lips quirk to the tiniest of smiles. "I don't think I've taken advantage of them enough, this trip. Perhaps we—" But then she cuts herself short, glancing toward the door.

I'd forgotten we were in a crowded room. But the moment she looks away, all the music and conversation comes surging back. There's a girl with reddish-blond hair—a relative, I'm sure, though *her* nose is straight and perfect—descending upon my companion, a small entourage in tow.

"Lil, there you are," she says, scolding, and holding out her hand in a clear invitation. No surprise, I'm not included. The entourage swirls into place behind her.

"Anna," says my companion, who now has a name. Lil. "May I present Major Merendsen?"

"Charmed." Anna's voice is dismissive, and I reach for my book and my drink. I know my cue.

"Please, I think I'm in your chair," I say. "It was a pleasure."

"Yes." Lil ignores Anna's hand, her fingers curling around the stem of her champagne glass as she looks across at me. I like to think that she regrets the interruption a little.

Then I rise, and with a small bow of the sort we reserve for civilians, I make my escape. The girl in the blue dress watches me go.

"You next encountered her . . . ?"

"The day of the accident."

"What were your intentions at that stage?"

"I had none."

"Why not?"

"You're joking, right?"

"Major, we aren't here to entertain you."

"I found out who she was. That it was over before I even said hello."

TWO

LILAC

"DO YOU KNOW WHO THAT *WAS*?" ANNA TILTS HER HEAD toward the major as he slips out of the salon.

"Mmm." I try to sound noncommittal. Of course I know—the guy's picture was plastered across every holoscreen for weeks. Major Tarver Merendsen, war hero. His pictures don't do him justice. He looks younger in person, for one. But mostly, in his pictures, he's always stern, frowning.

Anna's escort of the evening, a tuxedo-clad younger man, asks us what we'd like to drink. I never bother to remember the names of Anna's dates. Half the time she doesn't even introduce them before handing them her fan and clutch and skittering off to dance with someone else. As he heads to the bar with Elana, Swann follows them, after a long, level look at me.

I know I'll catch hell later for slipping my bodyguard and getting here early, but it was worth it. You have to know to look for it, nearly invisible in the lines of Swann's skirt, but there's a knife at one thigh and a tiny pistol set to stun in her clutch. There are jokes about how the LaRoux princess never goes anywhere without her entourage of giggling companions— that half of them could kill a man at a hundred yards is not exactly public knowledge. The President's family doesn't have protection like mine.

I ought to tell them about the man who accosted me, but if I do, Swann will usher me out of the salon, and I'll spend the rest of the evening locked in my room while she verifies the man in the cheap hat didn't intend to harm me. I could tell he wasn't dangerous, though. It's hardly the first time somebody's wanted me to intervene with my father. All his colonies want more than he can give, and it's no secret that the most powerful man in the galaxy dotes on his daughter's every whim.

But there'd be no point to Swann hiding me away. I recognized the particular slump of the man's shoulders as the major guided him out. He won't try again.

"I hope you know what you're doing, Lil." I look up, startled. She's still talking about Major Merendsen.

"Just a bit of fun." I toss back the last mouthful of champagne in a way that makes Anna crack a smile in spite of herself.

She erases her smile with an effort, summoning a scowl far more suited to Swann's face than hers. "Uncle Roderick would be cross," she scolds, sliding into the booth next to me and forcing me to move over. "Who cares how many medals the major managed to wrangle in the field? He's still just a teacher's son."

For a girl who spends more nights in someone else's room than her own, Anna is a prude when it comes to me. I can't help but wonder what my father has promised her in exchange for keeping an eye on me on this trip—or what he's threatened her with should she fail.

I know she's only trying to protect me. Better her than one of my bodyguards, with no reason to cushion the truth when reporting to my father. Anna is one of the only people who knows what Monsieur LaRoux is capable of, when it comes to me. She's seen what happens to men who look at me the wrong way. There are rumors, of course. Most guys are smart enough to steer clear, but only Anna *knows*. For all her lectures, I'm glad she's here with me.

Still, something in me won't let it go. "One conversation," I murmur. "That's all, Anna. Do we have to go through this every time?"

Anna leans in so she can slip her arm through mine and put her head on my shoulder. When we were young, this was my gesture—but we've grown, and I'm taller than her now. "I'm only trying to help," she says. "You know what Uncle Roderick is like. You're all he has. Is it such a terrible thing that your father's devoted to you?"

I sigh, leaning my head to the side to rest it on hers. "If I can't play a little when I'm away from him, then what's the use in traveling on my own?"

"Major Merendsen *was* rather delicious," Anna admits in a low voice. "Did you see how well he filled out that uniform? He's not for you, but maybe I should look up his cabin number."

My stomach gives an odd little lurch. Jealousy? Surely not. The movement of the ship, then. And yet, faster-than-light travel is so smooth it's like standing still.

Anna lifts her head, looks at my face, and laughs, the sound a delightful, well-practiced tinkle of silver. "Oh, don't scowl, Lil. I was only joking. Just don't see him again, or you know I'll have to tell your father. I don't want to, but I can't not do it."

Elana, Swann, and the faceless tuxedo return with a hover tray in tow, laden with drinks and hors d'oeuvres. The girls have given Anna enough time to chastise me, and they're all smiles as they slide into the booth to join us. Anna sends the tuxedo back to the bar because her drink has a stick of pineapple in it rather than cherries, and she and the other girls titter to one another as they watch him walk away. It's clear why Anna's chosen this one—he'd give the major a good run for his money in the filling-a-suit department.

Anna begins describing the tuxedo's enthusiastic attempts to court her, much to the amusement of Elana and Swann. Sometimes this kind of conversation is all I want—light, easy, and not remotely dangerous. It takes the spotlight off of me and puts Anna at center stage, so that all I have to do is smile and laugh. Usually she'd have me in stitches by now. But tonight it feels hollow, and it's hard for me to let myself go.

I glance at the door now and then, but though it swings open and closed dozens of times, it's never to admit Tarver Merendsen. I'm sure he knows the rules as well as I do, and there's not a person aboard who doesn't know who I am. That he spoke to me at all is a wonder. Though my father made a show of letting me travel by myself for my birthday in New Paris, the truth is that he's always there, in some way or another.

There is one tiny comfort, though. At least he left of his own accord, and I didn't have to end him in front of all my friends. After all, on a ship carrying over fifty thousand passengers, the odds of ever encountering again the major's crooked smile and distracting voice are next to nothing.

The next two nights Anna and I skip the salon, and go straight to the promenade deck after dinner. We walk arm in arm, and talk out Anna's gossip. I know she'll still spend the entire night in our adjoining suites draped over the foot of my bed, chatting. Though she never seems to show the effects of not sleeping, I inevitably wake up with purple smudges under my eyes, standing out like bruises on my fair skin. Outside of these voyages, Anna and I never get to spend so much time together. Here, we can be like sisters.

And so we walk. Swann is with us as well, of course—I can barely get out of bed without her at my elbow—but if she listens to us, she doesn't comment.

Though Anna's said nothing else about the major, he hasn't been far from my thoughts. Most of the lower classes, when they speak to me, try to pretend they're on my level. They fawn over me, dancing attendance, so phony it makes my teeth ache. But the major was candid, genuine, and when he smiled, it didn't seem forced. He acted like he truly enjoyed my company.

We turn into the broad sweep of synthetic lawn that curves around the stern of the ship as the lights, timed to the ship's clocks, dim past sunset into dusk. The observation windows tint from their daytime image of sunny sky and clouds through gold, orange, pink, and finally to a starry sky more brilliant than any you could find on a planet. Back home on Corinth there are no stars, only the gentle pink glow of the city lights reflected in the atmosphere, and the holographic displays of fireworks against the clouds.

I'm watching the window and listening to Anna with only half an ear when her arm in mine tightens convulsively. I nearly stumble as she stops abruptly, but thankfully I catch myself before I can face-plant on the synthetic lawn. Tripping over my own feet would land me in the headlines for a week.

Anna's eyes aren't on me but rather fixed on something—or someone—some distance away. I look over, and my heart drops into my violet satin shoes.

Major Merendsen.

Has he seen us? He's speaking to another officer, head bowed to listen to him—maybe he's distracted enough that he won't notice me. I turn my face away, willing him not to spot me. I curse my unusual hair, too bright to be fashionable or subtle. And why do I insist on jewel tones? If I was dressed like the other girls, maybe I would blend in.

What awful backwater posting would my father have him reassigned him to, if Anna reported back that I'd been associating with the infamous Major Merendsen, teacher's son, scholarship student, classless war hero? If only the major realized he'd be lucky to make it out with a reassignment.

"Good heavens, he's actually coming over," Anna murmurs in my ear through a fixed smile. "What on earth ails him? I mean, does he suffer from some mental—"

"Good evening, Major," I interrupt, cutting off Anna's stream of insults before he's close enough to hear them. I hope.

The major's fellow officer waits respectfully some distance back, and my heart sinks even lower. Anna knows the rules, so she and Swann make their excuses and walk some distance ahead, ostensibly to look out the window. Anna glances back at me once she's passed the major, both brows lifted in concern.

Don't, her expression warns me. *Let him go.* I can see a momentary flash of sympathy in her gaze, but that doesn't change the message.

They stay within earshot, providing only the illusion of privacy. Swann leans back against the railing, watching us closely. Still, she looks more amused than concerned. She may be lethal when I'm in danger, but she's still right at home with the others, thriving on gossip and giggling and the intricate dance of society. Anna's used to this rotating roster of bodyguards, and she adopts them into our circle as readily as any of our other companions. My father chose well.

"Good evening," says Major Merendsen. Behind him Anna whispers something to Swann, who giggles loudly. The major barely flinches, merely smiles a little. "I'm sorry, I shouldn't have interrupted your evening with your friends. But I never got the chance to ask the other night if you'd be interested in seeing the observation decks some evening. You mentioned you hadn't been there much."

Anna is staring at me, her green eyes fixed on mine. There's no sympathy there now, only warning. That not even my best friend will keep my secrets is a truth I'd rather not face right now. Especially since the most painful part is that I can't even blame her. There's no one my father can't rule. Not Anna—not me.

And certainly not Tarver Merendsen. How arrogant can this guy be? Maybe he thinks the rewards are worth it. Men will do just about anything for a rich girl's attention. If he won't back off on his own, well—I've done this before. Nothing short of absolute annihilation will do. I have to choose my moment with care to maximize the damage.

"You remembered." I find my smile, feeling it spread across my face like a sickly grimace, and turn my attention back to the major. "I think my friends will understand if I miss out on one evening."

Behind the major, I see Anna's face freeze, genuine fear flickering there. I wish I could tell her to wait, not to panic. But that would give me away.

His face shifts, the cautious smile widening as some of the tension drains. It's a jolt to realize that he was nervous. That he really, truly, wanted to ask me. His eyes, the same shade of brown as his hair, are fixed on mine. God, if only he weren't so handsome. It's a lot easier with the older, fatter men.

"Are you busy now? Tonight?"

"You certainly don't waste any time, do you?"

He grins, clasping his hands behind his back. "One of the things you learn fast in the service is to act now, think later."

Such a change from the circles I travel in, the deliberate games and calculated slips of the tongue. Anna's mouthing something at me, but I only catch the end of it. Something about *now*.

"Listen, Major—"

"Tarver," he corrects me. "And you still have the advantage on me, Miss . . . ?"

It takes me a few seconds to understand what he means. He's watching me, brows lifted, expectant.

Then it hits me. *He doesn't know who I am.*

For a long moment I just stare at him. I can't remember the last time someone spoke to me who didn't know who I was. In fact, I can't think of any time at all. Surely when I was little, before I became the media's darling? But that seems so far away from who I am now, like a movie seen in another lifetime.

I wish I could stop, let it sink in, even revel in this moment. Enjoy speaking to someone who doesn't see me as Lilac LaRoux, heiress to the LaRoux Industries empire, richest girl in the galaxy. But I can't stop. I can't let this stupid, foolish soldier be seen with me a second time. Someone will say something to my father, and ignorant or not, Major Merendsen doesn't deserve that.

I've done this before. So why do I have to hunt for the right words to bury him? "I must have given you the wrong impression last night," I say airily, summoning my brightest, most amused smile. "I try so hard to be polite when I'm bored out of my skull, but I guess sometimes that backfires."

There's little reaction to be seen at first on Major Merendsen's face, merely a subtle closing down of the amused eyes, a tightening of the firm mouth. Even so, there's an irrational surge of anger toward him, for being so ignorant as to talk to me at all.

You smiled at him first, a tiny thought points out. *And let him retrieve your glove, and bring you a drink, and sit with you.* Beyond him I see Anna and Swann about to collapse with laughter, and my jaw starts to clench. The anger shifts.

End it now. Make him walk away. Before you break.

"Did you not understand me?" I toss my hair back over my shoulder. I can only hope that if my expression shows how much I'm hating myself right now, he reads it as disgust. "I suppose it's to be expected that you're a little slow. Given your . . . upbringing."

He's silent, his face utterly wooden. He just stares at me, as the seconds draw out. Then he takes a step back and bows. "I won't take up any more of your time. If you'll excuse me?"

"Of course, Major." I don't wait for him to leave but brush past him to rejoin Anna and Swann, sweeping them up with me in my momentum. I want nothing more than to look over my shoulder and see if Major Merendsen is still standing where I struck him down, if he's storming away in anger, if he's following, if he's talking to the officer he came with. Because I can't look, my imagination conjures a dozen possibilities—I expect at any moment to feel his hand on my elbow or see him out of the corner of my eye at the elevators away from the promenade deck.

"Oh, that was *brilliant*, Lil," gasps Anna, still laughing. "Was he actually asking you to accompany him to the observation deck? To see the stars? God, how cliché!"

The faster-than-light vibrations, usually undetectable, are giving me a headache.

He didn't know who I was. He wasn't after my money; he wasn't after my father's business connections. He wasn't after anything, except an evening with me.

Suddenly Anna's hysterics are like sandpaper on my nerves. It doesn't matter that her laughter helped drive the major away, that she saw me hesitate and understood, that she's only doing her best to protect me from something unthinkable happening again. All that matters is that I had to slap that poor guy in the face, and now she's laughing.

"If you're jealous, get your tuxedo of the week to take you," I snap.

Leaving her and Swann staring after me, I aim for the elevator. There's a pair of techhead guys there already in their flashing, circuit-laden suits, waiting for the doors to close. When I sweep inside, one of them whispers to the other, and muttering something like an apology, they skitter out and leave me alone.

In the sound of the doors rushing closed, my mind conjures up the techhead's words. It's happened enough times that I don't need to have heard him to know what he said.

Oh, spark it. That's LaRoux's daughter. They catch us in here with her and we're dead, man.

I lean back against the synthetic wood paneling lining the interior of the elevator and fix my eyes on the symbol emblazoned on the elevator doors. The Greek letter lambda, for LaRoux Industries. My father's company.

Lilac Rose LaRoux. Untouchable. Toxic.

I should've been named Ivy, or Foxglove, or Belladonna.

"You next saw her when the incident occurred?"

"That's correct."

"Did you try to figure out what was happening?"

"You're not military, you don't understand how we work. I'm not supposed to ask questions. I was just following orders."

"What orders were those?"

"We have a duty to protect civilians."

"So there wasn't a specific order that drove your decision?"

"Now you're nitpicking."

"We're being exact, Major. We'd appreciate it if you tried to do the same."

THREE

TARVER

THE AIR LEAVES MY LUNGS WITH A RUSH, PAIN SHOOTING
up my back as I slam down onto the practice mats. The other guy falls
with me, and I realize I've still got a handful of his T-shirt. I suck in a
quick breath as I shove my weight to one side, coming up to my knees
in one movement so I'm looming over him, instead of the other way
around.

I can't *believe* I made such an idiot of myself tonight. Everyone in the
galaxy knows who Lilac LaRoux is, and I couldn't have glanced at one
lousy newscast, watched one of those damn gossip shows, and learned
what she looked like? I must be the only guy alive who doesn't know.

Normally you couldn't get me near a girl that rich and entitled if you
held a gun to my head. What was I *thinking*? I wasn't thinking at all. I had
my mind on dimples and red hair and—

The guy underneath me pushes up against my shoulder, and I roll
it back so he can't get purchase, planting a knee in his chest and drawing back my arm. My fist makes it halfway to the guy's cheek before he
catches it, gripping and twisting so I have to throw myself backward to
break free. He scrambles after me, grinning and panting.

"That all you got, kid? Try harder."

That's all I ever hear. *That all you got? Try harder.* Be richer. Be smarter.
Learn which damn cutlery to use. Speak like us. Think like us.

Screw that all the way to hell.

A ragged chorus of shouts and swearing in a dozen different languages erupts from the blur of fatigues and faces around us. The only officer down here is the sergeant overseeing the sparring, and he's not about to tell us to watch our mouths. Well—the only officer other than me. But they don't know that. It's only upstairs that everyone recognizes my face from their magazines and newspapers and holovids.

Still, I bet they would have recognized Lilac LaRoux.

I can't get my mind off of her. Did she think it was *funny* to play with me like that in front of her friends?

I lash out so quickly we're both surprised, and there's a crunch, and then the other guy's rolling away, hand up in front of his face, blood seeping through his fingers. I draw a breath, and before I can move, the sergeant is leaning down to stick his hand between us, showing me the flat of his palm—bout over.

I lean back on my elbows, chest heaving as he helps the other guy to his feet and hands him over to one of his buddies to head for the sick bay. Then the sergeant turns back to stand over me, arms folded across his massive chest.

"Son, one more like that, and you're off the mats, you understand? One more and I'll be speaking to your commanding officer."

Down here it's all plain fatigues, khaki T-shirts and pants, and I can ditch my stars and bars and pretend I'm a private. Down here I'm just eighteen, not an officer, not a war hero. He doesn't imagine for a moment that I could be a major. I prefer it that way. Some days I wish it *was* that way. That I could earn my stripes in official training, rather than out in the field like I did, where mistakes cost more than marks on a piece of paper.

"Yes, Sergeant." My breath's still coming quickly, and I climb to my feet carefully. I want to stay a little longer.

The military quarters are utilitarian, the metal skeleton of the ship showing, but I'm more at home down here. The air is humid with so many bodies working and sweating, the filters chugging on overtime without much result. These guys are on their way to one of the colonies to put down the latest rebellion. Take away my medals and my field promotion, and I'd be traveling in military quarters too, waiting to see what terraformed wonders and pissed-off rebels were waiting for me. I wish.

The sergeant sizes me up a moment longer, then turns his head to bellow, parade-ground style. "Corporal Adams, front and center. You're up next."

She's a few years older than me, a couple of inches shorter, blond hair spiked. She shoots me a quick grin as she shakes out her arms and readies herself, and I suck in a breath and square up. I'm going to do this until I'm tired enough to sleep.

Turns out she's fast, shifting her weight nimbly as we circle each other. This is the sort of girl who suits me, quick and direct, none of that upper-decks intrigue. The way she moves reminds me of a line from one of my mother's poems. *Quicksilver light and motes of dust.*

She smiles again, and for an instant I can see Lilac LaRoux's smile, and those blue eyes.

But next thing I see is the metal grating across the roof of the deck. Corporal Adams has her bare foot on my throat, and it's over. I lift my hands carefully, think about grabbing her ankle, and show her my palms instead. She got me. I should have had my mind on the job at hand.

She lifts her foot and leans down to offer me her hand. I grip it, she hauls, and I come up to my feet.

Now Miss LaRoux's getting my ass kicked on the sparring mats as well. *Is there any part of my life that girl can't mess with?*

I lace my hands together behind my head, arching my back until the stretch tugs at sore muscles, looking over at the sergeant. He directs the corporal to the next mat over, and closes the distance between us.

"Son, I don't know what you're working off there, but you might want to try the weapons range," he begins.

I don't want my gun. I want someone I can lay into, here in person. "Please, Sergeant, I—"

The ground bucks and heaves beneath me and we both stagger backward—for an instant I think someone's tackled me from behind, and then I realize it's the ship herself shaking beneath us.

I plant my feet wide apart, waiting to see if there's going to be another tremor. The sparring hall is eerily silent as everyone turns their faces up, waiting for information from the loudspeakers. The *Icarus* hasn't been anything but perfectly stable in the weeks I've been on her.

Nothing breaks the silence, and I exchange glances with the sergeant.

Slowly he shakes his head, broad shoulders lifting in a quick shrug. Where's the announcement?

There'll be more information upstairs. For sure, someone will be telling the rich folks what's going on. They'd expect nothing less. I toss off a quick salute, and stomp into my boots.

When I push through the doors of the silent sparring hall and out into the network of gangways beyond, it's like entering another world. It's all soft luxury upstairs, but down here they don't waste an inch.

The gangways crisscross over and under each other like spiderwebs, populated by techheads in suits that pulse lights in time with the music around us, emigrants heading for new colonies, tourists taking the cheapest route to other planets, folks making the long haul for family visits. I hear a snatch of worried Spanish on my left, and an Irish curse nearby. A cluster of missionaries bent on bringing comfort and relief to the unenlightened rebels on the new planets stands watching the bustle of humanity like it's their first time off-world. Amid all the sound and movement, there's not a top hat or a corset in sight.

Footsteps clang on the metal gantries, voices echoing in a dozen variations on Standard, lesser languages woven in. Everybody's wondering what's going on, but nobody knows.

Brightly lit screens flicker nonstop advertisements at me—they line the walls and the ceiling, blaring words and songs and jingles. As I work through the crowd toward the first set of stairs, a 3-D holograph springs to life in front of me, a woman in a hot-pink catsuit throwing her arms wide open to invite me to a club at the aft end of the ship. I walk right through her.

My stomach lurches as though I'm in for a bout of spacesickness. I notice I'm not the only one looking uncomfortable—there are other faces in the crowd turning pale as well.

I can't be spacesick. I've been shunted around the universe on ships so badly tuned you could barely hear yourself over the chugging, and all that time I kept my insides on the inside. I must have overdone it on the sparring mats.

I can feel the metal gangway beneath me vibrating to the hundreds of sets of footfalls banging down on it, but there's something else under that—a tremor that doesn't feel right. Abruptly the vid screens all around me freeze, the jingles and voice-overs cutting out so a woman's voice can broadcast up and down the hallways, smooth and professional.

"Attention all passengers. In a few moments we will be cycling the ship's hyperspace engines. This procedure forms a part of our routine maintenance of the Icarus. You may notice some minor vibrations. Thank you for your understanding as we carry out this routine maintenance."

She sounds calm, but I wouldn't use the words *routine maintenance* twice in one announcement myself unless I was trying to keep people from noticing it's not. In two years of space travel, I only ever saw a ship cycle her drives once, about six months back near Avon. By the time we got that tub landed, she was more or less held together by spit and good luck.

This is the *Icarus*. Newest, fanciest ship to come out of orbital dock, built by the one corporation in the galaxy big enough to terraform planets all by itself. I'm quite sure Roderick LaRoux made certain that spit plays no part in the way she holds together.

I jog along the gangway, ignoring legs that feel like they're weighted down after my sparring session, and start on the next staircase with one hand on the rail, just in case. It's a good call—I'm halfway up when another one of those "minor" vibrations hits.

The ship shudders so violently this time that a ripple runs along the gangway beneath me. I can track its progress by the way the civilians ranged along it shout and grab at the handrails, knees buckling.

The crowd's growing frantic, and I turn my body to push through a gap and make for the stairs, then break into a run as I head for the next flight. At the top, I press my palm against the ID plate, and the door slides soundlessly open.

I hurry through to the richly carpeted hallways of my own deck. Lilac LaRoux's deck. It's more crowded than usual as folks emerge from their cabins like they're going to discover some kind of collective wisdom out in the hallways. Another time I'd pause to admire these women showing off their unlimited sleepwear budgets, but just now I'm moving.

I turn for my own cabin as three sharp alarm blasts cut through the soft music that plays in the hallways. The woman's voice comes again, this time high with fear, and tense with the attempt to conceal it.

"Ladies and gentlemen, your attention please. We have experienced difficulty with our hyperspace engines, and the Icarus *has suffered substantial damage as a result of the dimensional displacement. We will attempt to keep the ship in hyperspace, but in the meantime, please follow the illuminated strips in the corridors and make your way to your assigned emergency pods immediately."*

The hallway comes to life. It's clear most of these people wouldn't know their assigned emergency pod if it bowled up, introduced itself, and offered to tango. I'm firmly in the camp that reads up on all the safety information the moment they get a chance. You develop that attitude after your first this-is-not-a-drill emergency evacuation, and I've had more than one.

We military types are all trained to travel with a grab bag. The things you need to take with you if you evacuate, survival gear. None of it is much use out here in deep space, of course, which is the only place you'll find this ship. She was constructed in orbit. Like a whale, she'd collapse under her own weight if exposed to real gravity. Still, I'm doubling back before I have time to think about it.

I jog up the hallway toward my cabin, fighting my way against the crowd, which is surging along in a panic.

I palm my way into my cabin and unhook the bag from where it's hanging over the back of the door. It's a basic hiking pack from my cadet days, designed to fold down small. I hesitate, then grab my jacket as well.

I need to get three hallways along to my right, then take a left and keep going, though with the crowd growing louder and more unstable by the minute, it's going to take a while. I make it to the first hallway, passing by the doorway that leads out to the observation deck. I glance out sideways through the door.

I know what the view's meant to be—and it's not like this. The stars beyond the clear screens blur, then lurch, then come back into focus.

They're not the long, graceful lines that should be visible in dimensional hyperspace. They're in focus for a moment, white pinpoints of light, then long blurs again. I've never seen a view like this before—it's as though the *Icarus* is trying, and failing, to claw her way back into hyperspace. I'm not sure what will happen if she's torn out prematurely, but I'm pretty sure nothing good.

For a moment something huge and metallic is visible out the corner of the observation window, and then it's gone. I crane my neck, trying to catch sight of the object again. It's so massive that it would have its own significant gravitational field, enough to pull the *Icarus* out of her flight path.

I turn back to work my way through the crowd toward my pod. The press of bodies is too thick, and I duck to the side to slide along the guard railing. On these back passages, the railing is all that stands between us and a nasty drop, all the way down at least a dozen levels. As I turn the corner I collide heavily with someone smaller than me, and I'm instinctively putting my arms out to keep the person from toppling over.

"Excuse *me*!" says a breathless voice. "Sir, watch where you're going!"

No. *Oh, hell no.*

A pair of blue eyes meet mine, flashing shock—then outrage—before she's shoving me away with all her strength, staggering back against the walkway railing.

I unclench my jaw with an effort. "Good evening, Miss LaRoux." *Drop dead*, my tone says.

In spite of everything—the screaming of the crowd, the jostle of bodies, the blaring of the ship's alarms—I take a moment to savor the shock and dismay on the faces of Miss LaRoux and her companions as they register my sudden reappearance. I'm not expecting the surge of people that comes flooding from a side passage.

They knock me off balance, but the crowd is so dense that I don't fall. As if I'm caught in a violent river current, it takes me a moment to get my feet onto the solid floor again. I catch a glimpse of Miss LaRoux's friends as they're swept down the corridor. One of them is trying to battle the crowd, make her way back toward me, shouting Miss LaRoux's name and slamming into people right and left. I realize she's had training—not just another pretty face. A bodyguard? But even she can't make any headway. The others are already almost out of sight.

I see one of them scream—mouth open, sound drowned out—in the same instant I realize Miss LaRoux's not with them. I shove my way through to the railing, trying to catch a glimpse of that brilliant red hair.

This panicked crowd is enough to trample the unprepared. With a wall on one side and the balcony railing on the other, they're channeled wilder and faster every moment, like beasts in a canyon. I see people lifted off their feet, slammed against the wall. She's not here. I'm about to stop fighting the crowd and follow the current when a cry pierces the chaos.

I shove my way toward the sound. I'm in time to see a flash of green dress and red hair and white face vanish over the railing, as some frantic man twice her size goes barreling down the walkway.

I'm moving before I have time to think. I swing out over the railing, shifting my grip so I can angle my momentum toward the floor below mine, and jump after her.

"So you knew which escape pod was yours?"

"Yes."

"Did she?"

"Know which was mine?"

"Know her own, Major. Please cooperate."

"I suppose she did. I don't know."

"But neither of you ended up where you were supposed to be."

"Some of the passengers didn't handle the evacuation well."

FOUR

LILAC

PAIN LANCES THROUGH MY SHOULDERS, AND I TASTE BLOOD as I bite the edge of my tongue—but I'm not falling anymore. I've hit another railing, the bar catching me under my arms. I have no breath, no strength. The crowd surges past, paying no attention. Spots dance before my eyes as I try to force my lungs to work before my grip gives out.

I can't have fallen more than a floor or two, or surely I wouldn't have been able to catch myself without jerking my shoulders out of their sockets. Below me stretches a drop that will shatter my body beyond any surgeon's ability to repair it.

A ragged cry tears out of me as my lungs finally expand and contract, but nobody hears. The people around me are a blur of color and sound, the smell of sweat and fear, the feel of hips and elbows connecting with my face and arms. They're too terrified to even dodge the girl clinging for her life to the railing—much less help me. "Swann!" I scream, trying to make my eyes focus on anything long enough to recognize faces, but it's all moving too quickly.

And then a voice snarls at them to keep back. Not Swann. A male voice.

Strong hands wrap around my arms, pulling me from the railing back onto the catwalk. Someone hurries me down the walkway, moving with the flow, his body between mine and the screaming people scrambling for safety. My feet don't even touch the ground.

He jerks me into a side corridor free of traffic and sets me on my feet.

All I can see are brown eyes staring into mine, stern, urgent. With an effort I recognize him.

"Major," I gasp.

"Are you all right? Are you hurt?"

My shoulders are shattered. My tongue is bleeding. I can't breathe. I gasp for air, fighting the surge of nausea that threatens to overcome me. "I'm okay."

Major Merendsen leans me against the wall like a sack of laundry and goes to the mouth of the corridor, where the crowd whizzes by in a blur. As we watch, a man in an evening coat goes down, pushed by someone behind him; in an instant he's gone, before the major can even reach for him.

This isn't a crowd—it's a riot. And a deadly one. Swann might be able to take care of herself in this chaos, but— "Anna!" I cry out abruptly, lurching away from the wall. I lunge for the crowd. I only know I need to find them.

The major grabs my arm with an iron grip. I beat at his hand, but he pulls me away and swings me around before letting me go, sending me staggering backward, heels skidding. "Are you insane?" he gasps.

"I have to find them." I raise a hand to my lips, wiping away the hint of blood from my tongue. I recognize where we are now—a maintenance corridor, one of the many that thread through the private areas of the ship. "They're out there—I need to make sure they're—"

Major Merendsen blocks the way between me and the torrent of people rushing for the lifeboats. The ship lurches again, the floor buckling and heaving beneath us, throwing us both against the wall. The sirens start up, and we have to raise our voices to make ourselves heard over the urgent wailing.

"There's nothing you can do for them," he says, when he's regained his balance. "They're two decks up and half a klick away by now. Can you walk?"

I inhale sharply through my nose. "Yes."

"Then let's move. Stay between me and the railing. I'll try to keep them from flattening you, but you have to keep your feet under you."

He turns toward the crowd, squaring his shoulders.

"Wait!" I stagger forward and grab his arm. "Not that way."

He sucks in an irritated breath, but he stops. "We have to get to an escape pod. Much more of this shaking and she'll tear herself apart."

I'm still struggling to breathe, and it takes me a moment to get enough air to reply. "I know this ship," I gasp. "There are pods for the crew nearby."

He stares at me a moment, and though I know he must be debating, struggling, none of it is written on his face. "Then let's go."

The service corridor is empty, only the emergency lighting strips along the walls to tell of any problem. The crew must be at their stations, assisting the passengers into their pods before heading for their own. Or else there's no way for them to get back here, all pretense of civilization gone.

The major follows me in silence, though I can feel his tension. For all he knows, I could be leading him to his death. I'm sure he doesn't want to follow me anywhere. But he doesn't know this ship like I do. He didn't spend his childhood in her skeleton as she was being built.

We turn down a maze of branching corridors. I head for a door marked *Authorized Personnel Only* and shove it open with a slight whine of unused hinges. My shoulders still ache, but I can use my arms—maybe I'm not so shattered after all. The door opens onto an escape bay, a five-seat pod waiting with open door for its refugees.

"Thank you for the escort, Major," I say crisply, stepping over the lip of the entrance and turning to face him. He's just behind me, stopping abruptly to avoid running into me. I want to burst into tears, thank him for what he did, but if I do, I'm not sure I'll ever stop crying. And he doesn't know what it would mean for him if we got picked up in the same pod. My father would never believe there was an innocent explanation.

"Excuse me?"

"There's another pod a little ways down the corridor. It won't take more than five minutes to reach it."

The soldier lifts both eyebrows. "Miss LaRoux, there are five seats in that pod, and I mean to use one of them. We may not have five minutes. It seems like something's pulling the ship out of hyperspace before it's supposed to."

For a moment fear freezes me. As my father's daughter, I know better than most what happens when the fabric between dimensions is disturbed. I take a deep breath and step back so as not to have to crane my neck. "Major, if they find you alone in a pod with me when the rescue ships arrive—"

"I'll take my chances," the major replies through gritted teeth.

He doesn't want to be in this pod with me any more than I want him to be. But the ship gives another horrible lurch, sending me crashing into one of the chairs. The major braces himself in the pod doorway. From somewhere in the distance comes a terrible metallic shrieking.

"Fine!" I pull myself up with the straps on the chair. This is no cushy first-class pod. This is bare-bones, designed for mechanics' crews. The floor is a grid, and as I try to stand, the heels of my Pierre Delacour pumps wedge down into the holes.

Two thousand Galactics' worth of shoes, destroyed in an instant, the silk stripped from the heels. I stare at the floor, trying to catch my breath. What difference do the shoes make? And yet I can't stop my mind turning it over, can't stop staring at the ruined shoes. My mind seizes this tiny detail and clings to it.

The major palms the pad by the door, sending it hissing closed behind him. Then he punches the auto-eject launch button, starting a count-down that gives us enough time to strap in. A trio of lights goes on overhead, blinding me. His boots clomp across the metal floor to a chair opposite mine, and he starts clipping himself in. With a jerk, I wrench my heels out of the grid floor and turn so I can sit in the chair.

I take a full breath for the first time since the alarms started blaring. Safe. For now. I'm trying not to think of the fact that there's no way the screaming crowd can all be safely inside escape pods.

The ship's autolaunch will send us speeding away from the *Icarus*, and in no more than an hour or two a rescue ship will pick us up. I just have to get through the next few hours, with only Major Merendsen for company.

His face is blank, locked down. Why did he even bother to save my life if he hates me so much? I wish I could apologize to him for what I said on the promenade deck. Tell him that what I say and what I mean are never the same, because they can't be. My throat feels tight, my mouth dry. I never should have given him another glance in the salon.

"How much would we have to pay you to *not* spread this story around once they pick us up?" I fumble with the harness. It's not the elegant and comfortable lap belts of the passenger pod—this is a five-point harness that chafes at my bare shoulders.

The major snorts, turning his head toward the tiny viewport, which shows only a scattering of stars that blur and lurch as the ship does. "Why do you assume I'd ever want to tell anyone about this?"

I decide to bury the major in icy silence until this is over, for both our sakes. If we don't speak, he'll have nothing to report.

The countdown to ejection continues, blood roaring in my ears out of annoyance with the major. Forty-five seconds. Forty. Thirty-five. I watch the numbers over the door click down one by one, trying to make my stomach settle. A LaRoux doesn't show weakness.

Without warning, we're slammed down into our seats as the entire pod jerks. A ripple of white-hot energy shoots through its metal frame. I taste copper, and then the universe goes black with a sound like a thunderclap in my ears. All the lights, the countdown, even the emergency lighting . . . gone. We're left in utter blackness but for the stars outside the viewport.

Stars that are no longer stretched thin. The *Icarus* has been torn out of hyperspace.

For a few moments there's no sound. Even the background hum of the engines and life support are gone, leaving us in the depths of the most crushing silence either of us has known since we came aboard.

The major starts cursing, and I can hear him fumbling with his straps. I understand his haste. Without power, we're going to run out of oxygen before anyone out there even realizes the *Icarus* has had a problem. But that's not our most immediate problem.

"Don't!" I manage, the words tearing out of a throat gone dry and hoarse. "There could be another surge."

"Surge?" I can hear the confusion in his voice.

"There are huge amounts of energy involved in interdimensional travel, Major. If there was another surge and you were standing on the metal floor, it could kill you."

That makes him pause. "How do you know—"

"It doesn't matter." I close my eyes, trying to concentrate on breathing.

And then, the emergency lighting comes back online. It's not much, but it's enough to see by. And it means the emergency life support has engaged.

The major's face is drawn, tense. He looks back at me, and for a moment neither of us speaks.

And then a scream of metal tears through the ship, making the pod shudder; it's still attached to the *Icarus*. We both look up at the countdown clock—still blank. We're stuck. I look across at the major, then down at the metal grid floor. If there's another surge while I'm standing on it, I'll die—but if there's another surge while we're attached to the ship, it could destroy the pod anyway.

Just do it. Don't think.

I jerk my straps open and drop to the floor. The major protests but I ignore him and make for the control panel by the door. I don't know what's happening to the *Icarus*, but I know that the last thing we want is to be attached to the ship if another surge goes through it like the last one. I just have to get the separation and ignition sequence going using the emergency power, buckle myself back in, and we'll be safe until the rescue ships show up.

You can do this. Just imagine Simon, and his tools, and everything he showed you before. . . . I take a deep breath, and open up the panel.

So much for not giving him a story to take back to the tabloids. They'd go crazy for a month with just one picture of me up to my elbows in circuits. No man, woman, or child of my class would own up to something like this.

But none of them would know what they were doing. Not like I do.

I reach in for the bundle of rainbow-colored wires behind the panel, pulling them out and inspecting them. No doubt they're coded in some way, but lacking knowledge of this particular system, I have to trace them out manually, deciphering amid the tangle which are the two I want.

"Need any help?" The question is tense but civil, revealing nothing.

I jump, jolted out of my concentration. "Not unless you were an electrician out there on the frontier, and given I've heard they don't even have lightbulbs, I doubt it."

A faint noise behind me, a muffled exhalation. Is he *laughing* at me?

I glance over my shoulder, and he's quick to avert his eyes toward the ceiling. No wire cutters, so I use my fingernails. One advantage Simon never had—he couldn't strip wires bare-handed. And he never would've dared use his teeth on live circuits.

The major is silent behind me, and when I sneak a second peek over my shoulder, his eyes are still on the ceiling. A little of my annoyance fades. He did save my life, with no guarantee he'd have time afterward to make it to an escape pod.

I shouldn't say anything to him. I should make sure there's nothing for either of us to tell when we return. I should make sure he continues thinking I'm the worst person he's ever met. But for some reason, when I've got a section of the green and white wires stripped, I find conversation fighting its way out of me. I mean to be conciliatory, but despite my best intentions, it comes out as acidic as ever.

"On the frontier, isn't this how they hot-wire a hover—"

I brush the two wires together, and instantly the rockets ignite, catapulting the pod away from the ship. I have only the briefest glimpse of the wall in front of me careening at my face before the universe goes utterly black.

"What did you think was happening at that point?"

"I didn't know. There was no communication equipment in the pod."

"You didn't try to guess?"

"We're trained to work with solid information."

"But you had none?"

"No."

"What was your plan?"

"Sit tight and hope. There was nothing to do except wait."

"And see what happened next?"

"And see what happened next."

FIVE

TARVER

THE POD'S STILL WOBBLING AND STABILIZING AS IT SHOOTS away from the ship, but we're not spinning, so I risk unclipping my harness. The gravity's fading out to half strength already and I know it will go completely soon, so I hook a foot under one of the grab straps on the floor as I kneel beside Miss LaRoux. She's on the ground, stirring and groaning, already complaining before she's fully conscious. Somehow, not surprising.

There's a tempting view down the front of her dress, but I can practically hear her snapping at me like she did before. So I jam a hand under each of her arms and rise to my feet, lifting her and setting her down in one of the five molded chairs. She lolls against me, murmuring something indecipherable as I shove her arms through the straps, yanking them tight around her.

Resisting the urge to yank them tighter still should earn me another damn medal. I check the chest strap, then lean down to grab her ankles, pushing them into the padded plastene clip waiting for them. Closer than I should be to Miss Lilac LaRoux's legs. And how the hell does she even walk with those things on her feet?

The pod lurches again, and I swallow hard as I stretch over to dump my grab bag in one of the storage alcoves, slamming the lid shut on top of it. Then I thump down into my own seat opposite her, pulling on the harness and strapping in, pushing my ankles back into the clips. In my hurry, I bang my legs into place too hard—the left clip breaks with a snap, the right one holds. The last of the gravity fades out, and I have to strain the leg that's not secured to stop it lifting up.

I study her bowed head. *Where did you learn how to do that?* I've never met a rich kid in my life who even knew how wiring worked—much less how to hot-wire a state-of-the-art escape pod. She must keep this side of her buried so deep that even the relentless paparazzi don't find it.

She moans again as the stabilizer rockets fire, throwing us both sharply against our restraints. The pod vibrates, and the constellations visible through the viewport behind Miss LaRoux's head become fixed points. I can see the ship silhouetted against the static stars. And she's rolling.

"What did you do?" My sleeping beauty is awake, glaring at me with the eye that's not swelling shut. She's going to have a shiner, black and blue in a few hours.

"I fastened your safety straps, Miss LaRoux," I say. Her scowl deepens, bordering on outrage, and I can feel my own temper bubbling up to match. "Don't worry, I kept my hands where they belong." I've mostly managed bland so far, but I can hear the subtext in my tone as well as she can. *And you couldn't pay me to try anything else.*

Her gaze hardens, but she offers no retort except cold silence. Over her shoulder I still see the *Icarus* rolling, and in my mind's eye I see the stopping and blurring of the stars through the viewing deck window, and the books in the first-class salon falling out of their shelves as the room tips and the tables and chairs topple.

The *Icarus* is spinning when nothing should be able to cause her to do so, and I can't see any other detached escape pods in the fragment of deep space beyond the viewport. Are the others out of sight? I catch a glimpse of something impossibly huge—the same thing I saw before—reflective and bright. Where is the light coming from? The next instant the pod spins and all I can see is starry darkness.

I study the metal grid on the floor, then the circuit boards overhead that the builders didn't bother to cover, the metal plates riveted into place. Not like the rest of the escape pods, I'm sure. They'll be cushy and expensive. I'd rather be in this sturdy, utilitarian pod than one of the others, somehow. Our pod jerks again, when it should be using sensors and thrusters to keep us floating gently in space. Something's causing it to ignore its programming.

I look across at Miss LaRoux, and for a moment our gazes meet. She's some combination of tired, pissed off, and just as sure as I am that something's not right. Neither of us breaks the silence, though, or names the things it might be.

Her hair's coming loose from the fancy loops and curls she had it up in, and in zero gravity, it's fanning out around her face as though she's underwater. Even with a black eye on the way, she's beautiful.

Then a violent shudder tears through the pod, shattering that moment of peace. The metal begins to hum as the vibrations increase, shaking me through the soles of my boots. I look up to see a glow outside the viewport, and then an automatic shield slides across it, prompted by some reading from outside.

That glow. I know now what was casting that light. I know what's shaking the pod, causing it to twist and turn and ignore its instructions to laze about in deep space waiting for the cavalry.

It's a planet. That glow is some planet's atmosphere reflecting a star's light, and its gravity is dragging the pod down, interfering with its guidance systems. We're landing, and that's if we make it down in one piece. We're landing if we're *lucky*.

Miss LaRoux's mouth moves, but I can't hear her—the humming's too loud, lifting to a rumble and then a roar as the air inside the pod heats up. I have to shout to make myself heard.

"Press your tongue against the roof of your mouth." I'm bellowing instructions, and she's frowning at me like I'm speaking Old Chinese. "Relax your jaw. You don't want to break your teeth or bite your tongue. We're crashing." She understands now, and she's smart enough to nod, instead of trying to shout back. I close my eyes and try, *try* to relax.

The gravity inside the pod falters, then slams back again, so my harness cuts into my chest and my breath is pushed out of my lungs with a hoarse shout I can't hear.

The air outside the pod must be white-hot as we rip through the atmosphere. We're within the pull of the planet's gravity now, but suspended as we're pulled up against our straps by our acceleration toward the ground below. For an instant Miss LaRoux meets my eyes—we're both too shocked, too shaken to communicate.

I have only that instant in which to register that she's silent, not screaming her head off like I would've expected. Then there's an impact that jolts my head back against the pad behind it so hard my teeth clash together. It turns out I'm holding my chest strap, because I nearly dislocate my thumb.

The parachute's deployed. We're floating.

We're both tense as the sudden silence draws out, waiting for the pod to connect with the ground, wondering if the parachute will reduce the impact enough that we won't end up smeared across the planet.

There's a deafening crash, and something scrabbling across the outside of the pod, and then we're turning over, upside down. The storage locker bangs open, sending my grab bag flying. I pray to whatever might be listening that it doesn't connect with us.

The pod jerks again, ricocheting wildly, tumbling end over end. I'm stuck in a world where I'm jerked against my straps over and over, thrown back and forth, until finally we settle. It takes me several quick breaths to realize we've stopped moving. Though I can barely tell which way is up, I realize I'm not hanging from my straps, so we must be upright. I feel like I've been trampled in a stampede, and I swim back toward reason, trying to understand what's happened. Somehow, unimaginably, we've landed. Right now I couldn't give a damn where. I'm alive.

Or else I'm dead, and I've ended up in hell after all, and it's an escape pod with Lilac LaRoux.

Neither of us speaks at first, though the pod's far from silent. I hear my own breathing, harsh and hoarse. Hers comes in little fits and gasps—I think maybe she's trying not to cry. The pod pings audibly as it cools, the sound slowing and softening.

I'm hurting all over, but I flex my fingers and curl my toes, shifting and stretching within the confines of the straps. No serious damage. Though Miss LaRoux's head is down, her face hidden by a sheet of red hair, I can tell she's alive and conscious from her breathing. Her hand moves, feeling around for the release on her straps.

"Don't," I say, and she freezes. I hear how it sounds—like an order. I try for something a little softer. There's no point bullying her. For a start, she won't listen to me if I do. "No point in both of us going flying if it rolls again, Miss LaRoux. Stay where you are for now." I release my own straps and ease them away, rolling my shoulders as I push carefully to my feet.

She looks up at me, and for a moment I forget what she's done, and I'm sorry for her. It's the same white, pinched, blank face I've seen in the field.

Two years ago, I was a brand-new recruit myself. A year ago, I was hitting the field for the first time. That was me, freezing up until my sergeant grabbed my arm and hauled me down behind half a brick wall. A laser burned a hole right where my head had been a moment before.

Thing is, though some of the kids who react this way get blown to bits, some of us come out the other side and make good soldiers.

There's blood on her neck where the backs of her earrings have punched through the skin, and her face is so pale that I know what's coming before she speaks.

"I think I'm going to be sick," she says in a choked whisper, and then she's pressing her lips together again. I reach up to hold on to the hanging straps and stand with my feet apart, shifting my weight. I can't rock the pod, which means it's probably wedged in firmly.

"All right," I say, in the same gentle voice that worked on me the first time I froze, dropping to one knee in front of her and helping her with her straps. "All right, hang on a moment, breathe in through your nose." She whimpers and scrambles free of the straps, dropping to her knees on the metal grid floor. That'll leave a mark later.

I flip up the seat of the spare chair, and sure enough there's a storage locker underneath it. I lift out the toolbox and set it aside. She understands my intention and leans past me to grip the edges of it, back arching as she retches. I leave her to it, getting to work hauling open the hatches of the lockers and storage compartments built in all over this thing. There's a water tank, the silver wrappers of ration packs, a first-aid kit marked with a red cross, the toolbox. I find a slightly grubby rag stashed inside one, and hold it out to her as she lifts her head. She stares at it dubiously—still blessedly silent—but finally takes it gingerly, using the cleanest corner to wipe her mouth.

Crash-landed on an unknown planet, a black eye on the way, and the contents of her stomach now in the underseat storage locker, and she still feels the need to act like she's above it all.

She coughs, trying to clear her throat. "How long do you think it will be before the shuttles will find us?"

I realize that she thinks the *Icarus* is still okay—that they're doing repairs as we speak. That her surface-going craft will come scoop us up at any moment, that this is all some fleeting nightmare. My annoyance fades a little as I think about telling her what I saw. The *Icarus* dipping, wallowing in the atmosphere of this planet, fighting a losing battle against gravity.

No, telling her will just send her into hysterics, like it would any of those people I met in the first-class salon. Best to keep some things close to my chest.

"First things first," I say instead, hunting for something I can use to pour her a cup of water. This works with the recruits too—a firm, businesslike tone, cheerful but not quite friendly, pushing them toward tasks they can focus on. "Let's learn what we can about where 'here' is."

As I speak, I'm watching the heat shields retract on the windows, and something releases inside my chest as I look outside. Trees. "We're in luck. This place looks like it's terraformed. There must be sensors for checking the air quality outside."

"There are," she agrees. "But the electrical surge fried them. We don't need them, though. It's safe."

"Glad you're so sure, Miss LaRoux," I retort before I can stop myself. "I think I'd rather an instrument told me so. Not that I don't trust your extensive training."

Her eyes narrow, and if looks could kill, then toxic atmospheres would be the least of my problems.

"We're already breathing the air," she replies tightly, lifting one hand to gesture toward the lockers by her feet.

I crouch to get a look at where she's pointing, and for an instant I stop breathing, lungs seizing. You can't see it unless you're down low, but the pod's been ripped like a massive can opener ran along one side of it. I remind myself that nobody's started choking and force myself to inhale.

"Well, look at that. Must have happened on landing." I listen to my own voice. Sounds calm. Good. "So the terraforming is in advanced stages for sure. And that means—"

"Colonies," she whispers, closing her eyes as she completes my sentence.

I don't blame her. There's a crack on the tip of my tongue about how soon she'll be able to find company she prefers to mine, but the truth is I'm just as relieved. The companies that own this place will have colonies all over the planet's surface. Which means somewhere on this planet, maybe even nearby, folks are wondering what the hell is going on up there. They'll probably show up ready to fight, expecting hijackers or raiders, but I don't think we'll have a hard time convincing them we're crash survivors. I could live without being in my fatigues, though. Most of the settlers on the remote colonies aren't too fond of my kind.

"Keep sitting," I say, rising to my feet and filling the canteen from my pack at the water tank. "I'm going to stick my head outside and see if the communications array is okay."

She raises an eyebrow at me, her mouth curving to a tiny smile that somehow manages to be superior, despite the hair everywhere, and the blood, and the black eye. I feel myself bristle as that smile echoes every condescending moment I've ever experienced at the hands of her people.

"Major," she says, speaking slowly, as if to a child, "all we have to do is stay put. Even if the communications array is gone, the colonists will have seen the crash. My father's teams are probably already on their way."

I wish I could afford to be so sure someone was going to swoop down and save me, but I've never been able to count on that in the past. Then again, I'm not Roderick LaRoux's only child.

I leave her sitting on one of the seats, arranging her skirt artistically and clasping her hands in her lap, and head for the door. It takes the weight of my whole body behind my shoulder to ram it free of its warped frame. It gives with a screech that the uncharitable might suggest sounds just like Miss LaRoux, when displeased.

Outside, everything's quiet. The chilly air is rich—not thin and spare like it is on some of the younger colonized planets. In fact, I don't think I've ever breathed anything so pure, not even at home. I shove that thought away. I can't let myself be distracted by thinking of home, of my parents. I'm stranded with the richest girl in the galaxy, and I need to make sure that when her daddy shows up to find us, we're out in plain sight.

I can't hear birds, or any of the small scuffles that might suggest there's local wildlife on the move. Then again, our pod's cut a furrow through the surrounding woods that stretches nearly a klick, huge trees laid out flat and ground into the mud along the length of the scar. Perhaps the local fauna's just hiding up trees and down holes, waiting for the end of the world to continue.

The trees are tall and straight, their lower trunks mostly devoid of limbs, their foliage a dark green with a distinctive smell, crisp and clean. I've seen them before. I don't know their technical name, but we call them pole trees. They're the first trees the terraforming crews get in, once all the organic muck has provided a basic layer of soil. They grow quickly, and make good building material with those tall, straight trunks. It's later that the ornamental and the harvest trees are planted. So, perhaps this is my first hint at where we might be. Since I see pole trees and not much else, we're probably on a newer planet, despite the rich air.

But they're large enough that the ecosystem has clearly had a while to take. In fact, they're huge, bigger than any pole trees I've ever seen. They stretch up skyward at least half as tall again as usual, their spindly tops bending under the weight of the branches. How did they get so big? By this point, the terraformers should have introduced all manner of other species that would've edged the pole trees out of the ecosystem.

Any hopes I had for the communications array are answered with a glance. It's been ripped off, and if it wasn't fried by the surge or burned up when we entered the atmosphere, then it's probably lying somewhere back along our swath of destruction, reduced to its component parts. So my cranky heiress might be right, and her father might show up any minute, but more than likely we're going to look like one of ten thousand pieces of debris scattered across the planet. We need to find a bigger crash site, a more prominent place, so we'll be somewhere the rescue party will definitely land.

I study the trees around me that are still standing. Like regular pole trees, they get narrow toward the top, so there's no way I'm climbing high enough to see any distance. She's lighter and might manage, but I'm grinning just thinking about it. *Come on, Miss LaRoux. Your evening gown will match the trees. The nature goddess look is all the rage in Corinth, trust me.* I wonder if she's ever even seen real leaves.

That's when I realize, standing there in the middle of this disaster, aching all over from being jerked back and forth against my restraints, but grinning like an idiot—I kind of like this. After weeks trussed up on board the ship, chest covered in medals and days taken up by people who don't like their war too real, I feel like I'm home.

There's a hill some way off to what I arbitrarily call the west, because the sun's setting in that direction. The land rises, and with any luck it'll offer the view we need. It'll be a long walk, and as I climb back up into the ruined pod, perhaps it's my newfound good mood that has me feeling a little sorry for the girl inside. I might be back in my world, but she's out of hers. I know well enough how it feels.

"Our communications are gone," I tell her.

I half expected tears—instead she just nods as if she already knew. "They would've been useless anyway. Most of the circuits got shorted during that electrical surge."

I want to ask her how she knows, where she learned to do what she did, but instead the question that emerges is: "What was that? The surge?"

She hesitates, her eyes on the trees visible outside the viewport. "The *Icarus* came out of hyperspace when it wasn't supposed to. Something happened, I don't know what. Didn't you learn about hyperspace jumps in school?" There's disdain in her voice, but she doesn't stop long enough for me to reply. Just as well, because all I know about hyperspace is that it gets you from A to B without taking two hundred years.

"The way ships skip through dimensions, folding space—there are huge quantities of energy involved." She glances at me, as though trying to figure out if I'm following. "Usually when a ship leaves hyperspace there's a long series of steps that prevent that energy from backlashing. Whatever's going on, the *Icarus* got pulled out of hyperspace early."

I shouldn't be surprised that the daughter of Roderick LaRoux, engineer of the largest, finest hyperspace fleet in the galaxy, knows any of this. But it's hard to reconcile her vapid laughter and scathing insults with someone who'd pay two seconds of her attention to physics lessons.

I certainly never knew there was this level of danger involved with traveling via hyperspace. But then, I've never heard of this happening before. Ever.

I'm turning over her explanation in my mind. "Since we came out of hyperspace early, we could be anywhere in the galaxy, then?" No communications. No clue where we are. This just keeps getting better and better.

"The *Icarus* got emergency power back," Miss LaRoux says coolly. "They would've gotten distress calls out."

Assuming there was anyone alive in the comms room after that surge. But I don't say it aloud. Let her think this will all be over sooner rather than later. I know she has to be struggling. "There's a rise to the west. I'm going to climb up before it gets dark, figure out where we should head. I can get some of the ration bars out for you, in case you get hungry while you wait."

"No need, Major," she says, climbing to her feet, then grimacing as one of her heels falls through the grating in the floor. "I'll be coming with you. If you think I'm giving you the opportunity to abandon me here, you're sorely mistaken."

And just like that, I'm not feeling sorry for her anymore.

Abandon her? If only my duty or my conscience would let me. The galaxy would be better off, if you ask me. Who'd even know we were in the same pod?

Except that I would know. And that would be enough.

"I'm not sure your shoes—" I try, before she cuts me off.

"My shoes will be fine, Major." She comes sweeping across the floor and miraculously keeps her heels from sliding through again, then descends the steps. Her head is up, shoulders back, movements ludicrously graceful—like she's descending a staircase to a ballroom dance floor. I leave her to examine her new kingdom, and climb up to open up my grab bag, rifling through the contents. This is the emergency gear we all carry, and I've never been more grateful for all the time I've spent lugging it places over the last two years.

Mine has all the usual—my classified intel on encrypted memory storage, flashlight, water-purifying canteen, matches, and razor blade, plus a few personal items: a photograph of home and my notebook. On board the *Icarus*, it held my Gleidel as well, since it was uncouth to carry a visible sidearm.

I haul out my gun, curling one hand around the grip and quickly checking the charge to make sure the kinetic battery's working properly. At least I don't have to worry about it running down while we're here. I settle it back into its holster and strap it on to my belt, then scoop a couple of ration bars out of the overhead storage locker. After picking up the canteen from where Miss LaRoux dumped it on the floor, I head back out and wrestle the door closed behind me. No need to offer the local wildlife the opportunity to take revenge for our invasion by feasting on our rations.

The hike is one of the most goddamn awful things I've ever done.

It's not a difficult walk, though the underbrush is thick, and there are fallen trees to scramble over, rough bark grabbing at my clothes and scraping my skin. The temperature's not cold enough to keep the sweat from dripping down my spine, but the air carries a chilly bite that aches in my lungs. None of the plants are quite familiar, but none of them are completely unknown—just a little different, a twist on what I'm used to. There are dips and hollows waiting to wrench my ankles, and prickly plants snag my shirt, leaving little barbs to stick my arm later.

None of these things is the problem.

The problem is Miss LaRoux, who's trying to keep up with me in heels. I wish she'd just stayed behind, because I could move a lot faster without her. But every time I turn to ask if she wants to head back, she gives me a frigid look, lips set, stubborn.

I offer her my hand to help her clamber over obstacles, though it's getting to the point where if she fell down a hole, I'm not sure I'd bother fishing her out. At first she looks at my hand as though she might catch something from skin-to-skin contact. It's like she's determined to make it through this hike looking like it's no more difficult than a stroll through a meadow. But after a few near misses, she's gingerly resting her fingers on my palm every so often, doing the very least possible to accept my assistance. She's still looking white despite her squared jaw, and I stay close enough that I'll be able to get between her and the nearest hard surface if she decides to top it all off by fainting.

Eventually I give up. "Would you like a rest?" I'm trying not to be too obvious about checking the progress of the sun toward the hill. I don't want to be out here once the sun sets. It's hard enough dragging this brat through the woods without her breaking an ankle trying to walk in the dark.

She considers the question, then nods, reaching up to tuck her hair back where it belongs. "Where will I sit?"

Sit? Why, on this comfortable chaise longue I've carried here for you in my pocket, Your Highness, so glad you asked.

I clamp my mouth shut, struggling not to say it aloud. Miss LaRoux notices me biting back a response and her expression darkens. But I can see where the holes punched by her earrings are still oozing, and that her nose is swelling up from the blow she got while hot-wiring the escape pod, and that her lips are chapped and raw. It's a wonder she hasn't completely fallen to pieces—it's what I would've expected of someone like her.

So instead, I haul off my jacket and lay it out on a log for her. She twitches her skirts into position and then lowers herself onto it, accepting the canteen and taking a delicate sip. She averts her gaze as I take it back and lift it for a long swallow, before capping it once more. I walk the edge of the clearing, pausing every so often to listen. The rustle of small creatures in the undergrowth has returned, and I'm hoping against hope she doesn't hear—let alone see—anything making those noises.

The fact that I can hear the local wildlife adds another layer of information to the picture I'm slowly building—it wouldn't be here unless the planet was in the final stages of terraforming. It ought to be brimming with colonies, the skies full of shuttle craft and planes. So why are the only sounds the rustle of the undergrowth, the whispering of the wind through the leaves, and the sound of Miss LaRoux trying to catch her breath as quietly as she can?

I'm about to suggest she turn back and retrace our path, when she rises to her feet of her own accord, leaving the jacket for me to retrieve. I half expect her to stalk off back toward the escape pod without a word, but instead she actually gestures for me to precede her, in the direction we were traveling. Her jaw's squared as we set off, and as she takes my hand to climb over a log in those ridiculous shoes, I'm forced to concede that she's tougher than she looks.

It's a relief—the idea of keeping her safe weighs me down, my shoulders tense and my gut roiling. No matter how irritating she is, she's a long way from home. If she's going to get through this, it's all on me. Sometimes I feel like I spend my life trying to keep other people safe.

By the time we reach the base of the rise, she's panting despite her clear intention to look like she's got it together. But we can't afford to rest again if we want to get back to the pod before dark. We both scramble up the incline, and when I take her hands to haul her with me, she doesn't bother to look scandalized, too exhausted to waste time on pretense.

It turns out to be a craggy hill, the land sloping up one side, then falling away steeply down the other in a rocky cliff. The crest provides exactly the vantage point we need, and we stand side by side to take in the view.

I wish I'd come alone.

She gasps, breaking her panting for a noise that's part sob, part wordless distress. Mouth open, she's staring, and so am I, neither of us capable of processing what we're seeing. It's quite possible nobody's ever seen something like this before.

I try her name. "Lilac. Lilac, don't watch." Low and gentle, trying to cajole that recruit in the field into lifting her foot, taking a step, getting out of there. "Look at me, don't watch it happening, come on." But she can't drag her gaze away any more than I can, and we stare together, turned to stone.

Before us, pieces of debris are streaming down from the sky in long, slow arcs, burning as they fall like a meteor shower or incoming missiles. They're only a sideshow, though.

The *Icarus* is falling. She's like a great beast up in the sky, and I imagine her groaning as she wallows and turns, some part of her still fighting, engines still firing in an attempt to escape gravity. For a few moments she seems to hang there, eclipsing one of the planet's moons, pale in the afternoon sky. But what comes next is inevitable, and I find myself reaching out to put an arm around the girl beside me as the ship dies, pieces still peeling away as she makes her final descent.

She comes in on an angle, heading for a mountain range beyond the plains. Debris the size of skyscrapers goes flying, and one side begins to shear away as the friction becomes too much for her. Smaller shards of fire stream off of her as she goes, arcing across the sky like shooting

"You'd been in survival situations before."

"That's true."

"But never like this?"

"I never had a debutante in tow, if that's what you mean."

"I meant that you didn't know where you were at that stage."

"I wasn't focused on that."

"What were you focused on, Major?"

"Working out where the rescue party would land, and getting there."

"And that was all?"

"What else was there?"

"That's what we'd like you to tell us."

SIX

LILAC

HE'S LEADING ME AWAY FROM THE BLUFF, HIS HAND WRAPPED around my wrist. His fingers are five individual points of contact, rough and hot, too tight. I think my eyes are closed. Whether they are or not, the only thing I see is the fall of the *Icarus*, a river of fire in the sky, great storm clouds of smoke and steam. It's burned into my retinas, blinding me to anything else. He could pull me off the cliff and I wouldn't notice until we hit the ground.

My ankles wrench and twist as I stumble along in his wake, the heels of my shoes rolling on the uneven ground or else sinking into the earth and tripping me. Why don't ladies dress for such occasions? Surely the occasional hiking boot with evening wear would make a statement.

A bubble of laughter tears out of my throat, and he pauses only long enough to glance over his shoulder at me before shifting his grip on my arm.

"Only a little farther, Miss LaRoux. You're doing well."

I'm not doing much at all. I might as well be a rag doll. Comes complete with matching shoes. Spine sold separately.

I've got no clue where we are or how far behind we've left the pod, but as a branch hits me in the face, I'm forced to close my eyes again. The ship is still there, a painting of muddled afterimages. The sunlight's lancing almost horizontally through the trees, alternating flashes of glare and shadow that shine red through my eyelids. How long were we on that bluff?

My father's ship is in ruins. I watched her fall from the sky. How many souls fell with her? How many couldn't launch their pods?

My legs stop working. He nearly jerks my arm out of its socket in his attempt to keep me on my feet, and some detached part of my mind notes how much that's going to hurt later. Another tug, and I can't quite help the moan that squeezes past my lips. After a second he seems to accept that he cannot drag me through the forest without some assistance from me.

He drops my arm and I collapse in a heap, barely catching myself on my forearms before my face hits the half-rotted gunk coating the forest floor. It smells like coffee and leather and garbage—nothing like the sweet, homogenous earth in the holo-gardens on Corinth. So much for trying to get through this with some dignity. So much for making him think I haven't fallen apart.

I'm given a moment to pant, the force of my breath blowing bits of leaf and dirt away. When he crouches beside me, I can't help but flinch back.

"Lilac." The gentleness in his voice is more arresting than any barked order could be. I lift my head to find his brown eyes not far from mine. It's like I can see the *Icarus*'s fall etched on his face, the way I know it is on mine.

"Come on. It's going to be dark soon, and I want us back safe in the pod before that happens. You're doing so well, and it's only a little farther."

I wish he'd kept being an ass. Dislike is so much easier to handle than sympathy. "I can't," I find myself gasping, something tight and cold inside me cracking open. "I can't, Major. I won't do any of this. I don't belong here!"

He lifts his eyebrows, the expression taking away some of the grimness about his face. There's a curious warmth to his features when he lets them relax. This, more than anything, jars me from my haze of grief and denial. Then he speaks, and ruins it.

"Just try to stay on your feet. Do you think you can manage that much, Your Highness?"

Much better. "Don't patronize me," I snap.

"Only an idiot would patronize you, Miss LaRoux." The warmth is gone again, and he stands up in one smooth motion.

He takes a few steps away, scanning the forest around us as though he recognizes something in it. He's at home here. He can read this place like I read the tiny shifts in a crowd, the back-and-forth of couples and conversation, society executing its slow revolutions around me like the stars in the heavens. Known. Charted. Familiar.

The forest has nothing of this. To me it's a haze of green and gold and gray, every tree like the next, nothing of sense to be gleaned from them. I've been in nature before, but then, all it took was the flick of a switch to change the holographic projector from perfectly sculpted and manicured garden terraces to a sunny, songbird-filled forest. It smelled of airy perfume, and all the trees were hung with flowers. The earth was rich and uniform and never stained my clothes, and the ground was soft enough to sleep on.

When I was little my father used to bring me to that forest for picnics. I'd pretend the forest with its cathedral canopy was my mansion and I was the hostess, serving him invisible cups of tea and sharing the inconsequential secrets of my life. He was always solemn, playing along without hesitation. As the light waned I'd pretend to fall asleep in his lap, because then he'd carry me home in his arms.

But this forest is thick and alien and full of shadows, and the ground has rocks in it, and when I try to use a nearby tree for support, its bark scratches my hands. This can't be real—this is a nightmare.

And yet the major nods to himself, like he's read the next step from some instruction manual I can't see. A surge of jealousy runs through me so violently that my arms quiver where they're holding me up.

"I don't know how much battery power the pod has," he says, "so we'll use as little as possible. I'll get you a bed set up in there and we'll keep the lights off, and tomorrow I'll figure out if there's any chance at all we're sending a signal for rescue ships to read."

He's still talking, taking so little notice of me that he might as well be talking to himself. "I think for tonight we'll concentrate on taking stock, having something to eat, getting some rest. I promise you the pod is only a short distance away. Can you stand?"

I push myself onto my knees. Now that we've stopped, my ankles have stiffened, and I'm forced to bite down on my lip to keep from letting out a sob. I've sprained an ankle or two on the dance floor while smiling as though everything was fine, but it was never like this. Then, all I had to do was summon a medic and the discomfort melted away.

I swat his hand away when he extends it.

"Of course I can stand." Pain makes my words come out clipped, angry. His expression locks down tight, and he turns to lead the way back.

He's true to his word, and in only a few minutes the pod comes into view through the trees. From this direction I can't see the impact of our crash: the flattened trees and the deep groove in the earth carved by the pod as it rolled and skidded to where it rests. I see only trees, hear only incomprehensible rustling and shuffling. Even the stench of scorched plastene and corroded metal is fading, swallowed by the smell of green and wet and earth.

I drag forth enough energy to look up. Not a single rescue ship in sight—not even a shuttle or a plane from a colony. The sky is empty but for a pale sliver of moon overhead, and a second moon just clearing the trees. Shading my eyes with my hand, I look for the beacon light that should indicate that we're broadcasting our signal to the rescue ships. There's only the broad expanse of pitted, twisted metal. So much of the pod is wrecked—how did we survive?

How could anyone else? But I push that thought down, lock it away. This will all be over in a matter of hours—a ship as famous and as respected as the *Icarus* can't go down without setting off a thousand alarms all across the galaxy.

The major has continued on into the pod without a word, but he is only a few steps away, and I cannot let myself grieve yet.

I cannot think of Anna, and her face as she was swept on down the corridor by the panicked crowd, stripped suddenly of its coy confidence. Maybe she got into a pod. Maybe there was a mechanic who got hers free in time.

I cannot think about the fact that we have no signal light, no beacon, nothing to tell our rescuers where to look for us. My father will come for me, no matter what. He'll move heaven and earth and space itself to find me. Then I'll never have to see this soldier again, never have to feel so incapable.

When I step over the lip of the doorway into the pod, the major is going through his pack again, doing one of his supply checks. Like he thinks he can somehow make rescue come more quickly by taking inventory.

How can he just stand there, hunting through that stupid bag? I want to shake him, scream at him that our rescue ship isn't in that bag, that nothing's going to have magically appeared inside it to put the *Icarus* back into the sky where she belongs.

"Well?" I manage to sound civil. "You always know what the next step is—what now?"

He doesn't lift his head until he's finished his check, infuriating in and of itself—but when he does glance over at me, he only gives a slow blink. "Right now we sleep. Then tomorrow, if we're not broadcasting, we'll head out and find a better place to be seen. Maybe the wreck itself, if we don't come across a colony between here and there."

The wreck? The man's insane. It's days away at least. "Head *out*? Speak for yourself. I'm not going anywhere. They'll see our crash site. If we leave, my father won't know where to look for us." And he *will* come for me.

His look is dubious, almost insolent. "You may be content to wait for your white knight, my lady, but I'm not going to sit around while our supplies run out."

My lady? Does he know how crazy his faux courtesy makes me? Surely no one could be so aggravating by accident or coincidence. I cling to that anger, trying not to let it fade as I look at him. It's safe, this fury. I can't afford to feel anything else.

The anger is a shield, and if I relinquish it, I'll shatter.

A tiny piece of me wonders if he knows that. On the ship he was out of his element, awkward and almost tentative. Here, he's certain. Everything he does has a purpose. Maybe some part of him is deliberately goading me, keeping me strong.

Or maybe he's just an ass.

I stew in silence as he goes through that pack of his again, and then the lockers. He piles a coarse reflective space blanket with a softer one he finds in a locker near the roof, then looks across at me expectantly.

When I just gaze back at him, confused, his jaw tightens.

"Abhorrent though it may seem to you, we *are* going to have to spend the night together. Brace yourself."

With a jolt, I realize it's not supposed to be a random pile of fabric, but a bed. Just the one bed. The words fly from my lips before I can stop them. "Absolutely *not*." My voice has the same cold steel my father's does—at least I can put what I've learned from him to good use. "If you will leave me some water, you can take the rest of the supplies and sleep out there, in the forest you enjoy so much."

I'm watching him carefully, so I see his hands curling slowly into fists. An odd flare of pleasure runs through me. If he's infuriating me on purpose, then at least I can give as good as I get. "Maybe while you're at it you can stand on top of the pod and flag down the rescue teams when they come in the night."

He throws his pack down, making me jump. When he speaks, though, his voice is calm, controlled. "Miss LaRoux," he says softly. "All due respect, but I'm not sleeping outside when there's a perfectly good shelter here."

My satisfaction at having stung him falters. If the rescue teams do find us in the night, Merendsen's war hero status won't last long in the face of my father's wrath.

I take a deep breath, trying to backtrack. Maybe anger wasn't the way to go. "Major, the circumstances might be unconventional, but that's no reason to abandon—"

"Screw the circumstances." Despite everything, the flash of annoyance across his features prompts an answering surge of satisfaction in me. At least there's one thing I can do well in this godforsaken wilderness. "It's going to be cold out there, and it'll be warmer in here with two. I'm as tired as you are and I'm not going to stay up all night on watch. I also don't think much of being eaten."

That makes me pause. "Eaten?"

"Tracks," he says shortly. "In the woods, a ways back. Big ones."

He's trying to scare me, I know. I saw no tracks, and he certainly never pointed them out to me. Besides, terraforming companies would never introduce large enough predators to their ecosystems to endanger human inhabitants. I grit my teeth.

Even if he was telling the truth, the risk of predators would be less than the risks he'd face if found with me. "Major Merendsen, believe me, if my father finds us together—"

"—then you'll have to find a way to explain it to him. I'm not going out there in the face of all good sense. You can have the bed, I'm fine in one of these chairs. Sleep or don't sleep as you like, but if we have to move out tomorrow, I expect you to keep up a decent pace. Good night."

It's an order: *Good night, Private, or else.* Without another word, he jerks the string tight on his bag, slouches in his chair, and stretches his long legs out in front of him. His chin to his chest, he closes his eyes and clicks the flashlight off, leaving me in darkness. The only sound is his breathing as it immediately begins to slow.

Without his face distracting me, it's easier to be furious. How can he have been so abrupt with me? Doesn't he realize that I'm only trying to keep him from losing his commission—or worse? I struggle with the urge to wake him up and insist. I wish I were brave enough to sleep outside, but lie or no, his talk of big animal tracks is enough to keep me from moving.

I take a deep breath and try to think. My father isn't completely unreasonable—surely he'll understand. Especially since it's quite clear the major doesn't want anything to do with me. Perhaps it isn't the end of the world if he stays here, just for tonight.

And a tiny, tiny part of me points out that I'd rather have him here, beside me, in case anything does come in the night.

I slide between the two blankets, trying not to wince at the coarseness of the space blanket against my skin. It's barely better than sleeping on the floor, the metal grid cutting into my hip, and I begin to think maybe the major has the smarter idea. I'll be damned before I imitate him, though, so I curl up beneath the blanket, pillowing my head on my arm.

Maybe there's something I can do with the remnants of the communications array. Get some sort of signal transmitting, to tell people we're here. If I can prove we're signaling, maybe the major won't drag me across this nightmare of a planet.

I'm inching toward sleep when my cousin's face flashes in front of my eyes. My throat seizes so suddenly it's as though invisible hands are strangling me. She was only doing what my father forced her to do; she was still my best, my only friend. I should have gone back for her, tried to find her in the crowd, brought her with us. And instead, I left her there.

My lips shape the words in the darkness. *I left her there to die.*

I think of Elana, her mindless devotion to chasing the trends I set. I think of Swann, the ragged edge to her voice as she tried to fight her way back through the crowd to get to me as the *Icarus* began to break apart. Did they find escape pods that worked? Or did Swann spend too long trying to find me in the midst of the crowds, and go down in flames with my father's ship?

It isn't the first time someone's death has been my fault, but that doesn't make it any less impossible to bear.

My father is light-years away, perhaps being told at this moment what happened to the *Icarus*. And he has no one there to lean on, without me. Since my mother's death when I was little, we've never been apart for more than a few weeks at a time—and never without the ability to speak to each other at the touch of a button on a console.

And now I'm stranded on an alien planet with a soldier who hates me and everything I aspire to.

For the first time in my life, I'm alone.

I cover the sounds my tears make, tossing and turning in my make-shift bed, so the space blanket crinkles noisily. I expect him to chastise me for being such a princess, but he says nothing and his breathing doesn't change. He doesn't even hear me. I give up and just let myself cry.

"At that stage your expectation was that you would be rescued promptly?"

"I was with Miss LaRoux. I imagined she'd be their top priority."

"What did you make of your companion?"

"It was a change of pace from a platoon."

"That's not a substantive response, Major Merendsen."

"I hadn't had long to form an opinion. The situation wasn't ideal."

"For you or her?"

"For either of us. Do you know anyone who'd have been pleased in our places?"

"We'll ask the questions, Major."

SEVEN

TARVER

I'M ABOUT TEN SECONDS AWAY FROM TURNING ON THE flashlight and searching the first-aid kit for a way to sedate her when she finally stops crying. Eventually, I sleep.

It's late when I wake, sometime after midnight. For a long moment I sit perfectly still, letting my senses inform me. I feel cold metal and hard lines pressed against my skin, I smell the lingering odor of melted plastene. I hear some creature give a croak outside, and closer, inside the pod, a small sound as someone moves.

Memory bubbles to the surface and spreads out through my body, racing down my arms so my fingers tighten around the armrests. I haven't opened my eyes yet, and as I let my mind drift and deliver information, I hear the soft scrape of movement again. Light flashes across my eyelids. She's got the flashlight.

Dammit, doesn't she need to sleep? I sneak open one eyelid. She's at the electrical panel again, fussing with the wires. She's backlit by the flashlight, nibbling her lower lip. She looks different in this light. I can't make out the fancy hair or the remains of her makeup, and the black eye is concealed by the shadow. She looks clearer, cleaner, younger. More like somebody I could talk to.

I wonder what my parents would make of her. Their faces swim up, and my throat tightens. If the *Icarus* lost contact with LaRoux Industries when she fell out of hyperspace, then maybe my parents haven't heard anything about a crash yet. Maybe they think the ship is just missing. *I'm okay*, I think, wishing I could beam that thought straight to them. I don't even know which way to aim it—this planet could be anywhere in the galaxy.

As I watch, the girl expertly snaps a wire into place. I remember the way she stripped them with her fingernails before takeoff. We would have gone down still attached to the ship if she hadn't. My mind's eye conjures up the image of the other escape pods, streaming ribbons of fire as they split off from the *Icarus* during the crash.

Without a doubt, Lilac LaRoux saved our lives. That's a little hard to swallow.

I clear my throat to give her some warning before I speak. "Miss LaRoux?"

Her head snaps up. "Yes, Major?" She's keeping her voice polite and even, like she's at a garden party and I'm some annoying aunt who just won't back off.

Maybe if I shut up, she'll electrocute herself. "Need a hand there?"

She huffs a soft, derisive breath. "Unless you know how to bypass the comms relays, I can't see how you're in a position to help. If I can force the enviro circuit board to take over for comms, maybe I can use the pod itself as an antenna. It's made of metal."

We're silent for a moment. We both know that I couldn't point out the environmental controls circuit board with a gun to my head.

She takes my silence as a victory, and smiles that infuriatingly superior smile at me. "If I can get us a signal, *then* will you admit it's better to stay put and wait, rather than go trekking across unknown territory by ourselves?"

I take a deep breath through my nose and let my head fall back again. She turns back, crouching in front of the panel. I watch her covertly out of the corner of my eye, as much fascinated by her unlikely expertise as by the sight of the LaRoux heiress absently moving the flashlight to her mouth so she can hold it in her teeth as she works.

It's another glimpse of the girl I saw in the salon, the one who stood up for a man accosting her instead of letting her lackeys deal with him. Where's that girl the rest of the time? With a wrench of my stomach I realize that the man in the salon, the reason I talked to Lilac LaRoux in the first place, is probably dead now. Did anyone else survive? Did any of the escape pods break away before the *Icarus* hit the atmosphere?

At some point, between one blink and the next, I fall asleep.

"What did Miss LaRoux think of the situation?"

"I didn't ask her."

"What was your impression, then, of the way Miss LaRoux was coping?"

"Better than expected."

EIGHT

LILAC

I WAKE CURLED UP AGAINST A WALL, A BLANKET AROUND me, my face aching. For a moment I lie there trying to remember what I did the night before, dreading the return of memory, certain that my hangover will be the least of my concerns. Then the unmistakable smell of half-melted plastene jerks me awake, and I wish it was a hangover making my head pound—not the aftereffects of having a spaceship hit me in the face.

I glance at the broken communications array I tried to salvage last night. The wires are fused and melted beyond repair. The whole mother-board short-circuited, leaving nothing an entire team of electricians could salvage, much less me.

I should have just left well enough alone and gotten some rest.

The morning is quiet, which terrifies me. There has always been noise around me, even in our country house. The sounds of air filters and the garden shifting from roses to daffodils with the deft, mechanical click of its holographic projectors. Servants bustling here and there, Simon tossing pebbles at my window to wake me in the night. My father on the holowire at the breakfast table, delivering orders to his deputies back on Corinth while pulling faces to make me laugh.

Here, the only sounds are the faint noises of birds, and leaves whispering against each other high above.

Knowing that the major is going to insist we move out, I brace myself, trying to summon courage or strength or, at the very least, some dignity.

A whole day of him marching me along, telling me every five minutes that I need to keep moving, walk faster. A whole day of slowing him down.

A sudden dread prickles in my stomach. I'm sitting up almost before it registers—I already know its source. The chair the major had been sleeping in is empty, and his bag of supplies is gone.

I'm not ready for the panic that washes over me. I want to scream his name, and only fear tightening my throat prevents me. Yes, I was alone even with him there, but he knew things—the forest, how to walk, how to live—that I could never hope to learn.

My glares and jabs have driven him away. I lurch to my feet and stumble to the door of the pod, pushing it open and clinging to the frame. It's barely dawn, and I can see only a few meters into the dark woods. There's no pattern to the trees—each one is slightly different, undergrowth haphazardly scattered. There are no paths, no flowers. Nothing moves but for a branch waving gently in the breeze.

Every scowl of his, every irritated twist of his mouth flashes before my eyes. *Tarver*, screams my mind. *Come back. I'm sorry.*

With a rush, the pain of my twisted ankles, the weakness of having slept so little, the fear—it all sweeps over me and I fall heavily against the wall of the pod, eyes still staring at the unreadable mess of leaves and branches.

And then the clang of my body hitting the door frame isn't the only sound. A twig snaps, electric in the silence, and somewhere in the shadow something moves. I freeze, breath catching in my throat like a sob.

Tracks, he said. *Big ones.*

I'm given only a moment to imagine what creature might make even a war hero pause, before the source of the sound comes looming out of the dark wood.

Major Merendsen raises his eyebrows at me, and I know he can see my panic in the moment before I school my features. His mouth quirks in faint amusement. "Sorry to disappoint you, but it's going to take more than a few dirty looks to drive me off."

All my panic and helplessness and relief collapse into red-hot humiliation. This time there's nothing to stop me from lashing out at him. "Don't flatter yourself, Major." I sound like Anna, instantly superior. The thought makes my throat constrict, my voice strangle. "Your whereabouts are the least of my problems. But what exactly do you think you're doing, traipsing around out there? Anything could have come in! I could have—" My throat closes as I run out of words. I know I'm not angry with him. But screaming helps.

Major Merendsen watches me mildly, slipping his pack off his shoulder and settling it at his feet before arching his back in a stretch. I watch him as my anger ebbs, leaving me ashamed. It's a few seconds before I look away. The shirt of his casual uniform stretches in a way I can't ignore, and the last thing I want is for him to notice me staring. I glare at the furrow in the ground caused by our crashing pod instead.

"Breakfast, Miss LaRoux?" he asks blandly.

I could slap him. God, I could kiss him—he hasn't abandoned me. If I were home I would stalk out of the room in deafening silence, finding a place to gather my composure in peace. But if I were home, I'd have no reason to be relieved at the presence of someone I'd so much rather never see again. *If I were home* . . . I close my eyes and try to pull myself together.

His footsteps move past me, soft in the thick springy bits of leaf coating the forest floor. I can almost smell him, something sharp and different behind the assault of green smells I'm not used to.

"If you're not hungry," he adds, "then I suggest we get moving."

"What were your views of the planet at that stage?"

"Obviously it was in the advanced stages of terraforming. We were waiting for rescue teams to arrive."

"What made you so sure they'd come?"

"Why spend the resources to terraform a planet if you're not going to profit from the colonies? We were sure the settlers would have seen the Icarus crash, and somebody would be along to investigate."

"Your key concerns at that stage?"

"Well, Miss LaRoux had a party she didn't want to miss, and I–"

"Major, you don't seem to understand the seriousness of your situation."

"Sure I do. What the hell do you think our key concerns were?"

NINE

TARVER

THE SUN'S SLANTING THROUGH THE TREES BY THE TIME WE get moving. I'm aching, covered in bruises from the dozens of times I was thrown against my straps as our pod screamed in to land. My grab bag's on my back, stuffed with everything I could find use for in the pod's lockers—ration bars, the blanket, a pathetically inadequate first-aid kit, a length of spare cable, and a mechanic's suit I haven't yet dared suggest Miss LaRoux substitute for her totally impractical dress. My silver photo case, my battered notebook full of half-written poems. The canteen, with the built-in water filter we'll need so badly now. For better or worse, we're walking, following a creek through the forest.

I'm walking, anyway. She's hobbling along, grabbing trees for support when she thinks I'm not looking. She's still clinging to the idea that she's fine, that this is all simply some horrible inconvenience, and her regular life is going to resume at any moment. God forbid she drop her airs and graces for five minutes. If she'd just accept some damned help, we'd be moving a lot more quickly.

At this rate, we're not going to have to worry about the owner of the big paw prints—though I wish I knew what left them—or the risk of injury or starvation. We're going to die of old age before we make it a klick.

We're on a deadline, and that knowledge drums through me like a pulse. If we can't find a colony, we're going to *have* to get to the wreck as quickly as we can.

Our pod will just be one of a thousand pieces of wreckage strewn through the forest, with nothing about it to show there are survivors nearby. And even if they do recognize it as a downed escape pod, there's nothing to distinguish it from those that fell still attached to the *Icarus*. Nothing to say, *We're alive, come get us.* We can't rig up a smoke signal, because all around us are chunks of debris sending up columns of black smoke like an endless procession of funeral pyres.

The only place we can guarantee we'll be found is at the wreck. That's where the rescue crews will go, looking for survivors and salvage. That's where they'll set up their base of operations.

We have days of walking ahead of us. I don't think she realizes how deceiving vast distances can be—but if she knew it'd be a week or more, I'm not sure I could get her moving at all. And I can't afford to waste a moment. If we're too slow, depending on whether they're finding other survivors, they could pull out before we even arrive. I could make better time on my own, but if I leave her behind, I'm not sure she'd survive until I make it back.

It's only through an exhausting combination of frequent rests and liberal insults that we make it through the next few hours. I could tell myself that I'm doing it because she'll get back to her feet just to spite me—but the truth is, I really just *want* to piss her off. Keeping her moving is a bonus. I'm starting to think we might be able to make some progress when I hear a particularly loud gasp for breath.

I pause, staring ahead. It looks the same in front as behind, the same behind as to the sides. Uneven ground, underbrush with burs and scrub to catch at you, leaf litter, and straight, even tree trunks, like they were laid out with a laser sight. Slow breath in, slow breath out, then I turn.

She's standing still again, leaning against a tree for support. I know she's struggling, but does she have to stop *every* fifteen minutes? I open my mouth to try a new method of prodding her onward, but then I see her face—twisted with pain, not anger.

"How are your shoes?" I ask.

She swallows, regaining enough composure to scowl at me. "My shoes are fine."

I consider the heels I saw slide through the metal grating on the pod's floor. I know she's lying, and she knows I know.

"Well," I reply, using the calm tone I know gets under her skin. I wish I was noble enough not to enjoy it, but I came to terms with my lack of nobility long ago. "Way I see it, we have two options. Either I can take a look at your feet and try to patch them up a little for walking, or you can press on, descend into agony, get blisters, bleed, contract an infection, lose anything from a toe to your life, and end up being too slow for either of us to reach a colony or the wreck before we starve. Which do you fancy, Miss LaRoux?"

She shivers, looking away and wrapping her arms around her middle, squeezing herself tight. "Is this what you did on Patron? Terrorized them all with graphic threats?"

Kill me. She's acting like I offered to shoot her, instead of telling her the truth. "Call me unsophisticated, Miss LaRoux, but it works." I gesture toward a fallen tree, and she reluctantly sits.

Her feet are a mess, and I have to bite back a hiss when I see them. The straps have rubbed her skin raw, and her toes are puffy with blisters. The skin's red and shiny, and there'll be blood sooner, not later. Both her ankles are swollen.

Luckily for me, she's busy staring into space, as though she's too embarrassed to look at her own feet. That's good, because I'm pretty sure she's not going to like what comes next. I'm gentle as I slide the little straps through the buckles, unthreading the shoes and easing them off. I turn them over in my hands—such delicate things, probably worth a month's pay each—and snap the heels off.

She looks down to see what I'm doing and gasps, one hand lifting to cover her mouth. But in whatever passes for reality for her, even she must see the shoes have done their duty. She's silent as I hunt through the first-aid kit, carefully wrapping and taping the worst parts of her feet. In the end I have to let out the straps, and fasten the newly flat shoes around her swollen feet as best I can.

I offer her my hands, and she lets me help her to her feet. She does this without a groan, without a whimper. I'm not sure I could've made it this far on feet that badly torn up. Lilac LaRoux's handled a forced march with more determination than some of the recruits I've taken out in the last couple of years, even if she seems to be doing it out of spite more than anything else.

"Did you have any goal other than reaching the crash site?"

"You make it sound as though I conspired to get myself landed on the planet."

"And why would you do that?"

"That's my point. We wanted nothing more than to get out of there."

"Very well. What happened next?"

TEN

LILAC

I'M TOO OUT OF BREATH TO TALK AND WALK AT THE SAME time. Major Merendsen keeps upping the pace, so I'm forced to pant and struggle along behind him, with very little opportunity for complaint. Eventually, after the fifth or sixth time that I've tripped over a low-lying root, I let gravity finish its work and claim me. I hit the ground harder than I'd like, but I'm too tired to care.

Ahead of me his footsteps come to a halt. There's a long, long silence before he speaks. "Take a break. Rest your feet, have some water. Let's move again in fifteen minutes."

From somewhere I find the energy to push myself up on my arms. My legs are made of lead, and each movement rubs the straps of my shoes against raw skin despite the tape. I can't help but wonder how long it will take the blisters and calluses on my feet to fade when we're rescued. How soon will I be able to wear proper shoes again without displaying my battle scars?

He's standing some distance away, not even winded. Does he have to rub it in, how easy this is for him? I'm determined not to give him the satisfaction of pitying me. I'll show him how much a LaRoux can handle.

For all I know, there are rescue craft headed for our pod's crash site as we speak, but because of his idiocy, we're out in the middle of the forest instead of somewhere they might see us.

A tiny voice at the back of my mind tries to point out how much better suited for this situation he is than I am—how much more he knows.

But I'm tired of being weak. I'm tired of being led. I'm tired of having this soldier decide my every step. I'm *Lilac LaRoux.*

"Major, we need to rethink our plan." I try to keep my voice even, but I'm not doing a very good job. "The *Icarus* crashed behind a mountain range. There's no way we can make this sort of trek. I know it worked for you on Patron, but you had a whole team of soldiers and field researchers there. Just because it worked once doesn't mean it's the solution now. We can do something to make the pod more visible."

"There's nothing we can do that will guarantee us anything," he replies, shaking his head in quick dismissal. "We *can* be sure there'll be rescue craft at the wreck site."

"*If* we make it there," I snap. "We have to go back, it's our best hope."

"I prefer to make my own hope," he snaps right back, wheeling around to look me up and down, as though he finds me wanting. "Listen, I can't drag your ass through the forest for you. You have to work with me."

"I'd thank you not to do anything at all with my ass," I reply, glaring at him. "You're not the lord and master of this planet, and you're not the lord and master of me. My opinion is as valid as yours!"

"Are we going to discuss every single step we take?" I've reduced him to a frustrated roar, but there's no lick of satisfaction in response—I'm too furious myself. This stupid, arrogant *boy.* How old is he? He can't be more than a couple of years older than me, yet he acts like he's got a lifetime of experience just because he liberated one tiny outpost *once.* A one-trick pony with a chest full of medals.

"Are you going to listen to reason, Major?"

"If that's what you call reason, then hell, no."

"No!" I echo him in frustration. "That's all you ever say—no, you can't rest again, no, we have to keep moving uphill, no, you can't use the filtered water for bathing."

We stand, both locked in place, waiting for the other to break.

"Miss LaRoux," he says eventually, "I'll do my best to protect you if you'll let me. My duty demands that much. But I'm not going to sit here and die for you, waiting for rescue that may never come. And I'm certainly not going to beg to keep you safe, on top of everything else you've been serving up. If you refuse to come with me, that's fine. I'm going, and you can come or not as you wish."

"Not." My hand is itching to slap him, but I force myself to remain in place, spine stiff. "Leave me half the supplies and a blanket to carry them in, and you can be on your way. Relieved of duty," I add nastily.

"Fine," he spits. He throws his pack down with unnecessary force, and without another moment of hesitation starts unpacking things and laying them out on a blanket. He makes two even piles of everything— the contents of the first-aid kit, the ration bars, the cable scavenged from our pod. Then one pile, plus a small metal case, a tatty jumpsuit from the pod, and a notebook I haven't seen before, goes back into his pack, and the other is left on the blanket. I feel like telling him to keep the ration bars, since he seems to enjoy them so much.

The major straightens, casting me a dismissive look. "Best of luck."

He's waiting for me to cave. We both know he's not going to leave me alone in this forsaken wilderness—it's a question of who will admit it first. He may be an ass but he's a chivalrous one, and he's not going to let me die to prove a point. I know it, he knows it—and as we watch each other across the blanket, I have to admit a flare of pleasure shoots through me. This is a game I know.

"To you, as well," I offer graciously. After all, I can afford to be gracious now, can't I? I stoop and gather up the corners of my blanket. It's ungainly and awkward as I sling it over my shoulder, and my battered feet nearly trip on the ragged hem of my dress, but a LaRoux doesn't let those things stop her from making a statement. If it were my father, he'd have walked off into the forest hours ago, head held high. He'd have found a way to handle this.

Snatches of sound rise up from the awful, untidy forest all around me, for a moment sounding just like voices, high and distressed. He doesn't even seem to notice them—clearly at home surrounded by so much dirt—and just stands there with a scowl as I turn away.

I hope I have enough time to make it back to the pod before sundown, but either way, he'll probably catch up with me before then. I hear nothing behind me, but I can't risk a look over my shoulder to see what he's doing. It doesn't matter—he'll come back for me, I know it. I imagine him standing there, watching me go, and wish more than anything that I could see the expression on his face.

I wonder how long he'll last.

"The situation was foreign to Miss LaRoux."

"Yes, though I had some experience handling civilians in the field."

"Ah, yes. The intelligence and research teams on Patron."

"Yes."

"What was your assessment of her state during that part of the walk?"

"I thought she was handling it all right."

"There were no disagreements?"

"No, we were getting on fine."

ELEVEN

TARVER

I TAKE CARE TO KEEP MY PACE SLOW AS I START WALKING, breaking off branches and scuffing up the leaf litter so even a society girl should be able to tell which way I went. Important not to go too fast, otherwise she'll never catch up to me. Part of me wants to sit down on a log to wait, maybe write something in my notebook, have a snack. Wait to enjoy the look on her face when she turns around and comes back with her tail between her legs.

This little insurrection has been coming, and though I'd rather she tried it on the plains, where I could keep an eye on her, waiting until we were out of the woods was definitely too much to ask.

The arrogance, the sheer—what is she, sixteen? Amazing that she's had time to get through all that military survival training.

I've been walking ten minutes or so when I hear her. Not right behind me, where I'm expecting her to be by now. She must have stayed in the clearing, or even walked away from me, because she's something like half a klick back.

She's screaming.

I'm sprinting before I know I'm moving, grab bag banging against my back, Gleidel hauled out of my holster and fitting into my hand without any conscious decision to draw it. You develop instincts. Like my drill sergeant used to say: *Learn fast, or don't.*

Branches whip my face and tear at my clothes as I crash through the undergrowth, churning up mud along the edge of the creek as I choose speed over caution.

I burst into the clearing without any pretense of stealth.

I see it immediately—a giant creature, some kind of wild cat, solid muscle beneath tawny fur, teeth bared in a snarl. I've never seen anything like this in my life—not on any planet. Long canines, dark, intelligent eyes. This thing outweighs me easily, and one bite will do for Lilac.

It's got its front paws up against the trunk of a tree, growling low in its throat as it rakes them down the bark, leaving a row of parallel gashes. Lilac's up the tree, screaming, though how she got up there I don't know. I lift the Gleidel and brace it with both hands. Closing one eye, I draw a breath, wait until I steady. The shriek of the laser mixes with the frustrated yowls of the beast as the gun leaps and quivers in my hands.

The creature hits the ground with a crash, twitching and snarling as it kicks up the leaves and sends up clouds of dry dirt. It thrashes around for the count of ten and then lies still, the clearing filling with the horrible smell of burned hair and flesh. Up in the tree, Lilac's screams descend into a series of ragged gasps. I stand and watch the cat for the count of thirty after it stops moving.

Keeping the Gleidel in one hand, I walk slowly across the clearing to where the creature lies still. There's a moan of relief from the tree, and I realize she hasn't been able to see me until now. I can't focus on her yet.

"Stay up there," I call. "It's dead if it keeps its brain where it's supposed to. Did it touch you?"

There's no reply, but she hasn't fallen out of the tree yet, so I can only suppose she's unharmed.

I loose an extra bolt into the creature's head for safety's sake, the Gleidel shrieking again. I take my time over it, nudging it carefully with the toe of my boot, waiting for a response, and eventually stepping in for a closer inspection. The eyes are glassy; its side doesn't rise or fall. Dead.

What kind of a terraformed planet is this, with a thing like that running around? There's no reason to introduce a higher-order predator into a place like this; the felines should be a quarter this size or less. Their part in the ecosystem should be attacking small rodents, not chasing socialites up trees. This one has the same stripes around its face as the kind I'm used to, but it's a man-eater.

So how did this thing get here? I study it for a few moments longer, then give up—it's dead, and that's what matters. When I look up, Lilac's white as a sheet, clinging to the lowest branch. She stares down at me, blue eyes wide, shining. She's not even crying, which tells me how bad the fright has been.

No kidding, Miss LaRoux, I'm pretty shaken up myself. As I stare up at her, a rush of relief overtakes me, my hand trembling where it holds the gun.

I fight the urge to drag her down from the tree. I could shake her. I could kiss her. I can't let myself do either. I can't believe I was so moronic as to let her go off alone after I'd seen those paw prints. I have to be smart, handle this next part carefully. I swallow, clearing my throat to make my voice even.

"That was some climb. Do you need a hand down from there?"

She ignores my offer, which reassures me more than anything else that she's suffered no permanent damage. I'd be more concerned if she let me help her. She more falls down than climbs down, sliding sideways, dangling for a few seconds, then letting go so she can hit the ground with a *thump*. She crumples to sit on the dirt, then scrabbles backward away from the dead creature.

I know this moment too well, I've seen it in the field. Hell, I've been there myself. I could rub it in that I was right, and she was wrong—that I saved her life, that she needs me to survive. But there's no point. She knows it. I'm not going to force her to come crawling back. I'm the one with field experience. I should have stopped this from happening.

"Let's go," I say, listening to her ragged breathing. "We can cover a little more ground before we have to make camp."

A part of me wants to reach down and take her hands, and hold them until she feels safe. But I can't. If I do, she'll start crying, and she won't stop. I need her to stay tough. It's the best thing I can do for her. So I speak again. "Are you ready?"

She nods, climbing to her feet, not even bothering to dust off her hands. I'm aching, and I hate this, but damned if I'm not getting this girl to the crash site. She can hate me for the rest of her life once we're rescued—at least she'll be alive to hate me.

We leave the big cat behind and slowly backtrack to gather up her abandoned supplies. From her path, she would've caught up with me if she'd kept running. The beast was chasing her *toward* me—if it had chased her the other way, I might not have reached her in time.

I hope Lilac doesn't realize this. That it was only a coincidence that saved her life. She's already jumping at shadows as we walk—now and then she looks over her shoulder as though she's hearing things, seeing things. It doesn't seem to comfort her that there's nothing there. I hope she's not thinking about what other impossible creatures could be out there, just beyond the trees.

And I *really* hope that thing doesn't have a mate.

When we make camp by a creek, I estimate we've spent the better part of the day walking and taking breaks, and we've made it maybe ten klicks. So if we're lucky, we're halfway to the edge of the trees. After we make it to the plains, we'll have to cross them and get over the mountain range somehow before we reach the *Icarus*.

Lilac is lying on the blanket I spread for her, arms out to each side, staring up at the slowly darkening sky through a gap in the canopy. I wonder what she makes of the sky. I've never seen these stars, and I've memorized the charts for all the colonies. That's my only hope—that the rescue might be taking a little longer because the *Icarus* wasn't where she was supposed to be when she crashed.

I shake my head, trying to get rid of the creeping sensation of wrongness. Rescue will still come. This place is terraformed, however distorted it seems. The people *must* be somewhere, and they can't have missed the destruction of a ship like the *Icarus*.

Lilac's been silent since the incident with the cat beast, and against all logic I find myself missing the sound of her voice, even when it's insulting me. At least being annoyed at her is invigorating—this new quiet hopelessness is infectious.

"Not exactly the five-star accommodations you're used to," I call, in the cheerful voice that infuriates her so. She doesn't move—nothing. I retrieve the canteen, set aside earlier to filter water collected from the creek. "I'll give you a comment card when this is all over so you can complain to someone."

She stirs, propping herself up on her elbows. She glares wearily at me for a long moment. "I do hope you're assembling two beds, Major." Her voice is tired, but there's still a hint of that edge in it.

Fighting the brief and insane impulse to smile, I duck my head and start dividing the leaf litter I'm gathering into two piles. Too quickly, she lapses back into silence and stillness. And without her there to aggravate me, my mind wanders to places it shouldn't go.

I can't let myself think of home for too long. I can't let myself imagine my mother hearing about the *Icarus*, the way my father will try to find something to say.

I remember how the air was thick with grief after they told us about Alec, how the three of us made it from one day to the next without ever exchanging more than a handful of words. My mother didn't write a poem for months, and my father stared uncomprehendingly at the piles of food the neighbors dropped around. I skipped school and went out every day to risk my neck climbing forbidden cliffs, forcing my way through overgrown forest until I was lost and exhausted. Though never quite exhausted enough to sleep at night.

Slowly we learned how to talk about him—sometimes—with something other than sadness. Mom picked up her pen, and even though her poetry was irrevocably changed, she was writing again. Dad went back to his classroom, and I went back to mine.

I waited impatiently for my sixteenth birthday, so I could enlist, as though somehow by getting into uniform and doing what my big brother couldn't, surviving the trenches, I could bring him back.

I still don't know if he believed in what he was doing—if he felt like he was making a difference, controlling rebellions in a new colony every few months. I don't know if he thought the rebels had a point—occasionally I do—or if he just liked the rush, or wanted to see new places. I was too young to think to ask those things when he went, and once he was on assignment, we just wrote back and forth about trivial, everyday things. You don't mention death when it's hovering near someone you love. You don't want to attract the reaper's attention.

My parents and I fought when I told them what I wanted to do, and though we negotiated a kind of peace around my decision, I know they still wait for my message every week, for the words that will tell them I'm still alive.

I have to get home.

I can't listen to the part of my mind that points out I might not make it back.

I can't let this happen to them again.

"At that stage had you reached the plains?"

"No, we camped in the woods that night. We didn't make much progress those first few days. Can I get something to eat?"

"In good time, Major. How was Miss LaRoux's emotional state?"

"Still stable."

TWELVE

LILAC

I'M POSITIVE HE KNOWS HOW MUCH I HATE IT WHEN HE goes ahead to "scout." He probably does it just to provoke me. I suppose he's wandering off to imagine how much nicer it'd be not to have me around. Perhaps he's even wishing he'd let that beast eat me yesterday.

I'm sitting in a patch of afternoon sun on one of the blankets, spread over the nasty forest floor. Not that it matters all that much, as I'm already carrying half the forest along with me in my dress. The hem is hanging in tatters and the skirt is muddy. I can only imagine my hair and skin are as dreadful, but as the major scarcely glances in my direction at the best of times, and there's no one else around to see, I must try to bear it as best I can.

I know he'll come back—he always has—but tiny eddies of fear swirl in my subconscious anyway. What if he doesn't? What if he falls down some unseen gully and cracks his head open, and I'm left all alone? What if my last insult was one too many?

The forest is full of sound and movement I can't track, things that flicker out of the corners of my eyes, vanishing before I can focus on them. The major doesn't seem to notice—or if he does, he isn't bothered. But it's as though the forest is whispering all around us, saying incomprehensible things in my ear. Sometimes I almost think I can hear voices, though logic insists that I'm searching for the familiar in this alien world. I'm used to being around other people, and my mind is turning the sounds of the wilderness into sounds I find comforting.

Except none of this is comforting.

If my father were here, he'd tell me to stand up, pull myself together. He'd tell me not to let anyone see me fall. He'd tell me to find the power in this situation and get it back.

That makes me smile, however weakly. The only power I have in this horrible wilderness is getting under Major Merendsen's skin. It's so easy to undercut his know-it-all attitude, and score a point in our endless battle.

I can imagine Anna beside me, close and real for a moment. *Choose what you let them see,* she'd say. My throat closes as I think of her.

His opinion of me is already a lost cause—years later, when he looks back at this escapade, I'd rather he think *bitch* than *weakling.*

The sounds of branches cracking and leaves rustling alert me that he's returning. He makes a point of making a little noise now, after the first time he appeared soundlessly behind me and ended up with a scream and a canteen thrown at his face. My heartbeat quickens, mind turning over a dozen ways to pick a fight.

But just as I'm about to speak, I see his face.

He doesn't look at me, but there's a rawness in his gaze as he drops into a crouch that wipes my mind clean of insults. He rubs his hand over his scalp, fingers fanning through his dark hair, lips pressed tightly together. My eyes sweep across the telling droop of his shoulders as he crouches there motionless.

I was wrong—there is one thing for me to read in the middle of this alien forest.

I'm afraid to ask, but my lips form the question anyway. "Did you find something?"

He doesn't answer right away, pushing up from his crouch to collect the canteen from me and give a jerk of his head to indicate that I should get off the blanket and allow him to pack it away. Only after he's done that, leaving me standing there awkwardly with my arms wrapped around myself against the chill, does he speak.

"Yes. We're going to have to stop for a while so I can take care of it, but I want you closer so I can hear you if you shout. I need you to just do as I say for once, all right, Lilac?"

When he gives orders, my first instinct is to blast him with some kind of insult for his arrogance. But now he's so sad, so tired, that the thought barely flickers through my mind before I dismiss it. He's watching me, expressionless.

I nod, and a tiny bit of the tension in his shoulders drops away.

"Good. I'll find you a spot a little ways back from where I am. You can keep resting your feet, or if you want you can help by gathering some rocks."

"Rocks? What for?"

He turns away to shrug his pack back onto his shoulders. "There's another downed escape pod over the next ridge."

I'm about to fall into step, ready to follow him, when his words halt me mid-stride. "There's a *what*?" The torrent of relief and hope is so tangible it nearly drives me to my knees. I don't have time to analyze the tiny stab of disappointment—company means the end of this strange, private partnership—before words come pouring out of me. "How many people? Was it a first-class pod? Do you know anyone who was inside? Is their rescue beacon working?"

He's shaking his head and tightening his hands around the straps of his pack. "No, no," he says, cutting across the flood of questions. "There's no one."

"Maybe we can catch up with them!" I cry, plucking the hem of my skirt out of dirt and crossing toward him. "They must be heading toward the ship like we are."

"No," he says again.

"Well, you ignore them if you like, Major, but I'm going to go find them."

"There's no one to catch up with," he says shortly, tone sparking with annoyance.

"How do you *know* there's no one?"

"Because no one survived!" he snaps, turning finally so I can see the fierceness in his features, the rawness of dashed hopes, and the weariness that has replaced them. He takes a slow breath, not unlike the way he usually does when trying not to rise to my bait. This time, though, the tension drains when he exhales.

"They're all dead, Lilac."

My hands are starting to dry, the skin threatening to crack. The hours spent digging stones out of the earth and carrying them to the pile at the edge of the forest clearing have left me exhausted, sweating through my dress despite the crisp air. I never knew it was possible to be so miserable in so many ways.

I keep looking up at the sky through the trees, as though a rescue ship might fly over at any moment, but the sky stays empty, blue, clear. My father has to be coming for me. It's just the two of us, and has been since I was eight years old. I'm the only one he has in the world—just as he's the only one I have. And when he gets here, cracked, dry skin will be a dim, unpleasant memory.

Major Merendsen refuses to let me see the crash, demanding that I come no closer than the clearing's edge. This is what he meant when he asked that I do as he says. He doesn't want me to see the bodies.

I tried to protest that it couldn't make much difference, that all my time spent watching medical dramas on the HV meant I was immune to that kind of shock. Surely the three-dimensional gore and excitement of watching holographic limb-replacement and thoracic surgeries would prepare me for anything a crash could throw at me. But my protests sounded weak even to my own ears. I couldn't have understood it before, but I do now. It's different.

He urged me to rest, sit down and stay off my battered feet, save them for walking. But when I sit, I think, and I don't want to make it any easier for my imagination to conjure horrors in front of my eyes.

And so I'm collecting rocks for markers while he finishes digging the graves.

He's returned once or twice to check on me and drink from the canteen, face grimy with dust and sweat, hands as red and raw as my feet. I've yet to see him tired like this—hiking seems to him no more difficult than a light stroll around the promenade deck—and the sight of him dirty and out of breath is sobering. Major Merendsen is human after all.

I hand him the canteen quietly, and wait beside him while he rests until he's ready to continue the task.

It's edging into late afternoon when he returns carrying his pack in one hand and his shovel, a makeshift thing rigged from a branch and a piece of debris, in the other. He tosses both down beside my pile and gestures for me to have a seat.

"I need you to put these on for me," he says as I sink down beside him, skin crawling at the feel of the springy leaf litter underneath, but not quite ready to demand a blanket to sit on. I'm confused at his request, until he opens his pack and pulls out a pair of boots.

I'm recoiling almost before I have time to register what he's suggesting. "No. Tarver, no. I won't."

He rubs a hand across his eyes, leaving a streak of dirt on his forehead. "Please don't argue with me. You can't possibly make it much farther wearing those monstrosities." He jerks his chin at my feet, mostly hidden by their cocoons of tape, nestled inside the ruins of my Delacours.

This isn't about practicality, though. My skin crawls and I shut my eyes. "Please," I whisper. "I can't wear a dead woman's shoes. Please, please don't make me." My stomach roils, nauseous despite being empty.

I'm braced for one of his sarcastic remarks, designed to get me moving before my brain kicks in, like I'm one of his soldiers. Instead there's a light touch against my chin, startlingly gentle, and I open my eyes in surprise.

"If they could, these people would tell you to take what you can," he says quietly, crouching next to me with one hand on the ground for balance and the other outstretched, urging me to lift my head. "They can't use these things anymore. We can. I don't know how you've walked so far without decent shoes, but that, at least, can change now. I believe that rescue is coming, but we have to be in a place they'll find us. I'm not going to leave you behind, but that means you've got to do what you can to keep up."

The dizziness sweeps on past me, leaving me drained and tired, but no longer about to throw up. "I'm trying."

His sudden grin is as startling as the gentle summons to lift my head. "Believe me, I know. Come on, let's see if they fit."

No wonder he managed to take the remnants of an intelligence outpost on Patron and lead them to safety. There's not a person in the central planets who hasn't heard tales of his heroism, but no one actually believes in the stories that come from the border—suddenly I see in the man in front of me the qualities of *the* Major Merendsen, war hero. He could probably lead water uphill if he wanted to.

Later, when he's helped to cut my feet out of the tangle of tape and ruined shoe, and laced me up in the boots (he didn't mention having to wear a dead woman's socks as well), we share a drink from the canteen. Together we carry the rocks I've gathered over to the site of the crash. The grave is one long mound, no way to tell how many are buried beneath it, and I don't ask. We scatter the stones over the top as markers. I don't need to investigate the pod to know that its beacon isn't working—a whole side of the wreck is destroyed, circuits exposed and scorched where it was torn from the *Icarus* when it hit the atmosphere. These people were probably dead before the pod even broke away from the ship. It's a first-class pod; I have no idea where the boots came from. Maybe a few soldiers were mixed in with society in the chaos.

Suddenly I wonder if Anna was among its occupants. Would Tarver have recognized her? Perhaps all of us are only blurs of color and hairstyles to him, one rich person very much like the next. Even if he had recognized her—would he have told me?

"Could I say something?" I say, surprising myself.

He blinks and looks over at me as he shifts one of the stones and straightens. "Go ahead."

"I mean—alone. To them." I tilt my head toward the grave.

"Oh," he says, looking down at the disturbed earth and stone. "Of course. I'll be up at the tree line when you're ready to keep moving."

I listen to his footsteps moving away, my eyes on the stones I've gathered and placed. Always, my ears are tuned for the sounds of engines, the whine of a flyover jet, the hum of hovercraft. But they never come. It's always this silence. A world of quiet broken only by my footsteps and Tarver's, and the whispering of the woods.

I know he has no reason to lie. Still, it's hard to connect the long mound with the reality of people resting beneath it, actual flesh and bone. The sky is as empty as it always is—the world is quiet. My ears pick out the wind, the sighing of the leaves, the distant chirp of a bird. The stillness of an undisturbed wilderness. I can't help but wonder how long it'll take for the grass and the trees to consume these graves—how long until it's impossible to tell anyone ever rested here.

How long until we too are swallowed up?

"I don't know who any of you are," I whisper, eyes blurring with sudden tears. "I wish I did. I wish I could keep pretending none of this is real. That my father will swoop down, pick everyone up, and everything will go back to normal. That this is all some terrible dream."

I crouch, reaching out to lay a hand against the stones warming in the sunlight streaming through the clearing. The surface is rough and smooth at once, irregular but soothing. Nothing like the stones in our gardens, polished and placed with perfect artistic balance. I'm hungry and tired, and there's sweat rolling down my back. Tears drip from my chin, splattering against the stone, leaving uneven patches of darkness against the gray rock.

"I could have fit a lot more people in that maintenance pod. Maybe it could have been you. I'm sorry."

I straighten and look back, toward where Tarver waits at the tree line, adjusting his pack. From here the trek to the *Icarus* seems endless—I can't even see the mountains, much less the plains, or the rest of the forest that lies between us and our only chance at rescue. Maybe it would have been better to have died in this crashed pod. Easier than dying slowly out here, alone but for this man who hates me, so far from the one person who cares about me. Fear, icy and sickening, roils in my stomach.

Tarver lifts his head as if sensing my gaze across the distance between us. If he heard any of what I said, he gives no indication, merely hefting his pack and inclining his head to suggest we get moving.

I swallow, glancing down once last time at the freshly dug graves. "I think you might've been the lucky ones."

We walk.

My feet are nothing but a dull ache as Tarver marches me through the woods. He takes my hand sometimes to help me over logs and rocks and lifts me over the creek when we cross it. Other times he makes me drink from the canteen. I let him, because what else can I do? The day morphs into eternity, a nightmare from which I cannot wake. As the hours stretch on, not even the sounds of the forest make me jump. I see nothing but the ground before my feet. I cannot turn back because there is no back, only the next step, and the one after, and the one after that.

I used to think that my name would always keep me safe. That those two words—*Lilac LaRoux*—would be the only password I needed no matter where I ended up.

I had been so sure my father was coming for me, but now it's hard to find that certainty. This is a wilderness waiting to swallow me; I'd barely make a dent trying to fight it. There are no rules for me to learn, no points to be scored, no bluffs to be called. This is a hell I've never imagined.

And I think I'm going to die here.

"Nothing of note happened when you camped that night?"

"If you'd tell me what kind of thing of note you're wondering about, I'm sure I could be more help."

"Are you saying that nothing unusual happened?"

"Nothing at all."

THIRTEEN

TARVER

THE CAMPFIRE'S DOWN TO COALS WHEN I WAKE. MY EYES snap open, and as always, there's that brief moment of disorientation as I soak in everything around me, wait to know where I am.

This time it doesn't take long to remember. Our camp is near the end of the woods and the start of the plains. I built the fire up high before we slept, still thinking of the monster that nearly killed Lilac.

I roll over onto my back to find her blocking out the unfamiliar stars, standing above me like a ghost in the night. Something must have prompted her to come around to my side of the campfire—she's still insisting on separation—and I'm reaching for my Gleidel as I blink up at her.

"Miss LaRoux?" I ask, quiet and careful. I don't want to give her a fright and get a kick for my troubles. Assuming she's real at all, looming up there like a specter. Even as a ghost, she's something to see.

"Major, there's somebody out there," she whispers. "Can you hear? There's a woman crying out there in the trees."

A shiver of apprehension runs through me, and I tilt my head to one side, surprised the noise didn't wake me. As far as I can tell, there's nothing to break the silence. I shift and sit up, noticing I've still got my boots on. I think I remember deciding to sleep in them.

"There it is again, Major," she insists, still soft.

"I can't hear it," I whisper, stretching my protesting muscles.

Her eyes widen as though she's having trouble believing that's true.

"What direction?"

She lifts a hand to point unhesitatingly toward where the trees give way to the plains, and I climb to my feet, reaching out to scoop up my grab bag and sling it over one shoulder. Oldest trick in the book—lure folks away from their fire, then swipe their stuff. I've done it myself more than once, stuck out on the border planets, pitched against the latest colonist rebellion. If they're lurking out in the woods and not approaching us directly, I don't trust them.

It's my turn to lift my hand, and I raise a finger to my lips to signal she should be silent. She nods and follows as I ease away from the fire.

Once we're a short distance from the flames, I pause in the shadows, looking back at her. Miss LaRoux is focused on the task at hand, not even seeming to register discomfort from her bare feet. I tilt my head at her. *What about now? Hear anything?*

She shakes her head, perplexed, neat brows drawn together. "She's stopped," she whispers. "She sounded like she might have been hurt, Major. She could be unconscious now."

I open my mouth to reply—*or she could be a trap*—but I don't get a word out. Miss LaRoux's decided to take matters into her own hands.

"Hello," she calls out, stepping away from the tree. "Are you—"

She gets no further than that. She only makes it to three words because I'm so appalled it takes me a few moments to mobilize. I lunge, clamping a hand over her mouth and hauling her in against me, holding her tighter than I should. She makes a muffled sound, then goes still, frightened and tense. We stand like statues, straining to listen. I keep hold of her, and despite the danger, there's a part of my mind that insists on noticing her closeness, her body pulled against mine.

Out in the woods, there's no sound. Not the snap of a twig, not the brush of one branch against another.

Very slowly, she presses a finger against my hand in a silent request to be released. I ease my grip an inch or two and she breathes out. I tuck my chin to whisper in her ear. "Still hearing her?"

She shakes her head a fraction, leaning up to whisper in mine, breath tickling my skin. "Nothing. What if she's passed out? She could be hurt, she could be—"

I know what she really means. She could be one of her friends. She could be one of those girls who looked at me like some kind of specimen. If she exists at all. I can't believe that in a place like this, with my every nerve on edge, I could have slept through what woke Lilac. It's more likely she woke herself from a dream. Still, there's only one way to be sure.

"Stay here," I whisper, my cheek brushing against hers. She's still flushed with sleep and her skin's warm, so much smoother than mine. I'm sure she's never encountered anything as uncultured as a guy in need of a shave before. But she only nods in silent understanding. She's shaking violently, and I realize she's left her blanket behind. I take off my jacket and wrap it around her shoulders, and she sinks down to sit in the shadow of the tree to wait.

It's not the worst night of my life. I'm sure that prize will forever belong to a particular night on Avon. The whole platoon, me included, were so green we were practically sprouting leaves, and the night's entertainment was a group of rebels with an oversupply of pulse lasers. Not a nice thing on watery ground. To top it off, I missed a date with one of the local girls, and it's not like recruits get a lot of those lined up.

Still, on my list of worst nights, this comes close.

It's almost impossible to move through the undergrowth without making a sound, with great thorny arms reaching up to tangle in the fabric of my pants, and dry twigs concealed under the leaf litter waiting to crack and snap like bones breaking in the dark. On any other planet I'd be confident, but here I know anything could hurt me, anything could be just a little different from the way it's supposed to be. I'm forced to move forward a fraction at a time, with frustrating slowness. The hairs on the back of my neck are standing up, and I'm alive because I'm not in the habit of ignoring that.

I pass by Lilac three times in the first hour of searching. She's obediently huddled at the base of the tree, wrapped in my jacket, her legs tucked up inside it. She insists she can still hear the voice. I stand in the shadow of a tree and look out across the moonlit plain, in the direction she swears the voice is moving. Except that there's nothing there, and even the smallest critter would cast a shadow by the light of the two moons.

When I return to her a fourth time she shakes her head at me—the noise is gone. She seems so small inside my jacket, but I can tell she's trying to look like she's bearing up well. She doesn't want me to stop searching.

I hold up a hand to warn her to remain in place, and she nods as I back away from her. Time to try a different approach. I walk fifty painstaking paces, then settle with my back against a tree, the Gleidel in my hand on full charge. "Is anybody out there? We're friends." My voice splits the silence. Nobody within a klick could have missed it. Lilac and I both stay frozen in place, listening as our heartbeats count away the seconds. Nothing.

So I resume my search. It's another hour of wading through the undergrowth and past the smooth-trunked trees before I have to concede that if there's somebody out here, I'm not finding her until daylight.

I make my way back to where Lilac, miraculously, is actually dozing against the tree. She was trembling for hours—the strain must have finally worn her down. She starts when I crouch down beside her, and blinks at me apologetically—or it could be apology, anyway, and I choose to believe it is. I don't need to tell her we're staying away from the campfire, which shines in the darkness like a beacon to anything with sinister intentions that might be out there.

I ease in to sit beside her, Gleidel in hand. She's still half asleep, and she shifts her weight to settle her head against my shoulder. Looks like I've been promoted from the other side of the fire, for one night only. I wrap an arm around her, and with her leaning against me—small and warm and alive—I tip my head back to rest it against the tree trunk.

I bite the inside of my cheek to keep myself awake, fighting the urge to lean my head on hers, and settle in to wait for dawn.

"So then you made your way across the plains toward the mountains?"

"That's correct."

"What were your thoughts at that stage?"

"It was clear we were unlikely to find other survivors, but I remained alert. I didn't expect them to be kindly disposed toward a LaRoux, if they were around."

"Why was that?"

"Her father built the ship we'd been on. Terraforming companies are rarely popular with the colonists, and you know as well as I do that Central sends in the troops to back up the corporations' rights. Colonists hate us, too."

"Did you have any other thoughts?"

"I was beginning to wonder why we weren't seeing rescue flyovers."

"Did you mention that to Miss LaRoux?"

"No."

FOURTEEN

LILAC

"TELL ME AGAIN WHAT YOU HEARD," HE ASKS FOR THE eighteenth time after we complete another of his ever-expanding search perimeters around our campsite. In the light of morning, it's hard to keep insisting that what happened was real.

"It was a woman crying. She sounded desperate, afraid, maybe hurt, I'm not sure. She sounded—" But I cut myself off, pressing my lips together.

"She sounded?" he prompts, leaning back against a tree.

"She sounded like me," I finish, realizing how the words sound— even worse than I'd expected.

He's silent for a while, scanning the forest. "Right," he says after a few moments, pushing off from the tree and leaning down to retrieve his pack. "If there was someone here last night—"

He pauses a moment, as if expecting me to say something. I want to interrupt, insist I heard what I heard, but something keeps me quiet. I've lost the right, if I ever had it, to protest his declarations. I'd die out here if it weren't for him.

When I remain silent, he continues. "At any rate, she's gone now. We need to keep moving. How are your feet?"

Maybe I did invent her. The admission, even to myself, causes an uneasy tension to settle throughout my shoulders. But I have no choice. If he's decided it's time to move on, then I have to move on with him. The worst part is that I have to admit that he's right. There's no sign of anyone here, no trampled earth, not even a snapped twig to show that someone passed by.

"They're fine," I mumble, despite the throb from the matching blisters on my heels at the reminder.

"Once we're out onto the plains, we can find a place to rest, stop a little earlier today. Neither of us is going to have much stamina after such an interrupted night."

I know he means that *I* won't have much stamina. My jaw tightens in protest, and for an instant I want to retort. But then my ears fill with the memory of a cat's hunting snarl, and I smell the burning fur and the blood and I close my eyes.

The voice was moving toward the plains, which is the direction Tarver proposes to hike in order to reach the wreck. Perhaps if we just start moving, we'll be able to track down whomever I heard.

"Fine."

Silence from Tarver, which stretches long enough that I'm forced to open my eyes again. He's watching me with an odd expression on his face, one I can't read—his eyes aren't quite on mine. With a start, I realize I'm still wearing the jacket he wrapped around my shoulders last night.

When I start to scramble out of it, struggling with the way the material swallows up my hands, he's roused from whatever trance he'd been in. "No," he says abruptly. "Keep it for now."

Then he turns his back and moves out, sure in the knowledge that I'll follow.

What else can I do?

Somewhere in the back of my mind, a tiny, unbidden voice whispers, *Would you actually want to do anything else?*

The pace seems easier today. Perhaps he's being gentler on me, but I suspect I'm growing accustomed to walking.

We make better time on the flat ground of the plains, pausing only to choke down a ration bar each. I choke, anyway; Tarver tucks in as though it's a three-course steak dinner.

He calls a halt again after another hour and a half of walking, looking around the plains in each direction. Behind us the forest is a smear of gray-green on a ridge, dropping down into the broad, golden expanse of the plain. I've never seen anything so immense as this, such a vast sweep of empty land. The creek we've been following fans out into a network of silvery streams, marking the small dips in the land. They're all narrow enough to jump across, but large enough that Tarver can dip the canteen into them, filling it up and letting the water filter do its work. The wind ripples the grass of the plains in waves, for all the world like the oceans I've seen on the HV. On the far side of all this are the mountains that stand between us and the *Icarus*.

But we don't see any signs of life. No rescue craft roaring overhead, no colony traffic crisscrossing the sky the way the streams divide the plain. I can't understand why there aren't colonies here. Where is everyone? Neither of us says a word about it, but I know it can't have escaped him.

Tarver makes camp more quickly than he did the night before, and it takes me a few moments to realize why—he hasn't dug a fire pit this time. No wood on the plains for a real fire. Why hadn't I thought about that? Until I leaned against him last night, I was halfway to freezing, even with a fire close at hand. And after shoving him away so quickly this morning, I can't rely on his warmth again. I shiver, my mind on the miserable night ahead.

Tarver gathers up a bundle of the wire he stripped from the escape pod, mumbles something about setting snares for food, and strikes out across the plain in a straight line. At least I can see him here, without the trees of the forest to block my view, and know I'm not completely alone.

I'm watching him and exploring my face with my fingertips, wishing I had a mirror. My skin is warm and flushed despite sitting still; sunburn, something tells me, swimming up from some childhood experience when I got lost on a simulation deck emulating a tropical vacation. Then, my father just summoned a physician, and the burn melted away under her care. Now I trace its damage across my cheeks. The skin around my eye is still painful to the touch, and I imagine that it's at least a little bruised—it's had the four days since the crash to bloom. At least Tarver has the decency not to mock me about it.

I hear his voice not far behind me. Didn't I just see him in the distance, crouching to set a snare? I turn, chest tightening in surprise, only to find an empty plain. How could he have gotten behind me so fast? I squint back over my shoulder and see him straighten up, too far off for me to have heard him speak.

The hair on the back of my neck lifts, and I scan the plains behind me. There's no sign of anyone, and yet as I stand there, heart pounding and ears straining, I hear another murmur. It isn't Tarver's voice after all—it's not quite as deep. It carries some emotion I can't identify, and I can't understand at all what it's saying.

My body begins to shake, my fingertips tingling and itching, my breath quickening. *Fear*, I tell myself, but it doesn't abate even when I force myself to take deep breaths. My skin runs hot and cold and hot again, itching with restlessness until I feel like I must move or explode from the sensation. My head spins as though my blood sugar's low, as if I'm wearing a too-tight dress, and not enough oxygen is reaching my brain.

I'm still standing when Tarver returns. I hear his footsteps through the tall grass long before he reaches me, so when he announces with uncharacteristic cheer, "Burrows—we're in luck," I manage not to jump.

I glance over my shoulder to find him standing there smiling, his arms full of plants and long grasses. The sight's distracting—but not so distracting as what I heard. I turn back toward the plains.

"Did you hear anything while you were out there?" I ask, squinting into the afternoon light and trying as hard as I can to keep my shivering to a minimum.

"Wind," he replies, punctuated by a rustle as he drops his armful. "The grass, the occasional scurrying critter. There won't be anything larger out here, there's nothing to feed it."

"I heard a man."

The sound his monster of a gun makes when he takes it out of its holster is getting to be familiar. I sigh, shaking my head. "I don't think he means us any harm. He didn't sound angry."

Tarver comes up next to me, peering in the same direction I'm facing. "You sure? There's not much room for someone to hide out here."

"Positive." He can't accuse me of dreaming this time. I'm wide-awake, every nerve on edge. "I thought it was you at first, but you were too far away. It sounded really close, like he was nearby."

Tarver's frowning now. I catch him shooting me a sideways glance, before taking a few steps forward to turn in a slow circle, scanning the area. "I guess a voice could be carried a ways on the wind. What did he say?"

I hesitate, clenching my jaw to keep my teeth from chattering. "I don't . . . know. I couldn't quite tell. It was like listening to voices through a wall. You know they're speaking a language you understand, and you know you could hear them if you could *just* . . ." I don't know how to explain it.

He stops watching the plains, turning his attention fully on me. "Well, which was it? Was he distant or right next to you?"

"I don't know!" The burst of frustration escapes before I can control it, and my voice is shaking with whatever's seized my body. "He was right here, but muffled. Like—the sounds were clear, but there was no meaning in them."

He's staring at me, and I feel my face starting to burn.

"I'm realizing how this sounds," I whisper.

"Not good," he agrees. But then he surprises me, and turns around to holster his gun and cup his hands around his mouth to bellow across the plain. "Come on in if you're out there. We're armed, but we'll play nicely if you will."

He drops his hands, turning his head slightly to better listen for a reply. My own ears strain, skin prickling at each rustle and whistle of grass and wind.

Then, from only a few feet away, comes the voice, clearer than ever. I still can't make out what he's saying, but this time I can tell he's excited.

"There!" I dart forward to stand at Tarver's side. "There, it's the same voice. I *told* you."

He isn't smiling. He's not looking out at the plain, but rather down at me, his expression more troubled than annoyed.

"I heard nothing," he says quietly.

The words are like a punch in the stomach, leaving me gasping. Even he wouldn't be so cruel. "That's not funny."

"I'm not laughing." Carefully, Tarver reaches out and takes hold of my shoulder. "I've been working you too hard. You're exhausted. Let's just sit and rest, and you'll feel better tomorrow."

I jerk my shoulder away with such force that I wrench the muscle, although I scarcely notice the pain. My spine tingles uncomfortably. "I'm not hallucinating, Tarver!"

He smiles, though it doesn't touch his eyes, which remain grave, fixed on mine. "It's no big deal," he says dismissively. "I've done it myself, once. Come, sit down for me, and I'll see about finding you something to eat besides those ration bars."

"I know what's real!" I want to smack him, shake him, do whatever it takes to convince him that I know what I heard. My shivering slows, my dizziness ebbing. As a breeze skitters past and touches damp skin, I realize I've been sweating.

"Lilac," he says, voice soft and weary. "Please. Rest."

I wonder if he knows how easily he can win this way—how can I fight him when he's so tired, so sad? The relief at having heard another human voice has shattered into a thick misery, so dense I can barely breathe. I sink back down onto my blanket, eyes burning. I refuse to cry, not while he can see me. But was it too much to ask to have been proven right, just once? Instead he thinks I'm going mad, that Lilac LaRoux's so traumatized she can't even tell dreams from reality. I wish Tarver were here alone.

And the worst part is that I know he does too.

"Sudden trauma can manifest in any number of ways."

"That's true. We receive extensive training."

"Did you notice any of those manifestations in Miss LaRoux?"

"No. Well, only that she was off her food, but I think that was an objection to the ration bars, mostly. Not quite what she was used to."

"Otherwise nothing?"

"That's what I said. Are you having trouble understanding my answers?"

"We just want to be certain, Major. Exact."

"Any chance you can tell me exactly how much longer this is going to last?"

"Until we have the answers we require."

FIFTEEN

TARVER

SHE STAYS CRUMPLED ON THE BLANKET, AND I DELIBERATELY putter around, giving her a little time to pull herself together. If I've learned anything about Lilac LaRoux over the past few days, it's that she doesn't like to fall apart in front of people, even when it's justified. I find the razor in my grab bag and shave, clawing a couple of steps back toward civilization—a comfort to her, maybe. The rough rasp of the blade on my skin keeps me focused, and the silence draws out.

There's some good news among the bad. The plains make for easier walking, the ground even and flat. I'm confident we've left our feline friends behind in the forest. I've found burrows that tell me something will end up in my snares for sure, and the armful of unfamiliar plants and grasses that I foraged is bound to yield up something edible. I'd hoped that giving Lilac a break from the ration bars might cheer her up.

But now there's a horrible weight in the pit of my stomach that won't shift. I saw how she was shaking, sweating, how dilated her pupils were. Hallucinations can be a sign of a number of things, but I can't help thinking that in Lilac's case, it's simply all too much. I just need her to hold on long enough to make it across the mountains to the *Icarus*.

"Give me an hour or so, and I might be able to get some variety into your diet, Miss LaRoux," I say briskly, running out of things to pretend to fiddle with and sinking down beside her. "When they terraform, a lot of the flora that goes in is edible, more or less. Once you're on a steady diet of ration bars, your definition of 'edible' changes pretty radically, I'd say."

Her gaze flicks up to me, still blank, glazed. I know that our ongoing battle isn't what she needs right now, and in the face of such misery, I try the only thing left that I can think of. I offer her a small smile—and though she doesn't quite smile back, she looks at me, absorbing the human contact.

"I'll test them," I continue, "and if any of them are edible, we can gather up some extras and have a proper meal tonight. These aren't the standard plants I usually see come out of terraforming, but I can't see why the principle wouldn't be the same. There's enough grass here for a tiny fire, so we can heat up the canteen for some soup, at any rate."

She nods, which is a small improvement. My efforts are beginning to calm me down, as well. I set to work, breaking open the first stalk of grass—a stout, woody thing at the base, green and juicy at the tip, about the same thickness as one of her fingers. I don't want to highlight to her how strange it is that I don't recognize these plants—terraforming flora and fauna are completely standard. The corporations don't mess with a formula that works . . . but the plants here are only tangentially related to the ones I'm used to. As the sap on the broken grass stalk begins to appear in tiny beads, I rub it across the sensitive skin on the inside of my forearm.

"What are you doing?" She's still subdued, but at least she's looking at something other than the ground in front of her.

"Checking for an allergic reaction. If it doesn't make me red or itchy, then it makes it through to round two, the taste test."

She nods, watching my forearm for a moment, then looks away.

I try again. "There's a dip in the land to the east, looks like a river. We'll cross over and follow it across the plains so we've got plenty of water. We can even wash, if you like, make ourselves presentable for when the cavalry arrive."

She bows her head and takes a deep breath. "I expect you to check it thoroughly for me, Major. Knowing my luck, there'll be space crocodiles hiding in it."

Pay dirt, it's a joke. I'm grinning like an idiot, more than her attempt at humor deserves. She doesn't seem to notice. "Space crocodiles are no problem," I say. "You just tickle them under the chin and they roll over. I was posted to New Florence last year, and I met a guy who kept one as a pet, shipped it home from his posting in his luggage. He punched airholes in his bag, and the croc made it just fine."

She treats me to a faint smile. Now we're getting somewhere. If I can find a way to sustain it a little longer, we can leave the voices behind. She can get some rest, some sleep, and we'll keep walking. That's what matters. Getting home.

There's a sudden stab of longing at the thought of home—it's why I need to try not to think about my family. I've always known something might happen to me in the field, but I never saw it happening like this, with time to remember my mother's face when they came to tell us about Alec.

"Smuggling crocodiles. What adventures you've had, Major," she murmurs, sounding oddly wistful. The smile's fading out.

"Well, I've seen plenty of places in the last couple of years, but not many as beautiful as the plain out there." I sort through my piles of plants. "Look at these." I hold up a handful of small, delicate flowers with purple petals that stand out unevenly against a brilliant yellow center. Their underside is the same gray-green as the grass of the plains, so that when they close as the sun goes down, they can hide. "Just like us, a little rumpled, but still doing all right, yes?"

She breathes out slowly as she reaches for them. "It's hard to believe these things are just growing here." She picks one flower out of my hand, her fingertips brushing mine as she does. The one she's chosen is warped, two of the petals growing together, asymmetrical. I realize she's probably never seen the imperfect beauty of the natural world.

"I've been to cultivated gardens before," she continues, "but to see such precious things here, with nobody to care for them, simply growing. It's hard to fathom."

"My mother lets nature just come right up to our cottage. She plants flowers, but they grow among whatever else shows up." I have no idea why I'm telling her this, but she's listening, intent on my words in a way she never has been before. "There's a huge field of poppies by the house, a sea of red. Flowers grow all over the house on vines. It inspires her."

"It would inspire anyone," Lilac agrees with a soft sigh, finally distracted. Her face has softened, and for the first time in days—the first time since we met—she's unguarded. I want to bring her smile back.

When she smiles, she looks like somebody I could know. We both need this.

I reach for my grab bag, sifting through the cable, the ration bars, past the first-aid kit and the solar-powered flashlight, and the toughened leather of my notebook full of half-scribbled poems. I'm looking for the small, metal case I know will be at the bottom. It's cold when my fingers close around it, about half the size of my palm, almost as thin as the plastic sheet inside it.

"Does your mother spend much time in her garden?" she asks, and I know she wants to continue the distraction—this cease-fire between us—as much as I do.

"Every day." I pull out the case. "My mother's a poet, my father's a history teacher. I grew up surrounded by sonnets, and spent most of my time climbing trees and falling into rivers. Turned out to be pretty good practice for joining the military."

"Sounds lovely," she murmurs. "Is your mother published? I'm not sure I remember reading anything by a Merendsen, but I might have done."

"That's my father's name," I say, opening the metal case and pulling out the picture. Now I have to speak a little more slowly, spacing out my words to keep my tone even, because my throat wants to close looking down at it. A wave of homesickness rises up inside me like a physical force. "Her name's Emily Davis."

I look down at the picture in my hand. It's home, the image slightly dog-eared after two years in various grab bags and holdalls. There's the house, white walls covered in the blue flowers she loves, red poppies stretching away in the background. There's my mother, small and fair, hair falling out of its bun as usual, glasses—one of her many eccentricities—perched on her nose. There's my father beside her in a waistcoat as always. There's Alec, gangly, and me on his shoulders, holding on to his hair. If you don't know better, it probably looks like he's smiling, not grimacing. I ache, looking down at them.

"You're not serious." Her smile is in her voice, and when I look up, her gaze is waiting for me. When she sees my expression, her amusement falters. "Emily *Davis*?" she's saying, as though perhaps I got it wrong.

"If I'd known you cared, I'd have said so right away." Except I wouldn't have. I reach for the next plant to break open a broad leaf and check it against my arm. I know my mother's name impresses, but I refuse to use her as a password. It was one of the reasons I agreed to that stupid public relations trip—they said they'd keep her name out of it. I don't want to be acceptable because of who my parents are, or have her garden invaded by paparazzi. I guard the secret of our connection as fiercely as I guard my own writing. Nobody who looks at me sees poetry there. But somehow this moment with Lilac is different.

I look down at my arm. The third plant is stinging a little, and I carefully pour water from the canteen over the spot, watching as the skin reddens—not too much, though, not too bad.

Lilac's still staring down at the picture of my family. "I *love* your mother's poetry," she whispers, almost reverent. "I had a book of her poems when I was a little girl, a real book. There was one about a lilac bush, and you know how you love things with your name in them when you're a child. But I got older, and the words . . . they're so beautiful and sad. *She weeps, perfumed and pale, at summer's end.*" She looks up at me, eyes shining. "Is there really a lilac bush?"

"Hell yes, there is." I ignore the stinging on my arm. It's already fading. "I nearly killed it when I fell off the roof and landed in the middle of it, but it was tougher than it looked. Kind of like another Lilac I know."

The words come out before I can stop them, the compliment bypassing my better judgment entirely. But she smiles instead of brushing it off as condescension. It feels like the first hint of warmth all day, and suddenly I'm talking again. I want to keep her smiling.

"People come to our house to see things from the poems. Half the time the fence is broken and the shingles are falling off the roof, but my father puts the visitors to work helping him keep the cottage in one piece until my mother's done working for the day. Then she comes downstairs to see them."

She's coming to life as I watch, laughing in her delight. "Oh, Tarver."

It still feels strange to hear her say my first name. Not strange—thrilling. It's as though I'm in an actual conversation for the first time in days.

She's shaking her head. "I can't believe it. Wait, no! The one about the tin soldier boy. Tell me that's not you, I'll die. I learned to recite it!"

I shake my head, leaning forward a little to look down at the photo she holds. "That was Alec." And perhaps because I'm looking at the photo, I can smile when I say his name. I point to him. "That's him there in the picture, with me on his shoulders."

"He's in the military too?" She leans down to get a good look at his face.

"He was," I say, quieter. "He was killed in action."

She looks up at me, eyes wide. "I'm so sorry."

In this moment I know that this is what I wanted. This is what I wanted that night in the salon, and it's what I've wanted every day since then.

She's not looking at me and seeing a guy brought up on the wrong type of planet. She's not seeing a soldier, or a war hero, or an uncultured lout who doesn't understand how hard this is for her, or an idiot who knows nothing about the right kind of anything.

She just sees me.

"The two of you were becoming closer."

"And?"

"You confirm it?"

"You made a statement, I thought you already knew it was true."

"Can you elaborate on how that came about?"

"I thought the purpose of this debrief was to discuss my impressions of the planet."

"The purpose of the debriefing is for you to answer whatever questions we choose to ask you, Major. We're asking about Miss LaRoux."

"What was the question again?"

"Never mind. We can come back to it."

"I'll look forward to that."

SIXTEEN

LILAC

I KNOW A THOUSAND DIFFERENT SMILES, EACH WITH ITS OWN nuanced shade of meaning, but I don't know how to reach the few feet away to touch this person next to me. I don't know how to talk to him. Not when it's real.

I settle for smiling at his stories, and spreading ointment from the first-aid kit on the rashes he's getting from some of the plants. As dusk threatens, he heads out to check his snares. The second he leaves my side the world seems darker, bigger, and I brace for a new voice to slice the quiet. But instead there's only the wind sighing through the tall grass and, in the distance, the sounds of Tarver moving across the plain.

I avert my eyes as he tends to the small, furred creatures he brings back, the fruits of his traps. I'm hungry enough that I'll eat them, but that doesn't mean I want to watch him gut them. He keeps up a steady stream of his stories as he works to distract me and cover the sounds, stories about his platoon, each more outrageous than the last. In the growing dark I can almost feel as though we are comfortable together, as though he enjoys my company rather than merely tolerating it—as though he's volunteering these stories because he wants to make me laugh, not just keep me moving.

I watch as he builds the fire, paying attention for once. I should have been doing this from the start, in case he did leave me on my own—but now I don't watch out of fear. Now I just want to know so I can help. He's able to have only the tiniest of fires here due to the lack of fuel, nothing to help keep us warm tonight. But it's enough to cook minuscule slivers of the meat, and for the first time since crashing on the planet my stomach feels as though it's full of something real.

My eyes grow heavy as I huddle by the smoking remains of the fire. Tarver sits writing in that notebook of his by the last of the light, head bent low and close to the pages. The sun has set while we cooked, and what was a mildly unpleasant evening chill has turned into a piercing cold mitigated not at all by the tatters of my green dress. My cheer has plummeted with the temperature, and with his absence when he puts away his notebook and goes to deposit the remains of our dinner far enough away to avoid attracting visitors in the night. He doesn't think the giant cats come out on the plains, but as he says, better safe than sorry.

I can't help but wonder how many times over I would've died out here without Tarver keeping me alive.

When he returns I lift my head, but I'm too tired to try harder than that. Though I can feel the dynamic between us changing, I still don't quite know how to talk to him. Wounded pride and bruised confidence keep me from saying what I wish I could say. I drop my head back onto my knees.

"Miss LaRoux." Tarver crouches down beside me, a movement I know now so well I don't need to see him to register it. "Lilac. It's too cold out here on the plains. There's not enough fuel to keep a fire going, and the wind is that much colder than in the forest."

"No kidding."

He laughs, and I realize I've borrowed his words. I sound like a soldier. I feel my cheeks beginning to heat. "If you insist," he continues, watching me, "we can sleep back-to-back. But it'll be warmer if you let me put an arm around you and tuck the blankets around us. I promise to think only the purest of thoughts."

Surely he can see my face burning even in the darkness. I turn it away, letting the chilly wind cool my cheeks, as the rest of me shivers. "You don't have to do that."

"What's that?"

"Pretend I'm—" I shrug, shake my head. I'm not angry with him, but there's anger in my voice anyway. At my body's betrayal, the way I can't control my blush. How awkward he makes me feel, as though we're partners in a dance where I don't know the steps. Like I'm the ignorant one.

I try to summon some dignity, a last-ditch effort. At least I don't have to look like I'm foolish enough to think he's an admirer. "I know I'm not your choice of—of companions. This is as much a trial for you as for me."

At that he laughs again, this time not bothering to do so quietly. It's a full laugh, rich and without restraint, nothing like the genteel twitters and chuckles in society. My mouth wants to respond with a smile, even as the rest of me recoils, certain he's making fun of me.

He gets to his feet, shaking out the blankets and making up a bed. One bed, tonight. "Miss LaRoux, before you martyr yourself, I should warn you that I've had to curl up with my large and hairy corporal under certain undesirable circumstances. By comparison, a beautiful girl sounds like a vacation."

Beautiful? I've always been reasonably pretty—but enough money would turn even a cow into a catch. Still, aside from those first days on the *Icarus*, he's never looked at me that way. He's made it clear my status and money mean nothing to him. The opposite, in fact.

I'm grateful for the darkness, that he can't see my face. For him to see me incapable of concealing my smile for one tiny compliment? That would be the ultimate humiliation.

I turn around, and he's kneeling at the edge of the bed, hands braced on his thighs. He gestures for me to lie down first, barely visible through the darkening night. The first of the moons is yet to rise, and the stars overhead grow brighter by the second. The air is clear and cold and sharp.

He's right. Neither of us will sleep if I insist on separation. Part of me recoils from the very thought, too well trained. But who would know? There are no rescue teams flying over, no sign of my father's cavalry coming for me. I can cave, just for one night. And it is so—tempting. To be warm, that is.

I swallow and creep forward to slip beneath the blanket, making myself as small as possible. "Only while we're on the plains and can't have a fire." The words come before I have a chance to stop them. He'll think I'm disparaging his gesture. Why can't I just accept his offer?

But he just nods, readying himself for bed, unhooking his holster to set it beside us and placing the flashlight nearby. When he lifts the edge of the blanket to lie down, it brings a rush of cold air, and I curl up more tightly.

"Sorry," he murmurs, voice not far from my ear. "Close your eyes, you'll be warm in a minute."

He's not subtle about making himself comfortable, reaching out to wrap an arm around my waist and draw me close. His body is warmer than mine, and after a moment he lifts his hand to rub my arm. I try not to shiver at his touch, at the heat of his palm on the chilled skin exposed by my idiotic dress.

Eventually he stills again, ducking his head so that his nose brushes the back of my neck, and his breath stirs my hair. Already his breathing is slowing, lengthening—I envy his ability to sleep anywhere, in any position, without hesitation. Every nerve of mine is alive, tingling, feeling every shift he makes.

I've never been this close to someone like him before. I close my eyes with difficulty, stifling an insane urge to turn within the circle of his arm to face him. It's such a stupid thing to think, and guilt and anger surge in to follow the thought.

It's not difficult to see the way he looks at me, even though he tries now to hide his impatience and annoyance. How quickly one's delusions come crashing down—the soldiers aren't watching us society folk, wishing they could touch us. They're *laughing* at us in our bright dresses and parasols, our immaculately re-created drawing rooms and parlors. And what was funny in the sparkling world of the *Icarus* is simply pathetically ridiculous down here, in the kind of world they live in day to day. I'm not even close to the type of girl he'd want, just as I've been signaling at every opportunity that he's the last man in the galaxy I'd want to touch.

The only difference is that I was wrong.

How long I lie there, listening to the slow beat of his heart and the frenetic dance of my own, I'm not sure. One of this planet's moons has begun to rise beyond the trees, casting a cold blue light across the plain and edging the grass with a frosty glow. The wind has died, but over the whisper of Tarver's breath stirring my hair, another sound breaks the quiet.

My breath condenses in the cold air as I exhale. I squeeze my eyes more tightly, as if somehow I can block out the sound of the incomprehensible voice echoing across the night if I try hard enough.

"Go away," I whisper into the darkness, my body tensing, starting to shake. Bad enough these voices invade my thoughts—but they seem to invade my body too, destroying my control, leaving me a shivering pile of confusion and fear. Behind me, Tarver senses it and mumbles something against my skin, the arm around me tightening.

The voice continues unabated. I know Tarver doesn't hear it, or else he'd be awake and holding his gun in an instant. I turn my face into the pack we're using as a pillow, try to think of the music I used to listen to back on the *Icarus*, even cover my ears with my hands, trying to make them work despite the twitching of my muscles.

On and on it whispers, into the night, each passing moment multiplying the torment. A tear squeezes out beneath my lashes, rapidly growing frigid in the cold and tracing an icy path down my temple to join the cold sweat that's broken out all over. This time there's a strange taste in my mouth too, a metallic tang that doesn't go away no matter how many times I swallow.

I'm going mad.

"Tarver." My voice is barely more than a whisper, emerging as a tight and wobbly thing I almost don't recognize as my own. "Do you hear that?" I don't even know why I ask. I already know he doesn't.

If it had been one of my friends, I would have had to shake them; with Tarver, my whisper is enough. He comes awake instantly, body going from lax and peaceful to tense and alert.

"Sorry," he whispers back, his lips not far from my ear. "I was asleep. What was it?"

The voice is still murmuring some distance away, in the direction of the mountains that lie between us and the *Icarus*, as if beckoning me on. Meaning slips away as though I've forgotten how to comprehend language.

"I hear them now," I whisper. I barely register the fact that my body is shaking violently. I'm too ragged to care that he sees me so low. "Please," I add, my heart shrinking inside me, "please just tell me that you hear it too."

"Lilac," he begins, reaching up to curl his hand around my upper arm. Warm. Steadying.

"Please."

He reaches up and brushes the hair back from my face, an uncharacteristically tender gesture. As he drops his thumb to my cheek to brush away the dampness there, he murmurs, "Promise me that no matter what you hear, you won't go off on your own to investigate. I want your word." There's a command in his voice, soft as it is.

I want to tell him that leaving his side is the last thing I want to do right now, but my throat has closed completely, and I can do nothing but curl up more tightly and nod. He keeps his arm around me, holding me through the shivering. I ought to be scandalized at his closeness, demand he keep his distance, but my mind is too full of the things I wish I could say. His touch just feels right.

"We'll work it out," he says. "There's a reason for it. Maybe when you hit your head in the pod—that was a beautiful shiner you gave yourself. At least you don't have the taste of dead rat in your mouth, hmm? A soldier in my platoon got that on Avon. Couldn't taste anything else for weeks after she smacked her head."

I recognize his tone. He's trying to cheer me up as he did before. He needs me moving, and to keep me moving he has to keep me sane. He doesn't know that I'm tasting blood and copper at the back of my mouth. I draw in a shuddering breath.

"Well," I manage, summoning an even voice from God knows where, "if all she had to eat were those ration bars, maybe it's best she couldn't taste properly after all."

He laughs, the sound barely more than a quick exhalation by my ear. "You're really something," he says softly, giving me a tiny squeeze that nonetheless robs me of what breath I have left.

A thrill runs down my spine, the tiniest of sparks to remind me I'm not lost yet. The tears are still there, clawing to get free, clogging my throat and my voice.

"I think you're doing incredibly well," he continues. "Really, you're coping much better than half the soldiers I know would in this situation. We're both still on our feet, we're heading in the right direction. We're sticking together. That's why we'll be all right."

The lie is so blatant that it cracks my resolve. I can't stand his pity, not now after everything.

"I'm sorry," I whisper. My cold lips fumble the words.

"Don't be." His voice is a low rumble against me, the sound carrying through my bones, clearer than any of the voices I've been hearing. "You've got nothing to be sorry for."

"I do too." The dark of the night is like a shield of anonymity, despite the fact that we may well be the only two people on the planet. Curled up in these blankets, I might be in a confessional, and before I can stop myself the words that have been roiling around in my heart since he got me out of that tree come pouring out.

"I'm sorry I can't do things, I'm sorry you have to keep stopping for me, I'm sorry that you have to sit and watch me go mad. I'm sorry I ever dropped my glove for you to pick up." For a moment I'm choked by my own voice.

But none of this is what I really want to apologize for.

"I'm sorry I said those things to you on the observation deck because Anna was there, because of who I am. It was mean and petty and I only said it because I couldn't afford to let myself say anything else."

I can't find the words for what I want to say next—that I'm not what he thinks, that I wish I had a picture that could make him understand, the way he showed me his life in one snapshot. I gasp for breath and fall silent.

He doesn't answer me right away, and for a few insane moments I think maybe his ability to sleep anywhere extends to dozing while faced with semi-hysterical girls blurting out apologies.

Then his arm tightens around me, his breath warm against the back of my neck. The tangled words choking my throat ease, and let me take in a long, shaking breath.

"I appreciate the apology."

From anyone else I'd know it was a platitude. But there's a sincerity to his voice when he says it that tells me he means it.

I shift, trying to get comfortable, and my eyes fall on one of the moons, which has cleared the plains. It's the first time we've been able to see this one clearly, unobstructed by the forest canopy.

"Tarver."

"Hmm?"

"Look."

He lifts his head, and I feel the moment he sees it; his arms tense around me, his breath stops.

What I'd always thought was a smaller, second moon is actually a grouping of cold blue lights, too steady to be any kind of aircraft, too regular to be any kind of asteroid cluster. Seven in all, arranged evenly in a circle, one in the middle.

"What is it?" My voice is shaking, but this time it's not because of the voices.

Tarver props himself up on one arm, staring over me at the phenomenon. He says nothing, and after a moment I turn to look at him. His face is set, jaw clenched—but he doesn't look surprised. He looks thoughtful.

"When the pod was going down," he says slowly, "I saw something in orbit. Something other than the *Icarus*. Went by too fast for me to get a good look, but I could see enough to know it was man-made. How big would something like that have to be, to be visible like this?"

I draw in a slow breath, mind running through the calculations. "Each of those objects would have to be dozens of kilometers across at least, to reflect that much sunlight."

Tarver lowers himself down again, arm circling my waist. His voice is soft and warm by my ear. "What is this place?"

I have no answer for him, and we watch the false moon in silence. For a dizzying moment I see us as if from above, a tiny lump in the blue-black sea of grass, nearly swallowed by the vastness of the plains.

At some point while we talked, the voice out in the night fell silent, and the tremors racking my body have calmed. And so I listen to Tarver's breathing as it slows, and his heartbeat, and the breeze slipping through the long grass all around us, and eventually I sleep too.

"Every planet has its eccentricities."

"That's true."

"What did you notice about this one?"

"The lack of company."

"Major, that's unhelpful."

"I'm not trying to be unhelpful. I noticed it was a terraformed planet with no sign of a local population. I've been involved in six campaigns in two years, I never saw a planet without people before."

"What did you think of your prospects?"

"I was realistic about them. I'm realistic about them right now too."

SEVENTEEN

TARVER

I WAKE UP BECAUSE IT'S RAINING. A FAT RAINDROP LANDS right behind my ear, running down to somehow find a way inside my collar, freezing cold. I shiver and roll onto my back, and another smacks me right between the eyes.

Lilac's moving, stirring as I shift away from her, and she rolls over with a little protesting noise, reaching sleepily after me. Then she begins to register the raindrops as they connect with her skin, and she sits up straight with a gasp. I'm busy sitting up too, because when you go to sleep wrapped around a pretty girl, there are some things going on first thing in the morning that you don't exactly want making headline news.

So I'm shuffling into a slightly more diplomatic position and trying to look casual, and she's staring across at me, all confusion and dawning alarm. I realize in my surprise I've grabbed for the Gleidel, and she thinks there's some threat around.

"Tarver?" She looks up, eyes huge. One of them is still a little puffy, the skin bruised and dark where her face hit the side of the escape pod. Then a raindrop splats against her upturned face, and she jerks back. As I watch her flinch, lifting her fingers to her face and staring astonished at her wet fingertips, it hits me: she's never seen it before. In her world even the climate is controlled.

"It's raining," I say, voice hoarse from sleep. I clear my throat and try again. "It's fine. Straight from the clouds to you."

She frowns, still huddling over and trying to shelter from it. "Straight from the clouds? Is that hygienic?"

I can't help it. It starts out as a snicker, but I'm grinning, and there's a tension inside me that snaps and releases, and a moment later I'm laughing so hard I can't stop.

She stares across at me, wondering if I've finally cracked. I reach for her hand and wind my fingers through hers, turning them so the rain patters down onto her palm. I trace a circle there with my thumb, smoothing the water into her skin. I want to show her there's nothing to be afraid of.

Then her lips are curving slowly, and she's flopping back to lie down and let the rain hit her upturned face. I look across, drinking in her smile, some part of me noticing I'm still holding her hand, fingers tangled through hers. I notice she's shaking, and for an instant I think she's crying.

Then I realize she's laughing too.

I get exactly ten heartbeats to live in this perfect moment, before she blinks and lifts her head sharply, looking off across the plains, a heavier shudder running through her body. She catches herself a moment later and turns back toward me, trying to recover her smile, but I know what that was. I can see how large her pupils are, the trembling of her lips.

She heard another voice.

"I thought you said the rain was on the third day."

"No, that was the first time it rained."

"You're contradicting yourself, Major."

"No, you're trying to trip me up. I know how this works. The military invented these techniques. What's your next question?"

"What did you make of your relationship with Miss LaRoux at that stage?"

"What does that mean?"

"How did you see it unfolding?"

"I didn't. I'm a soldier. I'm from the wrong sort of family. I think it's more comfortable for everyone when guys like me are out of the way."

"Do you believe that? That you're from the wrong sort of family?"

"My family wasn't on the planet with me. I don't see a need to discuss them."

"There's no need to raise your voice, Major."

EIGHTEEN

LILAC

IT'S AMAZING HOW MUCH CAN CHANGE WITH JUST A FEW short hours, and a few million gallons of water.

I hate the rain and I hate this planet and I hate the cold and I hate my stupid, stupid dress. And I hate Tarver, for the way he strides ahead without a care, as if there isn't water *falling from the sky*, as if he doesn't even notice. I hate the way he offers me his jacket exactly when I've gotten so cold that I can't refuse. Just once I'd like to look like I've got myself together.

The morning stretches into a frigid, never-ending drizzle as we head for the river he spotted from higher ground. The mountains we're aiming for are concealed behind a soggy gray curtain. Darker clouds line the horizon, and Tarver glances over his shoulder to track their movement. I'm looking over my shoulder too, but there's nothing for me to read in the weather patterns. I simply can't keep myself from searching for the sources of the sounds I keep hearing. I keep turning to scan the plains behind us before I remember we're alone out here.

It's the rain, I tell myself. *The wind, flattening the grass. One of the grassland creatures like that thing we ate last night.*

But can an animal cry?

The sobs that surge over the rain shatter my heart, sounding for all the world like Anna, like me, like any one of the girls in my circle. With rain rolling down my cheeks and brokenhearted weeping so close at hand, I almost believe that I am the one sobbing so hopelessly. Head spinning and muscles shaking, I can barely put one foot in front of the other. It's no longer one voice—now I'm surrounded by a desperate, heartrending chorus. My eyes blur and I stumble again and again, muddying my ruined dress beyond recognition. More than once Tarver has to come back and haul me to my feet.

I despise him for how easy it is for him, the way surviving this ordeal is second nature. When he catches me staring across the plains, he grins as if to say, *Yeah, it's no big deal, I've been there.* His eyes, though, tell a different story. He's worried. Worried in a way he hasn't been since we crashed, not when the pod started to fall to the planet, not when I told him the beacon wasn't working, not even when we saw the *Icarus* fall.

And that scares me more than anything else.

Though the strange moon has set again, it's not far from my thoughts. It has to be a structure made by the corporations that terraformed this place—but what is it? Some kind of surveillance system, perhaps. Something to keep track of the colonists, should they rebel.

Only there aren't any colonists here. There's nothing to track.

There's just us, waterlogged and freezing, trekking endlessly across this planet, lives depending on finding the search parties when we reach the wreck.

Neither of us suggests stopping for lunch, despite our exhaustion. There's no way to make a fire in the steadily increasing downpour, no way to warm up if we stop moving. I wish I'd listened to his repeated suggestions that I put on the spare mechanic's suit he brought with us from the escape pod—my dress is so ragged by now and so soaked that it's as though I'm wearing nothing at all. Worst of all, I'm so cold and so tired that I don't even care about the way it clings to my body and winds around my legs, outlining my every feature.

The river swims into sight as a black smear in the distance. Tarver stops and raises a hand to shield his eyes from the rain, the picture of a soldier saluting some commanding officer. I drop into a crouch, wrapping my arms around my knees and trying not to shiver so visibly. He'll be making some mental calculation about how long it'll take to get there. This isn't a real break, I know. But it's all I have.

I don't open my eyes until I feel his hands on my arms, trying to warm skin so chilled it makes him grimace at me. "Not much farther," he promises, water cascading from jaw and nose and brow. His features have become so familiar in only five short days. I'm staring bemusedly at the rivulets meeting under his chin when he gives me a little shake.

"Lilac? You in there?"

I blink, trying to remember how to speak. My lips are sluggish, refusing to obey me. "Yes. At least I think so."

Tarver grins, that lightning-quick shift of expression, and pushes my soggy hair back from my forehead. He's about to speak when I hear something behind us, a low, rising susurration like a thousand different voices.

I'm turning before I remember that he'll see more evidence of my descending madness. It's a half a second before I realize that he's staring in the same direction too.

I open my mouth, heart constricting with sudden hope, but he beats me to it.

"More rain," he murmurs, so soft I almost can't hear him.

Not my voices, then. I cast my gaze back toward the horizon, and this time I see the thick gray curtain advancing across the plains toward us. More rain. *If there's any more rain than this*, I think, *we'll need gills.* We could swim up to the sky and leave this place with no need to wait for a rescue ship.

I want nothing more than to lie down in the mud, but as my knees buckle, his grip on my upper arms tightens, holding me up. When he stands, he pulls me with him.

"Can you run?" His face is close to mine.

"What?" I can't do anything other than stare.

"Come on, Lilac, focus. Can you run for it? That rain is too heavy. We need shelter."

Heavy? How can rain be heavy?

I know there are blisters on my feet because I saw them there this morning, but right now I can't feel them. I can't feel my feet at all. I keep staring at him, at the water running down his face, never the same path twice. It ought to follow the same pattern over and over, but instead it splits and cascades and dances off his cheekbones. Like it wants to touch all of him.

"Goddammit," mutters Tarver, glancing at the advancing monsoon over my shoulder. "I'll pay for this when you warm up enough to hate me again."

What? I don't have time to consider the words any further before he's wrapping his hand around my wrist and jerking me forward, forcing me to break into a run before I'm yanked along after him like streamers on a parade car. I get my heavy legs moving somehow, reaching inside myself for one more effort.

My feet slide and skid in the mud behind him, and the bones in my wrist click under the tightness of his grip, but he doesn't let go. He's making for the dark smudge of the river on the horizon, and as we grow nearer, the darkness resolves into trees, and I don't even care that we're returning to forest again, because trees means wood and wood means fire and fire means warmth and I think I've forgotten what that feels like.

I open my mouth to say something, but before I find any words, the roar of oncoming rain overtakes us and the sky comes crashing down on our heads.

Tarver is cursing, swearing like I've never heard him do. The sudden torrent of water pries my wrist from his grip, my skin slipping free like wet rubber, and I go crashing to the ground. I'm more surprised than hurt, because I can't really feel my legs, and I didn't realize they weren't working.

He scoops me up and carries me the last few meters to the shelter of the trees bordering the river, then dumps me unceremoniously on the ground.

"Stay there," he shouts, putting his face close to mine until I push him away, because he's dripping on me. The sound of the water hurling itself at the canopy is almost as deafening as the roar of the rainstorm outside, but the branches are thick, and they keep most of the water off us.

He throws his pack to the ground and rummages until he pulls out the mechanic's suit, and shoves it at me. "Put that on," he orders, retrieving the jacket he gave me earlier. Then he's leaving again, pulling his gun out of its holster as he goes.

The mechanic's suit stays where he put it, resting half in my lap, half draped over my folded arms. I'm too cold to take off my dress, wet as it is. I press myself against the tree trunk and wait for him to come back. Whispers rise at the edge of my hearing, somehow distinct from the sound of the rain on the trees overhead. The voices are no longer crying, but I still can't make out the words. I stretch out my shaking hand in front of me, pale, clammy, smeared with dirt. I never knew madness came with such a physical toll.

I don't know how much time has passed before I wake up to find Tarver gently tapping at my cheeks. "I'm going to try to get a fire going," he says, and I realize he's not shouting anymore. The rain must have lessened a little. "Get your dress off."

"Why, Major," I find myself whispering. "I never."

"Lord help me," he says, but this time he's rolling his eyes, and I know he'd be laughing if he were a bit less cold. That is a triumph far more satisfying than annoying him ever was. "Just do it, okay? No arguing with me this time. I promise not to look. Dry off with the blanket, then put on the mechanic's suit."

I take the blanket he thrusts at me, and lean on the tree as I get to my feet, stiff and cold. The voices have stopped, but I'm still shivering. I'm working at the knotted laces for a full five minutes before I realize that I haven't taken this dress off in five days, the laces are soaked and waterlogged, and my hands are so cold I can barely make them curl around the strings.

"Tarver," I whisper. "I need help."

There's a spark of heat left in me, because I feel my cheeks beginning to burn as he turns to me, confused. Understanding dawns as his eyes fall to where my hands are fumbling at the neckline of my dress.

Muttering something foul-sounding in a language I don't recognize, he closes the distance between us again and directs me to warm my hands under my arms while he tries to unknot the laces. Eventually he's forced to pull out his knife and saw through them while I look away and try to think of something else. The dress was already so far past saving anyway. This is just one more tiny casualty in the name of survival.

I had the delicate purple flower that he gave me on the plains tucked down my bodice, and as I peel away the remains of the dress, I find it crushed against my skin, almost beyond recognition. I'm forced to let it go, drop it in the mud.

What does it say about how I've changed that I feel more for the loss of one tiny flower than for the loss of the dress?

He turns away to start finding kindling that isn't soaked through, careful to keep his back to me, and I let the dress fall to the ground. Leaving it where it is, I grab the blanket and wrap it around myself, gasping in the cold. I drop to my knees so that the blanket will cover more of me as I huddle.

A tiny flicker of orange against my closed lids prompts me to open them to see Tarver nurturing a fledgling fire so carefully that his hands are shaking with the effort.

The trees above us have thick, broad leaves, but even so, it's raining so hard that some water finds its way through. I can't quite stop the inarticulate sound of relief that he was still able to find enough dry wood to burn. He looks up at the sound, eyes flickering down when he sees me in the blanket, then jerking away.

I must not be as covered as I think I am. Clearly I'm warming up, because suddenly I actually care, and hunch more carefully into my cocoon.

"On with the mechanic's suit, Miss LaRoux. You'll be the height of fashion, I promise. Then give me the blanket so I can dry off as much as I can."

That's what finally convinces me to give up my claim to the blanket. He's still dripping, forced to lean away from the fire as he works so that he doesn't swamp it. We'll never be completely dry with the rain that makes its way past the canopy, but damp is better than soaked. I get to my feet and let the blanket fall so I can shove my legs into the bottom half of the suit and zip it up. It's made for a man, and I draw my arms inside the loose material to cradle them against my chest, letting the sleeves hang empty. The material's so rough that when it comes time to move out, I'll have to wear the dress underneath or risk rubbing my skin raw. But for now, it's comparatively dry, and that's enough.

It isn't until I crouch down next to the tiny fire that Tarver looks up again, cautiously. He adds another stick to the flames before standing to retrieve the blanket and start stripping off his own wet clothes. I am not as honorable as he is. My mind goes blessedly blank as I watch him drop his jacket and his shirt to the ground. His dog tags leap and gleam in the meager glow from the fire. His skin is taut with cold and covered with goose bumps, reddening as he scrubs at it briskly with a fistful of the blanket.

The jacket goes back on, and he lays his shirt out on the other side of the fire to dry before retrieving the blanket from the ground. He wraps this around me, and I don't even care anymore about its coarseness—it's warm despite being damp, and though all I can feel right now is the chill of my own body radiating back at me, I know in a few moments I'll be better. My eyes follow Tarver as he goes through the motions of setting up camp, jerky and quick. It's not until he's got the canteen set to boil over the fire that he joins me, ducking abruptly inside my cocoon of blankets and wrapping an arm around me before I can react.

The fire's still too young to give off much heat, hissing unhappily at the drops that squeeze past the sheltering trees overhead. After a time I stop shivering, but he keeps his arm around me nonetheless. There are no voices to be heard above the popping fire and the splat of raindrops on the canopy above, and in a rush my sleepless nights catch up to me with all the force of a mag-lev train. I ought to disentangle myself from Tarver, go to sleep properly on my own. I ought to wait for dinner to boil. I ought to let him rest without having to take care of me.

But I'm warm now, and for once there's no one calling to me in words I can't understand, and for reasons I don't care to examine, the thought of pushing Tarver Merendsen's arms away makes my stomach twist unhappily. And so I stay still, and let my head drop onto his shoulder, and if he minds the way my wet hair drips on him, he says nothing, and lets me sleep.

"You told us that Miss LaRoux suffered some minor head injuries as a result of the crash."

"That's right."

"There were no side effects? She was able to travel without difficulty?"

"I'd like to see you hike across a planet in a ball gown and the type of shoes those girls wear. I don't think I'd say the walk was without difficulty."

"It's a relevant question, Major Merendsen."

"And?"

"And I'd be obliged if you'd answer it."

"I'm not aware of any difficulties she had that were a result of the knock to her head."

"What about you?"

"It was a walk in the park. What do you think?"

NINETEEN

TARVER

SHE WAKES EARLY, THIS GIRL WHO PROBABLY USED TO SLEEP until noon and lie abed until three. I roll over into the warm spot she leaves behind, eyes closed, but I can feel her watching me. She pushes away the dirt I used to bank the fire, stirring up the coals. Warmth flickers against my face as she builds the fire up again with the kindling I gathered last night.

Moving slowly, probably stiff and sore from our drowning dash last night, she crouches down beside me and rests a hand on my shoulder. When I crack open an eyelid to peer up at her, she looks tired. Both her eyes are marked underneath with dark smears of blue and purple, and one is still marbled black and yellow as her magnificent black eye starts to fade. She's pale, with new freckles from the sun overhead standing out like punctuation on a page.

But she's captivating too, maybe more than she was before, with the tale of our survival written on her features.

"I'm going to get us some water." Her whisper's barely audible—she wants to let me sleep. "I won't be long."

I clear my throat a little, and she takes that as a sign that I've heard her. I wonder for a moment if I should let her go alone, but she's not the girl who crashed with me. She'll be careful.

I didn't see any paw prints while I was gathering the kindling last night. I don't think there's anything big living around here. It's an isolated clump of trees by the bank of the river, surrounded by open plains.

A predator wouldn't make the trip this far, or be able to live on what could survive here.

As I watch her through my lashes, she straightens and turns away, and I let myself drift again. Apparently I'm not going to be punished for the fact that she woke up wrapped around me. The cold shoulder would have been worth it, but it seems she's accepted our sleeping arrangements as a necessary evil. Sleep reaches for me, and I let it take me for a little longer.

When I wake, I have no sense of how much time has passed—seconds or minutes, or longer. The thing in orbit around the planet has set, which means at least an hour or two has passed since dawn, but how long ago did Lilac leave?

The air's so damp that my shirt still hasn't dried. I give up trying to avoid smelling like smoke, though I know she'll wrinkle her nose at it, and hold the shirt directly above the fire. When she gets back with the water, I'll try hot soup for breakfast. Some of the plants that tested okay should add some flavor, and we've still got leftover chunks of the latest small, scampery thing. I don't know what to make of its elongated snout, or the oversized ears. It's like a parody of the small fauna I usually see on terraformed planets.

Then Lilac comes crashing back through the undergrowth like somebody told her there's a shoe sale going on here at the campsite. It honestly doesn't occur to me that something might actually be wrong until I get a look at her face.

She's white, breath ragged and hair tangled. Her eyes are huge, and the knees of the mechanic's suit are covered in mud—she's fallen on her way back.

Part of me wants to drop my shirt and reach for her, but my hands know better, and first they're setting it aside where it can't catch fire, then reaching for the Gleidel.

Lilac flinches at the soft whine as the gun powers up. "No, you don't need to—it's nothing, it's fine."

"It's not nothing." I keep my voice low, lifting one arm to invite her over. As though a barrier's suddenly come down, she trips the three steps across to lean against me like she's falling. I pull her in close, keeping hold of the gun as she presses her face against my chest. My shirt's still on the ground, but I'm not cold anymore. "Tell me what happened, start at the beginning. You took the canteen to the river, and . . . ?"

She's trembling violently, gripping the canteen with white knuckles. I can see where she's spilled some of it down the leg of the suit. My heart sinks. I recognize this now, her scattered gaze, the way her body shakes. Last night I'd begun to think that the worst had passed, when she slept without any interruptions. But now she looks worse than ever.

"Tarver, you're just going to think I'm crazy." She's staring past me, and I focus on keeping my expression calm as I wait. She'll fill the silence eventually; she doesn't like the quiet. "Crazier," she amends herself, then tucks her face back in against my chest, as if the effort of speaking normally has cost her. I'm practically holding her up.

"Tell me anyway," I say quietly, flicking the power switch on the Gleidel and tucking it back into the holster. Now I'm free to wrap both arms around Lilac, and she tucks in underneath my chin like she's meant to be there. I close my eyes. "Never mind what I think, tell me what happened."

It takes her a little while to answer, and though the trembling is starting to fade, she's not calming down any. I can feel the way she's breathing, in short, sharp jerks. "I saw them," she mumbles eventually. "The voices. And yes, I know how it sounds. You don't have to point it out."

It's like something's turning to stone inside my stomach, heavy and painful. She's right. Crazier. *Please, no.* "People? You saw people?"

She nods, though it's such a small movement that I only feel it against my skin. A tiny part of my mind registers just how distressed she must be, not to notice that I'm half naked, holding her against me—that her cheek is resting against bare skin. "On the far bank of the river. One minute it was just me, getting the water, and then . . ."

"What did they look like? The people?" I still want there to be an explanation, something I can understand.

"I know who they were." Her voice cracks. I wish I could go through this for her, spare her. "They were all looking at me, and pointing that way." She tips her head in the direction we've been traveling, toward the mountain pass and the wreck beyond.

"You could see the mist right through them, and when the sunlight hit, they disappeared." She pauses to swallow, her voice tightening and breaking again. "One of them wasn't wearing any boots."

It takes me a moment to understand what she means. Then it hits me, and I tighten my hold on her. "They're not real, Lilac. I believe you saw them, but you know you hit your head when we landed. Once we're back in civilization, it'll be the work of a moment to fix this. For now, I need you to promise me you won't go chasing after anything you see. You could get hurt."

She goes still. I wonder if she was expecting me to believe her, that I'd find visions more convincing than voices in her head. "Tarver, how many people did you bury in that pod?"

"We didn't kill them, Lilac. We treated them with respect. If you're feeling guilty about what happened—"

"There were five of them, weren't there?" She pulls back to look up at me, intent. Her pupils are huge, the blue of her eyes nearly drowning in the black. Her gaze is so raw it's frightening. "You didn't let me see them. How could I know that? Tarver, don't you see? I'm *not* crazy after all. I'm being haunted."

I don't know how to deal with this. You can't reason with insanity, and you can't bark orders at a girl who's not a soldier. I keep up the calm and patient face that used to annoy her so much, allowing myself a slow breath before I speak again. "I'm sure I told you how many people I buried." But we both know I didn't. "Even so, five's a reasonable number. That's almost capacity for a pod. Let's get moving, Lilac. I want us to have plenty of time this afternoon to find a safe, warm place for camp. Let me have the canteen, I'll heat some water."

As I reach for the canteen, she pulls away from me. Her stare's unwavering as she puts distance between us. "There were two women," she says evenly. "The one with no boots was about my height. And there was a soldier. I could see his dog tags."

Something's blocking my throat, and for the count of maybe three, I can't breathe, my chest struggling to remember what it should do next. It's a mistake. She's making it up. She's seeing my dog tags now, that's how she got the idea in her head.

But she's not done. "The other two were men in evening dress."

I finally manage a breath, choking on it. *No. It's impossible. She can't know.* When I can breathe evenly again, I speak, keeping my gaze steady. "Of course you saw a girl the same height as you, Lilac. She had the same size feet as you. Those aren't the people we buried, though, if that's what you're thinking. It was all women in the pod. There were no men; there was no soldier." I don't even know why I'm lying to her, except that my mind's freewheeling, scrabbling for anything to grab on to, and all it can find is this: I can't buy into what she's saying. I can't make this any worse than it already is.

We stare at each other for long seconds. Her lips are parted a little, like she's been slapped, but she's trying to hide it. She knows I'm lying. Then her features settle, and she's giving me a blank stare that betters any of my efforts this morning.

"Right," she says softly. "Then let's go."

We're silent as we pack up the camp. Neither of us is thinking of breakfast anymore.

I don't know what else I could have said. I can't feed whatever's going on in her head.

It makes no sense.

She laid rocks on top of their grave, but she never saw the bodies. The bodies of the men in evening dress, of the women in the mechanic's suits, of the soldier not much older than me.

I have that man's dog tags in the bottom of my bag.

"You had nearly reached the Icarus."

"We still had to make it over the mountains. The crash site was on the other side of the pass. That's where we'd seen the ship fall."

"The reports say there was snow in the mountains."

"Yes."

"We've been at this for some time now, and you never mentioned the snow before."

"You think I'm lying about the weather?"

"I don't know what you're doing, Major. I'm trying to find out. There was snow?"

"Yes. If you have the weather reports, I'm not sure I can add anything useful."

"Try, Major."

TWENTY

LILAC

TARVER DIDN'T TELL ME THAT IT WOULD BE COLDER IN THE
mountains. Maybe it's always cold on mountains, I don't know. Maybe he
thought it was common sense.

As we leave the river for the foothills, I find myself thinking about the
girl in the salon. The one who flirted as easily as she breathed, the one
who dodged bodyguards and stayed up all night gossiping. I bear so little
resemblance to her now it's as though she no longer exists.

And as hateful as she was, I find I miss her. She knew where she
stood. She knew what she was meant to do. She had a father who'd stop
at nothing to protect her, a world that arranged itself to fit around her.
She never had to care about the opinions of one lowly soldier. And it
never used to matter when someone lied to her, because that's all anyone
ever did.

What had looked like clouds in the distance are, now, clearly snow-
capped peaks. The mountains lie between us and the wreck of the *Icarus*,
and Tarver says to go around would take more time than we can afford.
And so through we go, regardless of the temperature and the threatening
sky, to shelter in some crevice overnight and hopefully make the valley
beyond in the morning.

The pass he proposes to cross is not white with snow, but as the day
wears on, the temperature drops and the clouds gather low in the sky.
Even Tarver glances up at them, restless, picking up the pace so that I

stumble and bang my knees on the rocks. My hands are too numb to break my fall.

I ought to be surprised when the first flakes begin to fall—the closest I have ever come to snow is watching the Christmas specials on the HV—but I have no energy left for surprise. Some other Lilac, the one in the salon perhaps, would have found the snow beautiful.

With the sun retreating behind the clouds, the temperature is dropping faster the higher we climb. The snowflakes linger on my cheeks before they melt. The mechanic's suit provides little warmth, but the tight weave of the fabric gives shelter from the wind. Thanks to these cursed boots, my feet are the warmest part of me.

At least I know I'm no longer going mad. No, I'm being haunted. Is one better than the other? I've been the cause of death before. Why can't I dismiss the faces of those five lost souls?

If I hadn't seen Tarver's face when I described what I'd seen, perhaps I could go on believing I was hallucinating. But his expression was that of a man who's been mortally wounded, frozen in the few shocked seconds before he falls. He knew I had no way of knowing whom he buried. Perhaps he believes he's helping me in some way by leading me to believe I'm mad. But Tarver is not given to lying, and he doesn't fool me.

Maybe it's not the Lilac in the salon that I miss. Not the Lilac on the plains, or even the Lilac before she saw the *Icarus* fall.

I think I miss most the Lilac who trusted Tarver Merendsen.

"What?"

"Major?"

"I stopped listening there for a moment. What did you say?"

"I suggest you make every effort to keep listening, Major. You seem tired."

"Bright-eyed and bushy-tailed. Could I get something to drink?"

"We'll arrange that in a moment. Are you ready to continue?"

"Of course. Eager to provide whatever it is you're after."

"We're after the truth, Major."

"That's exactly what I've given you. You're looking for something else."

TWENTY-ONE

TARVER

THE MORNING DAWNED CLEAR AND PROMISING, AND I HAD let myself hope a little that the ascent wouldn't be as bad as I had anticipated. Streams of snowmelt run down the mountainside, and though they're gut-achingly cold, I never lack somewhere to fill the canteen. But the higher we climb, the faster the temperature drops. The sunlight feels pale and cold, but I know it's the only thing standing between us and a much bigger problem. A problem we'll face when the sun starts to sink.

Lilac works stubbornly to keep up, and my heart tugs at me to slow down and let her rest. But I press on, up past the boulders and the thinning tufts of grass.

As we climb, my mind circles back to how utterly alien this must be for her—as far from her experience as her life is from mine. What must it have been like to grow up with your face on the cover of every gossip magazine in the galaxy?

I can't stand to think what the paparazzi would say if they heard her mutter one of my curses under her breath, or saw the way she nestles in close to me at night. What they'd make of her strength.

I can smell the snow coming. We don't have time to waste in getting to the crash site, and the difference between slowing down and pushing on might be an extra night up here. So we keep climbing.

It's a few hours after we split a ration bar for lunch that the first flakes start to fall, so tiny at first that they almost look like a mist. Behind me Lilac makes a soft sound, and I realize she's probably never seen real snow before. She's had more reality since we crashed than over the rest of her life put together. Part of me wants to stop and appreciate the start of the snowfall with her, but I know it won't be long until it's coming thick and fast, so I park her in the lee of one of the huge rocks that litter our path and scramble up over it for a better view. We need a cave, or at least an overhang. The twisted trees up here have bare, spindly branches, and they're useless for shelter. I've never seen trees like this—combined with the thick, pale moss on the rocks, they make this place ghostly, unwelcoming.

I used to do a lot of mountaineering with Alec when I was a kid. Me and my hero. I've been thinking about him as we climb, and about my parents. By now they must think they have two dead sons. He's one of the voices in my head that keep me moving when I want to stop. A line of sergeants and commanding officers comes to life in my head when I get tired—big, wild men from the frontier who screamed at us until their instincts became ours. They keep pushing me on, instructing me on finding the right campsite, making sure I take the extra minute to make the bed as comfortable as I can so I don't pay for my laziness by tossing and turning all night. But Alec's voice is quieter, patient, the way he used to sound when he came home on leave and taught me the things he'd learned.

It doesn't take long to find a cave. The entrance is barely more than a space between two rocks, roofed over with earth and stone, but it extends farther in, and it'll do.

The cold cuts into my face and the rising wind pulls at my coat as I work my way across the mountainside to fetch Lilac. She's huddled against the rock, and her hands are freezing as I guide her up the slope toward the place I've found.

We make our way in past the first twist of the cave. It's dark, but we're sheltered from the wind. When I catch sight of her face in the flashlight, her gaze is dull and hopeless.

I wish she'd come alive and start listing my faults for me. I bundle her in blankets and build a fire with deadwood piled by old snowmelt at the mouth of the cave, then crawl inside the blankets with her. She's too tired to resist, maybe, because she leans in against me and rests her head on my shoulder. "Don't drowse," I say quietly, my voice hoarse from disuse. "Not until you're warmer."

"Mmm," she agrees, drawing the blanket in tighter around us. "Why am I always the problem? Just once I'd like to be the useful one."

"We happened to get stranded on my turf," I say. "That's the way it goes, sometimes."

"I just wish—" She shifts a little, getting comfortable again and sub-siding against me with a sigh. "Well, I suppose I wish a lot of things."

"Me too," I say quietly to the girl in my arms. *I know exactly what you mean.*

"I wish I had a really good cup of tea," she says, with a sigh. "And some scones, jam, cream."

"I wish I had a steak." We both dwell on that for a moment. "Or something to boil. There's a guy in my unit who can make food out of anything. He boiled up a shirt when we were in a tight spot on Arcadia. But he says it's got to be a general's shirt, because they use a better qual-ity dye on those."

"Major." She sounds like she doesn't know whether to giggle, or chas-tise me.

"Oh, don't worry, you remove the insignia first. Otherwise it would be disrespectful."

Talking again after the day's silence is like a truce after a long cam-paign. As we settle in to wait to warm up, I'm careful to keep my mind from drifting toward the people she saw by the river. All of them point-ing this way, at the mountains, or the wreck, perhaps. But why? I don't want to talk about it, don't want to think about it. For now, we're allies again, and I'm not about to mess that up.

My internal clock tells me I've been asleep for hours when something wakes me. The fire's burned down to embers, and the wind outside is howling in the way only a blizzard in full swing can. But we're wearing everything we own, including our boots, and I'm warm.

Then I realize what woke me. Lilac's sitting bolt upright, staring into space. Her eyes are wild and vague—she's been dreaming. Cold air's leaking in where she's pulled the blankets away from me, and I wait to see whether she'll lie back down, keeping one eye barely cracked open. I really want to sleep. I want her to sleep too.

No such luck. She scrambles out of the blankets and onto her knees, reaching down to shake my shoulder. "Tarver," she hisses. "Tarver, I know you're not asleep, get up."

Dammit. I open my eyes. Flushed and urgent, she stares at me. I see her trembling, a drop of sweat trickling down her temple despite the chill. She looks sick with whatever nightmare woke her.

"Lilac, please. Just kill me." I let her hear a little of the impatience in my voice, which I'm usually so careful about. But it's the middle of the night. I was finally warm. I *really* want to sleep. "What is it?"

She tries to calm herself, but I can still see the urgency in her eyes— she's hoping I'll listen if she hides away the crazy. "We have to get out of here." Her breath catches as she says it, as though she's surprised to hear herself speak those words. "It's not safe."

"No kidding," I say, hauling the blanket up underneath my chin. "And trust me, the first rescue ship I see, we're on it. But for now, we're as safe as we can be in here. We'll freeze out there. You don't screw around with blizzards."

She hauls back the blankets and grabs my wrist, throwing her weight into the effort. I can feel the tremors racking her body. Not just a dream, then—this was one of her visions. She's clearly beyond reason.

"Believe me," she says, teeth gritted with effort. I don't let her shift me, and without my cooperation, neither of us moves. "Tarver, I *know.* But we have to go, we have to go *right now.* Please, it's not safe in here, something's going to happen."

"Something's going to happen if we go out there," I say, pulling my wrist back, which jerks her closer. "We're going to start slurring our words and shaking, then we're going to stop shaking, then we're going to go mad and start pulling off our clothes, stumbling around, laughing. Then we'll collapse, and that's the merciful part, because that way we won't feel it when we freeze to death. For once, please just make things easy for me and lie down, all right?"

This is the thing I've been afraid of. This is why I made her promise not to go running after one of those voices she hears. That's how I could lose her.

"Please!" There's an edge to her voice, hoarse and desperate—whatever's scared her so much, she believes in it completely. "I don't know how, but I swear to you, I know." She closes her eyes for a moment, gathering calm, gathering steel. I know that look. When she opens her eyes again, her voice shakes with passion. "I know you lied to me back there, and I don't care. I've trusted you with my life every second, Tarver. Can't you trust *me* for one second? Just once?"

My heart's breaking, and I reach out for her hands, but she snatches them back. "It's not about trust," I tell her. "I don't know what's happening, I can't see what you see. But there's a difference between making some educated guesses about who died in that pod and thinking you can see the future. Lilac, if we leave in the middle of this blizzard, we risk dying from exposure. It's insane. We're not going out there, if I have to hold you down myself. Give yourself a few moments to calm down, and you'll see I'm right."

"We don't *have* a few moments!" Lilac is breathing hard, agitated. "You're wrong. It's *all* about trust. You just don't believe me."

I don't know what to say, and I'm still searching for words when she snaps into action. She scrambles to her feet, grabbing my pack and wheeling around to dash for the mouth of the cave.

I can hear myself roaring in pure frustration. The blankets seem to come to life, wrapping around me and tangling my arms for vital seconds before I rip my way clear. I pound after her, leaving behind the blankets and the fire, the warmth and safety of the cave.

The cold hits me like a wall, cutting in through my open jacket. I'm thanking whoever's listening that we slept fully dressed. No light from the strange moon makes it through the clouds and the snow swirling through the air. For long, terrifying seconds I can't see her at all, the darkness leaching the color out of everything. Then there's movement—she's stumbling away from the cave, scrambling over rocks and dragging herself to her feet again—and I hurl myself after her, breath rasping, boots crunching on the snow.

I've been moving so slowly and carefully for days that for an instant it almost feels good to stretch my legs. I vault over a boulder and throw myself after her, driven by my fear that she'll disappear into the night, or fall, or I'll lose her in any countless number of ways. I'm not gentle when I catch her—I grab her upper arm and slam on the brakes, so she's pulled up short and jerked into my arms, to hold her still and keep her from escaping again.

She doesn't struggle, and my heart pounds as the two of us stand there, panting, the snow quickly coating our heads and shoulders.

Then a sound starts to rise above the howling of the wind, and the muffling blanket of the snow, and the harsh rasp of our breath. It's a deep rumbling, starting as a whisper and then building to drown out everything else as the ground trembles beneath our feet. I'm forced to let go of her to catch my balance, but she doesn't move away. She looks past me toward the cave, and when I follow her line of sight, I see the faint glow of our fire wink out of existence as the roof of our campsite collapses in an avalanche of rock.

We both stand for a few moments, still panting, still staring.

It's nothing but a pile of rubble and snow.

Our bed and blankets are buried beneath it all, as we would have been too, if we'd been inside. I know this, but somehow I'm disconnected from the knowledge. I know that our cozy shelter is somewhere under the debris, but I can't imagine that it's really true.

Or how she knew to run.

When I turn to walk away, she comes without a word. We can't move far in the dark, but we find a place to wedge ourselves between two rocks and build up some of the snow to shelter us from the wind. It creates a poor shelter, but lacking any alternative, we huddle down together. We sit on the pack and wrap our arms around each other, and I don't think either of us sleeps a wink in the few hours until dawn.

The sky's only starting to lighten when the snow stops. My arms and legs have long since gone through the agony of losing circulation, and they're out the other side into numbness. The feeling comes flooding back in bolts of fiery pain as I instruct my body to move.

She follows my example as I stretch, exhausted but uncomplaining. She must hurt as much as I do, but I note with a twinge of admiration that it doesn't show up in more than a tightening of her jaw, a careful slowness to her movements. Once we're both able to take a step without stumbling, we turn away from the cave.

The last of the stars are sparkling overhead, as they always do after snow, and the artificial moon hangs low in the sky. The world is crisp and beautiful. Every step is careful and testing—you never know what lies beneath the overnight crust of snow. I sink in over my ankles, and Lilac's breathing behind me quickly becomes labored. Our progress is slow.

I don't want to think about what happened, but my mind insists on revisiting it over and over.

She saw the folks I buried.

She dreamed, and knew to run from the cave.

I let myself skid in a controlled slide down a rock as big as a tank, then turn to lift my arms up so she can slither down to join me. I catch her, hands braced against her sides, and when I move to release her, she grabs the fabric of my sleeve, holding me still.

I look down at her, and though her skin's pale with exhaustion, and her eyes are two dark, sleepless circles, her gaze is locked on mine.

She wants what happened to be her proof. Proof her voices are real, proof of her sanity. She's waiting for me to admit she's not crazy, for my conversion.

But what happened last night was impossible. Nobody can know something before it happens. I can't explain it, can't let myself dwell on it. I have to stick to the task at hand, and get us out of here.

I've been trained to close my mind in order to keep functioning. I've been trained to keep moving.

I let my gaze slide away from hers, and I hear her breath catch as she stiffens. I can imagine her face closing over, but I can't let myself look at her. She releases my arm, and I turn back toward the path.

I thought yesterday was awkward and too quiet; it pales against today. The hopelessness in the set of her shoulders as she trudges through the snow is heartbreaking.

We struggle through the snow without speaking, legs made of lead and arms protesting every moment they're put to use. The things we don't say grow thicker between us, and by the time we've been walking a few hours, the silence has set like concrete.

When we stop I reach for the canteen, only to find it gone. I look up to find Lilac watching me, and we realize at the same time. The canteen is with our blankets, buried in the rubble. I close my eyes against the blow of it. Without a way to carry water, we're tethered to creeks and streams, left hoping our guts can take the local bacteria. Without water—

She starts moving again first, continuing on down the slope. Maybe she doesn't realize what the loss of the canteen means. Maybe she does know, and is just moving anyway.

When we finally make camp, we work side by side to clear a spot of snow and hunt for meager piles of grasses for our bed, picking out twigs and stones and scooping out a hole for our hip bones. Without the blankets, we'll have to bury ourselves in whatever we can find.

We melt snow in a strip of fabric torn from the too-long sleeves of the mechanic's suit, sucking at the water as it drips. It's precious little, but eating snow will only increase the effects of exposure. I reach inside the pack for the flashlight to lay it by the bed, and catch sight of the small case that holds my photograph inside it. I can't help wondering why she grabbed the pack before she ran. Why, in such a panic, would she think to get supplies?

Then it hits me. She wasn't sure I'd come after her, unless she had my prized belongings with her.

Half-formed words gather in my throat, but she won't even look at me, and I don't know what to say.

When I curl up behind her to sleep, the curve of her spine says everything she doesn't. Tense and unhappy, she only barely tolerates our proximity. If it were warmer, if we had our blankets, if she had a choice, she'd be on the other side of the fire. For a moment it seems like she's about to say something, her breath hitching with intention, but she remains silent.

Neither of us has spoken a word all day. It's a long time before we sleep.

We wake a little later than usual in the morning, paying the price for the night before. One of the many prices. It doesn't take long to clear up the camp—stretch, pack up our supplies, split one of the last few ration bars.

I stretch again as she tightens the laces on her boots, and when we set out it's clear she's determined to keep to the pace I set. But by the time we reach the crest of the pass she's breathing fast, lagging behind despite her best efforts, her gaze fixed on the ground in front of her.

The view of the rolling hills before us is spectacular. They stretch out for klicks before they level off and reach a forest that's only a dark line from this distance. Between the base of the mountain and the start of the forest lies the *Icarus*.

She's strewn out over a huge distance, ripped apart by her descent. Though sections of it have collapsed in the unfamiliar gravity, a large part of her hull is intact, with her trail showing where she came skidding in over the ground. My heart thumps in my chest as I run my gaze along the trail of debris—ruined escape pods that didn't detach until the ship broke apart, chunks of metal, burned streaks along the hillsides, half-melted things I can't begin to identify.

The *Icarus* held fifty thousand souls. I wish I could believe that any of them have survived this charred disaster. Not a single pod that I can see is intact, and the ship herself is beyond all redemption.

But it's what's *not* there that nearly drives me to my knees.

There should be rescue craft buzzing around the ship's carcass. There should be crews climbing all over her like so many ants. There should be people, life, salvation. But what lies before us looks like nothing more than a graveyard. I've been holding on to the hope that we could have somehow missed their approach, that if we could get as far as the crash site, rescue would be waiting for us there. But there's not even a hint of other survivors.

After everything we've been through, I finally admit to myself what I've been avoiding since we landed.

I don't think anyone's coming for us.

And I don't know what to do, except try to stay alive. The wreck and the broken pods below us must hold the soldiers I sparred with, the folks I met on the lower decks. The man who conned his way into the first-class salon to petition Lilac. Her gaggle of friends, her bodyguard, her cousin.

I take a breath, and turn to begin making my way down the mountain.

"Just—just *stop*." Lilac's voice cracks behind me, hoarse from dehydration and ragged with emotion.

She's staring down at the wreckage, stuck in place. She's flushed, or burned from the glare of the snow, more likely, her hair curling across her forehead, damp with sweat. When she turns her burning gaze on me, I flinch. "I need you to look. Look at me; look at *that*, Tarver."

"I see it." My own voice sounds nearly as bad, unused for so long. "But we can't stay here. We need to keep walking. There might be supplies in the wreck, some kind of communications equipment we can salvage."

She sways, then sinks to the ground in utter exhaustion. "When are you going to stop punishing me for *not* being crazy after all? I saved your life. We'd never have survived the cave-in."

Lilac, I know. I know we'd never have survived it. I know you heard or saw something before you ran, I watched it happen. I know you saw something real by the river. *I know.*

But I can't let myself admit it out loud. This goes so far beyond anything I've been trained for, and my training is all I have. I'm better equipped to drag a crazy person across a wilderness than cope with the possibility that she's receiving communications from—what? Ghosts? The thought is more than absurd; it's impossible.

If I let myself believe her, then everything I know goes out the window. And what I know has kept us alive this far.

She's still looking at me wearily, pain written clearly in her expression. "I'm not trying to punish you," I say finally. "But I can only work from what we *know*. I don't think I know everything, and in a place like this, I know even less than usual. But what I *do* know is that we need to keep moving."

She slumps over to rest her forehead against her knees, and my heart groans under the pressure. I wish I knew what to do, or even what to say. I wish I knew anything useful at all.

"So you're going to shrug it off again," she mumbles, fixing her tired glare on me. "I've been struggling for anything I could find to show you I'm not crazy, even when my own logic told me I must be, even when you *lied* to me outright. And now that we both know I'm not, you're just going to dismiss this?" She's crying, but the harsh edge to her voice is anger. "Just once, Tarver, just *once*, I wish you could see what I see."

She speaks the words like a witch in an old story, laying a curse on me. I look away, down the mountain at the wreckage below us.

"I'm sorry, Lilac. I don't know what you see. I only know how to keep us moving. I'm just a soldier. Once we get out of this place, you won't ever have to see me again. But I can't make myself see what you do."

She starts climbing to her feet, slow and painful, and if looks could kill I'd be dead and buried. "I hope that one day you're forced to believe in something for which you haven't got a shred of proof." Her voice is taut like wire. "And I hope someone you care about laughs in your face for it."

She stalks off down the mountain, and I wonder which one of her fancy tutors taught her this—the ability to make an exit without a door to slam, picking her way down the snowy path with her back ramrod straight in furious indignation. I wonder where she finds the strength for it.

"I'm not laughing at you," I whisper. I adjust the pack and start to make my way down the mountain after her.

She's learned a thing or two about trailblazing in the time she's spent following me, and she makes good time at first, though eventually she starts to slow from exhaustion.

I can almost see my younger self, marching along, trying to keep up with his big brother as we trekked near home. I think of my parents, and my throat closes as I conjure up our cottage in my mind's eye. My sanctuary, the place that's always safe. No matter how I try to stay focused on what's real, what's in front of us, I can't resist the thought of home.

The path—maybe a path, anyway—that we're following curves around the side of the mountain. As we clear an outcropping and a secluded valley becomes visible below, Lilac's head snaps up. She draws breath to speak, her eyes widening. Then it's gone, stamped out, and she's quiet again as she turns away to start working her way around a boulder. She has one last longing glance over her shoulder, as if whatever she sees, it's something far preferable to our reality. On cue I see her start to shake, shivering as though cold, fingers twitching before she shoves them into her pockets.

Another vision, then. A wave of dizziness washes over me, like a sympathetic reaction—I clench my jaw before my own teeth can start to chatter. At least she knows the difference now. I ignore the part of my brain that points out that if she knows the difference between visions and reality, she can't be that crazy. I follow in her wake, and I glance down into the valley below us.

It feels like the air's been sucked out of my lungs. I'm caught gasping for breath, grabbing thin air for something to support me.

There's a cottage in the valley. My parents' cottage. It's all there—the white walls, the rich purple of the lilac, the curving path and the red flowers in the field behind it. The faint wisp of smoke from the chimney, the black smudge to one side that must be my mother's vegetable garden.

The path winds its way out of the valley, vanishing into the distance, through the hills toward the wreck.

It's perfect, to the last detail. It's my home. It's not really there.

I can hear her voice in my head. *Just once, I wish you could see what I see.*

I feel her presence beside me, and she reaches out to slip her hand silently into mine. It isn't until her fingers wind through mine that I realize I too am shaking violently.

I'm going mad.

"As a member of the military, you've been trained to withstand a certain degree of shock."

"If we weren't, I don't think we'd last long on the front lines."

"At any point while you were on the planet's surface, did your training . . . falter?"

"I'm not sure I understand what you're asking."

"Did you ever experience any side effects from your exposure to such harsh conditions?"

"I think I lost a few pounds."

"Major, did you ever experience any psychological side effects?"

"No. Like you said, we're trained not to let that kind of thing happen. Solid as a rock, and just as dense."

TWENTY-TWO

LILAC

NEVER PUT YOUR HAND OUT TO A DROWNING MAN. I SAW that on an HV special once. If you do, they grab on to you and pull you into their panic and hopelessness, dragging you both into the same watery grave.

But I don't care. I step close to him and slip my hand into his. His fingers tighten around mine with a strength born of desperation. Which of us is shaking more, I can't tell, but where our hands are joined, we're steadier.

He's drowning. And I'll drown with him.

It's a long time before he speaks.

"I can't—" He breaks off, voice cracking. His eyes close against the vision of his family home in the valley. A vision both of us can see. The cottage looks just like it did in his picture.

I know from experience that he'll be dizzy, disoriented, tasting metal and feeling cobwebs on his face. I know from experience that he'll think he's mad. My own ears are buzzing, my body trembling, but I push it aside, force myself to focus. He needs me.

"I'm exhausted," he goes on. "I've had training on this. Your mind can—when you're tired enough . . ."

He thinks he's hallucinating. Maybe it'll be easier if he believes that. I squeeze his hand, wrapping my other around his arm. "You should rest, have some water. I'll sit with you."

He nods, eyes opening to fix on the house below like a starving man would stare at a banquet. He lets me pull the pack from his shoulders, doesn't protest as I tug him down to sit on the edge of the cliff, his face haggard and strained.

I've never seen him afraid.

I could be smug. I could rub his nose in the fact that he has no choice now but to believe me. Once upon a time, I wouldn't have hesitated. But now, one look at him is enough to kill that desire. He doesn't deserve it. And I know what it feels like to think you're going insane.

I sit beside him, quiet, waiting. This isn't like the silence of the past two days. For once, it's simply that there's nothing to say, not that there's no way to say it. I'd wanted him to see what I see—but now I wish I could take it all back.

"I don't know what to do." Tarver's voice, rough with emotion and exhaustion, trickles into the quiet.

I summon my steadiest voice. "I do. We'll stop for the day here, and you'll get some rest. I can make camp, I've watched you do it enough times. We'll have some dinner and sleep and in the morning we'll make for the wreck. We'll keep going, and figure out a way off this planet, so you can go home for real."

Tarver only swallows, the muscles in his jaw standing out briefly as he clenches it. He lets go of my hand and rakes his fingers through his hair in a quick, jerky movement. I stifle the urge to touch him again, and get quietly to work.

I don't do anything as well as he would've done it. I'm still shaking from the side effects of the vision, still fighting dizziness and nausea. The cottage is the most vivid, longest-lasting vision yet—and the side effects are worse. The fire burns dangerously low because I can't find much fuel, and the bed is lumpy. I pull out the food we have that doesn't require boiling, since we lost our canteen. Cold dinner, cold snowmelt, and it'll be a cold night, with no blankets. But if we have one night where nothing is right, at least it will be one night he doesn't have to be responsible for it all.

"You see it too, don't you?"

His voice after such a long silence makes me jump. When I look, he's still watching the valley. The house has faded, shimmering like an afterimage as the sun retreats behind the mountain ridges. It's a beautiful sight, even more so than the picture in his pack suggests. I would have loved to see it for real.

I gather up what I've pulled out for dinner and move back to Tarver's side. "Your parents' house?"

"Then it's not madness. I don't know what it is, but if we're seeing the same thing, I'm not crazy. And neither are you."

For a moment I want badly to remind him that I've been saying that all along. But I just nod, and drop down beside him to sit a few inches away. "Have something to eat." I offer him the larger half of a ration bar and a few of the grasses that taste okay raw. We only have two ration bars left.

Finally, he looks away from the vision and blinks at me. His pupils are huge—suddenly I can see what made him look at me the way he did, like I was mad.

He's quiet while he takes a few bites of the ration bar, and we settle into silence with the ease of familiarity. When he speaks again, his voice is soft. "We have to deal with a lot of crackpots who accuse the military of playing with mind control, telepathy. As cadets we would all joke about it, that the brass was in our heads, telling us to keep our bunks tidier. But maybe it's not a joke. Maybe this place is an experiment—something in the air, or the water, that makes us see things. Some artificial, psychological connection."

After days of silence with only my own thoughts for company, I have more than a few ideas about what we're seeing. And I don't think it's so simple. But just hearing him try to work it out, without suggesting I'm simply insane, is such a relief I almost don't want to contradict him. "But what about the cave-in? Neither of us could have known that was going to happen."

"More than once I've moved from a spot that was blasted out of existence a second later. Maybe you did know, subconsciously."

But he doesn't sound convinced.

"Can I share a theory?" I've known this wasn't a haunting since the cave-in—and now that Tarver is seeing it too, I can't dismiss the thoughts that keep coming to me.

"Of course."

Now I'm cursing myself. He's going to think I'm insane again. But when I don't reply right away, he turns to look at me as if seeing me for the first time.

"I think—there's something here." I lick my lips, anxious, trying to articulate it. "Life. On this planet."

His brow furrows. Skeptical. But he's not calling me insane—yet. "Like the cat? There's no way that thing belongs here."

"No—I mean, intelligent life. Maybe even something that was here before the terraforming. If it were only the visions, maybe it could be some kind of shared hallucination. But the cave-in? Neither of us could've known. I think something is watching us." The words alone cause a shiver down my spine, and I see his lips twitch as though he wants to dismiss me. I scramble to speak before he can. "There are whispers, everyone knows it. Even if nobody's ever proven anything, there are always stories about what lies beyond the edge of explored space. Even on Corinth, we hear them. The corporations that built this place must have abandoned it for a reason. Something had to drive them away."

He's looking less skeptical and more thoughtful now, watching me—the way he's looking at me, I'm not even sure he's listening to what I'm saying. The shock of seeing his parents' house must have been worse than I realized. He clears his throat. "Don't you think, if a corporation discovered intelligent life here, it would've been all over the newscasts?"

"Unless they're keeping it hidden for some reason." I try not to think of my father, of the rooms upon rooms of isolated, secret servers and data cores. I asked about them often as a child, but he had always managed to distract me with a gift or a story, until eventually I wasn't even curious anymore—his secrets were just a part of who he was.

Surely he wasn't the only corporate executive to keep certain things hidden from public view.

"You think the military are the only ones keeping secrets?" Tarver asks.

I take a deep breath. "I dreamed, right before the cave-in. That someone I couldn't see was whispering at me, warning me. When I woke up, that someone was still there, still whispering, but I couldn't understand the words. It's like they—whatever they are—are trying to talk to us, but they don't know how. They're pulling things out of our minds, the things that hurt us the most. I thought I was being haunted, but if they're seeing my thoughts, then they know how torn up I am about the people who died on that pod. Maybe it was the only way they knew to start a conversation, to pick up on the thing that was playing so much on my mind. And maybe this, your parents' house, is meant for you."

Silence follows my speech, my heart pounding as I try to catch my breath. I know he'll go back to thinking I'm mad. Any moment and he'll open his mouth to dismiss me as always.

But instead he just says softly, "If these whispers were trying to make me hurt, they managed it pretty well."

We sit for a time in silence. I can feel Tarver's warmth next to me, a finger's width away. Despite the comfort of his presence, my skin prickles with the unmistakable feeling that we're being watched. I don't ask him if he feels it too—the tension in his body says it clearly enough. The whispers are out there, and even though they're quiet now, we both know we're not alone.

After a time he gets to his feet and offers me a hand, and we make our way back to the campfire. I add a few of the meager bits of deadwood I was able to collect, and we settle in. He puts his arm around my shoulders, encouraging me to lean in against him. The distance that had grown between us has vanished, and I'm more than willing to comply. We sink into the quiet together.

My eyelids are drooping when his voice, barely more than a rumble against my cheek, rouses me.

"You shouldn't feel guilty about the people on the pod. There were plenty of pods for everyone. You had no way of knowing what was about to happen."

"Maybe you're right," I say, my chest constricting, but perhaps not quite as tightly as before. "But ours is the one that survived."

"Well, whether it's the only one or not, I'm glad I ended up in it with you."

I snort, a sound I never used to make. "Major, please. I know an outright fabrication when I hear one. I'm the last person you'd want to have with you here."

"Think again, Miss LaRoux." His voice is calm, earnest. I know him well enough to recognize when he's lying, and he isn't. "If you hadn't been on that escape pod when it jammed, I wouldn't be here at all."

He shifts, causing me to lift my head, and I find him looking at me, his face only an inch from mine.

I feel my face starting to burn, and I look away first. I can only hope that he dismisses the redness as heat from the fire.

"If only Swann was here," I say briskly. "She'd have killed that cat thing with her bare hands. Or Simon, he's the one that taught me about electronics, he was—" My voice cuts out. I don't think I've said his name out loud in nearly two years. "He was a boy I knew," I finish lamely.

I can still feel his eyes on me. "I think I'll take the girl I know, thanks."

By now the sun has vanished and the stars have come out, a scattering of light across the sky. I fix my eyes on them, grateful for something to look at that isn't the soldier with his arm around me. I never realized how unfamiliar the stars could seem until now.

"If it's true, then we know we're not mad," I say, keeping my eyes on the sky.

"And if it's true, we know we're not alone." He, however, sounds more troubled than relieved.

"The whispers haven't hurt us so far. I just think they don't know how to reach us except by showing us what's in our thoughts."

"If they're trying to communicate," Tarver murmurs, curling his hand around my arm, possessive enough to keep my face burning, "then the question is, what are they trying so hard to say?"

"This water bottle you gave me is empty."

"Indeed. I'll send for another. In the meantime, what were your goals when you reached the crash site?"

"Supplies. Safety."

"Rescue?"

"We hadn't seen a single flyover. I wasn't confident of rescue."

"Did you discuss that with Miss LaRoux?"

"No. We were tired. We just concentrated on the basics."

"What were the basics?"

"We were almost out of food, and she was quite pleased to find a change of clothes."

TWENTY-THREE

TARVER

IN THE MORNING, THE SILENCE BETWEEN US IS GENTLE, broken by our puffing and panting as we scramble down the snowy mountainside, our breath clouding the air. My throat's rough and my mouth's dry—it takes too much energy to melt snow in our mouths, and the cold leaves our stomachs cramping. The canteen's at the forefront of my mind. Losing the Gleidel would have been less of a blow.

I squeeze through a gap between two rocks, and before I turn back to help Lilac through, I glance down to make sure my feet are planted firmly—and there it is. A military canteen. It's in flawless condition, khaki sides smooth and unmarked. As though it just came off the production line.

I reach down, half expecting my hand to go straight through it, but my fingers connect with solid metal—it's real. When I flip it over, my stomach lurches. My initials are there, engraved by my own hand, impossible to re-create—and yet the dents and scuffs have been erased. The canteen is as flawless as the day I got it. I pull out the stopper, and there's the filtration system sitting in place, clear water just below. A shiver starts between my shoulder blades and runs down my spine.

We left my canteen behind in the cave, crushed under rock and snow. And now, as though we willed it into existence, here lies a replacement directly in our path. No, not just a replacement—this is the *same* canteen.

"Tarver?" It's Lilac, trying to look past me at what stopped me short. I step aside to let her through, but it takes her a moment to spot the canteen. When she does, her blue eyes widen, and she nearly falls the rest of the way through the gap. I wrap both arms around her. We pause for a moment with her tucked against me, holding still.

"You're touching it," she says, reaching out to press a fingertip against the canteen. "Tarver, it's solid. It's not a vision."

"It's mine, but brand-new." I flip it over to show her the initials, and her breath catches.

"How? No—all those soldiers on board. Someone was bound to share your initials. It's a coincidence."

I'm about to point out that there's no way the canteen could have ended up here, in our path, if thrown from the wreckage—but then I see her face, and the words die. She knows. But neither of us wants to say what's on both our minds. These whispers are capable of more than just visions, or premonitions. What else can they do?

I try the water—sweet, fresh, clean. We each drink, grateful it's not snow, icy cold and trickling down our faces as we swallow. When Lilac finishes, she holds the canteen in her hands, staring down at it. She keeps running her fingertips over its surface, as though it might change upon inspection. Then she lifts her hand, staring at her own fingers. It takes me a moment, but by the time she lifts her gaze to mine, I get it. She's not shaking. This is no vision. No image plucked from our minds and given to us by the whispers.

This is real.

I wish that I could take this as a sign of friendship from these beings, if that is indeed what we're dealing with. But despite my relief at having a canteen again, all I can think is this: Why work so hard to keep us alive? What do they really want from us?

We reach the grassy foothills at the base of the mountain by late morning, and it's an unspeakable relief to be walking across level ground again, able to stretch my legs and unbunch my muscles for a while. I realize as we walk that in just a few short days, I've become familiar with this place—the wildflowers we saw on the other side of the mountain are missing, and my eyes can pick out burrows where I can lay snares later. Any sense of comfort doesn't last long, though. I'm soon reminded we're walking through a graveyard.

The debris blankets the hills. We pass pieces of twisted plastene the size of my hand, and great, melted piles of metal that tower above us.

Most of the pods are too damaged to scavenge anything from, but we're down to our last ration bar. I think we could survive on the tiny critters and grasses here, but it wouldn't be pretty. And so I risk peeking inside the first reasonably intact pod we come to, its only major damage consisting of the panels on the side torn away where it was still attached to the *Icarus*. I'm relieved there's only one occupant. Her head hangs forward and her hair hides her face where she sits, still strapped into her seat, in about the same position Lilac took in our sturdier mechanic's pod. She's in her nightclothes, a pink silky wrap tied on over whatever's underneath. I imagine she died on impact. Her hair is brown, not red, but it's all too easy to see Lilac there instead. I keep my eyes averted from her as I climb through the gash in the pod and rummage through one of the underseat compartments. There—half a dozen more ration bars. Food for another couple days if we supplement with the local flora.

When I climb out again, Lilac doesn't ask whether anyone was inside. She knows from one look at my face what I found there.

The *Icarus* looks like someone's run a knife along the side of her and peeled her open. For nearly a third of her length her innards are visible, scorched framework laid bare. The plowed-up trail behind her shows where she skidded in to land, carving out a furrow you could lose a platoon inside. There's a faint chemical smell on the breeze.

"In the military," I say, "we call this proceeding with caution. Usually that's code for 'let someone else go first,' but since we're the forward scouts this time, let's just watch ourselves carefully. We don't know how bad the structural damage is inside. We don't know what breathing those chemicals in the air will do, and we don't have the medical supplies if we get hurt. Let's be careful, okay? Test every step."

There's no haughty reply or cutting glare. She stares at the ship, solemn, and simply nods. "We can avoid the heavy damage completely. That's the stern; it's mostly propulsion systems, apart from the viewing decks." A pause. Maybe she's thinking of our encounter there, as I am. That was another lifetime, and we were different people then. She pushes on, businesslike. "The bow's technical as well. That's where the communications were."

What she doesn't have to say is that the communications clearly aren't there now. The bow is hopelessly mashed from the impact.

She's scanning the wreck, gaze intent. "The middle third of the ship is—was—passengers and cargo. That's probably where we'll find supplies, and it looks like some of it hasn't been torn open."

The false moon has been getting higher in the sky, staying for longer and setting later. It sits just above the horizon now, visible even in broad daylight. Lilac sees me staring at the horizon and comes to stand at my side. "Do you think it had something to do with the crash?"

I can't help but remember the awful lurching feeling as the *Icarus* tried to phase back into hyperspace, and failed. Caught by gravity, or by whatever force had ripped it from that dimension in the first place.

"Seems too much of a coincidence not to," I reply.

I hear her breath catch. "I don't know whether your schools would have focused on this, but my father taught me endless lessons on terraforming and its history. It was the one subject he refused to leave to my tutors—I guess being a pioneer means you don't trust anyone else to get it right. Before the first emigration, when they were still trying to figure out how to terraform Mars, one of the ideas for heating up the planet enough to have liquid water was to set up a large orbital mirror to direct more sunlight to its surface."

My eyes flick from her face back to the false moon. "Or an array of mirrors. I think I remember something about that. They never tried it, though, because it was so impractical, right? If that's what's up there, why now? Why this planet?"

She shakes her head, looking over at me. She has no answers, and neither do I. I turn my back on the moon as it sinks toward the plains, and head for the ship.

It turns out the part of the hull that hasn't been torn open is sealed off almost completely by melted streams of an alloy that was never meant to go through atmo. The sealing off is a good sign, I guess—maybe whatever's inside will be intact—but that only matters if we can find a way to access it.

I keep the Gleidel in my hand as we work our way along the edge of the broken hull, two ants trooping along the base of a huge metal wall that rises to the sky above us. We don't see any sign of other survivors. Can we really be the only ones? Surrounded by the utter silence of the wreck, I realize all over again that Lilac's actions are the reason we're alive. I may have saved her life when it came to the cat monster, and I may have gotten her this far, but neither of us would be here if she hadn't found a way to wrench us away from the *Icarus*. I can't help but watch her as we walk, my attention divided between our surroundings and the girl at my side. Seeing her in all her finery on board the ship, could I have ever imagined her like this? Wrapped up in the dirt-stained mechanic's suit, ruined dress stuffed in underneath and hair tied back with a dingy piece of string?

It's Lilac who finds the fault line that lets us in. A sheet of metal has buckled away from the unbroken wall a fraction, rivets showing, only darkness within. We don't speak as we get to work, lining up side by side to take hold of it and lean back, muscles straining to bend it and make the hole a little bigger. I feel like telling her to take a rest, but when I glance down at her, her jaw's squared and her frown is determined. Maybe she's not quite as weak as I thought—and maybe I'm not as strong or as heavy as I was when we landed.

An instant after I finish that thought, red-hot pain cuts across my palm, and I let go, stumbling back from the metal sheet and whipping my hand free. The metal springs back into place and Lilac nearly gets her own fingers trapped. I should have been concentrating, heeding my own advice. Now there's an angry red line across my palm, and a moment later there's blood, oozing, then flowing freely.

"Tarver, are you—oh." She curses admirably, then turns businesslike, hauling the pack off my shoulder and dropping to the ground to dig out our pathetic first-aid kit. All I can do is lift my bleeding hand above my head, and use my free hand to squeeze the wrist, trying to limit the blood flow, but it's deep. I can tell already.

"Where did you learn to say that, Miss LaRoux?" I try, keeping my voice light.

"You just wait until it's my father asking that same question, Major." She pulls out the little kit and starts to unpack it. "Then you'll know what real trouble is. Come down here, I'll try to bandage it up."

"I plan on being far away by the time the subject arises." I carefully sink to my knees. "Exiled to some far colony to fight the rebels, in punishment for making eyes at his daughter."

"You keep your eyes to yourself." The wound's bleeding properly now, and she wads up one of our bandages with our only gauze pad to press it against my palm, then straps it all into place with the other bandage. I wince as the pain begins to register properly, burning its way up my arm.

"Baby," she teases, wrapping the bandage around my palm. Despite her best efforts, though, the blood starts showing through the bandages while she's still packing away the nearly empty first-aid kit.

It turns out we've bent the metal far enough that she can wriggle in, and I wait anxiously as she turns herself sideways and squirms, pulling herself inch by inch into the darkness. "Keep checking you can move backward," I say, squatting down to try to get a better look at her progress. "You don't want to get stuck. And check with your fingertips before you grab anything."

Her legs disappear, and I hold my breath, waiting. My heart hammers in my chest. There's a clang, and the metal sheet shudders as she kicks from inside, then kicks again. It bends more easily with force in that direction, and once the gap is wide enough, I stoop to crawl in after her.

The air inside the ship is cold and still, but it smells okay. It's not as dark as I'd feared—small breaks in the hull let in speckled daylight, though it won't be much good once we go deeper. I keep my hand tucked against my body, hoping the bleeding will slow.

"We should be in a storage area." Her voice startles me. "Cargo, luggage maybe. Some services as well."

"There were a lot of troops on board. I'd love to find some rations. They taste like cardboard, but they're nutritionally complete and they'll keep forever." I feel like biting my tongue as soon as I'm finished. I've been trying hard not to mention the possibility that forever is exactly how long we'll be stuck here.

"There's a proper hallway up ahead." She disappears from view again, and then I realize her body was blocking the light as she climbed out of the service duct we're in and into a passage. It's tilted at a forty-five-degree angle, but we can keep our footing if we're careful. I hold open the pack so she can fish out the flashlight, and suddenly we can see.

The first two doors we try are jammed shut by the warping of the ship, but the third one swings open. The room's full of crates that have tumbled and smashed, and piles of circuitry litter the floor. Useless.

Lilac pushes open the next door, and I try the other side of the hallway. "No use," she calls as I push my door open.

Inside, there are piles of fabric everywhere, sheets and clothes all down one side of the room, lying together where they fell. I've hit the mother lode. It's got to be the laundry. I don't know if the stuff in here is clean or not, but it's got to be cleaner than we are.

"Remember that ladylike behavior of yours?" I call out, letting her hear the smile in my voice. "This is the time for it. No pushing, shoving, screaming, or—"

I don't get any further. She's heard the shift in my voice and crossed the hallway in a heartbeat. She wastes only a moment in gaping, then shoves past me to dash across to the pile of clothes, laughing.

"Tarver, *Tarver*. There are—can you see them all?" She's running the flashlight over the offerings, revealing swaths of fabric of every color.

I've got my mouth half open to reply when she starts unzipping the mechanic's suit, and then my mouth falls the rest of the way open by itself. It's dark inside the room, but I catch a quick glimpse of pale skin beneath the remnants of her dress before I remember myself, and decide to take a good, hard look at my boots. To judge by the sounds over on the other side of the room, she's forgotten I exist. The mechanic's suit must have been *really* uncomfortable, even wearing it over her dress, if she's that eager to get it off while I'm standing right here.

"There's dresses," she whispers, and I catch a movement in my peripheral vision. Oh, God, come *on*. It's the mechanic's suit and the ruined green dress being kicked across the floor away from her. So what does that mean she's wearing right now? She didn't actually *say* I couldn't look.

"Don't look," she cautions me, as though she just read my mind. *Dammit.*

I turn away and hold my palm out to examine it in a small stripe of light that falls near the doorway. The bandages are red, and it's throbbing to the regular beat of my pulse. I wish it would stop. The scratch itself is nothing, and I've had far worse in the field, but never without any hope at all of a medic or stitches. It'll just have to be all right.

"There are sheets, we can make a bed. A proper bed, imagine. We won't know what to do with it." She's laughing as she speaks.

Oh, trust me, Miss LaRoux. I'd know what to do with it. I can think up a whole list of things, if you like.

"You can turn around now."

I turn slowly, sure I'm going to see her clad in something frilly and impractical, but I can't make out a thing because she's got the flashlight pointed at me. Then she changes the angle of the light so I can see her, and I find myself staring.

She's picked out a pair of jeans and a pale blue shirt, and standing there barefoot with her hair hauled back out of her face, freckles dusting her nose and cheeks, she looks perfect. She looks nothing like a princess, but she looks exactly like a girl from home. She smiles, and her dimples show, and my words get stuck in my throat.

She seems to take my slack-jawed silence as approval, and hands over the flashlight, politely turning to face the doorway so I can pick out some clothes for myself. I spare a thought for the man whose fatigues I find, but I'm most comfortable in khaki, and he was about my size. I find a new pair of pants and a T-shirt and ease into both using one hand, then call out to her so we can gather up some spares and extra layers.

I show her how to tear up a sheet to make bandages—I can't use my hand for much at all now—and we make up a better dressing for my gash. She works carefully, using a pillowcase to wipe the blood away, then emptying what's left of the tiny bottle of antiseptic over my palm. We've used most of it on scratches and scrapes, and now I'm regretting that. Once she's finished, she sets another pad gently against the gash, then swathes my hand in bandages, so my fingers poke out the top.

We fill the canteen from one of the water tanks in the laundry, then find big white bags and fill them to bursting with spare clothes and a pile of sheets to make up our bed, carrying one each as we make our way back out to the hallway.

"Do we have enough for dinner tonight?" she asks. "I guess we'll eat the rations you got out of the pod, then we can make camp. It's getting dark."

I follow her gaze and realize she's right—the daylight coming in through the cracks in the ship's hull is fading out. I should have been the one to notice that.

She starts toward the doorway dragging her bag of laundry, but I swing the flashlight over to where she changed her clothes. "Want me to grab your dress?"

Her eyes follow the beam of the flashlight toward the pile of dirty green satin. The corner of her mouth lifts in a rueful smile, and then she shakes her head briskly. "Leave it," she decides, turning her back on what's left of her old life.

We push and pull our laundry bags through the service chute once more and find a place to camp in the lee of a huge, twisted sheet of metal outside. There's a stream nearby, and if the wreckage has contaminated the water, the canteen's filter should take care of it.

We haven't seen any sign of a living soul, but I dig our fire pit deep anyway, trying in vain to keep my hand clean. It's still throbbing. Lilac busies herself making an elaborate bed, sorting the clothes into piles, then covering her efforts up with a sheet. After a moment's consideration, she stuffs a few items into the white laundry bags and makes us pillows.

We don't have a lot of fuel—a little we carried in, and a little we find nearby—but it's enough to heat a canteen of water and make ourselves some weak soup, and it helps make the ration bars a little more of a meal.

We talk about the things we want to try to salvage from the ship—medical supplies, food, warmer clothes, even a cooking pot—and study the silhouette of the wreck against the stars. I wonder whether we can climb her to get a better look at the terrain around us.

Lilac falls asleep with her head on my shoulder, and I carefully tug the sheets up over us, trying not to use more than two fingers.

No sign of the whispers. I can't help but wonder what it means. In coming to the wreck, have we done whatever they were trying to communicate? Or are they still watching, waiting? I don't understand—or trust—their intentions.

I suppose something could be preventing them from reaching us. Maybe now we're on our own.

"Significant parts of the ship were intact?"

"You've got the recon pictures."

"I'm asking a question, Major."

"You're asking a lot of questions you know the answers to. Is there a purpose to that?"

"Is there a purpose behind your refusal to cooperate?"

"I'm cooperating. Is that water coming anytime soon?"

"The ship. Significant parts of it were intact?"

"Parts weren't incinerated, but I wouldn't say they were intact."

"You conducted salvage without incident?"

"I cut my hand. That was about as exciting as it got."

TWENTY-FOUR

LILAC

EXPLORING THE SHIP IS A MIND-NUMBING TASK. EVEN THOUGH huge portions of it broke apart during its descent or were crushed on impact, it was originally large enough to hold fifty thousand people, with room to spare. Getting through just a fraction of it will take days. For every room we find with useful supplies there are dozens where everything is smashed, or where a fire swept through and left only shriveled plastene and unidentifiable char behind.

Tarver's been hiding his hand from me. At first, I assumed he was protecting me from the fact he's not invincible, for fear I'd fall apart.

But the morning of the second day, I know something's wrong. His face is white, with spots of red on either cheek, and his eyes take longer to focus than they should. He's too quiet. He's moving slowly. He doesn't even comment now when I turn his own foul language back at him. Just grunts and keeps moving.

We break for lunch deep inside the ship, sitting on an overturned cabinet in what was once an administrative office of some kind. There's no daylight, and we can see only with the help of the flashlight. He gives me two thirds of the ration bar. I give back the extra and he shakes his head, resting his elbows on his knees and letting his head drop between them.

"Tarver," I start cautiously. "We should take a rest day, maybe. We're low on rations, but not so low that we can't put off finding food here for a little while longer."

He shakes his head again, not bothering to lift it.

"Like we did on the plains, when I needed a break. We took a half day."

This time he does lift his head, and his eyes wander before coming to rest on me. "No. We need to keep moving."

"Tarver." This time my voice is firmer. I don't think I can bully him, but I have to try. "You clearly need rest. We should take a break, and I'll go find some of the grasses you showed me on the plains, and we'll eat those to stretch our food supplies."

He doesn't answer this time, but I can tell by the set of his jaw that he's determined to keep going. Then the fingers of his right hand tug at the grubby bandage covering his left, and suddenly realization hits me.

It's not the food stores he's desperate for. He needs to find the sick bay. He needs medicine.

I look at his hand again. It hangs uselessly off his wrist, fingers puffy and stiff. The color on his cheeks is visible in the half-light, and despite the chill in the air, he's sweating.

"Go back." I'm speaking fast, white-hot fear driving me. "Tarver, go back to camp right now. Go to bed."

This summons the first smile in hours. "Sound like my mother."

For once, I'm not in the mood for his jokes. "I mean it. Move, soldier." Though I can't quite inject the barking tone he employs when trying to jolt me into action, I hope the words will be enough.

He looks at me, hollow-eyed, then tightens his jaw as his gaze drifts off again. "Not going to let you wander around here by yourself. You get hurt, there's no one to help. It would take me ages to find you, if I did at all."

I get up and kneel on the floor in front of him, reaching up to turn his face toward mine and forcing him to meet my eyes.

"And I'm not going to let you get sick from an infection because you're too stupid to take care of yourself. I'll be careful."

His mouth twists, for all the world like a child refusing to take his medicine. He knows my chances of making any headway by myself are slim. If he weren't here I'd have died any one of a thousand deaths already on this godforsaken planet.

And then I know how to convince him.

"If you die," I whisper, my eyes on his, "then I will too."

By the time I return from the ship to camp again, night has fallen, and Tarver is only half-conscious. It didn't take long for me to find one of the food stores—but even the sight of dried pasta and spices and sugar couldn't relieve the knot of tension twisting in my chest. I ought to be relieved—we were on our last few ration bars. But hunger is no longer our biggest problem.

The packets are all stamped with the stylized upside down *V* of my father's logo—the Greek lambda, for LaRoux. My father and his stupid fixation on mythology. He told me all the old stories when I was little, of warring gods and goddesses, and I almost imagined he was one of them. All-powerful, all-knowing. Someone to be worshipped unconditionally. But who names a starship the *Icarus*? What kind of man possesses that much hubris, that he dares it to fall?

I've stopped waiting for him to come for me. There are no ships flying over the crash site. No one's looking for us here. With a jolt, I realize that by now my father must think I'm dead. There are no rescue ships, so they must not know where the *Icarus* went down—she could have fallen out of hyperspace anywhere in the galaxy. He already lost my mother. I've been all he's had since I was eight years old. I try to imagine him now, knowing I'm gone—and my mind just goes blank.

I wonder if the engineers who designed the *Icarus* are still alive, or if his vengeance has already destroyed them.

I shiver, tracing the shape of the logo with my fingertips, as I did countless times throughout my childhood. It would be easier not to connect this twisted heap of wreckage, this mass grave, with the flagship of my father's company.

I make three trips back inside the ship, my last lugging a pot full of spices and boxes of powdered broth. I make a fire, heat some soup, try to get Tarver to drink. He wakes up only reluctantly, and only after shoving me away in his sleep. I get a few spoonfuls of broth down him before he collapses again. I get the camp ready for the night, checking to be sure the fire isn't visible beyond our little hollow, that our belongings are all close, that Tarver's gun is at his side, where it belongs.

I lug some water from the stream nearby and use strips of the sheets to wipe his face and throat, which are burning hot to the touch. I'm afraid to unwrap his hand because I have nothing sterile with which to wrap it back up again, but the skin around the bandage is flushed red and painful-looking.

Eventually I run out of tasks and crawl into the bed beside him. He's so warm that despite the chill, it's uncomfortably hot under the blankets. Nevertheless, I slip close to him so I can feel his heartbeat and smell his scent, grass and sweat and something else I can't name. Familiar, comforting. In his sleep, his good arm curls around me, just a little.

I'm awakened in darkness by someone shoving me roughly off the makeshift mattress and onto the hard ground. My mind is slow to wake, and for a few moments I can only think another survivor has found us and is trying to see if we have anything worth stealing. My heart is pumping pure adrenaline, my every nerve screaming.

Then I realize it's Tarver who shoved me away. As I pick myself up I hear him murmuring to himself, and my heart leaps. He's awake. Surely this is a good sign. The sky is partially cloudy, blocking the light from the artificial mirror-moon.

I crawl toward the coals of the fire and throw on a few pieces of deadwood until it flares up, letting me see his face.

My heart sinks.

He's staring right through me, his eyes wild and glassy, and—I would've thought it impossible if I hadn't seen him above the valley with the vision of his house—afraid. His muttering is unintelligible, his lips dry and cracked.

"Tarver?" I crawl toward him. "I'll get you some water. Let me just—"

I start to reach for his forehead, to feel his temperature, when I'm suddenly knocked over, sent rolling in the dirt, my head ringing and throbbing. The stars overhead weave and waver as my vision clouds, and it's only with a monumental effort that I claw my way back toward consciousness, dizzily dragging myself back upright.

Tarver's half sitting up with his gun pointed directly at my face, though his eyes are staring into space. His face is set in a snarl far more fierce than anything I could've imagined from him. The spot where the back of his hand connected with my cheek throbs and radiates heat with each pulse of my heart.

"Tarver?" It's barely a whisper.

He blinks, and his head turns toward me. The barrel of the gun wavers and dips. His eyes focus, and my heart leaps. He swallows, speaks through dry lips.

"Sarah," he croaks.

"It's me," I say pathetically. I sound like I'm begging. I *am* begging. "Please, Tarver. It's me. It's Lilac. Your Lilac, you know me."

He groans and collapses back again, the hand holding the gun dropping. "God, I've missed you."

"I haven't gone anywhere." I should get close, feel his temperature again, but it won't do any good. I know he's burning up. The makeshift pillow under his head is soaked with sweat.

"Sarah, I feel rotten."

In his fever, he thinks I'm some other girl. His girlfriend, maybe— does he have one waiting at home? I realize I've never even asked.

"I know you do," I whisper, giving in. I can't reach him. The only thing I can do is get back inside that wreck, clear a path to the deeper, less intact parts, and find the sick bay.

He mumbles something else, and I slip in close enough to ease the gun out of his grip. He doesn't even twitch. I tuck it into the back of my jeans, my skin crawling at its presence. I don't know the first thing about guns, but I know I can't leave it here with him and risk him shooting me in his delirium.

I take a deep breath, locating the flashlight—and after a moment of hesitation, Tarver's notebook and pen. I need to make a map. It's going to be harder to navigate the labyrinth of sharply slanting corridors and broken staircases in complete darkness, but I can't afford to wait. Tarver can't afford for me to wait.

He's so thin now. I hadn't even noticed, seeing him every second of every day, but here, while he's asleep and flushed and delirious, I can see how lean he is. I brush the damp hair back from his forehead.

"I'll be back," I murmur. "Hold on."

He calls out for Sarah as I make my way back toward the ship, and it breaks my heart. I'd sit with him and be his Sarah if I could, if there were someone else to go look for his medicine. But I leave him with his ghosts and descend into the wreck, ignoring the voice behind me begging me to return.

In the darkness, the ship is a maze.

Over the last few days of searching I've still only found the one entry point, so every time I come back I have to retrace my steps, spending precious time going over the same ruined pathways. I try every possible turn, and each attempt ends in a crushed floor or a dead-end room.

I found an emergency fire station a few hours into that first night, with a fire blanket, an ax, an extinguisher—and a handful of chemical glow sticks. I've discovered that they shine steadily for about an hour and a half before they start to fade, and so I've been using them as timers. An hour and a half, and then wherever I am, I turn back. To check on him.

Three hours in and back, and then I can make sure he's not dead.

I've lost track of how many trips I've made. The flashlight is growing dim after so much use, so I turn it off, relying on the light of the glow sticks instead. I know this particular corridor, the pattern of its destruction, by heart now. I don't need light here.

To the right is the laundry room. I go straight. Farther along are more corridors branching off into dormitories for the staff. I discover a tiny gym with equipment so smashed it takes me long moments to realize what it is. What hope is there that, even if I can find the sick bay, there'll be anything remotely usable?

The darkness spins, exhaustion briefly threatening to steal my balance. I shut my eyes, stretching out a hand to grab on to the wall. I can't afford to think hopelessly.

I wait until the dizziness passes and make a mental note to eat something the next trip I make back to camp. When I open my eyes I realize I've made it to an intersection where I turned right, last time. This time I go straight ahead, into new territory.

Exposed steel spars and wiring make it impossible to move without deliberation, and debris strewn about threatens to drag me down at every step. I saw the *Icarus* dismantled like this once before, nearly a decade ago. She was my playground once, when she was little more than a steel frame and a sketch in the minds of my father's engineers. But then she was new and clean, bare with unrealized potential and promise. Not smashed beyond recognition.

I try to visualize the ship I played in. Did I know then what the rooms would be used for? I don't remember. Did I ever know where the medical wing was? Was I ever sick?

No. *But Anna was.* For the first time the thought of my cousin doesn't fill me with guilt so tangible I want to throw up. Instead, a tiny flicker of memory floods my mind, and with it, something like hope.

I remember the smell of soap as I brought Anna to the sick bay. And not the astringent scent of medical cleanser, but light, airy, clean-scented soap. The laundry.

I can't be far, then. Can I?

There's no smell of soap now, though I can smell something else. *Perishable food,* I think. It smells like a meat locker that's been without power for a week. But very faint.

The glow stick is getting dimmer. I have to move more quickly. Soon I'll need to go see if Tarver's still alive. Check his bandage, force some water down his throat, and hope he doesn't mistake me again for a threat. The bruise on my cheek throbs at the memory.

I can only see about a foot in front of me by the dimming light of the glow stick. Tomorrow I'll have to remember to set the flashlight out in the sun to recharge. *Tomorrow? It is night, isn't it?*

Maybe it's tomorrow already.

Go back, I tell myself frantically. *Just go back now.*

I have the strangest feeling, almost a superstition, that if I leave him for more than my arbitrary three-hour limit, those few minutes will be the death of him. And yet, the time it takes to go back and forth checking on him, instead of locating medicine, could be just as deadly.

I keep moving.

The path is clear enough here that I can break into a slow run. All that hiking has paid off, and though it's been a couple of days now since I slept more than an hour or two at a time, I still have enough energy for this.

Ahead of me yawns sudden blackness, not the grid of the floor. My mind, sluggish with lack of sleep, fails to process it. Before I realize I have to stop, I'm falling.

Something soft breaks my fall with a muffled crack. I drop the glow stick, gasping for breath as a sudden wave of nausea shudders through me. It's the meat-locker smell, not the fall, making me sick. The smell is stronger here. Too strong.

I roll away from whatever I landed on and push myself to my feet. Half in shock, my mind runs through an oddly detached checklist of my body, making sure everything's still working. Tarver would kill me if he knew I'd been so reckless. If he'd been here.

I turn back for the glow stick, which clattered out of my hand when I fell. I stoop to reach for it and freeze.

It's a face. A tiny patch of sickly green glow shines from the stick, lighting the hollows of the cheeks, the empty, staring eyes, glinting off the teeth just showing between parted lips.

I scream, flinging myself away until I hit the floor. My face presses into the cold iron gridwork, and I gasp for breath, trying to inhale shallowly through my mouth. The meat-locker smell—God, and it *is* rotting meat, isn't it?—is so overpowering I think for a moment I might pass out. I can taste it on my tongue.

I lurch to my feet and into a run. In darkness and fear, I keep colliding with walls and ricocheting around corners. I step on something that gives beneath my heel, and my ankle rolls, but I keep myself upright. I know that if I fall, what I fall on will be the end of me. Soft things. Rotting things. Dead things.

This ship isn't a maze—it's a tomb.

Exposed debris slices at my clothes and my hair and my face. Still I run, deeper and deeper into the dead part of the ship, helpless with the knowledge that after such a long fall, I can't climb back up to get out the way I came in.

A jagged rebar catches my arm and jerks me sideways, flinging me against a wall. My scream is a hoarse, desperate noise.

My hand finds a door handle and twists, and I lurch into the closet-like space behind it, dragging the door shut behind me. I slide down to the floor amid the clanking of buckets and mop handles and fumble for the flashlight. Its beam is warm and golden, if dim, and lights the inside of what seems to be a janitorial cupboard. It's strangely intact, mops and brooms neatly lined up.

My heart threatening to slam its way out past my rib cage, I put my head down on my knees and focus on my breathing. Anything but the thought of what waits for me outside, the dead eyes and bloated corpses.

One. Oh, God. Two. Three. Four. Something snapped when I fell on that body. I broke something in it. It was like a wet branch. No. No. Five. Six. Seven. He would have despised me for running. Eight. What if one of those bodies was Anna's? Oh, God. No. Nine. Ten. Eleven. Pull yourself together, Miss LaRoux. Twelve. You're no use to anybody cowering in a broom cupboard. Thirteen. Fourteen. Don't sell yourself short. I don't know many soldiers who'd have done better. Fifteen.

I make it to twenty before opening my eyes again. The beam of the flashlight shudders with each breath, the effort still enough to shake my whole body. But the darkness is no longer trying to strangle me.

Tarver's a liar, but he lies to keep me moving, and I can't fault him for that. The least I can do is try to prove him right.

I'll take the girl I know, thanks.

I force myself to stand up, opening the door again with an effort. I take a long breath through the collar of my shirt, trying to filter out the stench of decay, and step back out into the hallway.

The flashlight dies.

A tiny sound catches in my throat, but I keep from screaming again. Instead I stand still, gazing into the darkness and forcing myself to breathe.

I catch a whiff of something fresher, something untainted by the smell of death all around. I move toward it, picking my way in utter darkness slowly and carefully through the bodies and wreckage littering the floor.

It turns out to be coming from a tear in the side of the ship, where something ripped a long, narrow gash along its hull. I squeeze my body through, careful not to slice myself on the exposed metal and wiring nearly two feet thick in the wall.

It's night outside, but it's like walking out into the sunlight. The air has never smelled so sweet, the sky never seemed so full of stars. The clouds have cleared and the mirror-moon shines down, coating the world in its pale blue luminescence. I drop to my knees, gasping for air, as though I can wipe away my memories of what waits inside the ship with enough fresh oxygen. I can't go back in. How can I go back in? I *can't*. It's a tomb. We knew not everyone could have made it onto the pods in that frantic press of people, but now, faced as I am with the proof, the thought of returning to the ship makes me want to retch. I must have been near one of the evacuation points when I fell.

I let myself crouch in the darkness for the count of five, breathing deep, before I get to my feet and follow the outer hull of the ship back to camp.

Tarver's unconscious. It's almost a relief, though I don't know if unconsciousness is a bad sign, or if the rest is good for him. But it means he doesn't look at me with those burning eyes, doesn't reach for me unseeing, shout nonsense, speak to me as if I'm his mother, his lover, his corporal, anyone but me.

I bathe his face and chest in cold water, then lift his head and trickle some water from the canteen into his mouth. He swallows a few times, then moans and pushes me away. Angry red lines have begun to march their way from underneath the bandage up the inside of his arm. I trace them with my fingertips and swallow my dread.

He's so quiet, so still. I smooth his hair back from his brow, run the backs of my fingers along his cheek, rough like sandpaper with the stubble of the past few days. He looks younger than usual, no older than I am. I dampen my fingertips with water and run them across his mouth, which is dry and chapped. Even his lips are hot, flushed.

"Tarver," I whisper, cupping his burning cheek with my hand. "Please don't—don't leave me."

My whole body seizes up, my insides clenching with a horror and helplessness more profound than any I'd felt when confronted with the corpses in the wreck. Unable to breathe, unable to move, I crouch over him, my hands shaking as they try to somehow smooth away his illness.

"Please don't leave me here alone."

My fingers fan through the damp hair at the nape of his neck. My lips find his forehead, then his temple. I'm shaking, and I force myself to stop, dragging air into my lungs.

"I'll be back," I whisper in his ear. I say it every time I go. It's as much a promise to myself as to him. I try to make my feet move, make that promise real, but I'm so tired. All I want is to curl up beside him.

I stagger away, and as I wipe at my eyes, I spot something lying just inside the firelight. Something I know wasn't there a moment ago, because a moment ago I'd been stretched out in that spot, at Tarver's side.

It's a flower.

I pick it up, my fingers trembling, though I already know what it is. Two of the petals are grown together, a mutation, one in a million. Unique. Except that I've seen it before. And that flower is gone—it was destroyed in the downpour, crushed against my skin. I left the pieces behind where we camped by the river.

How is it here now?

I cup the flower in my hands, closing my eyes for a long moment. I brush a fingertip along the joined petals, and abruptly I see Tarver's quiet smile, the beauty in the moment he gave it to me. The memory spreads like a fire through my limbs, feeling and strength coming back to me. *I can do this.*

Whoever or whatever is watching us, I realize that this is a gift, just as the canteen was. I don't know what they intended, but I know what it means to me.

I'm not alone here. Perhaps I never was, even in the depths of the dead-filled wreck. These whispers, whoever, whatever they are, can see into my thoughts. They can see into my heart.

I shut my eyes, turning away from the empty space at his side.

Behind the camp looms the black monstrosity of the wreck, darker than the night and blotting out the stars. The tomb. The meat locker. I force myself not to look back at Tarver asleep in our bed again. I know that if I do, I might not go. That this time might be the one where I fail, and fall down, and can't get back up.

I walk back into the tomb.

"How did you divide up the labor?"

"What do you mean? The salvage?"

"Yes."

"She did most of it."

"Your sarcasm is uncalled for. How did you divide up the labor?"

"According to our strengths, I suppose."

"What were Miss LaRoux's strengths?"

"Hairstyling, eye makeup, spotting a faux pas at fifty paces."

"Major. Your lack of cooperation is being noted."

"She could fetch and carry, small tasks like that."

"And you?"

"I found that very helpful."

TWENTY-FIVE

TARVER

I KNOW IT'S STRANGE WHEN MY BROTHER ALEC SHOWS UP beside me, but I can't remember why. It tickles at the back of my brain like an annoying little itch. I give up for now and let my eyes close again.

I was watching Lilac before, but I think she's gone now. She keeps coming and going, coming and going, always carrying things. So many things. Where do they come from? This world doesn't have that many things in it. No things, no other people, no idea, no hope. Just her.

I really hope that when it comes down to it, she dies first. It'll be bad for her, if it's me.

"That's a pretty morbid thing to think, T." Alec's lying beside me on the bed, reclining on his elbows the way he always did when we lay outside on summer nights.

That doesn't make it any less true. What else should I hope for her?

"Don't look at me, she's your Girl Friday."

She's not my girl anything.

Then it comes to me like a splash of cold water in the face, quick and shocking, robbing me of breath. *You're dead.*

"Hey, no need to rub it in." Alec grins easily. "Happens to the best of us, T."

I concentrate for a moment, waiting for the shakes, the metallic taste in the back of my throat, the whispers across my skin. But my hands are steady. *You're not a vision.*

"No, I'm all you. You're delirious. Which means I get an afterlife for a while. I've got to tell you, I was anticipating worse. I can live with this. No pun intended."

That was dreadful.

"You missed it, though."

Yes. Every day.

"I'm sorry I left, T. I didn't mean to. What is this place?"

No idea. Abandoned planet.

"Abandoned? After all the money to germinate the terraforming? What the hell kind of thing causes them to pack up and leave?"

No idea, but something's up. Lilac thinks some kind of life-form is trying to communicate with us. No ill intent so far. Maybe they're harmless.

"Doesn't seem likely, T."

Doesn't, does it? Can't point that out to her. The corporations aren't the kind of guys to cut and run just because they accidentally set up camp in somebody else's living room.

"Hmm. What about the girl? She has seriously great legs."

I noticed.

"You hold her at night. That must be fun."

I've been trying not to notice.

"Ha. I'd sympathize, except that I can't touch her at all."

Nor can I, really. She's the kind that turns me down when they find out who I am.

"Well, T, if you ever wanted to take a run at it, I'd say now's your time. There's hardly any competition, unless you count me. Though I am of course very handsome, even dead."

No. She turned me down when she could. I know what she thinks of me. Don't really want to try again just because she's out of options.

"Is that what you really think?"

No.

"Safer, though, yes?"

Much.

"So what will you do?"

No idea.

"You're thinking that a lot lately, T. I've never heard it from you before, not once. When did you learn those two words?"

When the infallible spaceliner her father built came crashing down through atmo.

When Lilac started seeing the future, when Mom and Dad's house appeared in a valley halfway across the galaxy. No idea about a lot of things, now.

"You should kiss her. It looks like it would be fun."

Wait, what? Right, Alec. So what happens after this magical kiss?

"Who cares about after? You could die tomorrow, you don't think you should kiss her today?"

Perhaps I shouldn't kiss her today because I could die tomorrow.

"Boring. Also, illogical."

I'm delirious and hallucinating, now you want logic?

"I have only the highest standards for you, T. If you won't kiss her, have you at least written her one of your poems?"

Are you joking?

"You have, then. You just haven't shown them to her."

No. She likes Mom's.

"So yours wouldn't be up to scratch?"

Something like that.

"Rubbish."

Mmm.

"Mmm."

Alec?

"Yes, T?"

What do I do now?

"Keep trying. You have to get back to them. They can't lose us both."

I never really thought they would. I don't know why. I've nearly died a lot of times.

"I never thought they'd lose one son. Just keep putting one foot in front of the other, T. I know you can. You always do."

I look across at him, drinking in his familiar face, smiling, no older than he was when he died, watching over me with the same indulgent affection that allowed me to trail up hills and down mountains after him at home.

Don't go yet.

"I'll stay while you sleep."

I know something's changed when I open my eyes. My eyelids aren't heavy, and the sunlight doesn't burn. I suck in a breath through my nose, bracing myself to move, but when I shift my weight, it's easier. I know all this is different, but I can't put my finger on why.

I blink again, and when I try focusing my gaze, I find Lilac passed out beside me. When I clear my throat, she jerks awake, reaching out without opening her eyes to fumble for my wrist and check my pulse. Then she shoves up on one elbow to reach for my forehead, her own eyes still closed.

I see the moment she realizes my skin's cooler, and her eyes snap open as she stares down at me.

"'Morning." My voice is a croak. I reach up to brush my fingertips against her cheek. Her face is streaked with dirt, smudged where she's been sweating, and there's a dark bruise across her other cheek. Her eyes are red with exhaustion, purple circles marking the skin beneath them. I can't even see now where her black eye from our crash landing was.

"Tarver." It's more a question than a statement.

"I think so," I whisper. "What the hell . . . ?"

"You've been sick." She can't take her eyes off my face. She reaches for the canteen without looking at it and holds it up to my lips with practiced hands—but when would she have practiced this?—and I take a careful sip.

"How long?" My whisper's a little clearer now. She looks appalling. There's grime all over her blue shirt, and a brownish-red stain where she's wiped her hands clean.

But didn't she pick out that shirt from the laundry the day before yesterday? I thought it was clean when we went to bed.

"Three days." It's her turn for a hoarse whisper.

I feel like the air's gone out of me. "Are you okay? Anyone around?"

"No," she whispers, soft and raw. "Just me."

I don't know what to say. We stare at each other as seconds go by, my head swimming, her breathing slow, carefully controlled, that ragged edge held at bay. Hanging on by a thread.

Then her lips press together in a thin, firm line, and I see her take herself in hand. "I've got aspirin, and a ration bar for you," she says, suddenly purposeful. "I found antibiotics in the ship, in the sick bay. That's what made the difference." When she moves to haul herself to her feet, I see her exhaustion—it's there in the way she reaches out with one hand for balance, wobbles as she stands, bites her lip too hard.

I lift my head as she walks away, ignoring the momentary dizziness so I can get a look at our little nest. Our supplies have multiplied. I don't get a chance to see much more than that before she returns, peeling a ration bar out of its wrapper, watching my every movement—however small—with an unnerving intensity. She's almost possessive, the way she kneels down beside me to help me sit up, and holds the bar so I can reach out with my good hand to break off a piece.

It tastes delicious. God, I really must be dying.

Dying. Alec. The faces of my parents, a girl I dated on Avon. I remember . . . what do I remember?

I push that thought aside, and as she reaches for the canteen so I can take the aspirin, we're staring at each other again. I'm moving before I recognize the impulse. I ease my good arm away from my body, holding it out in a silent invitation, and after a moment she settles against my side and buries her face against my shoulder. A shudder runs through her, but she doesn't break down.

"You saved my life," I murmur. "Again."

"I had to. I wouldn't last a day around here without you." Her whisper's almost inaudible. Her arm snakes across my chest to rest over my heart.

"You lasted at least three, by the sound of it." While she's not looking I lift up my bandaged hand. My fingers aren't as puffy, and I find that when I wriggle them a little, there's no pain. The bandages look clean. "Did you wrap my hand up?"

"Mmm. You didn't like it much. You have the foulest mouth I've ever encountered, Major. I didn't even recognize half the languages you can swear in. I'm glad I'm not one of your soldiers. Still, it was rather educational."

"Been posted to too many places. You pick stuff up from the locals, wherever the old cultures have survived." I reach up to trace her hairline with my uninjured hand. "But if you're telling me you understood any of it, Miss LaRoux, I'm going to reevaluate my opinion of you."

"Well, the context helped."

We're quiet for a little, and I smooth down her hair with my good hand. She turns her head a little in response, and I see that bruise standing out on her cheek again, livid against her fair skin. I can actually see the faint imprint of knuckles there against her skin.

I'm the only one around here who could have done it. I swallow down the sick guilt that comes with that knowledge, and concentrate on something else. "Have the whispers shown up? I remember a lot of things that don't seem right, unless we did visit a restaurant, and you're holding out on me. I can't tell whether it was a fever, or visions."

"The fever, I think." She hesitates, eyes flicking from me to the fire, as though seeing something I can't. I want to press her, ask her what she's seen, but then she shakes her head. "I haven't seen anything since the valley, and your parents' house. You did, though. You called me all sorts of different people. I never realized how nice it was when you just called me Lilac."

"Lilac?" I smooth down her hair again as she settles closer. I don't want her to move. "I'd never be so familiar, Miss LaRoux. It would be highly inappropriate. I know my place, and apparently it's swearing up a storm at you, hallucinating wildly. My mother would be so proud."

"Inappropriate," she murmurs, that raw edge to her voice finally softening. She sounds amused, leaning into my hand where it rests against her hair. "When the cavalry comes, I hope it's not at night. Imagine what they'd think of this."

Yes, imagine. What a silly thought, that a girl like you would look at a guy like me. I'm a fool, lying here and holding her. This girl who, under any other circumstances, never would've given a guy like me a second glance.

"I have to move, tomorrow." My body resists the very thought, limbs turning to lead.

"Like hell you're moving," she replies, quick and sharp. There's a steel there I haven't heard since the early days of our stay here. "We're staying put. I'll go back into the ship and see what I can find."

There's something in her voice as she says it, a high note, full of tension. It makes me look at her again.

"We can both go in together tomorrow, or the next day at worst."

She shifts and sits up, shaking her head, chewing on her lip again.

I want a little to reach after her, and pull her back down next to me. "It's—not good in there. A few more days and I don't think you'd be able to spend much time inside without getting ill."

"What's in there, Lilac?" But the answer's settling in the pit of my stomach even as I'm asking the question.

"It's—you know, there's no power or anything. Everything's gone bad, rotting." She barely gets that word out before she cuts herself off, jaw clenching as she shuts her eyes. Her freckles stand out against the whiteness of her skin.

That knot in my stomach was right. Not everyone made it off the ship. "You can't go back in there, Lilac. Whatever you brought out, we have enough."

"Stop it." It's a strained whisper. "I'd have been eaten our second day here if it wasn't for you. Time for me to even the scales. I won't be long."

"You've already done that." I reach for her hand to wrap mine around it. "You saved us both, hot-wiring the escape pod. Let's just stop trying to keep track of who's saved who."

"Tarver, you're making it harder." Her eyes are squeezed shut now. "It's dark in there, and cold, and it's more silent than space itself, and being here with you is none of those things. But there are things we need in there. If I were the one who was sick—" I can see the wetness along her lashes, but she refuses to blink and let the tears roll down her cheeks. *What happened to her in that ship?*

I breathe out slowly and try to inject some calm into my voice, even though all I want to do is hold on to her so tightly she has to give up the idea of going back in there alone. "I wouldn't go in there. It's a pretty simple risk-reward analysis. Sure, there are things in there it would be good to have. What's better is to have two people functioning. What's worst of all is to have both of us down for the count. We need to be well more than we need more clothes or food."

Slowly, reluctantly, she begins to ease down beside me again, then stops. She draws the Gleidel out from the back of her waistband, offering the gun to me grip first. "I suppose I ought to give this back now. You should teach me how to use it, though. I wouldn't have known what to do with it."

It's a jolt to realize I was so sick I didn't even miss it. "You want to learn to use the gun?" I ask, setting it down beside me within reach and easing my arm around her once more. "Maybe when I'm a little better, and I can run to a safe distance."

"Come on, now." She pokes me in the ribs. "You know I run faster than you. So you'll do it?"

"After you've pointed out you're fast enough to hunt me down and shoot me when I upset you?" I tighten my arm around her and turn my head to tuck her under my chin.

"I'm stubborn," she warns as she closes her eyes. "Don't think you can just wait until morning and hope I'll forget."

"Of course not, Miss LaRoux. You'd shoot me if I tried."

I continue to lie there after her breathing has evened out. Alec wells up in my mind again, and I can hear our conversation. *I hope I die first.*

Has she been thinking about that too? About what would become of her? My throat closes as I realize that she's not talking about learning to defend herself if something happens to me.

I should give her a lesson. If I at least show her how to operate the settings, she'll have options. I can't think about it any further than that.

I turn my head to take a better look at her now she's asleep.

There's a rip in the leg of her jeans, running down by her knee and exposing skin that's turned grubby with dirt. Her blue shirt's untucked, marked with black grime.

Her hair's escaping the piece of string tying it back, framing her face in a halo of wispy curls that remind me of how it floated around her in zero gravity during the pod's descent.

There are dirty smudges mingling with the freckles all over her face, and that bruise on her cheek. Even in sleep, her mouth is pulled into a straight, determined line.

There are purple half circles underneath her eyes, and she's sweaty, beat up, and utterly exhausted.

She's never looked so beautiful.

"You didn't stay at the wreck."

"You already know that. We saw no option but to leave."

"Your reasoning?"

"There were no rescue craft in sight. There was a disease risk with so many bodies around. We needed another option."

TWENTY-SIX

LILAC

BY THE AFTERNOON OF THE SECOND DAY, I HAVE TO threaten to sit on Tarver's chest to keep him from getting out of bed. More than anything, the speculative look—and thoughtful silence—that follow that threat convince me he's feeling better. I don't mind. After hearing him call out for his ex-girlfriend in his delirium, there's not much that'll make me blush. I let him sit up and shave, as a compromise—it's nice to see him looking a little more like himself.

On the morning of the third day we agree that our best move is to get to a higher vantage point and scout the area. For the first time since we crashed we're talking about the long term. If they knew where we were, someone would be here, at the wreck, to rescue us. The *Icarus* must not have transmitted her location before she was destroyed. Not even the all-powerful Monsieur LaRoux could find us now—though I have no doubt he'll take the galaxy apart trying, even if it's only to mark my grave.

We need a place near the *Icarus*, in case anyone does show up and land to inspect the wreck in the future, but we can't stay this close. Not to all those bodies, not with the air full of burned chemicals and the ground littered with shrapnel.

We scale the outside of the wreck, aiming for the highest point. The wind has picked up, making the ship sigh and moan in protest. Tarver says that the *Icarus* will have done most of her settling already, and that it's safe enough. The way the hull has splintered, the path is relatively easy, with plenty of handholds and places to rest. Still, Tarver is pale and sweating by the time we near the top.

It isn't until I'm standing on the sloping surface of the top of the ship, steadying myself with one hand on the mangled communications array, that it hits me.

We're looking for a place to *live*.

And the thought doesn't hurt.

I could never admit it to him, but here in the sun, warm from the climb, waiting for Tarver to catch up, there's nowhere I'd rather be. After all, what waits for me on the other side of rescue? My friends would scarcely recognize me now, and the thought of filling my days with gossip and parties leaves me cold. The best six-course meal never tasted half so good as a shared ration bar after a long hike, washed down with mountain-fresh water. And while I wouldn't say no to a hot bath, I'm warm enough at night, with Tarver there at my side.

It's only the thought of my father, grief-stricken, that causes me any pain at all.

I set down the pack and rummage around for the canteen. When Tarver joins me, I offer it to him. It lets him hide the way he's breathing heavily, gives him something to hold so that I can't see the shaking of his hands.

To the east are the mountains we crossed, whitecapped and foreboding, and I wonder how Tarver ever convinced me to go into them. Maybe it was just that I was too naive to realize how hard the passage would be.

The camp below looks like a doll's play set. I can't see the dirty bandages, the ration bar wrappers. The river and its ribbon of trees lead away from the mountains and into the distance. Shielding my eyes from the sun, I can almost make out what seems to be an ocean, or some kind of salt flat, just visible at the horizon. In the other direction, the hills roll on like waves, growing smaller and gentler until they level out at the edge of a vast forest. It's like a painting, something out of a dusty museum. I've never seen so much open space in my life—for a moment I'm dizzy, lost in the tableau, struggling for breath in air that's suddenly too rich. A hand at the small of my back grounds me again and I grip the metal of the useless communications array more tightly. I turn and see Tarver, pale but smiling.

"The breeze is stiffer up here; are you cold?"

"What would you do if I said yes?" I grin back at him. "Offer me some of your fever?"

"Sharing is caring." He steps in close, and my chest tightens convulsively. But he's just reaching to grab on to the metal as well, steadying himself in the wind.

He doesn't look good. Despite his smile, his nonchalance, he's gripping the beam too tightly, leaning into it.

I kneel by the pack, pulling out his notebook. "Do you know how to draw maps?"

"Of course I do," Tarver replies. He's watching me, and then after a moment he moves to join me. I try not to show my relief when he sits down, some of the lines of pain around his eyes easing. I wish he'd let me climb by myself. But since he woke up, he's been reluctant for me to stray too far from him. Perhaps he's afraid I'll go back into the tomb of a ship despite my promise not to.

Maybe he just likes my company. I give myself a shake, trying to dismiss the thought before I can start blushing again.

He takes the notebook from me, flipping through. Belatedly I remember that I pressed the replicated flower between two of its pages to preserve it and keep it safe; I still haven't told him about it. But he flips right past it, unseeing, until he pauses on the pages I used while he was sick.

"Did you draw these?" His voice is unreadable as he looks over the maps I made of the twisted and broken decks.

"After the first day I started forgetting where I'd already been." I keep my eyes on the horizon, easing down onto my heels. "In the dark it all blurs together."

I realize he's turned back to the last page he wrote on before my maps begin—a page containing only fragments of a poem in progress. Scattered words and phrases describing one of the purple flowers we found together, something beautiful in a sea of loneliness.

When he was ill I tried to imagine he was writing about me. Now, by the light of day, it seems ludicrous. But he's staring at it. He knows I saw it. Reading everything would've felt too much like accepting he was about to die, going through his things, but I can feel him wanting to ask me if I did. If I violated that privacy while he couldn't stop me.

I had been expecting field reports, notes on wildlife, but every page was filled with poems.

He's silent, and I swallow, fiddling with the tear in my jeans, widening it as I pull at each thread. Unlike our usual silences, this one begs to be filled.

I crack first. "My drawing lessons were always more focused on flowers and lakeside vistas, but my maps served their purpose."

Tarver grunts and turns to a fresh page. The tip of the pencil hovers over the empty white space. His eyes are far away, staring through the page. The wreck beneath us gives a particularly wrenching shriek, and he blinks, and the moment's gone. He turns his attention to the horizon and begins sketching out the visible landmarks, expert and quick. I wonder where we'll go—if he'll suggest the forest, the hills, the river. I wonder if we'll ever go to the sea.

His eyes flick up and down from scenery to page—mine stay on him. If he notices my gaze he says nothing, concentrating on his task, letting me watch his profile uninterrupted.

He's still too pale, but he looks less likely to keel over. He's so thin it makes me ache, but I liberated some dried pasta and flour and shortening from the kitchens, all the things we can't find from the land. We'll eat better. He'll get stronger.

He sucks at the edge of his lip as he concentrates. The dimple there is hypnotic, fascinating me. I'm so focused on that tiny detail of him that I don't notice when he stops drawing, staring intently at something.

"Lilac."

I start guiltily, swimming up out of my trance. "I wasn't!"

"There's something—come look." His voice shakes—his gaze is fixed straight ahead.

I turn toward the hills, expecting an animal, other survivors, even a rescue craft. What I see instead is electrifying.

Before our eyes springs up a wave of flowers, the purple blooms from that first night on the plains, when Tarver tried to distract me from the fact that I was going mad. Just like the tiny purple blossom hidden in his journal. The narrow corridor of blooms extends as we watch, winding this way and that through the hills, toward the hazy green of the forest in the distance.

Beside me, Tarver is shaking. I can feel the dizziness myself, my skin tingling, itching, hot and cold all at once. "It's not real." I gasp, blinking my eyes hard and opening them again. The flowers are still there. "It's just a vision."

"The canteen—they made that, didn't they?"

I swallow. The flower was something they made for me, and just for me—to tell him would be to explain what it meant to me, in that moment of utter darkness. That it reminded me why I was returning to that shipwreck of the dead. That there's only one person in the galaxy I could've done it for. But I can't say those things to him, not yet.

The row of blossoms continues, the flowers growing thicker and brighter by the moment, until the entire corridor of the valley is shining with purple in the sunlight, leading toward the forest. It's a narrow, concentrated band, looking for all the world like a winding river of purple—or a road.

I gasp. "Tarver! They're—leading us. That's what they've been trying to—" But my voice sticks in my throat, my heart pounding.

He tears his eyes away from the flowers in order to look up at me. "Trying to what? What're you talking about?"

"The people I saw—they were pointing. The voice I heard was leading us away from the forest, toward the plain. Even your parents' house, the garden path led away—toward this spot. And now these flowers . . . I don't know, maybe I'm trying too hard to find sense in all of this."

"You think they're showing us the way." He turns back to face the hills. "Toward what?"

We stand, staring at the path before us, so clear and bright. All I want is to go find out if they're real, if they're as solid as the flower in his journal. If all of this is some dream in which the laws of physics don't exist.

"Lilac!" Tarver's voice is urgent, snapping me out of my daze. "Look!"

I blink, trying to catch my breath as he leans close to me. His cheek brushes mine, rough with faint stubble, as he brings his line of sight alongside my own. So close, I can smell him, feel the electric tingle where we touch.

This is no dream.

"Look along my arm, where I'm pointing." He stretches one arm out, toward the trees. "There's something there. See that glint?"

It's all I can do not to turn my face toward his, the way a plant grows toward the light. I draw in a deep breath and force myself to focus. I don't see it immediately, and my eyes strain along the strip of forest bordering the hills at its western edge.

And then, as sudden as a lightning strike, I do see it. A tiny glint of reflected sunlight, winking at me from the tree line.

"Wreckage," I whisper, staring at it, trying not to believe it's what I think it is. "It's a piece of the ship that landed there. Another crashed escape pod."

Tarver slowly lets his arm fall, but doesn't shift away again. He's staring at the thing too. "I don't think so." His voice is quiet too, barely audible over the wind. "It's tough to tell, but I think the trees around it are cleared, uniform."

I realize I'm holding my breath.

"I think it's a building."

There's no fuel for a fire out among the rolling hills, and it's bitterly cold, but I don't care. Tarver estimated a two-day journey to reach the edge of the forest, and as the sun set in front of us on the first day I could see the trees along the horizon, in the distance. The sea of flowers vanished into mist as we climbed back down the wreckage, but we know now where we're being led. To what end, or what purpose, we can't hope to guess, but if it's a building—and it's real—it might be the key to our rescue.

"Hot water!" I say cheerfully, eating cold, plain pasta with my fingers. I've never had anything so delicious.

"A roof," Tarver replies, munching at his own handful of the pasta I cooked before we left. The kitchen storerooms on the wreck were my best find—after the sick bay, anyway.

I glance over at him, the last of the light lending his still-pale face some false color. We're camped in the lee of a hill, as much out of the wind as we can be. Still, it'll be a cold night, even together.

"A bed," is my retort. "A real one."

"You win," he says, downing the last of his share of the pasta and leaning back on his elbows. He's still moving slowly, carefully. But he looks better, for all his trouble walking today. "I can't top that."

I hurry to finish the rest of my dinner and scoot over to where he reclines on the blanket, eager for his warmth and company. He folds his good arm around me, easy, comfortable. I don't think the old Lilac would've thought he smelled very good, but I turn my head toward him anyway, cheek rubbing against the material of his T-shirt.

We're quiet for a while, perhaps each of us imagining what might wait for us in the building Tarver saw on the horizon. His face has changed, a spark of hope where there had only been grim determination. How long has he been living with the belief that no rescue was coming? It's obvious that ever since we reached the *Icarus*, he's been aiming only for survival. Not for rescue.

Now there's a good chance we'll be able to signal for help. No remote outpost building would be without some method of communication.

I shift, pulling myself in more tightly. He inhales deeply, the rise and fall of his chest shifting my face where it's pressed against him.

"How long do you think we've been here?"

"Counting the time I was sick?" Tarver pauses, doing a quick mental calculation. "Sixteen days, I think."

So long? It knocks the wind out of me. Two weeks and counting. It feels like only two days and like a lifetime. "It was my birthday," I find myself saying, in a strange voice. "I turned seventeen a few days ago." *The day you came back to me from your fever.* But I can't bring myself to say that out loud.

Tarver's breath catches, then releases. "Happy birthday, Miss LaRoux." I can hear the smile in his voice.

I've become a year older while stranded on this planet. I swallow.

Perhaps sensing the shift in my mood, Tarver lifts his bandaged hand to trail his fingertips along my arm. I suspect the movement hurts him, but if it does, he makes no complaint.

I clear my throat. "What would be the first thing you'd do when we get rescued? A real meal? Call your family?" I smile against him, plucking at his T-shirt in distaste. "Take a shower?"

"My family," he says immediately. "Then they'll probably hose me down and interrogate me for a few weeks. The military will, I mean. Not my parents."

"Gosh." Now I'm trying to banish the mental image of someone hosing Tarver down. At least I'm not thinking about my birthday anymore. "I hope nobody tries that with me."

That earns me a laugh, my head jumping a little as Tarver's body quakes beneath my cheek. "I doubt anyone will try any such thing with you. It's pretty much just soldiers and criminals who get the high-pressure hose."

Even in the realm of imagination, we're already separated. Him, in his interrogations and debriefings—me, presumably taken somewhere for coddling and polishing. My heart twinges painfully, its beat rapid and strong against Tarver's ribs.

It's not that I don't want to be rescued. I do. I want to see my father again—and more than that, I want Tarver to find his family again, keep them from losing another son. But I had begun to imagine a life here, with him and me. A hungry, cold, barely-surviving-each-week kind of life—but a life together.

Before I can stop myself, the words come tumbling out. "What about me?"

"What about you?" Tarver echoes, one shoulder moving in a shrug. "Your family will scoop you up and quiz you on whether I compromised your virtue and whisk you off to strap you into one of those extraordinary dresses, and it'll be like this never happened."

My mouth is dry, my tongue heavy. Why doesn't he understand what I'm asking? If we're to be rescued, I don't want it to happen before we figure out whatever's happening here between us. I may not have many more opportunities.

I take a deep breath and lift myself up on one elbow. It's dark, but I can still make out his features through the gloom.

"You mean we'll never see each other again."

For a moment he just looks at me, unreadable as ever. The mirror-moon lights his face, silver on his skin, in his eyes. My heart threatens to slam its way out of my chest.

"Maybe not." There's a softer, less certain note in his voice.

The idea that someone will swoop down and take him away from me, off to fight some distant war in some distant system, makes me feel like my lungs are filling with water. I don't know how to reach him, how to make him see how I feel. I don't know what's going on behind the brown eyes I've come to know so well. I don't know what he's thinking as he looks at me.

But suddenly I do know that I'll never live with myself if we get rescued before I can make him understand.

"That's what I'm afraid of," I whisper.

I lean down, my hair falling forward around his face, and let my lips find his.

For an instant I feel him reach for me, and all I want is to lean against him, let him wrap me up, keep me close. All I want is for no one to take him away.

"What did you hope to gain by making for the structure?"

"Better shelter, at least. Some method of communication, at most."

"With whom did you wish to communicate?"

"Is that a trick question?"

"All our questions are extremely serious, Major."

"Anybody who could hear us. I had Lilac LaRoux with me. I knew her father would stage a retrieval at any cost, if he knew where we were."

"It was on your mind that you were with Monsieur LaRoux's daughter."

"It could hardly escape me."

"Just the two of you, alone."

"I noticed that too."

TWENTY-SEVEN

TARVER

I WANT TO SURGE UP AGAINST HER, TANGLE MY FINGERS through her hair, pull her down to meet me—and for a moment I find myself reaching for her, unable to resist. How long have I been wanting to touch her like this? A charge runs from her fingertips and into my skin, and all my careful self-control starts crashing down as I feel the heat of her near me. I want to lose myself in her, let this moment take me over completely.

My fingers find the edge of her shirt, and she makes a quiet sound as my hand curves against the small of her back. She shifts, and I realize it's my bandaged hand in the same instant that a white-hot line of pain runs up my arm. A groan tears out of me as I tense, pushing her away with my good hand.

We're left gasping, staring at each other—she, confused, uncertain why I stopped; me, trying to breathe, pushing away the need coursing through me despite the ache in my hand.

I know what this is. I recognize that desperate longing in her expression—I've seen it before, in the field. Lilac was very nearly left alone on this planet, and she's mistaking her relief for something else.

A girl like her would never look at a guy like me in other circumstances. If that building on the horizon is our ticket home, I'm not sure I could stand to see her waltz off into her old life and leave me behind. Not if I let myself—no.

I can't afford to show her how badly I want her.

Not when it isn't really me she wants.

Her expression is shifting with every moment I keep her at arm's length, eyes darkening, the confusion turning to doubt.

A treacherous part of me doesn't care that she's confused, desperately wants to kiss her anyway. Maybe one moment would be worth it, even if afterward it all dissolved into mist, like our trail of purple flowers.

I could be wrong. Maybe she does want—maybe—

I'm drawing breath again when she pulls away sharply, climbing to her feet to stalk off into the darkness. There's anger in her jerky movements, in the tense line of her shoulders.

My mind thunders with everything I should say, the words tangling in my throat. *Wait. Come back. Tell me you won't vanish the moment they find us here. Tell me if I touch you I'm not going to lose you.*

"Don't go far," I call instead, and silently curse my own cowardice.

She doesn't come back, but she does stop where I can still see her, choosing the cold, windy emptiness of the dark plain over returning to me. The mirror-moon gives off enough light that she probably won't break an ankle, but I wish I knew how to call her back.

In the end I unroll the blankets and stretch out on them—I'm too weak, too tired to sit up and wait for her. When she returns to lie down beside me, it's at the edge of the blanket, as far from me as she can get.

I have to say something. This will get worse overnight. I reach inside myself and find the part of me that's used to dragging the unwilling through all kinds of uncompromising landscapes, and I try for a lighter tone. "Stop that, will you come over here? I'm an invalid, I need you to keep me warm." If I can get my arms around her, maybe she'll understand.

She's silent so long it doesn't seem like she'll reply at all. When she finally does, her voice is hoarse and hostile. "You'll survive."

"Probably," I agree. "But I'd rather be comfortable."

She keeps her back to me, spine curved as she curls in on herself. "Tarver." Now she sounds like she's the one talking through gritted teeth. "I'm humiliated. I'll be fine in the morning, and we'll keep going and get rescued, and then this will be over. Just leave me alone right now."

"Lilac—"

She curls up away from me more tightly, tucking her head down as though she can block out my words. Eventually I stop waiting for her to roll over and join me. I lie on my back to stare up at the unfamiliar stars and the bright, blue-white mirror overhead, and wait for sleep.

It's bitterly cold without her.

She wakes up before me in the morning. I'm still feeling like the living dead, which is what I get for trying a forced march so soon after I've been laid up.

We eat a ration bar each in silence. I'm pretty sure giving me a whole one instead of splitting it is her version of looking after me while I'm sick, which perhaps means we're going to be civilized about what happened last night. It's not as though we have the luxury of finding someone else to talk to.

I know she's started hearing the whispers again—she shakes like a leaf whenever they show up. But they've declined to let me in on their secrets again, and if they tell her anything, she doesn't share it with me. I'm not sure I like the idea that they seem to be focusing on her—or targeting her.

I shoulder the pack and we set off in silence, but we do manage to talk a little as the morning wears on. It's not much, but the content of the conversation isn't the point. It's the gesture that matters, on both our parts—our way of telling each other that we're going to find a way to keep working together.

Seventeen days ago I'd have pulled out my own teeth with pliers before voluntarily seeking her out for conversation. Now I'm just tired with relief that we're not going to shut each other out completely.

It's late afternoon when we reach the trees. They're mostly pole trees again, like the forest where we crashed. This inexplicable landscape, none of the terraforming as it should be, is becoming normal to me.

Lilac's hand goes out when I stumble over a root. I'm so tired I'm not lifting my feet properly now, a combination of three days of fever and nearly three weeks of rationed meals. At least I started out with some condition on me. I have no idea how Lilac's still moving, but in some ways she actually seems stronger than she was before.

We emerge from the trees quite suddenly, both of us stumbling to a halt in the same moment.

A boxy, one-story building squats in the middle of the clearing. Hope surges up inside of me.

It's perfectly intact. This isn't wreckage, and it isn't ruined. It's real. It's an observation station, like dozens I've seen before on newly terraformed planets.

As we stand rooted to the spot, a carpet of purple flowers unfurls beneath our feet, racing away from us to ring the building. The path that led the way from the ship finishes here.

And then, in the next moment, disappointment cuts through me. I look again, and realize the clearing is dotted with young saplings. There are thick vines crawling up the sides of the building.

Nobody's been here in years.

"Are you reluctant to answer our questions, Major?"

"Of course not. It's a pleasure to assist you. I can see you're hanging on my every word."

"You seem uncooperative, Major. You're a highly decorated soldier. Your conduct doesn't match the favorable reports on your file."

"I suppose appearances can be deceiving."

TWENTY-EIGHT

LILAC

FOR A WHILE WE FORGET WHAT HAPPENED LAST NIGHT AND explore the building, working together again. Seeing an intact structure, something man-made, is electrifying. I try to imagine what my home looks like, my city, the buildings that touch the clouds and the cars on the skyways, and my mind draws a blank. I think if I were to somehow transport myself there now, it'd be overwhelming.

There'll be a generator inside this building, somewhere, and if we can get that working, I can get everything else working. Tarver insists there will be a communications system inside—though I've never been to a planet in any phase earlier than advanced settlement, he tells me that stations like this are common, and all alike.

Communications equipment would mean a way to send a signal. A way to get Tarver back to his family, where he belongs, even if I'm not so sure I want to rejoin the world anymore. And if there's any justice or decency in the galaxy, he'll get home in one piece.

I want so badly to tell him why I said the things I said when we first met. Why alienating people is one of my greatest talents. But to tell him would be to betray my father. To show Tarver just how monstrous I am. And so I bite my tongue, and try to ignore the way the truth is building inside me like water under pressure.

Let him hate me, and think I hate him back. It's safer for both of us.

We don't talk, but the silence is still easier than it has been. Neither of us asks why this place was abandoned, or what it was originally for. It's large enough that it can't just be to house monitoring equipment. It had to hold people at some point.

We haul on the doors, pry at the shutters over the windows, go so far as to attempt to bash our way in with a rock. The building is solid, despite its neglect, and sealed up tightly. We discover a shed not far away with a broken-down hovercraft inside. A quick look tells me it was probably broken even at the time this place was occupied. We poke around under the hood for a little, checking out the hopelessly gummed-up plugs and leads, then Tarver moves on to inventory the rest of the shed, leaving me to examine the circuitry.

He gives me a running commentary on what he finds: rusted tools, lengths of rope, cans of oil and glue, tanks of fuel in the back. Paint cans and a shovel in the corner. Drills and saws with plugs. This place once had electricity, then, which confirms my guess that there's a generator somewhere.

I wonder if some part of my brain will always look at things, now, and try to think of how they might be useful. If they're worth their weight, being carried from a wreck. I can't help but wonder if I'll always think of ways rope or oil or rusty hammers could save someone's life.

When I finally pry the circuit board's cover off to find half the circuits missing, it takes me only a few moments to realize the entire thing is useless. I slam the hood of the hovercraft down, and when Tarver looks at me, he sees the frustration in my face and doesn't ask. We head back out into the clearing, circling the building again, this time armed with tools. We set to work attacking the shutters, prying, trying to find a weak spot.

"At least you're human after all," Tarver says lightly. I'm still nursing the wounds from his rejection as I glance at him, expecting it to be a jab. He glances back, trying half a smile, and I realize it's an olive branch instead. "We've finally found circuits you can't fix."

He looks so tired, so weary, despite his weak attempt to bridge the gulf between us. I suppose I would be too, if I were him.

I sigh, rubbing a hand across my eyes. "I wish I knew more. If I did, maybe I could fix it."

"I still don't understand how you know any of this. Your father's the engineering genius, not you. I mean—you're not the sort of person who would've studied circuitry and physics in school. I mean—oh, screw it."

So much for the olive branch. Despite the temptation to leave him tripping over his words, I can't take credit for what I know. "When I was a little girl, after my mother died, I wanted nothing more than to be just like my father. Even then I knew I was everything he had, so I wanted to be . . . worthy of that, I guess. I asked someone to teach me." I swallow, feeling Tarver's eyes on me, knowing he can sense the tension in my voice.

"Who?"

"A boy named Simon."

Tarver's eyes go back to the shutter he's working on, focused, not looking at me. "You've mentioned him before. Who is he?"

My throat tightens. How can I tell Tarver, of all people, about the monstrous parts of my past? Why give him another reason to push me away? And yet, maybe he deserves to know why I said the things I said aboard the *Icarus*.

And maybe I deserve to relive it.

"If I tell you, will you just listen to me? Don't interrupt, don't say anything, just—let me get through this. Can you do that?"

His demeanor changes subtly, but he stays where he is, crowbar dangling at his side. "Okay."

I take a few deep breaths, like a diver about to jump.

"Simon was a boy who grew up near our summerhouse on Nirvana." I can't look at him while I'm speaking. I don't want to see the moment when realization hits.

"His family wasn't as well connected as mine, but whose is? He was absolutely brilliant, and not just in the subjects we were expected to learn. He's the one who taught me everything I know about electricity and physics. My father turned a blind eye to the time we spent together because he thought it was harmless, that I was too young to form any real attachment. I was fourteen then, but I loved him." I run my fingers along the edge of the screwdriver, fingertips learning its planes, the sculpted plastic handle. "The night before he turned sixteen he asked if we could stop hiding, and be a real couple. He said he was going to go to my father in the morning now that he was an adult, and ask for a position within the company. To earn the right to be with me."

Simon's sandy-blond hair and green eyes flash in front of me, my heart constricting even now. *Just keep talking. Get through it.*

"I said yes. When I woke I practically flew downstairs in anticipation, but when I got there it was like nothing had changed. My father said he hadn't seen him—he didn't even look away from the news screen. I went to his house, and found his parents devastated. All gentlemen's sons are in the reserves—you know that. As a matter of honor, I suppose, though it's never tested. It's all for show."

My eyes sting and the red and yellow handle of the screwdriver blurs. *Not yet. Hold it together.* I turn the tool over and over in my hands.

"Simon had been called to active duty. I went to the recruiting station, but due to some clerical oversight, he was shipped out to the front lines with a bunch of soldiers who'd been training for a year. By the time I got through all the red tape and found out where he was, he was already dead." *And I should have known better.*

Tarver keeps true to his word, not speaking, not even moving. But I feel his eyes on me, and I know he's listening. I swallow, suddenly uncertain. Will he understand why I'm telling him this story that no one in the galaxy knows, outside of my father and me?

"I live a life of utter privilege. I know that. I accept that." My voice cracks a little and I lick my lips. "But nothing's free. It comes with a price. I accept that, too. My father has expectations about where I'll spend my time, the company I'll keep, the connections I'll make to advance his interests. He always says that our name was hard won, and required sacrifice and work to maintain—but that if protected, it was all I'd ever need to get anywhere in this world. But sometimes—sometimes I slip."

I force myself to glance at him. He's standing where he was, his face shut down, as impassive and unreadable as I've ever seen it. I crumble a little, despite my resolve. This isn't just about how he sees me; that ship rocketed away long ago.

It's about how he thinks I see him.

"In the salon, when I dropped my glove, do you really think I didn't know who you were?" My fingers close around the handle of the screwdriver like it's a lifeline. "You were a hero, all over the news vids. I knew who your family was, that you were a scholarship case, all of it. I knew exactly who you were. I just—forgot, for a few seconds, who I was. Because I wanted to talk to you. Because you didn't look at me like I was Lilac LaRoux."

"So yes, I was cruel afterward. I'm cruel because it's the fastest way to get a man to lose interest, and trust me, I've learned how. My father taught me well." I swallow, making sure my tone is even. He'd be proud. "Tarver, you have to understand that everyone who approaches me— *everyone*—wants something. Men are after my money. Women are after my status. And men will suffer a lot for a rich girl's attentions, but not that level of humiliation. I've had to learn to use it over the years. And maybe I'm cruel because it's easy, and because it's something . . . something I can be good at."

He's still standing there, motionless. I've run out of things to say, and fall silent. My hand twitches, like it wants to throw the screwdriver at him. Anything to get him to move, speak. Say something. He stands there like he's been hit in the head with the canteen, staring at me, square-jawed and silent.

I toss the screwdriver down. "I'll find us a place for the night."

I can feel his eyes on me as I retrieve the pack of supplies and make my way back toward the stream.

The stream is cloudy where we crossed it earlier, so I follow it, looking for a place to refill the canteen and wash a little. A thread of an idea nags at me, but I push it away, my mind roiling.

Why, *why*, did I tell him? Why should he be interested in the sad saga of the poor little rich girl who had her boyfriend taken away? It'll be a great story for him when he ships out, something to laugh about with his platoon. I can just imagine him describing how this lunatic rich girl tried to jump him because of her daddy issues. Something twists uneasily inside me. Tarver isn't the type of person to share the story. But still, he must think me so self-involved. He's seen dozens of his friends blown to smithereens on the front lines, and I'm crying because a boy I once knew got sent away to war.

Still, now he knows. What my father is. What I am. That I'm responsible for the death of a boy whose only crime was falling in love. Now he knows how toxic I am.

I'm so tangled in my thoughts that I almost don't notice the cave. The entrance is narrow, barely wide enough for Tarver's shoulders. The source of the stream must be within it, but I can't hear any bubbling,

"Was there any significant time during which you and Miss LaRoux were separated?"

"Define 'significant.'"

"Are you able to account for her whereabouts and actions during the entirety of your stay on the planet?"

"You make it sound like we were on shore leave."

"Major."

"We were together the whole time."

"And nothing strange happened to her in that time? She didn't change in any way?"

"I think crash-landing on an unknown planet is pretty strange."

"Maj—"

"No. No notable changes."

TWENTY-NINE

TARVER

I PICK UP A ROCK AND CHOOSE A SPOT TO SLAM IT AGAINST the base of the metal shutters. There's a hollow metallic *thunk* that tells me there's nothing behind it, so I slam the rock home again, angling my body and finding a rhythm. My head's spinning.

Clerical oversight, my ass. Nobody's deployed by accident, least of all a rich man's son. I know twenty things that would keep that from ever happening.

Unless he had a girlfriend with a father who didn't like the idea of that connection. Unless the girl he loved was Lilac LaRoux.

Then I can see it happening.

Poor Lilac. She's lived with this secret locked inside for three years. I've never heard her sound so lost—like she really believes it's her fault that that boy was killed. What kind of father lays a burden like that on a fourteen-year-old girl? Lets her live her life thinking she's got blood on her hands?

I wish she'd told me sooner. But what would I have done, if she'd told me back on the *Icarus* that it was too dangerous to pursue her? Would I have been smart enough to walk away?

I realize that I've been pounding the rock against the same place for at least two minutes without a result. I drop it, abandoning my futile attempt to make a dent in the shutters, and head upstream after Lilac.

What can I even say to her? All I know is that I need to go to her, electricity coursing up and down my spine.

253

A flash of red jumps out at me, fabric tied around an outcropping. I'm so tired, my head so full of half-formed apologies, that it takes me a moment to spot the opening of the cave.

The Lilac I crashed with would never have thought of that. She'd have just disappeared inside without so much as a second thought as to how I'd find her. But my girl's changed so much since we landed.

The entrance is narrow, but I squeeze through it, splashing through the stream. The sunlight's fading when I spot the flashlight up ahead. The narrow passageway widens out into a larger chamber, like a bubble inside the rock, and I almost miss the big step down.

I stop myself from falling just in time, grabbing at the edge of the opening. She hasn't noticed me yet. She's in the middle of the cave, unpacking our things and carefully laying them out. She's gotten a fire going directly under a break in the ceiling, for the smoke to escape. Did I teach her that, or did she work it out herself? I can't remember anymore.

She's making up two beds, her mouth a thin, fixed line, her shoulders square and determined. She's reaching into the same well of discipline that she found when I was sick, I suppose. The same well that pushed her back into a ship full of the dead to find me medicine.

How did I ever think she couldn't judge the depth of her own feelings?

I climb down carefully into the cave, letting a couple of pebbles click together deliberately. She glances up as I walk over, then returns to her work, pushing a spare shirt inside the pillow she's making.

"Do you know what I thought, the first time I saw you, when you were telling off those officers?" There's an edge to my voice, a hesitation— I sound nervous. I'm not, though. I've never been so sure.

She looks up at me again, weariness etched all over her face. She lifts her chin a little as though bracing for a blow. "What did you think, Tarver?"

"I thought, that's my kind of girl."

Her expression doesn't shift.

I let myself smile a little as I ease down to my knees in front of her, every tired muscle protesting the move. "And Lilac, I was right. Forget everything else. Forget everyone else. You're exactly my kind of girl."

"Tarver, you were right to stop me before." Her blue eyes are dark and deep, her hair ablaze with firelight. "This can't happen."

Guilt is written on her features so clearly that it almost breaks my heart. Her breath catches as I reach for her arm to tug her up onto her knees, to my level. "What happened with Simon wasn't your fault. Your father did that—not you. You're not to blame for someone loving you."

She swallows, her eyes meeting mine, uncertain.

I can't stand it anymore, and before I even realize what I'm doing, I'm leaning down to kiss her. A jolt goes through me as our lips meet, and she drops the flashlight with a clatter. She hesitates for a moment, then pulls away from me. I want to lean after her, but I hold myself still, heart hammering. "But—on the plain, you acted like you didn't even want me," she whispers.

"If you really believed that performance, you're crazier than I thought. I've wanted you from the beginning. I thought it was better to keep away, to stay focused on getting us out of here." My voice is hoarse, now. "I was scared of having you, then losing you again. But it would be worth it a thousand times over. I was an idiot, I'm sorry."

Her face is flushing, lips reddening, her fair skin making it easy to see. The urge to kiss her again is overpowering. This time when I lean in she doesn't break away. I bend my head to hers and slide a hand around the small of her back to pull her in. I tease at her lower lip with my teeth and she gasps for a shaky breath.

I pull back a fraction, that tiny distance requiring a monumental effort. "You want me to stop," I manage, barely recognizing my own voice, "you tell me."

It takes me a moment to register her dark eyes, her parted lips, the way she leans after me. Her hand curls around the sleeve of my shirt, trembling. It's then I realize my hands are none too steady either.

"You stop now," she breathes, "and I'll never forgive you."

There's a soft moan as our bodies come together, but I'm not even sure which one of us made the sound.

If a rescue ship landed in the clearing outside just now, I'd keep right on hiding in this cave.

"What about physical changes?"

"Excuse me?"

"Did Miss LaRoux undergo any . . . physical changes to her person while in your company?"

"I think she got a little stronger from all the hiking."

"Major, to what extent did you act upon your feelings for Miss LaRoux?"

"Medium."

"Excuse me?"

"How am I supposed to answer that question?"

"We are attempting to discover what happened. It's in the best interests of all concerned that you answer with the truth."

THIRTY

LILAC

"YOU OKAY?" HE LIFTS HIS HEAD FROM MY NECK, LIPS grazing my jaw.

I shiver, choosing to answer with a small murmur, content. After a moment I open my eyes to find him watching me. His hair is stuck to his forehead, visible in the half-light from the dying fire.

"Happy," I add, just to see the line of his mouth curve upward, highlighted by the dim glow of the coals.

"Good." He leans down to kiss me, keeping his weight off on one elbow. I tilt my chin up, discovering the way it makes him lean into the kiss harder, uttering a sound of mixed satisfaction and surprise.

When he lifts his head again, he moves his hand from my waist to trail a fingertip along the edge of my brow, down across my cheek, nudging a few stray hairs away from my face.

"You've got no idea how long I've wanted to do that." His voice is still a little hoarse, and my stomach lurches in response.

"You took your sweet time." I try for airy and unconcerned, though I know my performance is not convincing.

He laughs, and I watch his mouth, distracted, and almost miss what he says next: "I'm pretty sure if I'd tried to kiss you while dragging you through the forest that first day, you would've thrown one of those ridiculous shoes at my head."

I expect him to put up a fight when morning arrives and I suggest, a little wistfully, that we take a rest day. I don't want to leave our bed, don't want to find clothes, don't want to be apart from him. The way he looks at me now is so different. Clear, unguarded, warm. I didn't even know there'd been a wall between us, until now, seeing it gone.

Instead of putting on his soldier voice and saying something about getting a march on the day, he just stretches and gathers me against him with one arm. The other, he tucks behind his head, looking up at the ceiling of the cave, where a little daylight comes through a crack. The light plays over the cavern walls, revealing formations carved over the ages—stalagmites reaching up from the ground for their twins overhead, vast curtains of gleaming limestone dripping down from the ceiling.

"I can't think of any way inside that building. For now, there's nothing we have to do that requires immediate attention."

I prop myself on my elbow, staring at him. "What do you mean, nothing we have to do?"

"Just what I said, beautiful." He grins at me, making my stomach flutter. No one in my old life would be permitted to grin at me like that. "You think I have any burning desire to get out of bed today?"

I can't help but smile back at him. He leans up and kisses me, a brief thing before he starts to pull away again. He pauses, eyes half closed, thoughtful, before leaning up once more, taking his time, his mouth warm against mine. By the time he pulls away, my heart is pounding.

"I'll get us some breakfast," he says, slipping out of our nest and tucking the blankets back around me. He hauls his pants on but doesn't bother with his belt, letting them hang low on his hips. I curl into the warm space beside me that he left behind and watch him as he moves around the camp. How is it that I can want him so badly when he's only been gone from me for a minute?

He rummages in his pack, searching for ration bars. After a moment he pauses, staring down at something in the bag. I see only a flash of silver as he picks it up, closing his hand around it, but I know what it is—the case containing the picture of his family.

It's then that I realize something that began to take root the day we climbed the wreck, looking for our next move. When I discovered that the thought of living here didn't hurt. The truth is that I don't *want* us to be rescued. I wish I could stay here, with Tarver, forever—even if forever is only a few short years, or months, or days, before the savageness of the planet overcomes us. Because the moment the rescue ships touch down, I'll never see Tarver Merendsen again.

And this is the thing I've been trying to fight, because I know it's not the same for him. I know he couldn't be happy here, not when his heart is in a little garden cottage with a teacher and a poet and the memory of his brother.

I watch as he sets the silver case aside, carefully, tenderly. He returns to his search, but I can see the grief lingering in his expression.

It doesn't matter that being rescued means the end of us—that it means a return, for me, to a life unlived, watched every moment and kept apart from anything that could touch me. All that matters is that he gets home. That his parents don't have to suffer the loss of their second child.

We have to get inside that building. By the time Tarver returns to me, I am smiling, and I wrap myself around him. But even as he murmurs in my ear, kisses my shoulder, twines his fingers in my hair, my mind is working. I'll think of a way.

It isn't until late afternoon that we finally drag ourselves from bed, and only then because we need to refill the canteen from the spring. We locate clothes and take a walk through the woods afterward, making our way back toward the building.

I try the shutters again; he taps at the door to gauge its thickness. We share a few ideas, each more improbable than the last. Tentatively we think about some sort of battering ram, but even if we use the rusted tools to chop down a tree, there's no way the two of us could lift and swing a log big enough to break a steel door. Whatever supplies or equipment might be inside stay firmly locked up.

I hear whispers of sound at the edge of my hearing, rising like rain hissing across the grass toward me. There's an urgency in the voices that moan in my ear, pleading, pained. They're always coming from the station itself—we're not the only ones who desperately want to find a way to get the station open. The whispers have been leading us here all along, and now they're beseeching us to come inside.

Eventually, as dusk approaches, we give up and return to our cave to rekindle the fire and reassemble our bed, which, over the course of last night, got scattered about the place. As I'm rebuilding pillows and settling blankets, Tarver's crouched by the fire. Tonight he's building it up high. Easier to be naked, he says, when you're not freezing.

"Slumming's not so bad, is it, Miss LaRoux?" he teases, flopping onto our makeshift bed and pulling me down on top of him.

Frustration flares, despite the urge to let it slide under the circumstances. "Do you really have to do that, after everything? Act like you're beneath me?"

He smiles again, shrugging, dismissive. "The whole universe knows I'm beneath you, Miss LaRoux. It doesn't bother me."

"Fifty thousand people on that ship, give or take." I choose my words carefully. "Three thousand of them soldiers. At least a dozen decorated war heroes. I looked at *you*."

He starts to speak, but I run my hand along his arm, and this is enough to make him hesitate, voice catching in his throat at my touch. This newfound power is intoxicating.

"Do you think I like you just because you saved my life? Because you know what to do and I don't, because you make sure I eat enough and you keep me from losing my mind? Because you're the only man on the planet?"

He protests, but I see it in his face. I'm not completely wrong.

"It is," I whisper. "It's because of all those things. It's because of your strength, but it's because of your goodness too, and your softness. You act like you inherited nothing from your mother, but that's not true. There's—there's poetry in you."

He inhales sharply, the arm around me tightening and his fingers twisting into my hair, tugging at it, tugging me close. I can't breathe—I don't want to. When he speaks his voice shakes a little, the way it did right before he kissed me for the first time.

"Sometimes you take all my words away from me." He leans back onto his elbow, then pulls me down to him so he can stop me answering with the press of his lips. When he breaks the kiss I end up blinking down at him, breathless.

"I'm still not sure you're right, Miss LaRoux," he murmurs. "I *am* beneath you."

It takes me a few seconds to see the spark of amusement in his eyes as he looks up at me. I realize he's laughing, in his way, not at my expense but because he's happy too. So I blurt one of the words I learned from him in his fever, and reach for the laundry bag that serves as our pillow to swing it at his head.

He catches my wrist before I come close, moving with such speed that I'm left gasping, laughing as he pulls me back down into our nest. He stops my laughter with his mouth, sending electricity crackling down my spine, like sparks resting in my belly.

Tarver tilts his head to kiss me behind my ear, teasing. I lift my chin and he makes his way down my throat, the softness of his mouth at a sharp contrast to the roughness of the stubble on his face.

Sparks, I think, something in the back of my mind stirring. The seed of an idea, the one I've been trying to ignore, leaps into a fully fledged plan.

"We should blow the doors off the station."

Tarver stops mid-kiss, lifting his head and looking absolutely baffled. "We should what now?"

"The doors! They're too thick to break open with any battering ram we could lift, but an explosion? That would do it, wouldn't it?"

He's blinking at me, half confused, half cranky. He doesn't like being interrupted. "You're being even more bewildering than usual."

I laugh, reaching up to run my fingers through his hair. "The hovercraft, in the shed? There are fuel tanks in the back. Stack a few of those up against the door, make a fuse out of some string, and we've got ourselves a party."

His expression is shifting from cranky to cautiously impressed, and I can't help but feel a thrill of excitement that he's impressed with *me*. Genuinely, without sympathy or surprise. Like equals.

"Who are you," he says eventually, "and what have you done with my Lilac?"

My Lilac. I want to stop and revel in that, but I'm too excited by my idea. "Anna has older brothers, and when I was little we'd blow things up all the time on our tennis court. My father had to have it resurfaced *so* many times." The memory causes a pang, my throat closing a little. For the loss of my cousin, for the loss of the way things were when we were children—for the loss of my own childhood.

Tarver's eyes soften, seeing my face. "We'll have to be careful. Clear the trees from the door, minimize the debris and the danger of a fire afterward."

There's an electricity in the air, a nearly tangible sense of purpose. We have a plan. I ignore the stab of pain that lances through me—now there's a limit on our time together. A countdown clock, set to some finite amount I can't see. Each moment is one we'll never get together again.

"Could we use your gun to set it off?"

His lips purse, thoughtful. "The Gleidel was designed to interact with organic matter—not metallic. Meant to prevent anyone dumb enough to fire it on a ship from breaching the hull. Wouldn't so much as scratch the tank." He reaches out to trace his fingers along my lips.

"A fuse, then. Like we used as kids." I close my eyes and kiss his fingers as they wander across my mouth. "I've never used fuel as an explosive, but the principle's bound to be the same. A sudden impact like that should blow the doors right open, leave the rest of the station intact."

Tarver makes a low sound in his throat, making me shiver. "Keep talking about blowing things up," he suggests, bending his head to resume what he was doing before I interrupted him.

It takes nearly an entire day to clear the area in front of the station doors. The power tools have long since lost their charge, so we're using rusty saws and a big pair of shears from the shed. We probably would have finished earlier, but I keep finding myself at his side without remembering the impulse to go to him. I keep demanding kisses, and he keeps dropping what he's doing to oblige. We don't make a very good team, distracting each other from what we're meant to be doing. We cut down the young trees, clear away the brambles, stack four of the fuel tanks against the doors.

I look over the dents and damage on the tanks, and finger the uneven length of rope we've found for a fuse. Suddenly I'm not so sure this is as foolproof as I'd thought. There are so many ways it could go wrong.

As the sun slants through the trees, close to the horizon, Tarver drags the last of the fallen saplings away and then arches his back until it pops.

I move toward him and he lifts his arm without looking, knowing I'll be there. I slip beneath it, wrapping my arms around his waist.

"Do we do it now?" I rest my mouth against his chest, eyes turned up to look at him. Let him be the judge of when we start being rescued. I can't see it objectively. I so badly want it and don't—I'm caught so tightly between staying and going.

"Depends on what you mean by 'it,'" he says, letting his fingers creep in against my arm under the edge of my T-shirt sleeve.

"Quit it," I reply, though I doubt he'll take me seriously with laughter in my voice.

"Not tonight," he says before leaning down to kiss me. It's a long moment before he speaks again. "We'll wait until there's good light, when we're sure we're ready. Tomorrow."

"If people were stationed here, there could be food inside. Hot water, maybe, if there's a generator inside. Beds too." I grin at him. "Though I suppose not having a bed hasn't really been a problem for us so far."

Tarver lifts an eyebrow, shifting his weight and wrapping both arms around me. "No, but the ground *does* have its limitations."

He leans down to kiss me again, his bandaged hand sliding up my side under my shirt, and that reminder of his injury—how close I came to losing him—sends a jolt through me. I can't let him be the one to do this. We don't know how volatile the fuel tanks are, or how fast the fuse will burn.

I let him kiss me for a while, wait until I feel him make the soft, growly noise he usually makes before he tries to remove some item of my clothing. Let him be as distracted as possible, before I try to do this. Because he's not going to like it.

I pull my mouth away a fraction and murmur, "I'll start testing fuses tomorrow morning. I don't relish the idea of losing a hand lighting this thing."

Tarver starts to lean in again, but then stops, frowning at me a little. "I don't relish the idea of you losing a hand either. I like both of yours. I'll do it."

"Don't be silly," I say, trying out my best, most capable smile. I can't let him see how desperately I need him to believe me. How much I need him to not get hurt if something goes wrong. "I did this all the time when I was a kid, my father never knew."

He's still frowning, something lurking in his expression—fear? I can't make it out. "I know how to take a hit," he says. "How to drop and protect myself in an explosion."

"But I won't *need* to do that, because I know what I'm doing. I'm not trying to be a hero or anything. I'll be perfectly safe. If something did go wrong, if something happened to you, I'd last a grand total of ten seconds out here by myself. But if something happened to me, you'd be just fine."

He's gazing at me like I've just offered to stab him in the gut. I can almost see him fighting with himself. But I'm right, and if nothing else he'll have to see my conviction. I can see his fevered face in my mind's eye, and my throat constricts just remembering how close I was to losing him. I can't let that happen again.

"It's a simple risk-reward analysis," I murmur. "You taught me that."

Tarver lifts one hand to touch my face, tracing the curve of my cheek. "Lilac, if something happened to you," he murmurs, "I would be anything but fine."

I reach up to take his hand, curling my fingers through his.

"Lilac, are you *sure*?"

I squeeze his hand, looking up at him, letting him see the confidence, the easy knowledge. I can do this. I will him to see it, with every fiber of my being. I can't let him light the fuse. I can't watch him put himself in danger again.

"Positive."

His gaze searches mine for a few moments as I hold my breath. Then he ducks his head to kiss my forehead, and turns to lead the way back to the cave.

There aren't many things my old life prepared me for. Not many skills developed in the world of society, of balls and dresses and intrigue, apply out here in the wild, with this man I would've never known but for this strange twist of fate.

But at least I'm still a good liar.

"You were found not far from the structure. Can you clarify what happened to it?"

"I was trying to get inside. Whoever left it last was inconsiderate enough to lock the doors, so we had to get creative."

"And was Miss LaRoux involved in this act of vandalism?"

"Vandalism? We were trying to survive."

"Shall I repeat the question?"

"Of course she wasn't."

"And yet you say you were together the entire time."

"Miss LaRoux isn't the kind of girl to get her hands dirty. She waited in the woods, out of harm's way."

THIRTY-ONE

TARVER

"I WONDER IF THE KITCHEN'S STILL WORKING. JUST THINK, real food could be on the other side of that door." She wants to distract me that night, keep us from revisiting the conversation about the fuse. I've considered telling her that if she wants to distract me, all she has to do is take her shirt off.

"I hope so." My head hurts with misgivings. I know it's smarter to let her light it. She's done it before. If she's hurt, I can help her better. She's less likely to *be* hurt.

And still.

"A bed too, no more sleeping on the ground."

I squeeze her. "You do keep ending up back at the bed. You have a preoccupation, Miss LaRoux."

"Any objections?" She's arch, smug, running a hand up my arm. If I were wearing a shirt, she'd be tugging on my sleeve, summoning me for a kiss as though she can't bear to be apart any longer. She's noticed she can make me forget my words halfway through a sentence.

"Objections? Hell, no." I'm so tempted to let her have her way, to just give in to her attempts to distract me. She can make my mind shut down faster than anyone I've ever met. But I'm still not sure. "Maybe we just leave the building," I suggest quietly. "Let it stay as it is. Do we really need to get inside this badly?"

Her hand stops, and she pulls back far enough to look at me. "Are you serious?"

"I'm not an idiot, Lilac." I trace her cheekbone with my fingertips, watching the color spring to her fair skin at my touch. "I know how dangerous this is."

"It's our only chance at being rescued. There has to be communications equipment inside, something we can use to send a distress signal."

Maybe being rescued isn't my top priority anymore. The words are there, just not the courage to say them. Instead, I pull her closer, tightening my arm around her waist. "I hope so. We don't even know why this place was abandoned. Something to do with the whispers, I suppose, but what exactly?"

"Secrets upon secrets," Lilac murmurs. Before I can ask what she means, she draws in one of those slow, careful breaths that mean she's organizing her thoughts before she speaks. "You said there were rumors about the military experimenting with mind control and telepathy. Maybe corporations are too. What if that's what this is?"

It's a little disconcerting that Lilac thinks best in bed. My brain pretty much flatlines under the same circumstances. "You think they discovered these beings, and then hid this place from the rest of the galaxy so they could study them."

"I don't know what's on this planet, Tarver, but whatever—whoever— it is, they can do things. See into our hearts, change our dreams, make us think things. They can create objects out of thin air. Who knows what else they can do? I know that any corporation, or the military for that matter, would stop at nothing for power like that."

I'm trying to ignore the sick feeling in my stomach, but I know she's right. There aren't many corporations with the resources to terraform planets that are known for their compassion and moral fiber.

"Whatever's going on," Lilac continues, "the whispers led us here. The answers are inside that building. We'll find out tomorrow."

I find a grin. "Tomorrow," I echo, giving her a squeeze.

She curls against me, tucking herself perfectly along my side. "What will we do, if we're rescued? After we've finished eating and drinking and smiling for the cameras?"

"*You'll* be smiling for the cameras," I correct her, laughing.

"You'll have your fair share," she tells me. "You're the one who saved the life of Roderick LaRoux's only daughter. It'll be hard to slip away."

"My commanding officer will sort it out. I'll get a week to go home and show my parents I'm whole, then a posting somewhere quiet for a while. Very quiet, if we've seen things we're not supposed to." Her skin's so impossibly soft. My hands feel rough against it as I run my palm down her side.

She's quiet for a little, holding still against me, not leaning into my hand as she usually does. I wait, and let her turn it over in her mind. Eventually she speaks again. "You'll just—disappear?" The question's very soft. "What about you and me? What happens to us, if you just vanish?"

I have no flippant answer for her, no deflection this time. I don't know what happens to us. It's the question I've been trying to avoid every second of every day since we saw the building on the horizon, and discovered the possibility of rescue after all.

"I'm not fourteen anymore." She lifts herself up on one elbow, gazing at me. "My father is powerful, changing the galaxy to suit him, but he's not going to change this. He's strong, but I'd fight him." Her blue eyes are grave, determined—calm. "I'd fight for you."

She's stolen my breath. My hand tightens at her waist until she makes a soft sound of protest, and it takes me a moment to realize I'm hurting her. I want to kiss her until she's as lost as I am. My heart fills my chest.

But I've seen what happens when people go back to the real world. I've seen what happens when they're reunited with their friends, their families. When the everyday rhythms reassert themselves, little currents pulling and tugging them back into the stream of life. Right now this is what she wants, but when she's back in a life with no room for someone like me? If I let her make these promises and then have to watch her return to her old life, leaving me and all we've gone through behind . . . I'm not sure I can survive that.

With an effort I force myself to start breathing again.

"Lilac." My voice sounds weak even to me. "Neither of us should make promises like that."

She swallows. "Are you saying that because you aren't sure, or because you think I'm not?"

"I'm saying I don't think it's as simple as either of us would like it to be."

"It's the simplest thing in the world," she whispers, leaning down to brush her lips against mine. "But I don't mind waiting until you're sure. You'll come around."

I want to tell her I've already come around, that I was there before she was—that I'd face down an army of paparazzi and her father to boot if she asked me.

But she doesn't know how it can all change when you get back to civilization. And I won't hold her to promises she can't keep.

She takes her time over preparations in the morning. At least this much was true—she does seem to know what she's doing when it comes to blowing things up. No wonder they kept this side of her under wraps—this is hardly an acceptable hobby for the well-bred.

She has me stack the fuel tanks six different ways, she paces out distances, tries different fuses. She dumps out some of the fuel—to leave room in the tanks for vapors, she says. I spend my time clearing anything that might cause damage if it flies through the air, until I'm combing the area for twigs and pebbles and even I have to admit none of them could so much as bruise her. After that I sit at the foot of a tree and watch her.

She's incredible. She's so composed, so determined, twitching the fuse with two fingers to change the angle a little. There are moments like this when I can actually imagine her at my parents' cottage. I can see her hauling wood with the rest of us, chopping vegetables, going for long walks and calling it entertainment. I think my parents would like her.

I can see her happy there. I just wish I knew whether I'm only seeing what I want so badly to see.

Crouched by the end of the fuse, she looks over her shoulder and smiles at me, and I smile back, helpless.

Then I realize that she's bending her head to strike a match, and something clicks together in my head. She can't. She mustn't. My daydreams scatter and I scramble to my feet, too slow, helpless—I don't know how I know, but every instinct I have is screaming at me as she leans down to touch the flame to the fuse.

The little spark races up the string fuse, too fast. The wind picks up, and the fuse burns quicker, leaping up toward the barrels.

She spots it as I do, and she whirls away from it. I stand helplessly by the tree. I can't move.

She makes it seven steps before the fuel tanks explode.

The flames blossom out behind her, and the *boom* comes an instant later. The building's tearing open like a tin can, and Lilac's thrown through the air like she weighs nothing at all. She hits the ground with a thud, rolling over and over as debris rains down around her. My body fails me, locking in place and keeping me from her. I rip my foot from where I'm rooted to the ground and finally start moving. She's facedown, unmoving, lying amid a dozen tiny grass fires as the last light particles fall around us.

I throw myself down beside her, turn her over with a hand at her shoulder and one at her hip. My throat is frozen, unable to even whisper her name. She lets me move her without protest, one arm wrapped around her middle, the other reaching weakly up for me.

Her face is white, but apart from the dirt smudges and the bruise across her cheek, she looks unscathed. For the first time since the explosion, I feel myself take a full breath.

"That was exciting," she murmurs, her eyes still closed. "Did it work?"

"I think they saw it from space," I whisper, leaning down over her to press my forehead to hers. "Are you all right?"

"Shh." Her voice is almost inaudible. "Tarver, I need you to—" She breaks off to groan softly, her mouth tightening, eyes squeezing tighter shut, pinched with pain.

My heart contracts. "Lilac, tell me what hurts."

Her hand curls around my sleeve, the way she usually summons me for a kiss. She opens her eyes with a visible effort, blinking until she can focus on me. "Just listen, okay? When you get inside—should be a generator. You have to—to get enough power for a signal."

"Lilac, stop, that doesn't matter." She's in pain somewhere, though I can't see where. My hands are shaking as I start unbuttoning her shirt. "We'll handle that when we get inside."

"Don't think we will," she whispers, hoarse. Then she lifts her hand away from where it's wrapped around her middle, and shows me what she's hiding, what she's holding together. A tangle of bloodstained shirt and skin, the glint of metal embedded deep.

I can't hear, can't see, can't think.

My body knows what to do, though. "Put the pressure back on, keep your hand on it." My voice snaps orders like I'm out in the field. I scramble across to our pack to haul out the first-aid supplies she salvaged from the *Icarus*, sending bottles and bandages flying in every direction as I dig for the one vial that matters. "Keep your hand on it, we have a coagulant."

"Don't." Her voice is weak, though she presses her hand back over the wound. "You'll need it later, until help comes."

"I need it now." Finally I find it, tearing the wrapper off a needle and scrambling back to her on hands and knees. Breathe in—one, two. Breathe out—one, two. My hand steadies. I fit the bottle to the needle, watching as it fills, lifting it, tapping it free of bubbles.

It's not enough. I know that as I slide the needle into her skin. It can't stop this kind of bleeding. The shrapnel went straight through her gut. This injection can't sew her back together.

"Please," she whispers, flinching.

I throw the empty needle aside and haul my shirt off over my head, lifting her hand and pressing the fabric against her abdomen. "I'm here, Lilac, I'm here. I promise. I'm right beside you."

She pushes weakly at my arm, shock overtaking sense as her gaze slides past me to the sky beyond. "This is why it's better. I'd be in pieces, if it were you."

I am in pieces, Lilac.

But my body keeps moving, my mouth keeps talking. "Stop it, I've seen this before. We can fix this." I press down on the wound and reach out with my other hand to touch her cheek, trying to guide her gaze back to my face. I want her to look at me.

She whimpers, and the sound breaks my heart. "Tarver, it's okay. Don't start lying to me again. I'm not afraid." But she's crying, tears leaking out the corners of her eyes and running down her temples, leaving pale tracks in the dirt.

I don't know what to say. Words abandon me.

"Tell my daddy—" She breaks off to cough, and blood trickles down from the corner of her mouth. I see the confusion start to take her. I've seen this before, too.

No. Please, no.

Her hand lifts to grab at me, finding my arm and clutching tight. "Tarver." Her whisper's a gurgle, the blood in her throat now. "I lied. I'm—I don't want to die." Her blue eyes are wide and terrified as she gazes past me.

I'm shaking as I ease down to stretch out beside her, pressing my forehead to her temple, whispering my words against her skin. "I'm here." I can barely make myself loud enough, but I think she hears me. "I promise, I'm right here, Lilac. I won't go anywhere. I won't leave."

She struggles for another breath, reaching across to touch my face, her fingertips trailing across my cheek. "I thought . . ."

Her hand goes limp, and I feel the moment the life goes out of her. For a moment we lie perfectly still together, neither of us breathing. And then my treacherous lungs contract, and send me gasping for air no matter how I try to stop.

She remains still, silent. Her eyes, like reflecting pools, show me the trees, the leaves, the sky.

"Are you all right, Major? Your throat seems a little dry."

"I'm sorry, could you repeat the question?"

THIRTY-TWO

TARVER

THIS IS SHOCK. I KNOW THAT FROM MY FIELD TRAINING. MY mouth is dry, and my hands are starting to tremble. I'm cold.

I stare down at her face, but it's like I'm looking at her through glass, removed. I find myself noticing trivial things—the length of her eyelashes, the new freckles that stand out on her pale cheeks. She never knew about those.

But I saw them, and I loved them, I loved—

I should close her eyes, I know that. There are steps to be followed. My body's trying to move, trying to do what it's done before, but I can't stop shaking. I observe the tiny cuts and blackened fingernails on my hand, and wait for it to stop trembling so I can brush her eyelids, but it won't. It worsens, and I stare at it, fascinated.

The brain places importance on these small nothings to distract itself from overwhelming trauma. Instinct causes it to start memorizing details feverishly when it's in danger. I've been trained for this.

No. No one trained me for *this*.

I know there's this other thing I should be thinking about, this other thing I know, but every time I try to approach it my mind reels away, shuddering. I can't think it. I can't know it.

The bile rises up my throat in a rush, and I wheel away from her to plant my hands in the grass as I cough, gag, then swallow hard. I'm panting, but I keep from throwing up. My elbows start to bend, and I lock them in place.

I know with utter certainty that if I let myself fold to the ground beside her, I'll stay there forever. The lessons they've drilled into me forbid it.

I stagger to my feet, movements clumsy. I'm swaying when I stand, looking around the clearing for something—anything—that will tell me what to do. The small fires from the explosion are burning out. Time must have passed. I don't remember.

And I don't know what to do. There's nothing here. No protocol, no notification, no debriefing, no—anything. Just me, standing in the middle of the clearing, Lilac at my feet.

The building is still smoking, one wall blown inward, debris scattered and metal twisted. The trees around the edge of the clearing bow inward, the forest beyond utterly silent. The tiny details of the scene clog my thoughts, dragging my attention away from this thing I can't understand.

I try again to push past the great wall of resistance in my mind.

Lilac is dead.

Nothing.

Lilac took shrapnel. Lilac bled out.

Nothing. I can say it to myself, I can push the words around in my mind, but there's not even a twitch of a response. They're just words. Stupid, impossible words—so ridiculous that I ignore them.

I try again, something smaller, like worrying at a loose tooth or picking at a scab.

Lilac won't talk to me again.

There's a tremor.

Lilac won't kiss me again. I won't hear her laugh.

My lungs constrict.

Why am I doing this to myself?

I don't know how to grieve. I've seen death before. I've seen it at close quarters, felt the heat of it on my skin. I've seen it from a safe, clinical distance, in the statistics on my intelligence reports. I've seen whole platoons die, too many to meaningfully understand.

I've seen my friends die, witnessed their final moments and accepted last messages to loved ones they never truly believed they'd leave.

When it was Alec, my mother needed me, and so I refused to succumb—but that didn't mean I stopped trying to grapple with what had happened. Soul of a poet, she always said. But I worked through it quietly, holding the grief inside myself, somewhere secure. Emotion had no place at my briefings. In the field, it was simply dangerous. You shut it away, mourned later, silently.

This is different. This is deafening, consuming. There is no next task. There are no other soldiers to see to. No parents who need me.

Just my Lilac, blood still seeping out across her shirt, even with her heartbeat stopped. Her skin, still warm, eyes open, face slack.

This is beyond comprehension. This is too much. I can still hear her voice.

If something did go wrong, if something happened to you, I'd last a grand total of ten seconds out here by myself. But if something happened to me, you'd be just fine.

I answered her. I remember that, too. *I would be anything but fine.*

In fact, I'm nothing. I don't exist. I'm lost.

I drop to one knee to gather her up in my arms, and she lolls horribly against me, head tipping back, arm slipping to hang down limply. Her skin feels different already.

I gather her in closer, so her head tips in against my shoulder. Her blood stains my skin. I carry her down the path to the cave.

I can't bury her today. I'm not strong enough to dig the hole. Some horrible, practical part of me knows that I'll dig until I'm exhausted, and it won't be deep enough. It will have to be tomorrow.

And I'm not ready to let her out of my sight yet.

I lay her down on our bed, carefully straightening her neck and folding her hands. I settle the pillow under her head.

I lie down beside her on the stone floor of the cave, rolling over on my back to stare up at the daylight coming in through the chink in the stone that serves as our chimney. I curl my hand around her cold one.

Sometime later, I realize there's no more light coming in through the crack in the ceiling.

I'll bury her in the morning. Not yet.

I feel like I'm observing these events taking place, without revealing myself or participating. I'm watching a boy lie on the floor of a cave beside a girl. In the darkness, they look like they're asleep.

The idea of the building drifts into my head eventually. I can picture the wall, forced in by the explosion. My memory of it is obscured by smoke and dust, so I can't see inside. I know, in a dull, uncaring way, that I should go and explore it tomorrow. Except that I can't imagine bringing myself to walk through the broken doorway.

A few minutes later, or a few hours, I notice the Gleidel digging into my back. I angle an arm to retrieve it, fingers wrapping around the familiar grip, sliding into place. I lift it and position the barrel underneath my chin. I nudge the barrel to the left so it sits in just the right spot.

The compulsion creeps up through me, starting somewhere in my belly. It travels up my spine, tingling down the length of my arm, until my finger tightens a fraction. It would be so easy to let it tighten just a fraction further. Nobody's coming. Nobody would find us. They think we're dead already.

Nobody would ever know what I chose.

It's dark when I wake, and cold. My bones ache, and I'm on stone, not blanket. Where the hell is Lilac? Has she pushed me away and stolen the blankets?

I smile faintly to myself. Unlikely. She's so insistent at night, snuggling in against me and teasing me that she'll steal all my warmth, leach it out of me. She presses her back in against my front, and I wrap my arms around her and bury my face in her hair, then—

The memory hits me like a body blow. My throat closes, muscles tensing, mind reeling. I can't remember how to move—my limbs are numb. Then, slowly, unwillingly, I reinhabit my body.

I push up onto one elbow, my back screaming a protest after lying on the cold ground for so long.

My eyelids are heavy and reluctant, but I blink to clear my vision.

Lilac's sitting in front of me, cross-legged, smiling.

My breath jams in my throat, and I roll onto one side, coughing, gasping for breath.

Lilac lies beside me, dead.

It only takes a moment to realize that the body beside me is barely visible, a silhouette to my night vision. The girl sitting cross-legged before me is sunlit, vivid, impossible. Shaking, choking on the metallic taste the vision brings to the back of my mouth, I drag myself upright. As I watch her, an image blossoms across the wall of the cave. My parents' house springs to life: white walls, green leaves, and the purple flowers that share Lilac's name.

I see the wooden front door, the windows and window boxes, filled to overflowing with herbs and yellow flowers. As I watch, a pathway appears, grass swaying on either side of it. It threads its way down to where she sits, curling past her so now she's relaxing in my mother's garden.

I can't do this.

I only realize I still have the Gleidel in my hand when I lift it, aiming it at the ceiling. The laser shrieks when I pull the trigger, and the room's lit for an instant by the bolt of energy, like a lightning strike. The image flickers, then solidifies once more. How *dare* they show her to me? How do they dare touch her memory?

"Get out!" My voice is hoarse, ragged, throat feeling like it tears with the shout. "Get out, get away from her. Get *away*."

I lift the gun a second time, and the blast of sound echoes again as the shot dislodges a shower of sand and pebbles. "Don't touch her. Where was your goddamn warning this time? What was the point in getting her out of that cave? What was the point in dragging her halfway across your forsaken planet, to do this? To let her bleed out? We should have died in our pod, like everybody else. You should've just let us die together."

I can't think about why they're showing her to me now, what purpose could be behind their torture. My voice is giving out, words jagged, slicing my throat. *"Go."* I close my eyes. "You could have saved her. You could have warned her. *You did this.*"

When I open my eyes again, the vision is gone, and I'm alone in the dark.

I crawl over to the pack, pulling out the last of the blankets, and I roll myself in it to lie back down. I close my eyes, breathing out slowly, waiting for the trembling to stop.

In the morning my body's stiff and sore from a night sleeping on hard stone, and I silently stretch out my cramped limbs.

I walk back to the clearing, keeping my gaze away from the blasted hole in the wall of the building. Keeping my gaze away from the blood soaked into the grass. I cross over to the shed where the fuel was stored, reaching past the paint tins for the shovel. I carry it back some distance from the mouth of the cave, and there I dig. The ground is sandy on top, the hole collapsing in on itself as the top crust keeps crumbling. Lower down the soil is darker, more densely packed. I set the edge of the shovel against it, then drive it down with my foot. It takes both hands to lever it back with my weight.

Three hours later, it's deep enough.

I wash my hands and face in the stream before I go back to her. Sometimes, a day later, the body is still stiff. It's mostly passed, though, and I lift her without trouble.

I climb down into the grave and lay her out carefully, wrapping her in a blanket. I crouch beside her, gazing down at her face, wishing I had words, or tears, or something to offer her. But this is beyond all of that.

I carefully lay the cloth across her face so the dirt won't touch her. Then I rest my hands on the edge of the hole and hoist myself up.

I've never been to a funeral that wasn't military, and that recitation doesn't fit. I don't know the words to any prayers. Eventually, thinking of Alec, feeling him beside me, I begin to scrape the dirt back into the grave, shutting my ears to the way it patters down onto the blanket.

There are flowers growing everywhere in the woods. I'd been planning, once we were into the building, to pick some of them and lay them all around our bed. A surprise for her when she woke.

I pick them in armfuls now, covering the low mound of dirt until not a glimpse of brown is visible. Now it looks no different from a patch of wildflowers growing in the forest. You could walk right by it, and never know it was there.

Except that I do. It's my landmark, now. I'll always know how far I am from this spot. From her.

I sleep, lying on one side of the blankets, as though there should be another body sharing them with me. I find that her scent clings to the pillow, and I bury my face in it at night.

I walk left of center along the path we wore through the trees, leaving room for her at my side.

I eat, breaking the ration bar in half automatically before I realize I have nobody to hand it to.

I go back to the mound of flowers, adding fresh ones, taking out those that die each day.

I can't count the days.

I can't think.

I can't focus.

I can't go into the building. I can't leave.

I sleep again. I eat again.

I fall asleep each night with the cold metal barrel of the Gleidel against my throat.

I see her again as I duck out of the afternoon sunlight and into the cave, arms laden with another load of wood. She's standing with her back to me, beside our bed—where her body lay for a night. This time there's no false sunlight, no vision of my parents' cottage. She's wearing the same green dress she was wearing when we crashed, as ragged and ruined as it was when she finally traded it for clothes from the wreck. She always wears that dress, in my memory.

She turns her head, and I feel a sick rush. They're doing it again. I'm not angry. Just tired and hurting. I don't want this vision. It feels like they're trying to force me to keep moving, trying to keep me from giving in. *Don't let her death be for nothing*, they're saying. But it is for nothing. I am nothing, without her.

"I told you to stop." My voice is a hoarse growl, roughened with disuse. It's been days since I've spoken. I don't know how many. "I'm not doing anything for you."

She jerks at the sounds of my voice, turning abruptly to face me. Her face is a pale smear in the darkness, but I hear her gasp, and the hitch of her breath. She doesn't speak. They never speak, these visions. The voices only came to Lilac on the wind, disembodied, incomprehensible. I never heard them. "Please, don't." I don't know if they can understand me when I speak, but maybe they'll read the grief in my thoughts.

She lurches backward, stumbling over the pile of supplies and knocking the canteen over to clang against a rock. She clamps her hands over her ears, crying out as she backs up to press herself against the stone wall, her breathing harsh, audible over the echoes.

There's something wrong. Something different. My mind is sluggish, struggling to understand what's changed. The canteen. The noise. This vision is solid—it can touch things.

"How did you do that?" I'm asking them, but she's the one that cringes.

I walk farther into the cave, slow and cautious.

She flinches at every footstep and presses herself back against the cave wall. She's watching me like a trapped animal, gaze skittering away from me, then drawn back again—as though she can't quite look at me, and can't quite look away.

I want to close my eyes at the sight of her. I want to drink her in. "Please." I'm not sure what I'm asking for.

I'm only a few feet away when she cries out like she's in pain, lurching sideways and stumbling away from me. She trips over a stalagmite, crashing down onto her hands and knees—she scrambles up with a desperate haste, and I tear after her as she disappears through the cave's entrance.

And then I see it, a thrill of shock running through me. A smear of blood where she squeezed through the narrow opening.

How could a vision be bleeding?

My tiredness falls away now as instinct sends adrenaline surging through my limbs, and I dodge through the trees after her as she runs along the bank of the stream. I don't realize where she's heading until we're nearly there.

She only halts when she reaches the center of the clearing, stopping sharply at the bloodstained, flattened spot in the middle of it where Lilac died. There, she drops to her knees, chest heaving as she struggles for breath, one hand lifted to shield her eyes from the pale light of the sun.

I stop at the edge of the clearing, resting one hand against the tree beside me. The bark is rough under my fingers, a contrast to the smooth grip of the Gleidel in my other hand. I don't remember drawing it. "What are you? Where did you come from?"

Her breath catches again, her long shadow quivering as she trembles. It's only then that I realize my hands are steady, my eyes clear. This is no vision.

She lifts her head to look across at me. Her face is flushed with exertion, streaked with tears. The eyes that gazed up lifelessly at the sky are wide and fearful now. Her mouth moves slowly, haltingly, as though it's an effort to speak at all.

"T-Tarver?"

"And you didn't notice anything unusual?"

"Unusual."

"About the structure, Major."

"Oh. No. Nothing unusual."

"Then why did you and Miss LaRoux remain at the station?"

"She believed that rescue teams might be aware of the building's location, and look for us there."

"And you?"

"I was tired of coming up with new plans."

THIRTY-THREE

LILAC

TOO BRIGHT, TOO LOUD. HARSH ON MY SKIN, IN MY EYES. The world tastes like ash and acid, and I am drowning in the air.

He sits opposite, against the stone. He led me here, this cave, made me sit where he could watch. The sun outside has gone while he stared at me, leaving us in darkness. The thing is still in his hand. *Gun,* my mind supplies. His gaze is burning me.

I press my shoulder blades against the wall at my back and clench my jaw at the pain. Every inch of me is raw. The fabric on my body scalds me, like I have no skin, like I'm only blood and bone and pain.

And he stares, always staring, watching me, waiting for something.

Tarver, I know. I know him. I know—

He shifts, the whisper of his shoe on the stone screaming across the distance between us. I gasp, try to retreat through the stone. But I am blood and bone, and I cannot pass that way.

He jumps as I flinch, the barrel of the gun retraining on me, a cold metal eye in the darkness.

"What are you?"

His voice—I can't hear it. It's all wrong. Not supposed to—

"Answer me."

He's so angry. So afraid. I remember—I want to take that fear away. But I don't know how. I can't move, pinned to the wall by his stare. I can feel him dissecting me, peeling me away layer by layer, trying to understand.

I swallow, trying to remember how to answer. "Lilac," I whisper, the name sounding strange. I try again, better this time. "Lilac."

His face ripples, muscles standing out as he clenches his jaw. He leans forward, gesturing with the gun.

"We both know that's not true. She's dead."

Dead.

Dead.

"Tarver." I try his name again, and it sounds better on my lips than my own. "I don't—"

"Don't say it!" He's on his feet, electrified, blazing in the glare of the dark cave. "You say it like—like her."

Then I remember. "Your Lilac."

He's across the space between us before my eyes can follow him, pushing me back against the wall; his hand grasps my shoulder, sending ribbons of pain down my arm.

"Don't say that."

The grief and horror on his face cut deep. I don't recognize my own hand as it reaches for his face.

"Tarver, it's me."

His hand clenching my shoulder shifts, slides up to touch my cheek. Fire. It's all I can do not to jerk away. Grief and anger battle on his features, banishing the flicker of hope that surges there.

"What are you?" he repeats, whispering this time. I realize the gun was pressed against me only when he lowers it, letting it clatter to the ground.

I wish he had pulled the trigger. It would have been easier.

I make myself look in his eyes, fighting every instinct to flee, to find some way back to the dark and the cold and the quiet.

"I don't know."

"Did you and Miss LaRoux wonder why the structure was abandoned?"

"We wondered, but there wasn't much we could do about it."

"Why is that?"

"We had no information."

"And no theories?"

"We had better things to do than speculate."

THIRTY-FOUR

TARVER

I HAVE TO KEEP HER CALM. SHE COULD BE ANYTHING. SHE could *do* anything.

I've brought her back to the cave, and she's been huddling in the corner for nearly three hours. When I come close, she flinches; when I move, she squeezes her eyes shut. Whatever she is, she doesn't feel like much of a threat.

That's not the problem.

The problem is that she looks like Lilac, and she sounds like Lilac, and I can't stand this.

I reach for the canteen and take a long swig. When I set it down on the rock floor of the cave, her breath catches. The sound hurts her ears. I try to remind myself that she's something created, not the original. Not her. *But is there really a difference?* My mind whispers the question.

"Are you in pain?" I can't use her name.

"Everything hurts." She speaks in a tight whisper, trying to keep her voice steady, failing. "The sun, the air. It's like when we came out of the snow in the mountains, so frozen you can't feel anything, until everything starts to burn in the thaw."

"Do you know what's happening?" My voice is rough, agonized. How does she know about the mountains?

"No." The word's nearly lost as she swallows. "What did you do?"

I didn't do anything. This is just another one of the ways this planet screws with your mind. "What do you remember?"

"I don't know." She's still whispering. "Nothing." And then a moment later: "I remember you. Your face. A picture of you . . . of your family. I remember poetry."

This is impossible. How can she know? God, if only she didn't sound like Lilac. My heart twists inside me. She's still huddled against the rock wall like she's trying to melt through it, and as I watch, one hand creeps down to her side, fingers pressing to the spot where her wound was. There's only the ruined satin of her green dress.

"It's okay," I whisper, because she looks just like my girl, and I can't help myself. I don't want her to be scared. "I don't understand either, but you're here, you're safe."

But is she? She came from nothing, will she dissolve right back? Creating a canteen's one thing. This is a human being.

I can be kind to her as long as she lasts, at least.

"How long was I gone?" Her voice is still quiet, quavering.

"A few days." *A few days. Forever. I don't know. You're still gone.*

We lapse into silence, each retreating to our own thoughts. Tiredness creeps over me until it can't be denied, and she watches me wordlessly as I unlace my boots, stretching out on the blankets.

I can't bring myself to imagine she's dangerous. If they wanted to create something that could harm me, one of those giant cats that chased her up a tree would have done.

What they gave me instead might make me want to die, but she won't kill me herself. I know a man can follow a mirage to his death, but at this moment that seems like a good way to die.

She stays curled up in her corner, and in the shadows I can hear her breathing. I don't know how much time goes by.

She's the one who speaks next, her voice echoing out of the black, soft and tired. "I'm sorry I left you."

This creature, or whatever it is, is so like her it's hard to remember she isn't real. Is there any harm in letting myself pretend, just for a moment? In the darkness, it's easier to say things I can't say in the light. "I'm sorry I let you set the fuse. I shouldn't have." Those words twist like a knife. Nothing else matters, except that I let her light that match.

I'll never be able to say these things to my Lilac, but saying it now is better than not saying it at all.

"Oh, Tarver." For a brief moment her voice takes on a hint of color. It's not amusement, but it's a faint upward tilt, the barest echo of a smile. It's even more heartbreaking than her fear. "You think you could have talked me out of it? You didn't stand a chance."

I don't believe that. I could have barked at her. I could have ordered her. I could have pulled the gun on her. She'd probably have done it anyway. My foolish, stubborn girl. I could have stopped her somehow. But there's no point arguing. "Are you hungry?"

"No."

I'm not hungry either, but I force myself to eat half a ration bar. I've been breaking them into pieces and putting them in my mouth and chewing and swallowing for days. I don't remember the last time I tasted one.

When sleep comes, I let it take me. She stays in her corner.

I wake once in the night, and her breathing's not slow enough for sleep, but she doesn't speak, and neither do I.

When I open my eyes in the morning, she's awake too. Maybe she didn't sleep at all. Maybe sleep is too much like the other thing. I can't allow myself to think about that. This isn't *my* Lilac.

We breakfast in silence. I break the ration bar in half automatically and pass it to her, and she reaches out to take the other end of the piece so our fingers don't touch. She's starting to look a little better—there's a hint of color in her cheeks, and it seems like the trembling's a little less. I eat a little and she nibbles, and then we rise without speaking to make our way out of the cave.

We both know without speaking where we're going.

She clears her throat as we step across the stream and start the walk toward the clearing. "I thought I'd seen the last of this dress. I threw away the pieces."

"Me too." I speak without thinking. I can't help but reply—I know she's scared, and she's trying. "It's what you're wearing, when I think of you."

My memory throws up a quick flash of my parents' house. They showed that to me covered in flowers, the way I always remember it. Is that why she's wearing the dress? Because this is the image preserved in my memory?

"Really?" She sounds faintly, briefly amused. "How mortifying." And then, softer, horror creeping into her voice: "I wonder if there are two of them, now."

"Don't think about that." I say it quickly, but it's too late. We both are.

The first room is bare, open to the elements. Our boots crunch on debris as we climb in through the twisted opening. I've seen a hundred outpost entrances like this one—room for a sentry if you need one, or your muddy gear if you don't.

An inner door opens into a larger room lined with monitoring equipment and file cabinets. It's dark, lit only by the light streaming in through the blasted entrance. At some point there was a fire, leaving half-burned pages from the files scattered all around the floor. I can see stacks of printouts, half intact. Some have been dumped in trash cans, where the fire burned out before the documents dissolved completely into ash. I wonder if they hold the answers to our questions about the mirror-moon above us, or the cat beast near our crash site—things that have no place being here.

"These could lead to a generator, or some other power source," she suggests, standing above a bunch of cables that plunge down into the floor. She crosses to a bank of circuit breakers on the wall, jerking open a small door and pumping the switches. For an instant I see her in the pod, stripping wires with her fingernails and hot-wiring our escape.

I close my eyes, trying to shake the image away. This isn't her. Instead I lean down, pressing my cheek to the nearest computer bank. With my eyes closed, I can feel the faintest of vibrations if I hold my breath.

There's still power here. A knot of tension releases inside me, and I stay where I am, letting the monitor take my weight. Power means some chance of a signal. Power means the game's not over yet.

The lights above us flick on one by one, dim from lack of power or long disuse. The walls and the far end of the room are illuminated, covered in something patchy that looks like wallpaper for a moment, completely out of place. Then my words die in my throat.

It's paint.

She turns, and together we stare, uncomprehending. Words and numbers cover the walls, incomprehensible equations and nonsensical half sentences. They start orderly, in marker, scrawled in even lines across the walls. But here and there they start to dip and slant crazily, the marker replaced by paint, until the words devolve into pictures crudely painted on by fingertips. Figures of animals, trees—and men. Handprints. Here and there a swirl of blue stands out amid the earthy reds and browns, electric—always the same shape, a spiral radiating outward. The blue spirals are a focus, but I can make no sense of them. The colors are as bright as if someone had painted them yesterday. With a jolt, I recognize the same reds, blues, and yellows we saw dried on the lids of the paint cans in the shed, back when we inspected the hovercraft.

Paint dribbles down from the walls to the monitors. Some of the paintings are orderly, almost artistic, painted with sensitivity and planning. Clearly identifiable. But overlaid on these murals are cruder, savage depictions of death and carnage, of men and animals fighting and dying. Gaudy crimson streams from a gash across one figure's throat. Another is impaled by a thick slash of black paint, some kind of spear. Red flames stream up from a bonfire laden with bodies.

"They went mad," she whispers, fearful, and I shove my hands in my pockets to keep myself from reaching out to take her hand.

I know what she's thinking—something about this planet sent the people stationed here insane. If an entire station of monitoring specialists, researchers, and whoever else was posted here fell apart so completely, what chance do we have? At least we're starting to get a picture of why this place was abandoned. Why the entire planet stands empty and forgotten. I tear my eyes away from the walls and focus on the lights overhead. We have to keep moving.

I clear my throat, and she startles. "If there's a generator we could turn it off. Disrupt the power, and if they're monitoring it, somebody might show up to do maintenance. Or maybe they're broadcasting updates, we could hack that and try signaling prime numbers to show someone's here?"

"I think we can do better," she says, swallowing hard. Her skin's pale beneath her freckles, but her voice is firmer. I can see it's still an effort to remain composed. Discussing the circuitry and power sources was the right move—like my Lilac, these things interest her. "I think perhaps we could send a real signal."

She drags her eyes away from the paintings and walks slowly back to the circuit breakers. Slowly, she closes the cover so I can see the mark stamped on it. It looks like an upside-down *V,* but everyone in the universe knows that symbol. Even I know it, out in the muddy far reaches of the galaxy. *Especially there.*

The lambda. LaRoux Industries. Not only was this an abandoned terraforming project—it was Lilac's father's.

She says nothing, turning her back on the symbol. We move around the monitoring room, exploring the hatches and machinery, trying to ignore the feeling that the primal figures in the paintings are watching us. We turn for the next door at the same time, and if it had been my Lilac, I would've reached down to wind my fingers through hers. Instead I just stand there, motionless, and let her through ahead of me.

The hall leads to a dormitory full of bunks, and a shower—I press the button and wait as long-disused pipes gurgle and groan a protest, then provide a stuttering flow of water. Half a minute later it steadies out, then begins to heat up. We both stare at it like we've never seen running water before.

"This isn't right," she says. "The lights, the hot water. A generator alone couldn't be doing this, especially after being abandoned so long. There must be another power source."

I reach out and hold my hand under the flow, watching hypnotized as the water curves around my fingers and streams off their tips. It's such a small thing, a shower—and then again, it's everything we haven't had. It's cleanliness and food on plates, and sitting in a chair instead of on a rock. It's civilization, safety. Of course, safety has come too late.

She crosses to inspect a bunch of cables where they plug into a bank of silent computers. "These cables lead downstairs. We should follow them and see where they go."

"Downstairs?" I glance around the confined room. "These places don't usually have an underground level. Are you sure it's not just wiring under the floor?"

"I'm sure," she says, tugging aside a panel to get at the keypad below it. "There's too many of them; there has to be more underneath us."

Observant and thoughtful, just like Lilac. I can barely look at her, and yet I can't look away. Her every word and gesture, every look she gives me . . . they're all Lilac's. But this isn't her. *I watched you die,* my mind screams at her. *I held you while you bled to death.*

In the end I have to leave, put space between us, on the pretext of looking for the underground level she insists is here. It takes me twenty minutes of searching the small base, but eventually I find it. The floor in the hallway is faintly worn, but only halfway. When I crouch to pull up the rubber floor mats, raising a small cloud of grit and dust, I find a hatch.

It's locked, and I try digging my fingers in and prying it out. That doesn't work, and after a few tries I give up. Time for a little gentle persuasion, as my first sergeant used to say.

I stomp hard on the hinges, the vibrations traveling up through my heel. The plastene cracks, but in the end I have to head out to the shed to retrieve the crowbar. In the main room, all I can see is a flash of red hair vanishing below one of the banks of controls as she tries to find out what's underneath. She doesn't look up as I pass by. I yank the hatch cover free. A ladder disappears down into the dark.

I've seen a lot of terraforming monitoring stations—this doesn't come standard.

I take a deep breath. "It's open," I call out, and a few moments later she walks through to stand beside me, looking down into the dark. There's no switch up here—the lights must be operated from down below. I grab my pack—I've gotten trapped in half-destroyed buildings before, and I'm not about to explore without food and water. I head down first and then reach up to steady her as she climbs after me, her breathing growing quick and shallow.

She drops down beside me and then steps away from my hand—still loath to let me touch her. I can't see my hand in front of my face, and the air is perfectly still. It doesn't feel close and stuffy, but that doesn't tell me much. It's bone-achingly cold down here.

We feel around in the dark for the lights and bump into each other, and I wince at the sound of her gasp.

"Where the hell is the switch?" I stumble against the ladder, stifling my curse as my elbow collides with the metal.

As if in answer, a light flickers on overhead. It's a pale, fluorescent ceiling panel that does little to illuminate anything beyond arm's reach. We seem to be at one end of a corridor; the rest of it is lost in darkness. We stand frozen by the sudden light, faces turning up toward it, blinking.

"Was that you?" I ask, despite the fact that she's standing in the middle of the corridor, nowhere near any switch I can see.

She shakes her head no. In the fluorescent light she looks even paler than she does by daylight. "It's like something heard you."

The light flickers, dropping us back into darkness for the space of a heartbeat and then creeping back to life again. I turn, searching again for the switch—but she's found it first. She stands to one side of the hallway, staring at the switch as I cross to her side.

"It's off," she whispers, glancing at me wide-eyed in the dim, wavering light.

"But how . . ."

She suddenly straightens, staring upward at the light. I know that look—it means Lilac's thought of something. But this isn't Lilac. It's a copy. Not real.

"If you can hear us," she says slowly, "blink the light three times."

On command the light cuts out once, twice—we wait, silent. I'm holding my breath. Then the lights click out a third time, and the bottom drops out of my stomach.

"Once for yes, twice for no." I swallow, my mouth dry. "Are you trying to hurt us?"

The lights flicker twice. *No.*

"Warn us?"

A brief pause, then three flickers. Is that a maybe?

"Communicate something else?"

YES.

"Where are you? Why won't you come out and talk to us?" I don't trust anyone who refuses to show themselves.

The lights remain even—there's no answer to that question. I lift both hands to scrub at my face. "Are you *able* to come and talk to us?"

No.

I look over, catching Lilac's eye. She looks back at me, face drained of all color. Then she takes over, her voice quieter than mine, echoing down the corridor.

"Are you what's been sending us visions? Leading us here?"

Yes.

"Did you bring the flower back?"

Pause. *Yes. No.*

Flower? What flower? I want to ask, but Lilac's riveted, her eyes on the lights, scanning them for signs of flickering.

"I don't understand," Lilac's saying. "You brought it back . . . but didn't? Not completely?"

Yes. "Are you even—" She shakes her head, tries a different way. "Are you capable of showing yourselves? Do you have a physical form?"

There's a long pause, and then the lights flicker twice. *No.*

Her voice drops to a whisper. "Are you ghosts?"

No.

She takes a slow, wavering breath. "Are you the ones that brought me back?"

The lights flicker once. Then we're plunged into utter darkness.

I hear her gasp. "No! Wait—come back! I have questions—what am I? Why did you bring me back?" She hits the switch on the wall and the lights come on for real, steady and cold. The switch clicks as she flips it on and off frantically. I can see her face as if flickering in a strobe light. "Please—come back!"

Eventually I tug her away from the switch. She's so distraught she doesn't even notice that I'm touching her for a few moments. Then she comes to life and jerks away, shoulders hunched.

"What were you talking about? What flower?"

She straightens. "Your pack—is your journal in there?"

"Yes, but—"

She reaches for it, sliding it off my shoulders and upending it, sending supplies and belongings everywhere. The case with my family's photo goes clattering across the floor along with the ration bars and the canteen—but it's the journal she reaches for.

"The flower from the plains—I put it here, in these pages." She flips through the pages, but when she gets to the end she freezes. There's no flower there.

She starts riffling frantically through the pages, over and over, searching. "It was here, I know it was here." She's afraid, her voice starting to shake.

"You left that flower by the river," I say carefully. She doesn't remember, and how could she? She's not Lilac. "It wilted and died, and you left it behind."

"No," she gasps. Her sudden distress pulls at my heart—if only I could understand the significance of this. "They brought it back. While you were sick, at the wreck, they brought it back, re-created it like the canteen. An exact copy. They did it to keep me going, to remind me how much I—" She chokes, closing her eyes. "I never told you. But I put it in here to keep it safe, and it's gone."

This time when I reach for the journal she lets me take it from her limp grasp, her eyes fixed somewhere beyond me, her body starting to shake. I flip through the pages but see no pressed flower there. She's mistaken, maybe given a false memory by the beings that created her. But my stomach twists uneasily, instinct fighting against my mind's attempt to keep her at arm's length. She remembered that I was sick, that I had this journal. For all I know, the real Lilac did find that flower, did slip it into my journal. Her fear is so real.

Something catches my eye, and my hands freeze. I flip a few pages back. There, hard to see against the backdrop of a poem I wrote on Avon—the faintest of stained impressions. It could almost be the outline of a flower.

In her distress, she forgets her fear of my touch and leans forward, one hand curling around my sleeve, urgent. My heart seizes and suddenly I can't breathe. The gesture is so familiar I can't bear it.

She takes the journal again, slow this time, tipping it up on end. A fine rain of dust patters down against our arms, but I'm not looking at the dust, our arms, or even the journal. I'm looking at her face. The way her every emotion is clear, the way her lips quiver, the way her eyelashes shadow her gaze.

"They re-created it, but didn't," she whispers. "The things they make are only temporary."

Clarity flashes like a torrent of ice water. Maybe fear kept me from seeing it, or grief—maybe I had to mourn before I could understand what was right in front of me. I don't know how it's possible, or why it's happened.

But this is my Lilac. And I refuse to lose her again.

———

We sit there on the floor of the corridor, sharing a ration bar and drinking from the canteen. Lilac isn't the only one who needs the break. My thoughts are churning so fast I can't make sense of anything. All I know is that this is her, my Lilac, and I can't live without her. We inspect the canteen, the only other thing we know the whispers have re-created—aside from Lilac. But it seems just as solid, just as real, as it was the day we found it. The flower is a fluke. It served its purpose and now it's gone, not worth sustaining anymore.

They wouldn't take Lilac back. They can't.

Eventually we're both calm enough to continue what we came down here to do, locate whatever the power source for the station is. If we can find that, we may be able to restore full power to the communications systems and send out a distress signal.

The corridor stretches away from us on a downward angle, lined with doors on both sides. Each door is stamped with the LaRoux insignia, the upside-down letter V of the lambda. We make our way down the corridor in silence.

I open a few of the doors as we pass, but they only contain more of what we found upstairs—dark screens, unresponsive. It's then that Lilac stirs from her silence, stepping past me. She points out a few dim orange lights here and there that I missed—the machines are in standby mode.

"It's like the whole station's on backup power. When my father's company pulled out, they must not have shut everything down, not completely." She steps back, following a tangle of cords that run up the corner of the wall to where it joins the ceiling, and then out to the main corridor. "If we can find the real power source and get it operating fully, instead of on this backup mode, maybe we can send a signal."

We head back out to the hallway, following the cables on down the sloping corridor. "You're sure it can't just be a generator?" I wonder aloud.

She shakes her head without looking up. "There's too much equipment here for that. There has to be something else here, something powering the hot water and the lights. And how did they power everything else, back when this place was operational? There's something more. I can feel it." Her voice is quiet, and there's a quaver there—weariness, or distress.

"What do you mean, feel it?"

"You mean you can't?" She pauses, swallowing hard, and presses a finger to her temple. "It's there. It's like having a headache—or, no, not a headache. It's like having something inside, something that shouldn't be there. Something's wrong here."

"You mean like the shakes when they send you a vision? Or a voice?"

She shakes her head. "Close, but different." Her voice drops to a whisper. "I think whatever's down here is what the whispers want us to find."

I try to shake the uneasy feeling that even though our light-flickering friends are quiet now, they're still watching us as we try to track down the power source.

Lilac does most of the work as we follow the cables through the rooms and hallways. This place must be four or five times as big underground as it is aboveground. Slowly, though, I begin to see her logic, and together we trace a path through a series of rooms along the first hall we saw, and then down a metal staircase to a second basement level.

When we round the corner at the bottom of the stairs, we find the door.

It's not square and chunky like everything else down here, but a perfect circle, sealed shut. I reach out to run my fingertips along the lines of its seams; it's made to dilate like the iris of an eye. With the sections interlocked, it's stronger by far than any normal door would be.

Lilac studies a keypad beside the door, its buttons glowing blue-white. "Can you feel it?" She's pale, shivering. And now I know what she meant before: I'm not taken by the full-blown shakes that herald a vision, but there's an almost unbearable shiver running down my spine, a coppery taste in my mouth. It's affecting her more strongly—I can see her swallowing hard, forcing herself to breathe slowly.

"It's behind this door." My voice is a whisper. "You're right. This is why they brought us here."

She tries the keypad with trembling fingers, entering a few arbitrary numbers and letters. The illumination behind the buttons flashes red with an angry, low-pitched drone. "And we don't know the password."

I could laugh, if our lives weren't on the line. All of this—the struggle to survive, to make it out of the forest, to dodge storms and snow and cave-ins. Staying sane in the face of the impossible. All of it—for this. Leading us to a door we can't open, a password we don't have.

I catch a quick, furtive movement out of the corner of my eye—Lilac, twitching a hand across her face. She's fast, and trying for subtle, but the shakes have made her clumsy, and I can see what she's trying to hide. Her nose is bleeding, leaving a smear of crimson across the back of her hand. She's clenching her jaw, one hand resting against the wall; she's trying to look casual about it, but her knees are buckling. Whatever's down here is making her worse by the second.

I'm trying not to think about what she said—that they brought the flower back to life, the way they brought her back. And that now that flower is no more than dust.

I stand there staring, unable to lift my feet. When you have so little left to lose, even the tiniest loss feels like a body blow. It's Lilac who eventually leads me away. Now that I know it's her, the touch of her hand alone is enough to make the blood roar in my ears. I never thought I would get to touch her again.

"You seem distracted, Major."

"Not at all. Just as focused as when we began this little conversation."

"Perhaps if you were more cooperative, we would be done by now."

"I'm being as cooperative as I know how. I certainly wouldn't want to inconvenience LaRoux Industries. If I knew what you were getting at—"

"We are attempting to determine the extent to which you explored the structure and its surroundings."

"Then I've already answered that question."

"So it would seem."

THIRTY-FIVE

LILAC

WE SIT ON THE FLOOR OF THE STATION'S MAIN ROOM, sifting through the half-burned pages, looking for answers. The nausea has passed and my head's not throbbing so badly. Most importantly, my nose has finally stopped dripping blood. If Tarver noticed what happened to me the closer I got to the locked room below, he said nothing, for which I am grateful. The key to this planet, to the whispers, to finding a way home . . . it all lies behind that door, and we're going to find a way through if it kills me again.

I fight to stay silent as a hysterical bubble of laughter tries to escape. *If it kills me again.* What difference does it make, anyway, if it does? For the first time I don't feel like the violent paintings on the walls in this room are staring at me. They used to feel like a threat, or a warning, of what might lie in store. Now they just seem to match the violence of my thoughts.

The records left behind were scattered around the room, some charred in fires that guttered for lack of fuel in the concrete building, others dropped, stacked, scattered, like this place was evacuated in a hurry. We've gathered as many as we could, and we're searching them line by line for anything that might help us.

Or, at least, for the password to the door below us. Tarver's shoulders are hunched, his eyes fixed on the singed page in his hand. Determined, focused. Driven. A fragment of me wants to go to his side, run my fingers through his hair, kiss his temple, distract him until that tension disappears.

But instead I just sit here, unmoving. No matter how hotly that part of me burns, the rest of me is frozen, unable to so much as reach for him. This half-life is torture—I'm little more than a prisoner in this numb, lifeless shell. All I have left, now, is to try to get Tarver home. I force my attention back to the records scattered all around us.

My father's lambda is watermarked on every page. I can't help but stare at it, thoughts dwelling on the man I thought I'd known so well. I want to believe he doesn't know about this place, that the mysteries and horrors of this planet are buried somewhere deep inside LaRoux Industries. But I know my father, and I know he has his finger on the beating pulse of the company he built. He's the one who hid this place. He has to be.

"They keep referring to a 'dimensional rift' here." Tarver's voice jars me out of my thoughts.

"Dimensional? Like hyperspace?" I look down at the page in my hand, trying to focus. But my paper is only a list of supplies and requisitions, nothing helpful.

"Maybe." Tarver's brown eyes scan the document. "The *Icarus* did get yanked out of hyperspace by something. Maybe there's a connection."

The overhead lights shine through the page he's holding up, silhouetting my father's insignia stamped at the top. "Then it's not coincidence that we just happened to crash on a terraformed planet, my *father's* planet."

"Doesn't look like it, does it?" He falls silent, then leans forward, suddenly alert. "It says here, 'Further attempts to re-create the dimensional rift using the super-orbital reflectors have failed, both here and on Avon.' What the hell does any of that mean? I know Avon, I was posted there for a few months."

I abandon my stack of pages and cross to Tarver's side of the room, where I start sifting through some half-burned documents.

"Are they talking about the mirror-moon? That must be what they mean by 'super-orbital reflectors.' Mirrors in the sky, to speed up terraforming. Even lifting the temperature a degree or two can change the terraforming timelines by decades."

"Okay, but then how does the mirror-moon cause a rift? Does it say anywhere what the rift is?"

He fishes out another page, blowing away a layer of ash and inspecting the text. "Dimensional rift collapse will release unpredictable quantities of energy, potentially fatal in nature. Do not attempt direct physical contact with any objects or persons."

"Then it *is* like hyperspace." I can feel the connections clicking together, and I trip over my tongue trying to explain. "The power surge when the *Icarus* was ripped out of hyperspace—remember I told you then that there's always a huge energy surge when a ship enters or exits hyperspace? There's usually preparation, better protection. The rift they're talking about must be like a hyperspace rift. A way of accessing another dimension, but without the need for a ship."

"They've found a way to reach into another dimension?" His voice is hushed.

"And it's unstable. What makes hyperspace travel so dangerous is that these rifts always want to close; it's their natural tendency. They've found a way to hold open this dimensional rift, but if you touch it, it'll collapse. There'll be an energy blast like the one that fused the circuits on the ship. Or worse."

He shakes his head, looking down at the sheet once more. "'Continued extraction of test subjects is dependent on rift stability.' The rest of it's burned, I can't read it."

"Test subject extraction," I echo. "They're pulling something out of the other dimension to experiment on? But what? And where is this rift?"

"Behind that door, I'll bet. I'm more interested in the test subjects themselves."

"What do you mean?"

"This." He reaches behind him, pulls a fragment of paper from a pile. It's barely more than a quarter of a page, the rest burned away, but there is some writing legible in the corner. He passes it to me.

"'Subjects display remarkable telepathic abi—'" I read, forced to stop where the page is gone, and skip down the remaining lines of text. "'. . . phased life-forms . . . energy-based . . . noncorporeal . . . temporary energy-matter conversion . . .'"

The rest of the text is lost in the crumbling ash, leaving black streaks across my palm.

"The whispers."

"The whispers," he agrees.

My head spins. There are answers in here somewhere, in the scorched remains of my father's secret research facility. These beings, experimental test subjects to my father's teams, have led us across the wilderness to this spot. If we're right, then Tarver and I are not so different from them—all of us castaways on a forgotten world.

"I wish we knew what they want. Perhaps they could get us past the door."

"We'll figure it out." He lifts his head, eyes meeting mine. His mouth twitches like he's about to speak, and I know what he's going to say. *Together. We'll figure it out together.*

I turn away before he can form the words. Just his glance is enough to set my very blood on fire. He's become so sure of me in such a short time. He thinks I don't notice when he watches me move, thinks I don't see the way he reaches after me, stopping just short of taking my hand. He's impatient, but not urgent—he wants me back, but he's waiting. He thinks we have time.

But I know what the whispers were telling me in the corridor below. They brought the flower back and didn't—like me. I am here, and not here. Perhaps the effort required to flicker the lights took their attention away from sustaining the flower. The words are there on the charred sheet of paper. *Temporary* energy-matter conversion. How long will I last?

Long enough to help Tarver get home? I try to imagine myself drifting to infinitesimal pieces on the wind, turning to dust like the flower did. It's easier to contemplate it if I'm not real after all—if I'm only a copy, a remnant of the girl who used to be here. I remember everything of my life, of Lilac's life. But is memory enough?

The question of the dress haunts me too, coming back to me at every turn. I know he thinks of it too. I left this dress behind in the wreck of the *Icarus*, discarded for more practical clothing. Each rip and run in the satin is identical to those the original had. I can trace my journey on it—here, the first tear, caught on a thorn as we watched the *Icarus* fall. There, rubbed raw as I climbed the tree to escape the cat beast. Each mark and stain bearing witness to what I've been through. Except that this isn't that dress.

So whose story does this impostor tell?

"I need to see the body."

We're both startled, heads snapping up. It's not until I see the horror registering on Tarver's face that I realize I was the one who spoke. The fragment of paper slips from my nerveless hand, fluttering to the floor, streaming ash.

"The—what?"

"The body." I assume he buried it—me. These thoughts ought to make me sick, ought to frighten me. Why do I think them only blankly?

"Lilac," he whispers. "No. *No*. What good can come of that?"

"I need you to take me there." My hands remember how to work again, clenching into fists pressed against my thighs. "What if there's a body there? What if there *isn't*?"

Tarver's face has gone pale, something I never thought I'd see again after he recovered from his illness. My heart breaks a little, but not enough for me to crumble.

"Where did this dress come from?" I press. "We both know I left it on the laundry floor, back at the *Icarus*. Tarver, I have to know."

"I don't," he retorts, suddenly fierce. He leans across the space between us, seeking my gaze. "Lilac, I have you back. That's all I want. I don't want to ask questions."

To look at us one would think he was the one who'd come back from the dead. Maybe in some way he has. The way he looks at me now, like I'm water in a desert—how can I take that away from him? I make myself nod, and he relaxes.

He believes in me now.

The only problem is that I'm not so sure I do.

"I made up a bed for us in one of the rooms," Tarver offers, leading the way down the hallway. When we reach the sleeping quarters, I see what he means—he's pushed two sets of bunks together side by side, making a larger bed on the bottom, the top bunks forming a canopy above it.

"Us," I echo aloud, halting on the threshold.

Tarver stops a few steps into the room and looks back at me. "Lilac?"

I swallow, shake my head. "Please. No. I'll sleep out in the common room."

Tarver turns and reaches for my hands. I manage to stop myself from jerking them away, but he senses the buried impulse in the way my skin twitches, and he lets them fall again.

"Why?" he says softly, his face bearing all the lines of grief and exhaustion and pain.

And why *can't* I grant him this? I shiver. I must seem so cold to him now. How can he think I'm the same as his Lilac? He doesn't know what I remember. He doesn't know how hard it is to inhabit my own body, to make myself speak, walk, eat. How much I feel like I'm a prisoner, able to see and hear but unable to do the things the old Lilac would have done.

"I can't. I told you—your touch, it burns. I can't, not yet."

He presses his lips together. Pain. The urge to go to him is so strong I think I must be tearing apart. I can't let it go on like this.

"I lied to you," I whisper, turning to lean back against the door frame. At least the pain of that pressure on my body is physical, distracting. "I let you think I don't remember anything from the time I was—gone."

I hear his intake of breath. "What—how—"

"I remember it all." The cold is leaching my voice away, frost trickling through my limbs, crackling in my lungs.

"You mean—when it happened?"

He doesn't deserve to know this. Kinder to let him think I just woke up myself again. Maybe the old Lilac would have protected him from this.

"I mean after." I close my eyes. For a moment all is quiet and I can almost believe I'm gone again, to the silence. "Cold and dark don't begin to describe it. Cold is just an absence of heat, dark an absence of light. There, it's like—light and heat don't exist, ever."

The scrape of his shoe on the cement floor. He's trying not to go to me. He's trying to hold himself back.

The frost in my chest creaks, something else trying to come through. "I remember being dead, Tarver." I swallow, and my breath comes out like a sob. "How do you live again, knowing what waits for you in the end?"

"You don't sound like you believe me."

"It's our policy in such cases to maintain a certain amount of healthy skepticism."

"You have a lot of precedent with survivors of serious trauma making things up as they go?"

"Considering the circumstances in which you were stranded and subsequently rescued, we don't have a lot of precedent for anything."

"What reason would I have to lie?"

"Now that, Major, is a very interesting question."

THIRTY-SIX

TARVER

WHEN I WAKE AGAIN THERE'S LIGHT CREEPING IN THROUGH the shutters, and I roll over to squint at the illuminated clock built into the wall. I've learned from it that this place has twenty-six-hour days. I haven't mentioned that to Lilac. It might seem a little too much like validation for every time she's told me the day really does seem to go on forever here.

The last thing I remember was thinking that I'd never get to sleep on this damn bunk. The mattress is narrow and confining, and there's a discomforting sense of being too far above the ground and in an unfamiliar space. I dragged the beds apart for her again and retreated to the top bunk, the frame screeching a protest as I hauled it across the floor.

The clock announces that it's not too early to rise, and I shove the blankets aside so I can lean over the edge of the bunk and check whether Lilac's still sleeping below.

She's gone.

A thread of ice runs through me, bypassing rational thought completely—somehow I make it from the top bunk to the floor, banging my shoulder against the door as I hurl myself through it, out into the comms room. No sign she was ever there.

An image flashes through my mind of the outline of the flower in my journal—the flower she said they created, the flower she said disintegrated. Why didn't I listen to her?

No, *please*.

I nearly trip on my way through the blasted entrance, stumbling out into the clearing and looking around wildly. She can't be gone. They wouldn't. *They can't.*

I'm only a few steps out into the clearing when she emerges from the trees, smoothing down the ruined dress she refuses to replace. I pull up short, and we stare at each other across the space for a long moment. My chest is heaving as I try to push the panic back down again.

"Tarver?"

"I thought—I woke up, and you were—"

Her mouth opens a little as she understands, and though I find myself rooted to the spot, she closes the distance between us and halts within arm's reach. When I hesitate, she reaches out to touch my hand, brushing it with the tips of her fingers. After so long without her touch, that little gesture is electrifying.

"I'm sorry," she whispers. "I'm here. I went for a walk. I'll leave a note next time, or a sign. I'm so sorry."

I want to turn my hand and wind my fingers through hers, to tug her in closer so I can fold my arms around her, tuck her in underneath my chin, stand in this place and on this spot, and hold her until the sun goes down and it's dark again.

Instead I nod, and clear my throat, and nod again. I'm realizing that my bare feet are stinging with the cold of the dew, and from sprinting across the debris by the entrance. I'm shivering without my shirt.

She gazes up at me for a long moment, then turns back toward the station.

She's gone the next morning when I wake up, and the morning after that. I lie awake for hours at night, listening for the sound of her departure, but I never hear it. After that first morning, she starts leaving the canteen hanging from the doorknob, a silent assurance that she's coming back.

Each day we work on finding a way to get through the door and power up the station properly, to transmit the signal we need. *We're here. Someone's alive. Come get us.* Each day she grows weaker. She keeps trying to pretend that whatever's behind the door isn't destroying her.

We've tried entering the word *lambda* into the keypad by the impassable door, but to no avail. Lilac's tried every word she can think of associated with her father's business. We keep sifting through the burned documents in the main room, trying to find some mention of a password. We've even tried random patterns of numbers, words from the records, but the door doesn't budge.

On the third or fourth morning after she started going for her morning walks, I climb down from my bunk and lace up my boots, reaching for the canteen where it dangles on the door. The morning sun's peeking through the clouds as I walk out into the clearing, glancing up at the mirror-moon, dimly visible.

I wish I knew what part it played in all of this. If it caused the *Icarus* to crash, if it caused the rift mentioned in those documents, why keep it a secret? Whatever's happening here is wrong. It would've cost a fortune to keep an entire planet hidden from the galaxy—and LaRoux Industries wouldn't spend that money if they weren't doing something worth hiding.

We've tried a few times to get the whispers to talk to us again using the lights in the underground hallway, but we've gotten only darkness and silence in response. Perhaps they wore themselves out that first time. Either they can't answer, or they won't.

We even tried last night to overload the door, assuming that if it had an electronic locking mechanism, zapping it might trick its systems into opening. But despite Lilac rerouting every system we could think of to pour into the door, it stayed shut. The entire station's power fluctuated and dimmed, but the door didn't budge. Lilac was unwilling to try again, pointing out that if we don't know what's powering the station, we don't know how much power's left. If we use it all up opening the door, there might not be any left to create a distress signal.

I turn the canteen over in my hands and find myself thinking of the fragments of meaning on that shard of paper Lilac read from. "Energy-matter conversion," it said. *Energy-based life-forms.* So, these things can manipulate energy. They can do it to the electricity in our brains, and the electricity in the lights. They can convert energy into solid matter, create physical objects. After all, I hold the evidence of it in my hands. They re-created the canteen. Lilac says they re-created her flower.

I shake my head and stretch, tossing the canteen up into the air and letting it tumble down again to smack into my palms. I toss it up a second time, seeing it rise as if in slow motion to the pinnacle of its arc.

I witness the moment it dissolves, crumbling into fine dust while I stare, paralyzed. The dust rains down on my outstretched hands, slipping through my fingers and falling to the ground. Shock holds me in place, and slowly I tilt my hands so the rest of the dust can slide off them and disappear into the still-scorched dirt and grass at my feet.

It's when I finally lift my gaze that I realize Lilac's standing at the edge of the clearing, staring at the place where the remains of the canteen fell.

It might be the fifth day, or the sixth, or the seventh, when I wake up and she's gone again. My boots have been moved over to the doorway as a signal that she didn't vanish in the night, and I climb down to stomp into them, making my way through the common room to grab a ration bar, and out into the clearing.

I've been trying desperately to push aside the thought of the canteen disintegrating just like her flower did. The whispers somehow re-created those two things, and Lilac's the only thing left that they've given us. Did they dissolve because it was too much effort to hold them together? Were they sending us a message?

All I know is that the things they create aren't permanent. If these beings, whatever they are, are behind that locked door, then that's where we need to go. The source of the energy that made her—if we can tap into it somehow, maybe we can stop her from falling apart. If there's a way to save Lilac, that's where I'll find it.

I'm chewing on the ration bar and standing in the doorway for nearly a minute, sleepily surveying the clearing, before it hits me. The door to the shed is standing ajar. Why would Lilac go there? I cross the clearing and stick my head inside. Something's missing.

The shovel's gone.

And in a moment of horrified realization, I know why.

The morning walks, despite her weakness; the way she waits for me to sleep before she slips out; the way she returns each day at dawn, before I can go looking for her.

She's looking for her grave.

The ration bar turns to ash in my mouth, and I throw the rest aside as I break into a run. I dodge through the trees and break out the other side, coming to a halt at the edge of the stream.

I'm too late. My mound of flowers—dead and wilted now—has been churned up and pushed aside. She's on her knees, shovel by her side, gazing down into the hole she's dug. From here I can see only a glimpse of red hair in the grave, but Lilac can see everything.

I want to drag her away, take away the memory, somehow get her to unsee what she's seen. I wish I could turn back time and stop her before she ever found the grave.

But I can't. And now we both know.

"You can glare at me as long as you like, Major. I am in no hurry whatsoever."

"Was I glaring? Must've drifted off there."

"If you'd care to answer the question, perhaps I can send for some dinner, and we can take a break."

"What question?"

"What reason would you have to lie?"

THIRTY-SEVEN

LILAC

I LET HIM LEAD ME BACK TO THE STATION, AND EVEN AFTER HE lets me go and retreats to the common room, I can feel his hand in mine.

Now, back in the dormitory, I'm standing in front of a mirror. It shows me freckles. Scattered across the nose, pointed up, too pert for real beauty. This nose I've always hated—now it doesn't even seem like mine. A tiny white line graces the edge of one cheekbone, a memento of the blow Tarver delivered in his delirium. The lips are chapped. The eyes sunken, the skin below them like a bruise. Under the freckles, my face is pale.

For a moment I'm standing again in the forest, looking into a shallow grave at the translucent gray porcelain skin, the long lashes sweeping the cheek, the hair a bright mockery against the dull gray earth. Her lips are violet, slightly parted, as though she might draw breath in another moment. My own breath stops, the sound of my heartbeat roaring in my ears.

For a dizzying moment I don't know which body I am: the one in the grave or the one in the mirror.

No. I'm not her.

I'm not her.

Then I am once again back in front of the mirror in the station, staring at this too-thin body wrapped in a towel. Not my body—something else, something other. Something created.

The towel chafes at me, an agony of sensation. I let it fall. Tarver isn't here anyway. There's no one to see this body but me.

I close my eyes, shutting out the sight of the face in the mirror. Before I found the grave, I was a prisoner in my own body, feeling the impulse to reach out, to touch, to love, but unable to act on it. Now it's like I'm an echo, inhabiting nothing more than a statue. A memorial to the Lilac who once lived here.

The old Lilac, the one Tarver loved, would have patted herself dry, combed out her hair until it dried shiny and smooth. She would have stood near enough for him to feel her warmth, for their arms to brush now and then, her hair to tickle his shoulder, until he could not help but turn and reach for her, on fire. She would have loved him.

For the first time in a life of balls and salons, designers and high fashion, flirtations and intrigue—that Lilac came alive inside her own skin. Who am I now?

Tarver is so certain I'm me, I'm his girl—but how can he know? I want to believe him. Sometimes I almost do. I want to believe I'm more than imaginary smoke drifting from an imaginary chimney. But for the scrape of fabric against my bare, raw skin as I dress, I would think myself no more than a memory.

By the time he returns I have forced myself into my clothing, put my wet hair into a knot that drips ice down my neck, cleaned my teeth, sipped enough water to give these chapped lips a semblance of color.

Tarver pauses on the threshold as he enters and smiles at me.

"Lilac," he says. He thinks I don't see how he starts to reach for me and stops, the movement so quick it's barely there. My thoughts scream at him not to use that name. *Lilac.* An echo.

Without him to say the name, I could just fade away.

He busies himself trying to make the bare dormitory habitable, oddly domestic. I know he's doing it for my sake, but he's also not used to being helpless. He sees me falling apart, little by little. He's torn, wanting my help to sort through documents and try to bypass the locking mechanisms, and wanting me nowhere near the underground station and its weakening influence.

He doesn't know I want him to touch me, that I want nothing more than to throw myself into his arms. My body's still raw but I don't care anymore. I want his fingers in my hair and his lips on my face—I want his warmth and his strength so much it hurts. I want it every moment, for as long as I can, before I'm gone forever.

But I am not his Lilac. I can't think about what I am or who I've become, or let him touch me—all I have is what drove me before I died in the clearing. All I have is the need to find rescue and get him home. If I'm to be dust at any moment, and I can't fight it, then at least I can finish what I started when I blew the doors off the station.

I can save him.

He's better able to tolerate the strange energy field in the bowels of the station, the power radiating from behind that door. He's not the one who knows electronics, though, so I'm slowly dismantling the wall panels, inspecting the circuits, trying to bypass the lock electronically. I think the only reason he hasn't forcibly dragged me away from the round door in the basement is that he thinks getting through is our only hope. Everything that's happened here has led us to that door, and he thinks he can use what's behind it, if only he can get to it. He thinks whatever's behind the door will save me.

But how can you save someone who's already dead?

I'm beginning to think I know what's behind the door. The shakes, the metallic taste, the dizziness that touched me every time I received a vision or a dream—the sensations are overwhelming when I come close to the door.

I can almost feel the whispers behind it. Desperately wanting something, but unable to do anything but reach for it in our thoughts. Trapped there. Waiting.

And I'm starting to understand what it is they want from us.

After all, I'm a prisoner now too, in a body that's falling apart. I understand better than Tarver what an agony it is to be so trapped.

I can't keep this up. It's harder and harder to focus. I can't help but imagine that their pain is like my own, trapped as they are between life and death, unable to reach past their own torment. When we get through that door it will be all I can do to use whatever's there to power the distress signal, and not succumb to the urge to give them what I know they want.

Because while that tiny part of me wants him, and only him, the rest of me wants what the whispers want. An end to it all.

During the day, at night, while we eat, he watches me, and I can't— my mind doesn't work. I can hear him trying to get my attention.

"*Lilac*, you okay?"

My spoon is in my hand. We're eating dinner, and a bowl of rehydrated stew sits in front of me. I'd forgotten.

I stare at him, blank, confused.

"Lilac?" His voice is softer, his brows furrow. His left hand twitches where it rests against the table, as though it might reach across the gulf between us and take mine.

"Don't call me that."

"What?" He's staring at me, bewildered. "It's your name, what else should I call you?"

"I don't care. But you can't call me that. I'm not your Lilac. I'm a copy."

"Are you *serious*?" Shock gives way to anger, hurt, confusion. His voice is ragged. "You're *you*. You have your memories, your voice, your eyes, the way you speak. I don't care how it happened, you're you. You tell me what the difference is."

Breathe. I force myself to watch him. Lilac would've looked away. Somewhere inside my mind she's desperate to get out, to go to him, stop torturing him like this.

"The difference is that she's dead."

I can see him warring with himself. The urge to go to my side. The urge to shout. The urge to give up, just for a little. I will him to let the latter win, let us both rest. Just for a little.

"You're you," he repeats, his eyes full of grief. "You're the same girl who crashed on this planet with me, who I dragged through forests and over mountains, who climbed through a shipwreck full of bodies to save my life. You're the same girl I loved, and I love you now."

Stop. *Stop*. No more. Please.

My throat seizes.

"I love you, Lilac." His voice is soft, intent. "I love you, and I should've told you before you—"

I listen to the way his voice catches, feeling the break in it deep in my own chest. I close my eyes.

"You're my Lilac."

I shake my head, find my voice. "I don't know what I am or why I'm here, but until I do, I'll do what she would've wanted. Which is to get past that door, power the signal, and get you home."

"Get us both home. I'm not leaving without you."

"My father is a powerful man, but we're talking about a corporation powerful enough to bury an entire planet. He may not even know what's happening here, and if someone else is the one to discover what's happened here—you think they can't bury us? I was *dead* . . . you think they're going to just let me walk back into a normal life?"

Tarver's jaw clenches. "They'll never find out what happened here. We'll lie."

I stare at him, my heart aching. "Tarver," I breathe. "You can't lie. They'll *know*. They'll run tests on me and find out. They'll court-martial you. You'll lose everything."

"Not everything."

He watches me calmly. Now that he's made up his mind about what I am—that I am his Lilac—it's as though nothing else matters. He looks so tired. If only he would sleep.

"She loved you so much," I find myself whispering. "I wish you could have heard it from her."

It isn't until later, when I've changed for bed and he's cleaned up the few dishes from dinner, that he speaks to me again. He stands in the doorway, watching me open the window shutters so I can look out at the night.

"Do you really imagine yourself staying here if they come for me?" he asks.

"No. But I know I'm here for you. They didn't bring me back to be nice—they brought me back because they need us both to get past that door and do what they've been trying to get us to do all along. Without you here there's no reason for them to sustain me."

I keep my eyes on the night outside, trying not to let him see how afraid I am.

"It's not that I imagine myself staying here when you go," I say softly. "I imagine myself ceasing to exist. You have to let me go, Tarver. You can't . . ."

"I can't what?" His voice is lower, tightly controlled. I've never heard him sound like this before. I turn to find him clutching the door frame, his grip white-knuckled, every muscle tense.

I swallow. "Lose yourself in a ghost."

For long moments he's quiet and still, the silence drawn between us as tightly as a wire. At any moment it will pull me from my spot at the window and draw me toward him at last.

I can't keep this up.

But he breaks first, and vanishes from the doorway. I hear his footsteps, angry and quick, crunching over the debris in the mudroom as he heads out into the night. The tension drains and I find myself falling, hitting the ground with bruising force, my skin fragile and paper-thin now. I can barely summon the energy to drag myself to the bed.

I can't—

I have to get past that door, and for the first time, as my eyes light on the LaRoux lambda embroidered on the blankets, I think I know how. I have to do it soon. I don't think I have much time left.

"This is insane. You're the one who imagines I'm being less than truthful, then you want me to explain why? You tell me."

"Perhaps we can both agree, hypothetically, that there may exist some reason for you to conceal the truth."

"Hypothetically."

"It means conditionally, conceivably."

"I know what the word means."

THIRTY-EIGHT

TARVER

IT'S LATE WHEN I MAKE MY WAY BACK ACROSS THE CLEARING, head clearer, step surer. There's something about going outside and stretching my legs that helps me line up my thoughts. When I make my way through into the comms room, it's empty—but different.

The monitors, usually black, are lit up like a city skyline, blinking incomprehensible lines of code at me in vivid red, lights dancing across the controls. We've got power. Proper power, not whatever we've been squeezing out of the backup power mode.

Hope surges through me. Maybe she found a way to get through the door, into the locked room. I've spent every waking moment trying to find a way in, hoping for something behind that door I can use to help her.

But if she got the door open, why didn't she come find me? My mind keeps replaying one image: the canteen dissolving to dust.

Stay calm. She's fine. But my heart's thumping wildly as I swing down onto the top rung of the ladder. I can hear my old drill sergeant screaming in my ear to keep me from trying some stupid, impossible jump to reach her faster. *Keep yourself safe*, he bellows at me from beyond his grave on another planet far away. *You can't help anybody else if you're in pieces. Don't rush in.*

But I can't help it. I scramble down, ignoring the stab of pain as I twist my ankle in my haste. The lights are on, and I hurl myself down the corridors and then the metal stairs, swinging around the corner.

The round door is open.

Lilac must have heard me coming—she stands framed by it, looking out, waiting for me. Her skin is nearly a dull gray, too pale, her eyes lost in the shadows. I can see her shaking as she grips the edge of the round doorway. I slow to a walk as I approach her.

"I guessed the password." Her whisper rasps.

I want nothing more than to go to her side, but I know she doesn't want me to, and I hold back with a monumental effort. "How?"

"My father. This is his station—his emblem is everywhere. He always said my name was all I'd ever need to get anywhere. So I did. I used my name."

"Lilac."

She nods, her mouth twisting. I understand the grief in her expression. If the password was her name, it means her father did this, and not some faceless person at LaRoux Industries without his knowledge or consent. He's responsible for whatever happened here, and for covering it up afterward. And he used her name as his key.

"I got a distress signal working, though it's weak." She says it quietly, tightly. "It'll only show up as static, unless enough relays catch it and boost the signal."

This news that once would've been some of the best I'd ever heard is instead twisted, dark. I don't know anymore whether I want them to come for us. Not if I can't find a way to save Lilac.

"Come through," she says. "There's more."

She steps back, and I climb through the doorway, unable to stop myself from reaching for her hand. When I grip her fingers, the squeeze she returns is just a weak flutter. I can feel my own strength draining away as the shakes start to take me. It's like the side effects from the visions, only ten, twenty times worse.

The room hums with power, lined on every side with banks of monitors, control panels, and machines. Thick cables stretch from the consoles into the middle of the room. Towering over us is a circular steel frame twice my height. Flickers of blue light snake back and forth inside it like lazy lightning strikes, creating a shimmering layer of air. The frame dominates the room, overwhelming.

I can no longer hear my heartbeat, my harsh breathing—all sound is lost in the crackle and hiss of electricity. The room beyond the metal frame is hazy. The air is thick and heavy and tastes of something metallic at the back of my throat. The humming in the room makes my very teeth ache.

Two large, yellow-and-black-striped warning signs are mounted on the steel frame, one at the top, one down the side. *Contact with subjects forbidden. Risk of rift instability*, they read, in blocky letters.

Subjects. The test subjects from the papers above us.

Whispers rise suddenly, swelling in my ears, insistent. They hover just on the edge of comprehension—as though if I could close the gap between us just a little more, I could understand them.

Without thinking, I step toward the frame, unable to resist its pull.

For a moment the room around me is gone, and blackness overlays it, pinpoint stars twinkling.

And then something jerks me back. I blink again, and it's gone—and Lilac is there, grabbing at my hand and pulling me away.

"Are you insane?" she gasps. "Don't you remember what those papers said? If you touch it, you could bring the whole thing to a fatal collapse."

"What?" I'm still shaking the vision of stars, the sense that I was a hairsbreadth away from understanding.

She gestures at the hypnotizing blue light inside the metal frame. "Don't you see? *This* is the rift. It has to be."

I open my mouth to respond, but before I can, the lights overhead flicker, leaving only the roiling blue electricity to light the room. The lights dim once. *Yes.*

"Oh, God," Lilac whispers, her eyes on the portal. She's sweating, her hand clammy in mine. She feels cold, too cold. I can't tell for sure in the flickering blue light from the metal frame, but it looks like her eyes have become more sunken, the dark circles under them more pronounced.

"Lilac?"

"It's them."

"What—" But I can see her staring at the frame. And I realize what she means.

"The creatures, the subjects. The whispers. *They* are the power source for the station. This light, this energy—this is my father's rift. A gateway between dimensions. And they're here, trapped somehow by this metal ring they've built around it."

The lights flicker madly, and overhead a number of the fluorescent lights burst, showering the metal floor with shards of glass. Within the steel frame containing the rift, the blue forks of lightning fluctuate wildly.

"Energy-based life-forms." My voice is a whisper.

Suddenly Lilac's weight sags, her clammy hand slipping from mine as she drops to her knees with a moan.

My heart stops, and I drop to the ground beside her.

Her pale skin is nearly translucent now—I can see the dark veins snaking up her arms. She lifts her head with an effort, gasping for breath. When I lay a hand on her shoulder, a part of her dress crumbles at my touch, drifting away. Like the flower; like the canteen.

Being this close to the whispers is killing her—the symptoms are a thousand times worse. I have to get her out of here. I wrap an arm around her and drag her to her feet, more of her dress turning to dust with every movement. The fabric flutters and flakes away, drifting through the air like ash. I haul off my jacket and wrap it around her, then swing her up into my arms.

They're the power source, I hear her voice echo.

And they're running out.

My mind shuts down, and I turn to carry her back out through the doorway. All I know is that I have to get her out of here.

She recovers enough to grab at the ladder a little as we climb back up to the surface, and I help her into one of the chairs in the common room. I'm as gentle as I can be, but she still winces. It's clear she has a link with the creatures in the rift that I don't. The energy flowing through the station is the same as the energy flowing through her, the life force keeping her here with me.

She fixes her gaze on the far wall as she tries to steady herself, and for a moment my heart stops as I see her go still. Then I realize she's staring at the savage paintings we try so hard to ignore.

I follow her gaze to a figure painted in red.

"Tarver, I know what the paintings are." Her voice is a cracked whisper now, quivering with intensity. "Do you see?" She lifts one hand, the effort obvious, to point at the next in the sequence, also in red, and then the next. "He's there again. See the handprint beside it? It's the same. In this first one, he breaks his neck. Here, it's the spear. Here, he's burning. It's the same man, over and over. Tarver, the researchers stationed here did this to themselves." Her voice is raw, and she's forcing the words out of her throat. "And then they were brought back, like me."

"Holy—you're right." My mind's whirling, freewheeling, trying to find something to latch on to. "They came back again and again."

The figures painted on the wall are clearly distinguishable, and suddenly I can see each individual going through death after death, the pictures surrounded by the handprints, and the LaRoux lambda, painted large and bold beside them. Suddenly the recurring blue spirals scattered throughout the paintings have a new meaning. The rift, and its prisoners.

Her gaze sweeps across the paintings, which become wilder, more frenetic, and slowly degenerate into primitive daubs I can barely make out. At the end of the stream of pictures is a single handprint, smeared.

Then nothing.

I know we're both seeing the same thing. *This* is what they found here.

They died, and lived again, and found madness somewhere in between. They came here to study the creatures that gave me Lilac again, or to kill them, perhaps, and discovered a kind of twisted immortality.

Until—what? Until the whispers were too weak to bring them back anymore and power the station at the same time, and the researchers died for good? Until LaRoux Industries pulled them out, and buried this place?

I'm still staring when Lilac brings one hand down against the floor with a dull smack. "Why would anyone choose this? Living in limbo, in constant fear that you'll crumble away?" Her voice is ragged, broken.

I wish I could reach out, wrap my arms around her. Instead the distance between us feels like a canyon. "Maybe it was different for them, when this place was at full power. We only have the remains, what the company left behind."

"And when I do fade away, they won't have the energy to bring me back."

She sounds as though that's what she wants. My breath fails me, and I'm left staring at her, aching.

"I just want to sleep," she whispers, eyes dark in her white face, transformed by her longing. "I wish it—because you'd be heartbroken, and you'd mourn, but you'd—you'd heal. They'd find the signal and you could go home. And you'd have your parents, and the garden, and . . . Then the station could die, and the whispers could rest. *I* could rest. That's all we want. Real rest, not that coldness, that—"

"Lilac, I don't *need* to heal. I don't want to." My voice is as broken as hers. "I want you. We'll find a way to stop this, get the power to keep you whole. I won't lose you a second time."

"You're not losing anything, Tarver. I was already gone." Her struggle's written all over her face, eyes closing tight, mouth pressed to a thin line that doesn't keep the tears from spilling down her cheeks.

For the first time I can see this other longing—the desire to stay. For the first time I realize that maybe she insists on us staying apart because *she* doesn't want to lose this all over again.

I slide my hand forward a fraction of an inch at a time, until I can slip my hand into hers. She closes her eyes, breath catching. If my touch hurts her, she doesn't pull away.

"Whatever they've done to me, Tarver, whatever I am—I love you. Don't forget that."

I gather her against me, her hair spilling over my chest, her face in the crook of my neck. I hold her until she falls asleep, her breath warm against my skin. It should feel like a victory: she's here, with me, finally coming into herself again. Instead, all it feels like is a good-bye.

The rungs of the metal ladder are cold against my palms as I climb beneath the station once more. Though it's night aboveground, down here the light is the same harsh, steady fluorescence. My footsteps echo as I walk along the hallway to the humming room.

The rift waits for me, blue light curling about inside the circular steel frame of the containment device.

Whispers rise up, and the metal frame crackles with the electricity of the beings trapped there. There must be a way these creatures can help me save Lilac. The images they showed us come flooding back—a valley full of flowers, my parents' cottage as large and colorful as life, a single blossom in Lilac's darkest hour to keep her going. I refuse to believe a species capable of such compassion could be so cruel.

I stare up at the snapping, electric-blue glow of the rift, desperate to somehow decode these beings, to understand why they reached out to lead us here from so far away. Frustration surges up inside me as I stare at the ever-changing blue light. I'm running out of time, and I'm no closer to saving her.

The whispers rush into my ears once more, shapes flickering at the edges of my vision. My heart pounds.

All this way, all this pain, and now they can't find a way to just give me their damn message?

"What the hell do you want from me?" My voice is hoarse.

The whispers surge, as if in reply. But of course, as ever, there's no sense to be found there. No answers. No way out for Lilac.

"Go on, then." I fight the urge to strike at the damned thing with my bare fists, to attack the problem the only way I know how. "You've got me here. I trekked all the way across your damn planet. What do you want me to do?"

Silence, broken only by the crackle and snap of electricity, and the humming of the machinery. If I can't figure out a way to stop this, Lilac's not going to last much longer. And this time it's going to happen slowly, and I'm going to have to watch her die all over again.

Like hell I am. Something in me snaps. I wheel around, slamming my hands down on the control box attached to the metal frame around the rift. I hit one of the dimly lit screens, the plasma rippling at my touch. I strike it again, and again, until the plastic cracks and the monitor frame warps and my arm throbs with the impact, and it's still not enough.

Every step of this journey, every ounce of pain, everything I've found in her. It can't end here. There's a chair in my hands now, and sparks fly as I slam it into the metal framework. My mouth tastes like copper, and the room reels around me. Someone far away is bellowing grief and frustration, the blood roaring dimly in my ears. I bring down the chair again, and again, caving in the control box and the monitors attached to the rift, sending up sparks and smoke, intent only on destruction.

Then there's another voice, shouting to be heard over my grief.

"Tarver. *Tarver.*"

I whirl around, shaking with fury and helplessness. Alec stands on the other side of the room, leaning against the wall, hands in his pockets. The air goes out of my lungs.

"Alec, you can't be—"

In the next instant I realize he's blurred at the edges, not solid.

My hands are still trembling, and I drop the chair with a clatter, swallowing hard against the sharp taste of metal in my mouth.

Alec steps forward. His walk, the slight cant of his head, the thoughtful look on his face: it's all so familiar, so hauntingly real. My heart shudders, constricting painfully in my rib cage. He doesn't answer me, but looks instead at the rift, at the swirling energy inside. With a jolt, I realize that his eyes aren't the brown that I remember. They're blue—bluer than Lilac's, bluer than the sky. They match the color of the rift perfectly.

"You're not my brother." My hands grip the edge of the console, holding me up.

"No." He hesitates. "We came here through the . . ." He looks past me at the blue light.

"The rift? How?"

He nods at the smashed console. "You broke the dampening field. We can reach more easily inside your thoughts now. We can find words, and this face. It's always somewhere in your mind."

I suck in a slow, steadying breath. "What are you?"

Alec—or the thing wearing Alec's face—pauses in a way so human I have to keep reminding myself he's not who he looks like. "We are thought. We are power. In our world, we are all that is."

"Why did you come?"

Alec's mouth tightens, as if he's in pain. "Curiosity. But we found we were not the only ones here."

"LaRoux Industries."

Alec nods. "They found a way to sever us, to cut us off from each other."

"But why don't you leave?" I ask. "Return home?"

"This is the cage they built around us. We cannot fully enter your world or return to ours." His face—my brother's face—is taut with grief.

His image flickers, and fear snakes through my gut. Their strength—*Lilac's* strength—is running out.

"Please! How can I help you? I can't lose Lilac again."

Alec's face is awash with sympathy. "This cage keeps us here, but we are stretched too thin. There isn't much time left. Less, now. If we could trade our—our lives for hers, we would. To find an end, to sleep."

"Why less?"

"Her signal.

"The distress signal? That's draining you?"

"Soon there won't be enough left." Alec flickers again, fading as his image sputters out. The next moment there's only me in the room, and I've never felt more alone.

I jog over to the bank of monitors where Lilac rigged her distress beacon, watching the signal jump brightly across the screens as I search for any way I can find to shut it down. In the end I simply yank out a handful of leads. The screens go dead, and for an instant the rift swirls a little brighter.

Alec's voice—the whisper's voice—is still ringing in my ears. *We are stretched too thin.* Lilac's only hope is tied to these creatures, and they're fading.

I walk back toward the ladder. I need air—I need space to move. Deep within me, I feel the weight the whispers carry.

They've poured what energy they have into reaching out to us, drawing us here with visions and whispers, giving us what we need—giving me my Lilac—so we could find them. Now they can barely keep her here.

I understand now why they brought her back. They needed me moving, exploring, trying to understand the mystery of the station. They couldn't risk me blasting my brains out in the cave, when I was their only hope at release. But they're still trapped, and I don't know how to give them the end they want. My head's spinning.

The fresh air outside the station is a relief as I step over the rubble in the doorway and out into the clearing. I tip my head back to stare up at the now familiar stars, tracing out the shapes I've come to know. I blink as my vision blurs for a moment, the stars shifting. Another blink, and I know what I'm seeing is real.

One of the stars is moving. No, not one—there's another. And another.

I've seen this before. I've seen it on every planet I've been posted to. Those are ships in orbit. They must have picked up on Lilac's distress signal and come to investigate.

Panic hits me like a body blow. If they find us—if they find Lilac— they'll take us on board, and if they take her away from the whispers sustaining her—

My body flows into action before the thought's complete, and I pound back into the station. We have to hide. If they drag us off this planet before I can find a way to save her, she'll die, and I'd choose any length of time here with her over a life at home, alone. I choose her. I choose whatever world has her in it.

I burst into our bedroom, and a moment later she's sitting bolt upright in bed, eyes wide and bewildered. "Tarver?"

"Quick—" Panic steals my breath, and I'm gasping. "There are ships in orbit. I don't think they know exactly where we are yet. We have to—"

She's scrambling to her feet before I'm finished, and I grab my bag and my gun as we bolt for the trapdoor that leads below the station. I'm praying they'll think that if we were once here, we're gone now.

She falls down the last few rungs into my arms, and I half carry her along the hallway to the control room. She breaks away from me, stumbling past the rift to the bank of monitors. I hear her horrified gasp as she realizes the distress signal is shut down, and next moment her fingers are dancing across keys and screens. An instant later a shrill alarm pulses, red displays flashing.

"Lilac, what the hell are you doing?"

She looks up at me, eyes huge, shadowed, gaze wild. "I've got it back up. I can overload the system. It might create enough electrical activity for us to show up on a scan."

My heart stops. She's trying to show them where to come and find me, using the last fragments of power that remain. The last fragments keeping her alive. I lunge for her. "Lilac, stop—"

She slaps at a screen, and another alarm starts, screaming an alert at us. Blue light flares in the rift, then fades to nearly nothing. I wrap my arms around her, pinning her arms to her sides, dragging her back from the screens.

Lights flash from screens, and the alarms scream their chorus.

I'm going to fail them all. Lilac's energy will drain away, and she'll crumble to dust. The aliens will stay trapped in the rift, neither alive nor dead.

There must be a way out. The blue light in the rift is twisting and pulsing, weaker than before, but trapped by the steel ring, the cage, unable to tip into nothing. My eyes light on the signs plastered to their steel cage. *Contact with subjects forbidden. Risk of rift instability.*

And then I remember the charred papers, the first time we found any sign of the rift's existence. The rift collapse would release energy, they said. The word *fatal* leaps up in my memory.

Fatal to an ordinary person, perhaps—but Lilac isn't, not anymore. Lilac is something different, created by the very energy inside the rift. All this time the whispers have been helping us—all this time we've only had to trust them.

Of all the people they could have chosen, they used Alec to speak to me. The one person in the universe I trusted more than my own self. The one person who always knew what to do.

I tighten my grip on Lilac and pull her away from the console. She cries out, fighting me as I drag her toward the blue light of the rift. It's like she senses my intention, using every last scrap of her remaining strength to pull away. In the end I wrap both arms around her and leap, sending us both plunging into the heart of the rift.

"LaRoux Industries has suffered huge losses as a result of this venture, Major."

"I didn't crash the ship."

"But the damage to the monitoring station. That was property of LaRoux Industries."

"How much did building the Icarus cost again? How many lives lost? And you're more worried about a monitoring station? You think the station was the huge loss?"

"Of course not. But we take any wanton destruction of our property seriously."

"Perhaps you could point out to Monsieur LaRoux that I was trying to save his daughter."

"It's at Monsieur LaRoux's request that you're being questioned. I believe he would point out in return that he has lost his daughter anyway."

THIRTY-NINE

LILAC

I'M FLOODED WITH GRATITUDE SO OVERWHELMING THAT IT becomes me, takes me over. There is no voice, but sensation wraps me up and carries me out of the jolting blue light surrounding me.

The world goes silent. All around me is power, and I feel it focus on me, pour into me and fill me up, heal me, restore me.

I straddle two dimensions, and I see all, know all.

I remember others of my kind, from a different time. Everything I am reaches out to them, longing for an end.

Not yet. They sound tired. Weak.

I try again to reach out, but they push me away. Gentle. Weary. Beyond them I can sense countless others, though I can't see them or touch them. They're behind some veil I can't push aside, and retreating farther and farther away.

I try to call out, to tell them to wait, but they are gone. All is cold and dark again, and I am alone. Dimly sensation returns to my body. I can feel something touching me, wrapping around me. My ears are ringing, blood roaring past my eardrums. Something warm and soft touches my face. The ringing in my ears is becoming a voice.

"Lilac?"

With an effort I swim up from the darkness.

Tarver gasps for breath, his hand against my cheek. "Are you all right? Can you move?"

I swallow, blinking. The only light comes from a series of monitors lining the wall, their glow slowly fading. With a rush I remember where we are: the basement of the station. I'm lying on the floor where we landed, looking up at an empty metal ring. The rift—Tarver, pulling me through. The blue electricity has vanished.

Whatever gateway between dimensions was here in this room, it's gone, and we're alone.

Somehow he's still alive. We both are.

I push myself up on my elbows, dazed, staring at him. "Tarver?"

His arms wrap around me, pulling me in against him. His lips press against my temple. "For a second there—" His voice catches painfully in his throat.

"What did you do?"

He releases me just enough so he can look at my face. "You needed a burst of energy. The papers talked about a vast energy surge if we made contact with the rift. I hoped it would give you what you needed—and they wanted to go. They wanted it to end."

"Are you insane?" I curl my fingers in the fabric of his sleeves, urgent. "I also seem to recall reading the word 'fatal' in there too. It could have killed you!"

Tarver looks down at where I'm grasping his arms, and then looks back up, grinning. I haven't seen him smile like that since before I lit that fuse. "I chose you. And I don't think they wanted me dead—I think they wanted us both to make it through."

I look over at the metal ring that circled the rift. The blue light is gone, leaving only the empty cage my father's company built to contain the whispers. Tarver follows my gaze, his own smile dimming.

"They wanted an end," he says softly. "They were stretched too thin to go home."

Power gone, the last of the monitors fade, leaving us in utter blackness. Afterimages linger in front of my eyes—but not of the screens. "For a moment I saw them. All of them. They were once all part of each other in a way we could never . . . it was beautiful, Tarver. I wish you could've seen it."

His arm tightens around me as he kisses the top of my head. Then he pulls away so he can get to his feet, keeping hold of my hand in the dark to help me up.

My head spins as I stand, but I can feel my strength returning. I open my mouth, but there's a low groan of metal that sends vibrations through the grid floor to our feet.

"What was—"

Another scream of metal interrupts me, the ground shaking beneath us. Tarver's hand tightens in mine, and I hear him turn away.

"The station—the shock wave from the rift collapse must've . . . come on!" He jerks at my arm, and though I brace myself, it doesn't hurt like it would've a few minutes ago. As soon as I move I can hear something huge—the metal containment device, perhaps—come crashing down where I stood.

Together we careen out into the corridor, sprinting up the slight incline in pitch blackness. There's not the tiniest scrap of light, though my eyes keep trying to adjust to the darkness anyway, picking out imagined shapes looming ahead. Tarver keeps his hand wrapped firmly around mine, and I find myself growing stronger with each step. My blood races, my heart pounds—my lungs work for the first time in what feels like weeks.

Tarver collides with the ladder, the clang of impact lost in a flood of curses. He shoves me up in front of him. The world is reduced to the sound of our harsh breathing and the clang of our feet on the rungs. The ladder bucks beneath us as shudders run through the station. I collapse on the ground just above the hatch, and Tarver scrambles up behind me and drags me to my feet. There's light here, just enough for us to make out the doorways and the rubble, and beyond it the clearing lit by star-light so bright it dazzles my eyes.

We scramble for the exit just as the floor caves in, and for a horrible moment it's like I'm in the escape pod again while gravity outside wars with gravity inside—my head spins and I can't figure out which way is up. Tarver's hand closes around my wrist, and then I find purchase on the grass, and we drag ourselves up and over the lip of the cave-in.

For long, labored moments all I can see are spots as my lungs heave for air, and though Tarver tries a few times to get back to his feet, eventually he's forced to concede defeat and we just lie there, listening to the last remains of the building collapsing in on itself.

After the underground darkness, the stars seem like fiery beacons, bright and promising. I drag myself up so that I can look down at Tarver, who's still half dazed, searching for breath.

"You stupid, stupid man," I murmur, reaching for his face, tracing the path the starlight takes across the bridge of his nose, over his cheekbones. "We have no way of signaling now. If those were ships up there, they'll never find us. You'll never go home."

Tarver presses a hand into the dirt and hauls himself upright so he can look at me properly. "I am home." He lifts his hand when I start to protest. "My parents would understand. If they knew what was happening here, they'd tell me so."

"Still, how could you do such a thing? The signal was working. They would have seen it."

"It was killing you," he says simply.

I'm already dead. The words hover on my tongue, but remain unsaid. Because now, here, for the first time, those words aren't true. I draw a long breath, watching the way it steams the air when I exhale.

Tarver eases closer, reaching for my hand. I'm still weak from so long eating next to nothing and sleeping so little. But my muscles respond to my commands. My hand, as I twine my fingers through his, doesn't tremble.

For the first time since I was brought back, something inside me flickers, warm and vital. Hope. Together we stagger to our feet and move away from the sinkhole that used to be the station.

Tarver starts to let go of my hand, but I tighten my fingers through his, and he watches me for a long moment. I don't pull away. He lifts our joined hands and kisses my fingers, his eyes closing as his lips linger against my skin.

I can't help but wonder which is worse: losing the girl you love suddenly or being unable to touch her while she wastes away.

"How do you feel?" he asks, watching me intently.

"Incredible. Alive. Tarver, how did you *know*?"

"I didn't." He's still watching our joined hands. "But I just—I sensed they didn't want us hurt. They just wanted to be free. I guessed."

A little chill ripples through me, and at my shiver, Tarver hauls off his jacket and wraps it around my shoulders. "Pretty big guess," I point out.

"I had to believe it."

"You picked a hell of a time to start believing in hunches and feelings." I pull the jacket more tightly around myself and flash him a smile.

His arm around me tightens, and for a little while we just listen to the breeze stirring the leaves overhead.

"What do we do now?" I let my head lean back, looking up at the sky.

"Hell if I know," he replies cheerfully. "Start building a house, I guess."

I laugh again, startling myself with how easy it is. I didn't think I remembered how. "Can it have a garden?"

"A dozen gardens."

"And a bathtub?"

"Big enough for both of us."

"Can I help?"

"I'm certainly not doing it all on my own."

I shift my weight and lean against him.

"We should get some rest first," he says, turning his head to touch his lips to my temple. "We can start on the house tomorrow. Shall we go back to the cave? Some idiot destroyed your bedroom."

"Some idiot," I echo, with a smile. "I don't want to sleep in that cave again. Can we just sleep out here, under the sky, the way we used to? Before all this?"

"Anything you like." He kisses my cheek again, still gentle, still hesitant, and disentangles his arm from mine so he can stand. "I'll get the blankets from the cave. Tomorrow we'll start planning our life as castaways."

"We've already been living a life as castaways," I point out. "I think we'll be fine."

He's merely a shadow through the starlit trees as he makes his way back toward the cave. It's not until he's out of sight that I let my eyes close, tipping my head against the tree at my back, imagining I can feel the gentle glow of the stars on my cheeks.

All is silent and still. The air is crisp, and as I draw in a deep breath it sears the inside of my nose, tingling and strong.

"Rest," I murmur.

Though whether I'm talking to myself, or to our absent friends, I don't think I'll ever know.

"Is that what this is about?"

"This is about the truth of what happened on that planet."

"I've told you the truth."

"None of what you've told us has explained the anomalies in Miss LaRoux's medical tests."

"Sorry, I don't do well with big words. What do you mean?"

"Major, you know to what I am referring."

"I'm pretty sure I don't. Sir."

FORTY

TARVER

I HAVEN'T BEEN ABLE TO SLEEP YET, BUT I DON'T MIND. I yawn, holding Lilac a little tighter. She murmurs in her sleep—one of those stubborn little sounds that melt me—and nestles in closer.

I've been looking up at the stars, familiar constellations now, and naming them. I squint at what I've decided to call the Lyre, tracing the shape of a harp over again as I learn it. From the bright star at the base, to the next above it, and then . . . the next star moves. So does its neighbor. I blink again, and they slide into focus.

They're landing lights.

"Lilac, *quick*, wake up." I scramble to sit up, reaching automatically for the Gleidel, though I don't know what use it could possibly be. I lift my other hand to shield my eyes as the huge ship eases down toward us, thrusters rising to a steady roar. She'll be landing no more than a klick or two away.

Lilac comes awake lashing out with one arm, and I catch hold of her wrist gently. "No—no, leave us alone! We did what you wanted!" Her voice is high with fear as she gazes up, blinking, trying to understand what she's seeing.

"No, Lilac, it's a ship. They must have registered the explosion or the energy surge. Quick, we have to move." The dread's heavy in my gut. If they find us, they'll take us on board, and who knows what her medical tests will show? "Let's try for the cave, they might have infrared."

She's still sitting there, staring, mouth a little open now. "A ship?" I can barely hear her whisper.

"We can't let them find us. Come *on*." I reach down for her hand to try to tug her up.

She resists, my stupid, stubborn girl, tugging back. How did she find this strength so quickly? "Tarver, what are you talking about? You can go home after all! We need to find them, make them take us with them."

I drop to a crouch beside her, taking a breath, trying to slow myself. "I'm talking about us not knowing what'll happen to you if they get their hands on you. Who knows what your father's company will find if they do tests on you? Come on, there's food in the cave. We can hole up there until they leave."

"Tarver, no." There's a hint of that old LaRoux steel in her voice, but it's tempered now, warmer. "We're getting on that ship. You're going home."

"Lilac, I've made my choice, we don't have time for this conversation."

Behind me, the landing lights are moving lower, and the whine of the engines is growing deeper. I've heard this a thousand times. Usually it's a welcome sound. They're nearly down.

"No." She's soft, but sure. "I'm going with you. You kept telling me you'd take me home with you, and that's what you're going to do." She squeezes my hand, climbing to her feet now.

I want so badly to believe her, but the bitter twist of fear inside me says she'll do anything to keep me safe. She'd lie to my face if she thought it would save me.

I know she would. I'd do the same for her.

She reaches up to curl a hand around the back of my neck, pulling my head down so her forehead can press against mine. "I know what you would've given up for me. I could never let that be for nothing."

We stand like that for an instant, forever, and I try to reach inside myself for that trust. She waits, watching me, sure I'll make the leap for her.

I straighten up, reaching for her hand to lead her toward the rescue ship. She sees my decision on my face and opens her mouth to speak when she's interrupted by a new sound—in the distance, there's undergrowth snapping, crunching, booted feet moving toward us. I realize the sound of the ship has vanished.

They've landed. We don't have much time before they find us.

Lilac turns back to me, suddenly intent. "They're going to ask questions." Her hand tightens around mine. "We need our stories straight."

"Too much risk in both of us lying. You tell them nothing. Be the girl they expect. Distressed, pissed off. Shout for your father, cry if you can, but don't answer their questions. Be a princess."

She's shaking her head, her eyes on mine. There are flashlights in the distance, but here there are only the stars overhead to light her face. "I don't want you to have to face them alone. You don't know what my father's company is capable of—"

"I won't be alone." I lean down to press my forehead against hers, quick and sure. "You'll be playing your part as much as I will. Say you're too traumatized to answer questions. I'll have to talk, I can't avoid a debrief, but if we contradict each other, we won't be able to hide what's happened here."

"Traumatized." She's nervous, but there's a hint of laughter in her voice. I drink it up. "I can do that."

I start to move toward the sounds of cracking underbrush and dead leaves, but she stays still and tugs on my hand to pull me back.

"Tarver," she whispers, her eyes on my face. "There'll be cameras all the time. More questions. Everyone will want to hear your story. Your life will be different, no matter how far from Corinth we go."

A flashlight flickers through the trees, broken and jagged as it shines past the trunks. The light glances off her face, illuminating her eyes for a brief, brilliant moment.

I step closer. "I don't care."

"My father will try to—" She swallows, then lifts her chin, mouth firming to a straight, determined line. "No. I'll figure out a way to handle him."

I can't help but grin down at her, this steely assurance, my Lilac through and through. "I'd pay to see that showdown."

She smiles, lightning quick, then squeezes my hand harder, holding on like she's afraid someone will come and pull us apart. "You'll face it all with me?"

The world narrows, the sounds of the oncoming search party fading, the lights blurring around us until it's just her and me, our breath condensing and mingling in the cold air. She's stolen my voice, this girl in my arms, and for a moment I can't answer. I have to gather my wits, try to remember how to breathe.

"Always."

Her smile is like the sun coming out. "Then you ought to kiss me while you can, Major Merendsen. It may be a while before your next opportunity."

Her cheekbones are still shadowed, her face still showing the signs of her weakness, but her eyes are bright too, her cheeks flushed with life once more. Her fingers curl around handfuls of my sleeves, as though she can't wait to pull me in.

I thought I'd never get to touch my Lilac again. Even when she came back, I thought I'd lost her forever.

I break away from her a heartbeat before the rescue parties burst into the clearing. I'm almost tempted to tell them to come back later.

"Why did you blow up the station, Major?"

"I could see the ships in orbit. I was hoping somebody would notice it. I didn't want to miss this little get-together."

"The damage was significant."

"Well, it didn't seem like anyone really needed the place anymore."

"That wasn't your decision to make."

FORTY-ONE

LILAC

THE SHIP THAT FIRST PICKED UP MY SIGNAL WAS A RESEARCH vessel on its way to A243-Delta. The researchers didn't have any luck deciphering the static, but cleaned it up the best they could and bounced it back toward the rest of the galaxy. Then it reached a larger transport, a few days later, and then on to a junk heap of fringe theorists trying to discover structure in the background static of the universe. They were the first to clean up the signal enough to know there was a woman on it, asking for help. In the end it took dozens of ships, picking up the fragments that reached them, piecing them together.

The ship that collected us was one of my father's vessels, an advance team scrambled to get here before the image in the signal was clear enough for them to know who I was. They confirmed what we already suspected—we are the only survivors from the *Icarus*. Imagining fifty thousand people dead is impossible—and so instead I see Anna's face, and Swann's, and the face of the weary man in the shabby top hat who only wanted to pass a message to my father. I only have so much room for grief.

Four days after our rescue, still in orbit around the planet, another of my father's ships catches up to us. Tarver and I are bundled into separate rooms, and I don't see him again.

My meals are monitored. Someone stays at my side at all hours of the day, even when I sleep. My questions about Tarver are met with polite evasions. *He's in the best possible hands. You'll see him shortly. He's doing just fine.*

Your father will be here soon. Why don't you wait and ask him?

Their attempts to question me are met with floods of tears. I have my part to play as surely as Tarver does, and I do it well. Tears don't forestall the doctors, though, and I'm stripped down and inspected. They draw some of my blood, take a lock of my hair, scrape under my fingernails. I'm connected to machines by electrodes at my temples, on my chest. They attach clamps to my fingertips and watch some readout I can't see, staring wide-eyed, faces lit by the pale green glow of the monitors as they crowd around them.

And then I'm ushered back into the exam room, where a new round of doctors takes more blood, more hair. They check their results again and again. They're leading me back to the room with the monitors and the electrodes when the doors suddenly burst open.

"What is the meaning of this?" A voice like steel cuts through the hum of the machines.

The doctor grasping my arm drops it like she's been burned. Unsupported, my legs wobble and I drop to the floor. She and the others back away, leaving me blinking in the light.

"Sir," one of them starts, "we were only following orders—"

"Shut it down," the voice says, and the doctors scramble to obey. I know that voice well, after all, and no one hears it give an order without complying immediately. From somewhere, someone gives me a navy-blue dressing gown, a welcome change from the paper-thin hospital gown they had me in.

Someone reaches up and turns off the blinding overhead lamp, and as my eyes struggle to adjust, a face ducks down into my vision.

"Darling?"

For a moment all I can do is stare. The blue eyes, reddened with emotion; the chiseled features that don't betray his years; the close-cropped white hair he's never bothered to dye. It's a face I never thought I'd see again—a face I never wanted to see again. But here, confronted with it—I remember how safe it is. How easy, how warm. I remember how much I want him to make everything okay.

"Daddy?" I whisper.

His mouth trembles, then tightens, as if he can't believe it's really me. He throws his arms around me, and after a second I remember

I'm supposed to cry—and once I start, it's impossible to stop. For long moments we sit there on the floor of the medical wing, me sobbing wildly into the shoulder of his suit jacket, inhaling the familiar scent of his cologne. I'm a child again, in a perfumed forest, secure with my father's arms around me. All I want to do is pretend to fall asleep so that he'll carry me home.

But eventually my tears dry up and he helps me stand. He leads me to a meeting room dominated by a long glass table, then sits me down in the first chair on the left. He drops into the chair at the head of the table and rolls it closer to me so he can take my hand in both of his.

"Tell me everything, my heart."

Sitting here, with my father gazing at me with red-rimmed eyes, I'm finding it impossible to connect him with the lambda symbol stamped all over the hellish prison for the creatures that gave me back my life. For a moment I want nothing more than to tell him what's happened to us, what's happened to me, that I remember death and rebirth and everything in between.

But Tarver's words are still ringing in my ears. *Tell them nothing*, he said. *We lie.* I can't let him down.

So I sniff loudly and drop my head, staring at my lap as I shake my head. "I don't know," I stammer. "I can't. It's all too—I don't remember, it's all a blur."

"Are you sure?" He pats my hand, soothing. His skin is cool to the touch, soft and smooth. His hands always were well kept. "Perhaps it would help to talk about it."

I just shake my head again. The tears that were so easy to locate earlier have dried up as my conviction returns, and so I have to pretend, keeping my eyes on the fabric of the dressing gown.

My father is silent for a while. I know him well enough to see that he doesn't believe me. But he wants to. Eventually he pats my hand again briskly and straightens. "Well, good. We'll just put all of this behind us, then. What you need is some quiet. As long as you're safe, that's all I care about."

It's all I wanted—him to just accept me back, for all of this to go away, for my life to go back to normal. And still, I'm uneasy. There's a tension here I haven't felt since I was fourteen, and I learned that Simon was gone. Some part of me knows he's only telling me what I want to hear.

My father clears his throat. "I understand the young man in the other room is partially responsible for bringing you back in one piece?"

"Tarver Merendsen," I correct him, nodding, keeping my head down. "Entirely responsible, Daddy. He's the reason I'm here at all."

"Well, we'll be sure to reward him handsomely for it." Pause. "All of this in the papers and the HV clips about the two of you—"

"Yes?" I finally tear my eyes from my lap and look up, heart pounding. I know what's coming. "What about it?"

"When we reach Corinth you'll deliver a statement in which you'll correct the media's assumption that you're a couple. You'll thank him for his assistance, and wish him a safe journey back to his parents' home-world. And that'll be the last of it."

My head spins. "Father—"

"We'll find our way through this, Lilac." He gazes at me, his heart in his eyes. "You and me, you know that. You're all I have. All I need. My darling girl, you have no idea what it was like to hear that you were safe."

Guilt twists in my stomach, metallic and nauseating. "I won't leave him."

"Oh, Lilac." He sounds so weary, so sad. He can't know about the planet; it's impossible. Some distant employee used my name for the key-pad as a joke. My father is not capable of such monstrosity. "You think these things now. But in a week, two weeks—in a month, in a year, that will change. I'm only trying to protect you."

"The way you protected me three years ago?" The words slip out before I can stop them. My father and I have never spoken about Simon.

The eyes I used to think of as twinkling, kindly—they're steely now, paler and colder than ice. "You will come to thank me one day," he says in a voice that quietly cuts me to the bone.

And then I know. This is the man who sent Simon to his death. This is the man who discovered the first intelligent life other than ourselves and buried it. This is the man who enslaved the first ambassadors of another universe for his own ends, who perpetrated a cover-up so huge that a ship of fifty thousand souls went down without a trace until one tiny distress signal caught the attention of a passing research vessel.

This is the man who has ruled me for seventeen years.

And what's worse—with a rush of clarity, I realize that he's only ever ruled me because *I let him do it.*

"No," I say, standing up as the word rings in my ears. Some part of my mind points out that I have the power like this, that standing, I am taller than he is sitting, that making him look up at me gives me the upper hand. But in reality I simply can't sit any longer; a frenetic buzzing rising in my limbs drives me to action. It's all I can do not to pace. But pacing is a sign of weakness. I learned that from him too.

"You will leave us alone. Forever. In exchange, we will keep your secret."

My father's watching impassively, giving me nothing. "Forever is not a very long time for a soldier." His voice is soft as velvet, and as dark. My heart tightens, shriveling with fear.

But Roderick LaRoux is not the only one who can threaten without threatening, bully without raising a hand. He's taught me everything I know.

"You were all I ever needed in my life," I say softly, watching his face. The dynamic in the air has shifted. I can feel it. And from the minute twitch on his cheek, I see that he can too. "But people uncover buried memories all the time as they recover from traumatic events. I don't know what would happen if I began to remember what I saw on that planet."

My father gets slowly to his feet. He's a tall man, with suits tailored to emphasize his stature in dark, powerful colors. He places one hand on the back of his chair, watching me impassively. He says nothing, but I know what he's thinking.

"When we get to Corinth, Tarver and I will issue a statement together explaining how we salvaged a downed escape pod to send a distress signal. We won't mention the station. Tarver's probably in a room somewhere right now, lying, keeping your secrets. No one will ever have to know what we've seen.

"But, Father—and this is the important part—I'm holding you personally responsible for his safety. Because if something ever happens to him, I'll know it was you. If he's transferred to the front lines, I'll know. If he comes down with a mysterious illness, I'll know. If so much as a hair on his head is out of place, I'll know. And if someday someone thinks to blackmail or threaten him into leaving me, I'll know that too."

"Lilac, I'm sure I don't know what you're implying." His tone is cold, but I can see something behind it—something I've never seen before. Uncertainty. "Why his safety should be my responsibility—"

"His safety is your responsibility the way Simon's should have been." For the first time the memory of Simon's green eyes and quick laugh don't hurt. And this time, when I look at my father, he's silent. "If something happens to Tarver the way it happened to Simon, it'll be the end of LaRoux Industries. The galaxy will know what you did here. And if that happens, all the power and the money in the universe won't be enough to save you."

My vision is blurring—not with tears, but with the effort of not blinking. I can no longer see my father's face clearly, and so I stare past him. *Just get through this. You faced a wilderness with monsters, a ship full of corpses, the emptiness of death itself. You can do this.*

"And if something ever happens to Tarver Merendsen, you will lose me too. You'll lose me forever. And you'll have no one left."

I finally let myself blink, and when my vision clears I can see my father standing there, quite suddenly old. His white hair seems thinner, his skin looser. I can see wrinkles around his eyes that I don't remember being there. The hand on the chair back is for support now, not to strike a powerful stance. His mouth quivers.

I harden my heart. This, too, I learned from him. "I'll never speak to you again. Do you understand?"

He lets out a long breath, head bowed. "Lilac . . ."

"Do you understand?"

"You're free to go."

"Excuse me?"

"The door is unlocked, Major."

"You're too kind."

"Major—you realize that your story and our findings don't add up."

"I don't know what else to tell you, sir. It's what happened."

"There's absolutely no evidence to back you up."

"You really think I could make something like this up?"

FORTY-TWO

TARVER

MY INTERROGATOR STANDS AND GESTURES TO THE DOOR, which swings open as if on command.

I stare at him for a long moment, trying to process the idea that I'm free to go, my mind desperately tumbling over itself as it searches for the trick. What's the next step, the next part of the game? My eyes are scratchy, aching, my head throbbing to a slow pulse. Hunger has faded out now in favor of a heavy nausea that sits like a weight in the pit of my stomach.

I push upright, knees protesting, muscles cramping. I walk out of the room without sparing him another glance.

Lilac's waiting outside in a long corridor lined with broad windows. It must be night, ship's time, because the lights are dimmed, and she's lit largely by the light of the planet beyond the windows. She's wrapped up in some sort of robe, but it could be a ball gown, the way she stands in it. Navy blue, the same color she was wearing the night we met. Straight and poised, skin clear and hair caught up in one of those fancy knots I'll never understand; all that's missing is her entourage. They must have attacked her face with some sort of treatment, because her freckles are already fading. It's as though the past few weeks never happened.

I've played my part. Has she played hers? *Could* she play hers, after having a glimpse of her own world again? I remember what I said to her once, about returning to the real world. *Best not to make promises. It's not as simple as either of us would like it to be.*

For an endless moment she simply stares at me, eyes raking over me, taking in my exhaustion. There's no hint of the Lilac I came to know on the planet.

My heart wants to stop, and I want to let it.

She's the one to break the silence. "Tarver, are you—"

I move toward her before I can stop myself, and halt half a pace away. "I'm fine. Are you . . . ?"

"My father came." She's still gazing at me, blue eyes intent. I must look like hell. "What did you tell them? Is it over?"

I drag my eyes away from her mouth, swallowing. We're alone in this corridor and yet I can feel the weight of the reporters waiting to photograph us, the incredulous people in Lilac's circles, and the soldiers too, the shadow of her father over us. Is it too much for her?

Is it too much for me?

"What could I tell them?" I say lightly, trying to ignore how badly I want to reach out, close the gap between us. "I'm just a big, dumb soldier. What do I know?"

Her lips curve a little, amused, and for the first time my heart flickers with hope. There are her dimples again. I scan her face, looking for traces of the black eye she used to have, for her fading freckles, for anything to make her mine, not theirs. "What about you, Miss LaRoux?"

"Me?" She takes a deep breath, and with a jolt I realize she's as fearful as I am. "I'm just a spoiled heiress, too traumatized to remember anything."

And then she smiles, for real, and just like on the *Icarus* the first night we met, it's all over. It's nothing like a smile she would have given then; it's lopsided and true, and full of anxious hope. I reach for her, on fire. For a moment I feel the curve of her mouth against mine, smiling before the hunger takes over. Then I move forward into her, and she grabs handfuls of my shirt, pulling me with her as we crash into the wall of the hallway. She's holding me in close and my hands are at her hips, her sides, framing her face as her lips part and I kiss her, my mind spinning with all the moments I thought she was gone.

But she's here, she's mine. I'm hers.

My heart's thumping when we break apart, and I lean in to rest my forehead against hers. "You want to get out of here?"

She wraps her arms around my neck, lips tugging up in a smile once more. "Think we can outrun the cameras?"

"I do have extensive training in the art of stealth and camouflage." I find I'm smiling in return, helpless.

She opens her mouth to speak, but a blinding flash from beyond the windows interrupts her and sends her reeling backward with a cry. I turn, half blinded myself despite having my back to the windows. The light sweeps on past the ship, rippling outward from the planet in a wave. Blinking away afterimages, I'm left staring at the planet itself, struggling to understand what I'm seeing.

Lines of fire are spreading over the surface of the planet like cracks in an eggshell, as if some massive creature is hatching from the planet's depths. Lilac makes a low sound in her throat and grabs for my hand. The chasms widen, whole chunks of landmass vanishing into fire.

There's no sound across the vacuum of space, and for a long moment we stand there in eerie, utter silence, witnessing the destruction of the planet before us.

Lilac is the first to move, the first to speak. "Now no one will ever know what happened here." She swallows, gaze still fixed on the window as a series of soundless explosions eject streams of molten rock out toward the mirror-moon.

In the darkened corridor, the red-gold fire consuming the planet is reflected in Lilac's eyes, transforming them. In her face I can see the echo of the planet's destruction, the loss of the last shred of proof of everything she went through.

I wrap my arms around her, as much to reassure myself as anything. Ducking my head until her hair tickles my face, I take a long, steadying breath. "We'll know," I whisper.

We don't move from that spot, not even when the ship's engines kick in. We keep watching as the shattered planet and the remnants of its moon recede into the distance, back and back into the infinite dark. Until our eyes have to strain to see them, until they're only jagged pinpricks of reflected light.

The hyperspace drive gives its telltale whine, and Lilac leans back into me, bracing as we prepare to jump, to fold space to get home faster. Home to cameras and reporters, and questions from people who'd never understand what happened to us. I haven't given up on finding answers, not yet, even if we only whisper those answers to each other.

But just now, as we wait for the engines to kick in, all of that is far away. For a moment the image before us is frozen: our world, our lives, reduced to a handful of broken stars half lost in uncharted space. Then it's gone, the view swallowed by the hyperspace winds streaming past, blue-green auroras wiping the afterimages away.

Until all that's left is us.

ACKNOWLEDGMENTS

WE WOULD LIKE TO THANK OUR AMAZING AGENTS, JOSH AND Tracey Adams, for support, sanity, and SCBs at all the right moments—we're so grateful we have you on our side! Thank you also to the foreign scouts, agents, and publishers who have helped take our book places we've never been.

Thank you to our fantastic editor Abby Ranger for taking on Lilac and Tarver's story, and teaching, challenging, and supporting us. Abby, it's truly been our pleasure every step of the way (and thank you to Sylas, for sharing his mom!). Many thanks as well to the wonderful Laura Schreiber for editorial excellence and geeking out with us whenever necessary.

We also want to thank Emily Meehan for asking for us. We're excited to be with you, and can't wait to see what's in store.

Many thanks to the Hyperion family—from sales, marketing, and publicity, to our copy editors and design team, we're so grateful to be working with you. Thanks in particular to Suzanne Murphy, Stephanie Lurie, Dina Sherman, Jamie Baker, and Lizzie Mason, Lloyd Ellman, Elke Villa, Martin Karlow, Monica Mayper, and Sarah Chassé. Thank you to Whitney Manger and Tom Corbett for our beautiful cover!

Sarah J. Maas and Susan Dennard—we're so lucky to have you as friends and critique partners, and we thank you so much for both! Lots of love. Kat Zhang and Olivia Davis, thank you for being right there when we needed you. Thank you to Michelle Dennis for never being tired of reading just one more time, and for boundless (and often tasty) support. You're irreplaceable.

We're so grateful to the other amazing people in the writing community who have helped us along the way. Ellen Kushner and Delia Sherman, our Story Godmothers—thank you for the push we needed! Jeanne, Corry, and everyone at Odyssey, your support means the world.

Beth Revis, Marie Lu, and Jodi Meadows: thank you for championing our book and being our cheerleaders at all the right moments. You're awesome.

To our Leading Ladies: Alison Ward, Amanda Ellwood, Ben Brown (though he's no lady), Dixie McCartney, Kacey Smith, Marri Knadle, and Soraya Een Hajji, thank you for lessons in storytelling we couldn't have found anywhere else, and treasured friendships.

Thank you to ship's science officer Ben Ellis and ship's demolitions expert Nic Crowhurst for helping us crash things and blow them up (all errors are our own), and to ship's doctor Kate Irving for reading, critique, medical advice, too many bushwalks to count (*mostly* without survival situations attached), and so many years of extraordinary friendship.

Thank you to our brilliant support networks: the ladies of Pub(lishing) Crawl, the Lucky 13s, the team at FOS, the Roti Boti gang, Jay Kristoff, the TJ/UVA/extended NoVA group, the Plot Bunnies of Melbourne, and the awesome YA writers of Washington, DC. Thank you to our fantastic friends, who never mind when we scribble on napkins, bring our laptops everywhere, or slip out because our co-author just woke up on the other side of the world.

And finally, thank you to our families for their love, enthusiasm, and encouragement. We're so grateful to you all. In particular, thank you to our parents for unstinting encouragement and filling our lives with books, and Flic and Josie, for being our earliest partners in imagination. Thanks to our extended families—the Cousins clan, the Miskes and our own Mr. Wolf. And last, but not least, thank you, Brendan. It would've been a Massive Crash without you.

And now for a sneak peek at
the second book in the Starbound trilogy

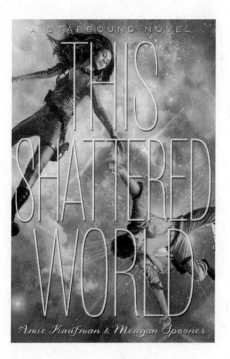

The girl is standing on a battlefield, and it's the street she grew up on. The people here don't know there's a war coming, and every time she opens her mouth to warn them, the city called November drowns her out. A car screeches past, a siren wails, children laugh, a holoboard starts playing its looped ad high above. The girl screams, but only the pigeons at her feet notice. Startled, they fly upward and disappear into the bright patchwork maze of laundry lines and lanterns crisscrossing overhead.

No one hears her.

ONE

────

JUBILEE

THERE'S A GUY STARING AT ME FROM THE OTHER END OF the bar. I can only see him because I'm in the habit of leaning forward, elbows on the plastene surface, so I can see past the row of heads. From here I can keep an eye on the whole place by watching the bartender's mirror overhead. And the guy I'm watching is using the same trick.

He's new. For one thing I don't recognize him, but for another he's got that look. Definitely a recruit, with something to prove, like they all do at first. But he's still glancing around, careful not to bump into the other guys, not too familiar with anyone else. He's wearing a uniform T-shirt, jacket, and fatigues, but the clothes are ill-fitting, the tiniest bit too tight. Could be because he's so new, they haven't ordered them in his size yet. Could also be because the uniform isn't his.

Still, the new ones know by the end of their first week not to hit on Captain Chase, even when she's at Molly Malone's. I'm not interested, and they know it. Eighteen is pretty young to take yourself off the market, but it's safer to send them all the same message from day one.

But this guy . . . this guy makes me pause. Makes me forget all of that. Dark tumbly hair, thick brows, dangerously sweet eyes. Sensuous mouth, tiny smirk barely hidden at its corner. He's got a poet's mouth. Artistic, expressive.

He looks oddly familiar. Beads of condensation form around my fingers as I hold my drink. Scratch that—I'd remember this guy if I'd seen him before.

"All good?" The bartender comes between us, leaning on the bar and tilting his head toward me. It's a crappy bar on a crappy makeshift street, wistfully named Molly Malone's. Some ghost story from the Irish roots claimed by this particular cluster of terraforming fodder folk. "Molly" is a three-hundred-pound bald Chinese man with a tattoo of a chrysanthemum on his neck. I've been a favorite of his ever since I landed here, not least because I'm one of the only people who can speak more than a word or two of Mandarin, thanks to my mother.

I raise an eyebrow at him. "Trying to get me drunk?"

"I live an' dream an' hope, babe."

"Someday, Molly." I pause, my attention returning to the mirror. This time, the guy sees me looking and meets my gaze unapologetically. I fight the urge to jerk my eyes away, and lean closer to the bartender. "Hey, Mol—who's the new guy down at the end?"

Molly knows better than to look over his shoulder and starts rinsing out a new glass instead. "The pretty one?"

"Mmm."

"Said he was just posted here, trying to get a feel for the place. He's asking lots of questions."

Odd. The fresh meat usually comes in herd form, entire platoons of wide-eyed, nervous boys and girls all shuffling wherever they're told. A little voice in my head points out that's not really fair, that I was fresh meat once too, and only two years ago. But they're so woefully unprepared for life on Avon that I can't help it.

This one's different, though—and he's all alone. Wariness tingles at the base of my neck, my gaze sharpening. Here on Avon, *different* usually means *dangerous*.

"Thanks, Molly." I flick the condensation on my fingertips at him, and he flinches away and grins before turning back to his more demanding customers.

The guy's still staring at me. The smirk is not quite so hidden now. I know I'm staring back, but I don't really care. If he really is a soldier, I can say I was sizing him up in an official capacity, looking for warning signs. Just because I'm off duty doesn't mean I can leave my responsibilities behind. We don't get much warning when we're about to lose one to the Fury.

He doesn't look much older than I am, so even if he enlisted the day he turned sixteen he won't have more than two years of service under his belt. Enough to get cocky—not enough to know he should wipe that grin off his face. A few weeks on Avon will do that for him. He's chiseled, with a chin so perfect, it makes me want to hit it. The shadow of stubble along his jaw only emphasizes the lines of his face. These guys invariably end up being assholes, but from this distance he's just beautiful. Like he was put together by an artist.

Guys like this make me want to believe in God.

The missionaries should really start recruiting guys like him before the military can get to them. After all, you don't have to be pretty to shoot people. But I think it probably helps if you're trying to spread your faith.

With my eyes on his in the mirror overhead, I give a deliberate jerk of my chin to summon him over. He gets the message, but takes his time about responding. In an ordinary bar on an ordinary planet, it'd mean he wasn't interested or was playing hard to get. But since I'm not after what people in ordinary bars are after, his hesitation makes me pause. Either he doesn't know who I am or he doesn't care. It can't be the former—everyone on this rock knows Captain Lee Chase, no matter how freshly arrived. But if it's the latter, he's no ordinary recruit.

Some stooge from Central Command, trying to lie low by dressing like us? A field agent for Terra Dynamics, come to see if the military's doing its job in preventing an all-out uprising? It's not unheard of for a corporation to send in spies to make sure the government is holding up its end of the terraforming agreement. Which only makes our job harder. The corporations are constantly lobbying to be able to hire private mercs, but since the Galactic Council doesn't exactly relish the thought of privately funded armies running around, they're stuck petitioning for government forces. Maybe he's *from* the Galactic Council, here to spy on Avon before their planetary review in a couple months.

No matter who he is, it can't be good news for me. *Why can't these people leave me alone and let me do my job?*

The dark-haired guy picks up his beer and makes his way over to my end of the bar. He puts on a good show of eager shyness, like he's surprised to be singled out, but I know better. "Hey," he says by way of greeting. "I don't want you to panic, but your drink appears to be blue."

It's one of Molly's concoctions, which he sometimes gives me for free as an excuse to actually mix drinks instead of filling pitchers of beer.

I make a snap decision. If he wants to play it coy, I can do coy right back. He's not exactly hard on the eyes, and this curiosity is tugging at me—I want to see what happens if I go along with it. I know he can't be interested in me. At least not the way he's pretending to be.

I fish out the plastic sword—it's hot pink—from the martini glass and suck the cherries off of it, one by one. The guy's eyes fix on my lips, sending a brief surge of satisfaction through me. Molly doesn't get much opportunity to mix drinks here—and I don't get much opportunity to flirt.

I let my lips curve in a smile and lean in a fraction. "I like it blue."

His mouth opens to respond, but instead he's forced to clear his throat at length.

"Got a touch of the swamp bug?" I feign concern. "Molly'll take care of that for you. His drinks'll cure anything, from wounded feelings to appendicitis."

"That so?" He's found his voice again, and his smile. There's a gleam behind the *aw-shucks* new-boy persona he's wearing: pleasure. He's enjoying himself.

Well, so are you, points out a snide little voice in my head. I shove it aside. "If you give it a second, we'll find out if it'll turn my tongue blue, to boot."

"That an invitation to make a personal inspection?"

I can see some of my platoon at a table in the background, watching me and the new guy, no doubt waiting to see if I rip off something important. "Play your cards right."

He laughs, leaning sideways against the bar. It's a bit of a capitulation, a pause in the game. He's not so much hitting on me as feeling me out.

I set my drink down on the bar next to a set of initials scratched into the composite surface. They were here long before I showed up, and their owner is long gone. "This is the part where you'd ordinarily introduce yourself, Romeo."

"And ruin my mystique?" The guy's thick brows go up. "Pretty sure Romeo kept his mask on when he met Jubilee."

"Juliet," I correct him, trying not to flinch at his use of my whole name. He must be new, not to know how much I hate that. Still, he's given me a valuable hint. If this guy knows Shakespeare, he's got to have been educated somewhere off-world. The swamp-dwellers can barely read an instruction manual, much less ancient classics.

"Oh, a scholar?" he replies, eyes gleaming. "This is a strange place to find a girl like you. So, who'd you offend to get stuck on Avon?"

I lean back against the bar, propping myself on my elbows. One hand fidgets with the plastic sword, weaving it back and forth through my fingers. "I'm a troublemaker."

"My favorite kind of girl." Romeo meets my eyes with a smile, then looks away. But not before I've seen it: he's tense. It's subtle, but I've been trained to notice the invisible currents, the ebb and flow of a person's energy. A muscle tic here, a line of tension there. Sometimes it's all the warning you get before someone tries to blow themselves up, and take you with them.

Adrenaline sharpens my senses as I lean forward. The air in here smells of spilled beer, cigar smoke, and air freshener—none of which is strong enough to drown out the invasive smell of the swamp outside. I try to shut out the sound of my platoon laughing in the background and look more closely at Romeo. I can't tell, in the low light, whether his pupils are dilated. If he's new to the planet, he shouldn't have had time to succumb to the Fury—unless he's been transferred here from somewhere else on Avon.

He shifts his weight under my scrutiny, then straightens. "Listen," he says, his voice getting brisker, "let me settle for your drink, and I'll leave you to your evening."

Somehow he's gotten a read on me. He knows I'm suspicious.

"Hang on." I reach out to lay my hand on his arm. It's a gentle touch, but firm. He'll have to jerk away if he wants to leave before I'm ready to let him go. "You're not a soldier," I say finally. "And not a local. Quite the little puzzle. You're not going to leave me so unsatisfied, are you?"

"Unsatisfied?" The guy's smile doesn't flicker a millimeter. He's good. He's got to be a spy from one of TerraDyn's competitors. Nova Tech or SpaceCorp, or any one of the neighboring corporations with space staked out on Avon. "That's unkind, Captain Chase."

I abandon pretense. "I never told you who I was."

"Like Stone-faced Chase needs an introduction."

Though you'd never catch my platoon calling me that, at least to my face, the nickname caught on like wildfire after my first few months here. I don't reply, scanning his features and trying to figure out why he looks so familiar. If he's a criminal, maybe I've seen his picture in the database.

He makes a small attempt to free his arm to test how badly I want to hold on to him. "Look, I'm just a guy trying to buy a girl a drink. So why don't you let me do that, and then we can go our separate ways and dream about what might've been?"

I clench my jaw. "Listen, Romeo." My fingers tighten—I can feel the tense muscle beneath my hand. He's no weakling, but I'm better trained. "How about instead, we go to HQ and chat there?"

The muscle in his forearm under my palm twitches, and I glance at his hand. It's empty—but then he shifts his weight, and suddenly there's something digging into my ribs, held in his other hand. He had a gun tucked inside his shirt. *Goddammit.* It's ancient, a tarnished ballistics weapon, not one of the sleek Gleidels I'm used to. No wonder he's wearing a jacket despite the heat inside the bar. The long sleeves are concealing his genetag tattoo, the spiral design on the forearm that all the locals get at birth.

"Sorry." He leans close to me to conceal the gun between us. "I really did just want to pay for your drink and get out of here."

Beyond him I can see my guys, heads together, laughing and occasionally peeking our way. Though half of them are well into their twenties, they still act like a bunch of gossips. Mori, one of my oldest soldiers, meets my eyes for a moment—but she looks away before I can convey anything through my gaze. Alexi's there too, his pink hair gelled up, looking way too interested in the wall. From their perspective, I'm letting this guy drape himself all over me. Stone-faced Chase, getting a little action for once. Troops cycle in and out of Avon so often that all of those here have only known the past few months' ceasefire—their senses aren't battle-sharpened. They're not suspicious enough.

"Are you kidding me?" My own weapon is on my hip, but we're close enough that he could easily shoot me before I reach it. "You can't actually think this is going to work."

"You haven't really given me much choice, have you?" He glances down at the holster on my hip. "You seem a little overdressed, Captain. Leave the gun on the stool there. *Slowly.*"

I roll my eyes toward Molly, but he's leaning back, drying glasses and watching the holovid over the end of the bar. I try to catch someone's eye—*anyone's* eye—but they're all carefully ignoring me, all too eager to tell stories later about how they saw Captain Chase get picked up at Molly's. My abductor shields me with his body as I reach for my Gleidel and set it down where he indicates. He wraps a hand around my waist, turning me toward the door. "Shall we?"

"You are the biggest icebrain ever." I clench my hands, the pink cocktail skewer digging into my palm. Then I turn a little, making a token struggle to test his grip and the distribution of his weight. There—he's leaning a little too far forward. I tense my muscles and jerk, leaning back and giving my arm a twist. It hurts like hell, but—

He grunts, and the barrel of the gun digs more sharply into my rib cage. But he doesn't let me go. He's good. *Damn, damn, DAMN.*

"You're not the first person to say so," he says, breathing a little faster.

"Fine—ow, I'm going, okay?" I let him steer me toward the door. I could call his bluff, but if he's stupid enough to bring a gun onto a military base, he might be stupid enough to fire it. And if this blows up into a firefight, my people could get hurt.

Besides, someone will stop us. Alexi, surely—he knows me too well to let this happen. Someone will see the gun—someone will remember that Captain Chase doesn't leave the bar with strange guys. She doesn't leave the bar with anyone. Someone will realize something's wrong.

But no one does. As the door swings closed behind us, I hear a low sound of whistles and catcalls in the bar as my entire platoon starts jeering and gossiping like a bunch of old hens. *Bastards,* I think furiously. *I'm going to make you run so many laps in the morning, you'll wish YOU had been carried off by a rebel.*

Because that's who this is. I don't know how he knows Shakespeare or where he got his training, but he's got to be one of the swamp rats. They call themselves the Fianna—warriors—but they're all just bloodthirsty lawbreakers. Who else would dare infiltrate the base with nothing but a pistol that looks like it's from the dawn of time? At least that means there's no danger of him snapping into mindless violence, since Avon's deadly Fury only affects off-worlders. I only have to worry about the average, everyday violence that comes so easily to these swamp-dwellers.

He tugs me off the main path and into the shadows between the bar and the supply shed next door. Then it hits me: I'm not going to be making anyone run laps in the morning. I'm a military officer, being captured by a rebel. I'm probably never going to see my troops again, because I'll be dead by morning.

With a snarl, I jam my hand back and down, sending the blade of the pink plastic cocktail sword deep into the guy's thigh. Before he has time to react, I give it a savage twist and snap off the hilt, leaving the hot-pink plastic embedded in the muscle.

At least I won't go without a fight.

Turn the page for a first look at
the Starbound trilogy eShort

"Hey—it's okay. Shhh. I'm right here."

"What? I—sorry, beautiful. I was dreaming."

"No kidding. Are you okay? Do you want to talk about it?"

"Mmm. You're warm. You've been stealing the blankets again."

"Stop trying to distract me. I thought I was supposed to be the one with the nightmares."

"You're not going to let this go, are you?"

"Do I ever?"

"Good point."

"Who's Sanjana?"

SIX MONTHS BEFORE
THE *ICARUS* CRASH . . .

ONE

THE SUN'S WARM ON THE BACK OF MY NECK, BIRDSONG filtering down from the trees lining the edges of the walking track. Unlike my last posting on Avon, surrounded by mud and swamp, this part of Patron is all blue skies and grassy hills. This far from the nearest town, I could almost forget I'm not home, that my parents' cottage isn't just beyond the next rise. Almost—except for the gun at my hip, the dim outline of Patron's rings faint across the afternoon sky, and Private Gil Fisk crunching along behind me.

"Listen," I tell him as we crest the hill, sweating a little under the heavy carbon fiber composite of my flak jacket. "All I'm saying is there's an argument to be made for coming in a little gentler. You lead by saying you miss *her*, not that you miss getting—look, it's about poetry, Private. Her eyes, her lips. Didn't you ever do poetry in school?"

Gil snorts, coming up alongside me, scratching behind his ear. "Yeah, but it was all roses and clouds, and if I start comparing her to a flower, she's gonna think I've lost it. You really get girls to go for you by talking 'bout their lips, sir?"

I hide a grin. This patrol takes almost as long by hover as on foot, and isn't usually sought after—but now I know why Gil traded two days of mess hall duty for this patrol shift: to get me to help him win back his girlfriend. "I know, it's a mystery. Listen, when we get back from patrol I'll show you a couple of poems, and you can try something based on those."

"Can't you just write it for me? Cole said you wrote his whole letter to his boyfriend on Babel."

"I wrote Cole's letter because he *can't* write," I point out. At this rate I'm going to have to start charging my men a fee.

"What about you, Captain?" Gil kicks a rock half-buried in the road and sends it skittering off into the grass.

"Nobody in particular," I reply. "I can't see myself settling down." I'm about to continue when the comm patch on my vest crackles to life. We both slow as we listen.

"Patrol three-six-five, this is HQ. Do you read? Over."

Fisk raises a brow as I thumb the talk-patch and reply. "HQ, three-six-five. Go ahead, over."

"Patrol, just a heads-up. VC-Delta opened a comms channel a few minutes ago, but we got no broadcast before it shut off again. They're not responding to hails. We think their system is glitching, but they may not be aware. Request you have them run a systems check on arrival."

"Will do. Thank you, HQ. Three-six-five out."

Fisk's pulling a face as we set out again. "How long's a full systems check gonna take, sir?"

"Long enough," I reply, trying not to grimace myself. "I had a card game tonight. That's shot, now."

Fisk shades his eyes against the setting sun, eyeing the hill ahead of us. "I can go check it out if you want to start heading back, sir. No reason you gotta miss your game."

But something about this doesn't sit right, and the prickle down my spine is one I've learned not to ignore. "No," I say slowly. "No, let's both go check it out. It's probably nothing, but if it's not, better to have two of us."

"You sure, sir?" Gil's impatient, and I suppress a smile—he *really* wants me to write that letter to his girlfriend. "Those things are always breaking. Scientists got their heads in the clouds, don't bother with maintenance. Call it my punishment for being late to the yard this morning."

I snicker. "You're learning to recite a sonnet for being late to the yard," I tell him, setting off to move a little quicker than before. "And then you can write to your girlfriend and tell her it reminds you of her."

He curses under his breath, and jogs a few steps to catch up with me.

We're still at least a quarter hour on foot from VC-Delta, the VeriCorp research facility we're checking on this evening's patrol. "What d'you think we'll find there?"

"Probably some idiot who spilled a drink on the comm set," I reply. "But that's what I think, not what I know. There are other reasons their comms could be down." And however long a shot, those reasons are why we're here.

We circle around to come in toward the base from the west—the approach up the road is completely open, and if anything's up, we'd be sitting ducks.

There's no reason it should be anything other than faulty equipment; Patron's been peaceful for years now, but for the occasional incursion by raider ships, and these patrols are more a courtesy than anything else. Part of the government's contract with the corporations that terraform these places. This isn't Avon—no rebels lurking in the wilderness, no discontented townsfolk to wrangle. It's supposed to be an easy posting, so I can recover from my time on the front lines.

We're both silent as we work our way through the scrub, climbing along just below the ridgeline to avoid our silhouettes showing, until we can get a better look at the valley below.

It dips down to a gentle bowl, trees scattering the slopes of the hills around the facility itself. A long mound bisects the valley and curves back around through the hills—it's the research facility's particle accelerator, a layer of earth and grass concealing whatever manner of science they keep inside there. Not my field of expertise. All I know is that they build their facilities out here because the land's cheap and they can make their equipment as large as they want.

Fisk starts to stride down the hill toward the compound, but I reach out and snag his sleeve, pulling him back. I know I've spent too long on the front lines, that the caution Avon drilled into me is still too fresh, but something's still warning me not to walk in blindly. We stop instead at the edge of a copse, crouching between the tree trunks to get a better look at the compound itself, the large courtyard visible within the walls from this height. I pull up my goggles from where they hang around my neck, blessing my commander for insisting we patrol in proper gear, and thumb the button to magnify the view. Two figures walk out across the courtyard, taking a curving path between the tables and chairs set out there to catch the sun, an old satellite dish dumped in the open space. The wind in the trees around me melts away, my world turning silent. They're in fitted body armor, but though it's almost like military issue, those aren't soldiers. I know every face on my base, and these two aren't among them.

"Gil," I murmur, looking across at him to find he's staring down at the compound, too. "Those look like our guys to you?"

"Not so much, sir," he replies. "We—" But he gets no further—he's cut off abruptly by a scream from the courtyard below, carried only faintly on the wind, followed by the quick, sharp shriek of a weapon rending the air.

Dammit. "Call it in, Fisk, use the sat phone. They could be monitoring our comm frequencies—we can't risk that. I'll try to get a better look at the approach."

"Yes, sir." Suddenly, he's all business—no longer the guy who tries to wheedle poems out of me, who can never get anything quite right no matter how hard he tries. In this, at least, he's sure of himself. He swings his pack off, dropping to one knee to pull out the sat phone, reaching up to adjust his goggles where they sit behind his ear. "Try the southwest entrance, I think the trees come in closest there."

I nod, using hands and feet to make sure I don't slide down the slope, keeping to the shadows of the trees. My mind's scrambling, competing thoughts and questions all shouting for attention. No sign of their vehicle; no military hovers, no chopper. Either they came on foot, like Fisk and me, or—more likely—they were dropped here. They're too well-organized to be raiders looking to strip the facility, and since they're not military, that means they're mercs. There's a reason that hiring mercenaries was made illegal decades ago: no regulation. No way to stop the people hiring them from forming their own private little armies on the edge of space.

It'll be impossible to know who hired them; a rival corporation after VC's tech, probably, but which one, I doubt we'll ever know. They'll be covering their tracks. People like these don't leave witnesses behind.

Assuming our commander mobilizes units the second he hears Fisk's call, there's only three ways the cavalry arrives—on foot, which will take an hour we don't have; via road, which will take even longer thanks to the winding roads of Patron's hilly countryside; or via air, which will give the game away completely. The facility's staff will be dead before our guys can land.

Which means it's on us. Me and a private I like just fine, but a guy I wouldn't choose to partner me in a game of cards, let alone a two-man military operation. I almost wish I was back at my last posting on Avon, with half a dozen soldiers I'd choose over Gilmore Fisk, who's never seen action like this.

He's just setting down the satellite phone and turning an anxious gaze on me as I return a few minutes later. I make sure I sound steady when I speak, completely sure of myself. "Okay, good news is there aren't many of them in the courtyard. Bad news is that shot was an execution. One of the civilians. We can't sit here and watch them take out the others while we wait for reinforcements."

Fisk nods, swallowing hard, and stows the sat phone before coming to his feet and pulling his Gleidel from its holster. "Yessir."

I draw my own gun and check its charge, then take point. We work quickly and quietly down the hillside, using what cover there is to get close to the wall, then easing in along it to make our way to the gate.

My brother Alec was caught alone when he died, and I've wondered countless times what he was thinking. Whether he knew he'd screwed up, getting himself cut off like that. Whether he kept trying, or knew he was done. Whether he was scared.

But I'm not alone, I remind myself, looking back at Gil, who's white as a sheet, but gripping his Gleidel in a steady hand. *And this is our duty. We can't sit up there and watch them be executed while we wait for backup.*

With my brother's face before my eyes, I ease in through the gate.

An Interview with Amie and Meagan

How did the two of you start writing together?

Meagan: Amie and I met online through a role-playing community that revolved around writing. We became instant friends in addition to writing partners, and a few years later I went to Australia to live with her and her husband while working on my first novel. While I was there, Amie and I started role-playing a new pair of characters—Lilac and Tarver—and we became so enamored of them that eventually our scattered scenes became a book!

Where did the idea for *These Broken Stars* come from?

Amie: We've both been space geeks since we were tiny, and we love survival and shipwreck stories, so it was natural to write a shipwreck story set in space. Our original plan was that Lilac and Tarver would be just two survivors of many, and we'd add others in once we got bored with them. Except a year later, we still weren't bored, and we realized we had the makings of a novel on our hands.

How did you divide the writing of the story?

Meagan: The fact that we began writing by role-playing characters made it easy to divvy up the writing. In our first draft, Amie wrote Tarver's chapters and I wrote Lilac's chapters. Once we got into rewrites and revisions, it was a bit more of a free-for-all, though. And while I may have written a given Lilac chapter, Amie may well have written Tarver's part of the dialogue in it. By the time we were done, there were significant chunks of the book where we couldn't remember who had written what.

You live on opposite sides of the planet—how do you work together?

Amie: The first draft of *These Broken Stars* was put together in our living room, but these days we're so far apart that we definitely have to embrace technology. We chat via instant messaging every single day, usually for hours. We also e-mail constantly, jump on video chat to brainstorm, or phone each other while we're out and about. The time zone difference can be a challenge, but there are also benefits— you wake up each morning, and it's like elves worked on your book overnight!

What drew you to write science fiction for teens?

Meagan: We've both been science fiction fans since we were tiny— from *Star Trek* to *Twenty Thousand Leagues Under the Sea*, science fiction was a huge part of our childhoods and teenage years. There's also a natural synergy between science fiction and young adult fiction that's too hard to resist. SF is all about mankind finding its place in the universe, while YA fiction is all about teens finding their place in the world. Putting the two together just feels right.

So what's next for the two of you?

Amie: As we write this, we've finished *This Shattered World*, which follows the mystery uncovered in *These Broken Stars* to the planet Avon, and introduces us to a soldier and a rebel whose lives depend on finding out more. We've also put together a short story that explains how Tarver came to be wearing those medals at the start of *These Broken Stars* (as well as explaining why he doesn't want the story told). Right now, we're hard at work on book three, which will follow the story to the center of the galaxy, the planet Corinth. We like to release sneak peeks and secret updates in our monthly newsletter, so if you haven't subscribed at www.thesebrokenstars.com, make sure you don't miss out!

10 Things You Didn't Know about *These Broken Stars* . . .

1. During revisions on this novel, our editor asked us to make a dossier of facts about the universe of *These Broken Stars*. It ended up expanding into a multipart encyclopedia covering everything from how planets are colonized, to politics, social classes, and a (future) history of space exploration!

2. The name "LaRoux" means "the red" in French, meaning someone with red hair. Each of Lilac's names is a color: Lilac, Rose, and LaRoux.

3. Amie invented the name Tarver—or so she thought. Later we discovered that it actually was an existing name in Old English that meant "tower" or "fortified hill," and we thought that fit Tarver pretty well!

4. A large chunk of the brainstorming for this novel took place in a hot springs resort near Melbourne, Australia. With all our talk about killing fifty thousand people in a spaceship crash, and heated discussion of topics like how long it would take someone to die of infection, we got a lot of weird looks from the other patrons!

5. The name of the ship, the Icarus, comes from a Greek myth about a boy with wings made of wax feathers who flew too close to the sun and fell to his death.

6. The dress Lilac is wearing on the cover of *These Broken Stars* was custom-designed for the photo shoot, and actually exists! It's toured the U.S. and Australia, on display in bookstore windows and featured in photographs with other popular young adult authors.

7. Tarver's gun, the Gleidel, might be a futuristic laser pistol, but the technology powering it already exists. Kinetic energy watches are a

product of the twentieth century, and charge themselves using the energy generated by the wearer moving his or her arm around.

8. One of the protagonists of book two is mentioned—though not by name—in book one. Only the most careful of readers will be able to spot it after having read both books. . . .

9. In order to get the facts and the science right, we consulted a whole cabinet of experts, including a doctor, a NASA engineer, a military demolitions expert, a particle physicist, and an ecologist, to name a few.

10. The original first draft ended with chapter 40, after the scene in which Tarver kisses Lilac as the rescue teams close in around them. Chapters 41 and 42 were added during revisions when our editor suggested adding the confrontation between Lilac and her father—now we can't imagine ending the book any other way!

———

ABOUT THE AUTHORS

AMIE KAUFMAN AND MEAGAN SPOONER ARE LONGTIME friends and sometime flatmates who have traveled the world (but not yet the galaxy), covering every continent between them. They are sure outer space is only a matter of time. Meagan, who is also the author of the Skylark trilogy, currently lives in North Carolina, while Amie lives in Melbourne, Australia. Although they currently live apart, they are united by their love of space opera, road trips, and second breakfasts. You can find them on Twitter at @AmieKaufman and @MeaganSpooner.